FOREVER YOUNG

A NOVEL

SCOTT KYLE & KARYN LANGHORNE FOLAN

FOREVER YOUNG

A NOVEL

LIV MAS PRESS

La Jolla, California

Copyright © 2014 by Scott Kyle and Karyn Langhorne Folan

All rights reserved. No part of this publication may be reproduced, distributed, or transmitted in any form or by any means, including photocopying, recording, or other electronic or mechanical methods, without the prior written permission of the publisher. For permission requests, write to the publisher, addressed "Attention: Permissions Coordinator," at the address below.

Publisher's Cataloging-in-Publication
(Provided by Quality Books, Inc.)

Kyle, Scott G.
Forever young / by Scott Kyle and Karyn Langhorne Folan.
pages cm
ISBN 978-0-9914949-0-3
ISBN 978-0-9914949-1-0

1. Man-woman relationships--Fiction. 2. Adventure stories. 3. Love stories.   I. Folan, Karyn Langhorne. II. Title.

PS3611.Y62F67 2014   813'.6
QBI14-600029

Liv Mas Press
888 Prospect Street, Suite 201
La Jolla, CA 92037

Copy edited by Lisa Wolff
Cover illustration and cover design concept by Kristie Langone
Text design and cover design adaptation by Gregory Smith

Printed in the United States of America

Scott's dedication:

"To my beautiful children Jet and Liv:
you keep me young at heart."

Karyn's dedication:

"For Kevin—and growing old together."

FOREVER YOUNG

A NOVEL

CHAPTER
One

Catherine Zeta-Jones looked like she was about to pass out—or throw up, or both.

Well, perhaps not Catherine herself—that was just Frank Young's nickname for his seatmate on this airbus from San Diego bound for Boston. When she sat down in the narrow middle seat between Frank and the cranky older man near the window, he'd searched the movie database in his mind and come up with CZJ in *Entrapment*—the French actress from *The Da Vinci Code* a close second. Even with her skin gone pale—well, turning kind of green, really—she had that same European beauty: a heart-shaped face of flawless ivory skin, blazing black eyes and an abundance of dark hair. He wrote her character synopsis in his mind: art history major from Radcliffe visiting girlfriends in San Diego, returning home to curate eighteenth-century Italian masters for the Boston Museum of Fine Arts.

In short, everything about her said "first class" and "out of your league"—and yet here she was beside him, squeezed into a middle seat in the very last row of the economy section, gripping the armrests so tightly her knuckles had lost all their natural color.

The plane shuddered. Not just a little bump or dip—Frank had slept through more of those than he cared to count—but a serious jerk as if the whole thing had been nailed by a giant flyswatter and knocked down a few thousand feet. Frank's stomach lurched and settled like he was on a roller coaster's front car.

Great, he thought. *As if I wasn't nervous enough about this trip . . .*

"We're experiencing some turbulence," the captain crackled over the intercom, stating the obvious in a no-problem-everything's-under-control tone Frank had concluded was an aviation requirement. "Looks like we've run into a storm. Normally, we'd try to get above it, but we're about an hour from Logan Airport now and starting our initial descent into Boston. Best thing to do, folks, is remain in your seats with your seat belts fastened and—"

Frank sighed. He folded up his tray table and settled his computer in his lap, peering down at the dim screen. He'd read the proposal for investment capital for his tiny travel agency a thousand times already, but the thousand-and-first couldn't hurt. Out of the corner of his eye, he saw lightning fireworking the night sky.

"Oh God," the girl beside him whispered.

At first he thought she was talking to him, but her eyes were squeezed shut. A rosary dangled from her wrist, the crucifix clutched tightly in her fingers. Her lips kept moving, silently now, as she turned the beads in her fingers. When she was finished with her prayers, she buried the cross under the sleeve of her jacket like a secret, opened her eyes and exhaled a long, determined breath.

He'd tried to speak to her before and gotten monosyllabic answers of supreme disinterest, but now she looked so scared and he felt so bad for her that he put his bruised ego aside.

"Are you okay?"

This time, she turned frightened eyes to him and tried to smile.

"Actually, I-I'm scared to death. I-I never like flying. Not even when the weather is good. But *this*? Th-this is—"

The plane dipped again. The cabin lights guttered out for a long slow count of three before illuminating again. The Catherine lookalike grimaced and closed her eyes, her jaw tight with the effort of maintaining her self-control.

"Hey . . ." The usual platitudes about the relative safety of air travel ran through Frank's mind, but he doubted it would make her feel better to think about all the ways she was more likely to die. "How about a movie?" Before she could refuse, he set his computer in her lap and reached for the case, dealing out DVDs like a Vegas croupier. "What'll it be? I've got *Blade Runner, Gran Torino, The Matrix*. If you like comedies, there's *The Forty Year Old Virgin* or *Groundhog Day*." He sorted the stash. "A bunch of adventure movies. I guess those are my favorites."

Curiosity rearranged her features. Frank saw himself reflected in her dark eyes: an average-looking guy with medium-brown hair on the longer side of conservative, a pair of bright blue eyes, and a rangy athletic build concealed under a nondescript polo shirt and a pair of khakis. He also saw that he'd succeeded; he'd pulled her attention off the shuddering, bouncing metal can hurtling through the rain at four hundred miles an hour.

He leaned closer to her, dropping his voice conspiratorially as he pulled a final selection out of its place. "If you want my recommendation, though, it's this one. *The African Queen*. It's old, but it's one of my all-time favorites. The ultimate romantic adventure. I've probably seen it a hundred times and I'll probably watch it a hundred more."

She grinned—and if he could have, Frank would have bottled that smile and stored it. It would always be too precious to sell, but he could have treasured it anyway, the way children kept scraps of shells or mothers kept their children's outgrown baby clothes—as something valueless and precious at the same time.

"That's smart. Bringing your favorite movies. If I—" She stopped, swallowed hard and corrected herself, "I mean, *when* I fly again, I'll try—"

The plane bounced and Frank's bottom left the seat. He was weightless for a moment, straining against his seat belt on a current of air before being dropped like a discarded toy. His laptop skittered off the tray table toward the floor.

"That was a big one. Looks like it's time to put this away after all," he joked, catching it and stuffing the machine back into its case. He turned back to his Catherine. "But movies are—"

Terror marred her features. Her eyes were scrunched closed and her lips were contorted in an expression like pain. A tear made a long, slow track down her cheek and paused in a fat droplet at the curve of her chin.

Crap, Frank thought, as a strange sense of panic choked him. He wished himself the debonair leading man in some movie from the 1940s—a hero in a dapper suit with a handy pocket square to offer the weeping damsel in distress. Instead, he had only the remains of his cocktail napkin.

"Hey . . . It's going to be okay," he murmured. "It's just a summer storm. We're really close to Boston now. In forty-five minutes you'll be on the ground."

The Mrs. Douglas lookalike nodded, but two more tears seeped from beneath a fringe of black lashes.

"Please don't cry," Frank begged, smoothing the napkin between his palms, struggling to make it acceptable. "I've probably been on three hundred or three hundred fifty planes in my life so far and—"

"Three hundred fifty?" she snapped, hysteria rising in her voice as the tears rolled in quick succession down her cheeks. "Then the odds are against you. Your luck is about to run out—"

"Stop it. I'm not going to die today—and neither are you," Frank replied firmly. It was a reflex from years of expeditions, kicking in as smoothly as a Marine's "oohra" or a boxer's left jab. He tucked the napkin into her fist, his anxieties about its sufficiency no longer relevant. "Take a deep breath and wipe your face. It's crumpled, but it's clean."

The woman glared at him, but she took the napkin and did as she was told.

"I-I'm sorry. That wasn't very nice of me, saying your luck was going to run out—"

"It's okay. You're just scared." Frank closed his eyes and exhaled, letting command ebb out of him. "And I apologize for yelling at you. It's a habit. One thing I've learned after a decade of travel is that panic never helps . . . but the truth is I'm a little scared, too."

She laughed, filling Frank's ears with bright music that forced him to smile again. "I wasn't expecting you to say that. It doesn't fit with that 'calm, controlled' thing you just did." She quirked an eyebrow at him like he was a puzzle she couldn't quite figure out. "My friends call me Jackie," she said, offering him a small, soft hand.

"I'm Frank—"

The airbus vibrated like a bridge shaken by an earthquake, filling their ears with the sound of shuddering metal. Jackie's fingers convulsed around Frank's hand.

"Talk. Tell me something," Frank said as the plane rattled as if the wind were peeling back its skin.

"Wh—what should I—"

"Anything. The time you fell off your bike when you were seven. Or when you wore braces and thought you would never smile again. Who's waiting for you in Boston? What did you leave behind in San Diego? Close your eyes and tell me about the first person who comes to your mind—"

"My father." Anger edged the fear out of her voice. "Isn't that funny? Of all people," she muttered.

"Funny? Why? What about him?"

"Horns and a tail."

"That's pretty bad!" Frank laughed. "Well, is the situation unredeemable—or do you think it might change?"

He thought she might at least smile, but instead Jackie considered him silently for a long moment. "I—I don't know," she said at last. "It's a long story. Never mind." She unlaced her hand from Frank's, slapped a few more tears away and aimed her piercing eyes at him again. "Your turn. Tell *me* something—"

"Like what?" Frank asked. His mind was suddenly blank, emptied of all the clever and witty remarks that might impress a woman in a circumstance like this.

"Anything," she said, her eyes dancing with mischief. "The time you fell off your bike when you were seven. Or when you wore braces and thought you would never smile again. Who's waiting for you in Boston? What did you leave behind in San Diego? Close your eyes and tell me about the first person who comes to your mind." The faintest grin ghosted her lips. "Wasn't that it? Did I get it right?"

"Cool trick," Frank agreed.

"Thank you. Now start talking, Frank."

The aircraft jerked sharply downward again and Jackie inhaled, this time her fingernails marking Frank's flesh. Across the aisle and a few rows up, a toddler wailed—the soundtrack of the anxiety of everyone aboard. His mother lifted him out of his seat, rocking him in her lap as she whispered soft reassurances. Clumsy images from his past flickered to life in Frank's brain.

The plane slowly leveled again. His beautiful companion stared at him.

"Tell me . . ." she murmured softly. "What you're thinking right now."

"Nothing, really. I was just remembering . . ." Frank let the sentence drop. He didn't want to remember. It was best if the past stayed buried—he'd learned that lesson. It was pointless to revisit it.

"You were remembering . . .?" the woman beside him prompted. Her fingers had been clamped around his, but now their pressure eased a bit. Her thumb circled a space at the heel of his hand, gentle and calming.

What's the big deal? another voice in his brain chided. *It was so long ago. You're over it. A grown man.*

"I guess I was a little older than he is," Frank began slowly, nodding toward the frightened toddler as the past's faded edges filled his mind. "Four or five. Flying with my dad. I don't remember where—we went so many places together. He was an archeologist and almost every year he'd take a bunch of his students on a dig and I'd go, too. Wherever we were going, it was a long flight. And often a bumpy one, like this. I remember scrambling into his lap and burying my face into his chest because I was so scared. He started telling me stories to calm me down. What's funny is it wasn't the stories that were calming. It was—"

Suddenly, his senses were engulfed with the smell of his father's clothes, the scratchy feeling of his sloppily shaved chin against Frank's five-year-old head and the sound of his voice. In a breath, time stopped and rewound. Emotions long suppressed bubbled dangerously close to the surface.

Stop, a voice inside him urged, throwing a red flag on the memory. *Stop now.*

"What?" Jackie asked. "Please . . . don't stop. Tell me."

This time when he stared into her eyes, he noticed the intelligence blazing in them. He saw not only the perfect symmetry of her features but the crease of concern folding between her eyebrows. She still looked something like Catherine Zeta-Jones . . . but she looked more like Jackie.

"This sounds strange, I know. But remember, I was a

little kid," he said, at last pushing down a feeling of inner turbulence stronger than anything he'd ever felt on a plane. "It was the vibration. I had my head on his chest and when he spoke, the words rumbled. It's funny how well I remember that. It was soothing, I guess." He glanced nervously at Jackie, expecting to read the diagnosis "mentally unbalanced" on her face. But Jackie simply nodded and waited for him to go on.

"Like I said, there was a lot of turbulence, and the flight attendant wanted me in my own seat, but I wouldn't let go. You'd have to know my father to understand this—he was an extremely easygoing man. I rarely heard him raise his voice. Usually the more emotional other people got, the calmer and softer his response. I'd seen him defuse all kinds of really tense situations on digs—culture clashes and the like—with that calm, firm voice. But that flight attendant got the full weight of his anger—and that's why I remember it. 'My boy is terrified! I don't care what your rules are—he stays with me!' And I did, too. These days, they'd probably land the plane and kick us both off. But this was 1984 or '85. The flight attendant wasn't happy, but that was that. And within twenty or thirty minutes we were out of turbulence and I got out of his lap and sat in my own seat. Like a big boy." He nodded toward the toddler and his mother, blinking back the stinging, wet pain in his eyes. "I hope they don't make her put him in his seat. If they do, I might not be able to mind my own business."

"Understood," Jackie said solemnly. "And don't worry. I've got your back."

Frank chuckled, imagining her assuming a fighting stance in the aisle of the airbus. Jackie smiled like she had seen herself in the same mental picture. They stared at each other for a long, silent moment.

"Sounds like you and your father were very close," she said at last. "Did he pass recently?"

Frank cleared his throat. "No. Fourteen years ago. This July."

"And your mother?"

"She died when I was born." He lowered his face. It was time to change the subject, time to cue up the tape on his struggling start-up, X-Treme Travel, and how badly he needed an investor. He'd even rather admit to being flat broke than—

"They're with you always," she said quietly. "You know that, don't you, Frank? The spirits of the people we love are always near."

Too late.

"Maybe. I just—I don't like to talk about this. It feels . . ." He shrugged. "Useless. Pointless."

"No. Not useless. It's comforting. I lost my little brother . . ." Her voice sank to a whisper before she mastered it and continued. "If I didn't believe that he was near me, I don't think I could stand it. If it weren't for his voice in my head and in my heart—" She shook her head, swallowing back some private pain of her own. "You believe that, don't you, Frank? You believe your father's with you now, don't you?"

"No." The word fell out of his mouth before he could edit himself.

Once again, Jackie laughed. "You're probably the most honest man I've met in a long time," she said.

"I'm sorry. I know my mother believed something like that, though," Frank backpedaled. "That the spirit never dies. She told my father that she'd always be near us, because the power of her love for us would draw her back. Maybe it's so, but . . ." If he could have spoken, he might have explained that his mother was a blank slate to him. But by the tightening in his chest and burning in his throat, Frank knew he could go no further. He put the past back into its dusty box and shelved it, turning toward his beautiful companion with a rusty but determined smile.

"Well, this is a strange conversation, isn't it? But look," he gestured, indicating the plane's relative calm. "We're nearly there. So, what do you do?"

Her eyes told him she'd read him to the very marrow of his soul, but she surrendered and answered the question, telling him something about a nonprofit and a speech in Boston on the two Ps—poverty and population control—while she distracted him with the soft pressure of her fingers stroking his.

"You?"

He queued up stories about his life: the college reunion he was traveling to, his troubled start-up and his many years on the road—normal airplane conversation stuff—and still felt like he had stripped down to his bare ass for a stranger.

I haven't said that much about my parents in a decade, he thought. *Why did I tell her that story about my father?*

"Thank you," she said when another brief silence fell between them.

"For what?"

"For everything. But mostly just for being so honest. I guess I'm not used to that anymore. Especially not from men. I wonder . . . while you're in Boston . . . if you'd like to—"

A massive basso of thunder exploded around them and the airbus buckled under it, trembling and tumbling downward for several agonizing seconds as a brilliant flash of lightning simultaneously made daylight of the night outside. The cabin lights guttered and extinguished.

The older blond flight attendant who had poured Frank a beer an hour ago bolted out of the galley and ran up the aisle. By the dim blue strips of the emergency lights, she jerked open the thin curtains separating steerage from first class and conferred briefly with the other attendants—a tall, thin young man and a younger-looking woman with a spiky haircut—before knocking on the door to the cockpit and disappearing inside.

"Something's wrong, isn't it?" Jackie's voice was a whisper in the general alarm surrounding them.

"I think we were struck by lightning," Frank began hesitantly. "But it's probably okay. Planes get struck all the time. Most of the time it's—"

The airbus began descending sharply, slicing the air at a steep decline. The flight attendant burst out of the cockpit and murmured a few words to her colleagues before striding toward the center of the plane. She switched on a flashlight, illuminating her face.

"Everyone, I need your attention!" she shouted. "Please! Quiet! So everyone can hear me! It appears that the aircraft's electrical system has been compromised. We'll be making an immediate emergency landing in Providence, Rhode Island!" She ignored the questions shouted around her and pressed on. "The captain is more than confident that we'll land safely, but as a precaution, we need for you to assume the brace position."

Anxiety rippled from the front of the plane to the back. The white-haired man in the window seat, who hadn't said a word since he boarded, dropped his paperback. "I know what that means!" he shouted, his voice rising in panic. "We can't land normally. The flaps are electric—"

"F-Frank—" Jackie began, clutching his arm. "Is that right?"

"Yes." Frank's stomach tightened. More than three hundred flights in about thirty years? Maybe his luck finally *had* run out. He turned toward Jackie's frightened, pale face and found ballast against his own fear. "Get your head as close to your knees as you can, Jackie." He bent, resting his head on his knees, his face still turned toward hers. "Rest the tip of your head—yes, just like that—"

"But—"

"Everything's going to be fine," he said squeezing her hand, hoping he wouldn't be made a liar. "It's just a precaution—"

She nodded, but more tears slid down her cheeks.

"It's just a precaution," Frank repeated gently. "Please don't cry. Please . . ." He touched her cheek, gathering up the wetness with a fingertip. "It's going to be okay—"

"Yes." She swallowed back a sob and her soft features sharpened with determination. "Yes, of course. I—I don't want to die . . . but I believe in God and a life beyond this one. I believe enough for both of us." She squeezed his hand, and Frank found himself staring into orbs darker and deeper than the violence of the night.

The aircraft hairpinned sharply, descending rapidly and steadily. Frank braced himself, contracting all the muscles in his body to keep himself in his seat. Over it all, the engine shrieked and strained and the darkness seemed to swallow up everything but hope.

I don't want to die today, either, Frank thought. *But if I do, I'm glad it's beside this woman. I'm glad—*

The landing gear smacked the ground. The airbus hurtled down the runway faster than the pilot could control, fishtailing wildly, throwing the passengers around like dice in a cup and sending the contents of the overhead bins flying down onto them like carry-on missiles. Something heavy scraped Frank's cheek, but he kept his head low and his eyes squeezed shut. Screams battled with the roar of the wheels against the tarmac and the hungry, fierce rush of the air as the aircraft split the driving rain. Jackie's fingers dug into his hand, but he wasn't conscious of pain, only of the shuddering feeling of the wheels out of control beneath his feet and the sickening anticipation of impact.

The aircraft listed dangerously, sending the older man in the window seat hard against Jackie and Jackie against Frank. Frank grabbed them both, straining every muscle in his body to keep them all from tumbling into the aisle. He felt the plastic of the armrest bite into his rib cage and drove his feet hard into the floor, using his legs to stabilize himself, sweating with the effort of grounding their weight. Jackie clung to him, her face pressed into his shoulder. He heard her screaming, felt her trembling, but he couldn't see anything. His eyes were squeezed shut.

Then, bit by bit, the plane wobbled and shuddered to a stop.

Frank lifted his head. Luggage scattered the aisles, but the cabin and its passengers appeared to be intact. Other heads lifted around him, one by one. And then, with spontaneous relief, the shaken passengers burst into applause. They were still alive.

"Frank!" Jackie threw her arms around him, her cheek buried in the warm skin at the side of his neck. "We made it!" And a moment later, Frank felt her soft lips touch his own.

He didn't know why he did it—probably he'd seen too many movies—but his body reacted faster than his brain could process. With a jolt of attachment, he pulled her closer, kissing her like an action hero in a summer blockbuster. She responded, her arms tightening around his neck, her palm nesting against his cheek. Frank sighed into her, relaxing into the feel and taste of her as though after many years of traveling, he'd finally found home.

"Fire! The plane's on fire!"

Screams of panic erupted around them. People dove toward the aisles, pushing and shoving each other as they pressed toward the exits. The little boy began sobbing again, his wails punctuated by short, hacking coughs. Frank glanced toward the ceiling. By the dim light he could see a thin veil of gray smoke wafting through the cabin, carrying an acrid chemical smell that burned his eyes and stung his throat.

"The rear door is stuck!" another voice hollered. "We're trapped—"

"I'm getting off this thing!" The older man in the window seat lurched over them, stepping on toes and belongings as he moved. "I'm getting off this thing—*now!*" he bellowed, stumbling into the aisle and shoving the elderly lady in the seat ahead of them aside. "I'm getting off—"

A blast of cold, wet air filled the cabin as the wing exits popped open and large yellow plastic slides unfurled, hissing violently like long plastic tongues of hungry snakes. Sirens sounded in the distance. Jackie twisted out of Frank's arms.

"Stay calm! Stay calm!" the spiky-haired flight attendant shouted angrily, sounding more like a mother disciplining her wayward children than a flight attendant in an emergency. "Everyone will get out in time. Just stay calm! Cover your faces with anything you can and stay low! Move toward the wing exits—"

From the galley behind him, Frank heard the desperate sound of someone working at the latch.

"There are one hundred and fifty-three souls on this flight." Frank recognized the voice as the blond flight attendant's. She had reminded him of Meryl Streep in *It's Complicated*. "We *need* this door!"

"I'm trying! It's jammed!" That sounded like the kid who had been sitting across the aisle from them—a no-neck, thick-muscled twenty-year-old in a UCSD hoodie and gym shorts.

"You lift up and over." Meryl's voice was urgent and on edge. "You must be doing something wrong—"

"*You* couldn't get it open," the kid snapped back. "And you're like—the professional—so what do you expect—"

Frank stood up.

"Wh-where are you going?" Jackie demanded. "They said we can't get out that way."

"We've got to get that rear door open, Jackie. I'm going to see if I can help—"

"But—"

"It's okay. I promise."

"No. No way, Frank." Her fingers tightened around his.

"If you're going, I'm going." She looked around them, taking in the rising panic of their fellow passengers with wide, frightened eyes. *Please don't leave me,* they begged. *Please.* "I-I don't think—I—" she stammered.

"It's okay," Frank told her. "Come on."

Meryl squatted near the kid, whose face had turned purple from straining against the door. She turned anxious eyes to Frank as he joined them.

"Let me try."

The young athlete shrugged dubiously as Frank felt along the hatch's frame.

"The clasp is here, I think," he called over his shoulder. "Turn your heads—"

Frank aimed the heel of his foot at the base of the exit door, kicking at it again and again until he'd shattered the plastic of the door's surface, revealing the mechanism of the lock inside.

"I need a lever. Something metal. Anything—"

Jackie's face disappeared into the deep well of her purse. A few seconds later she pulled out an expensive black fountain pen and a small flatiron. "I have this and this. The nib of the pen is steel—"

"I'll take it."

Frank wedged the pen into the pin of the clasp, then positioned his fingers at the rim of the doorway. He took a deep breath as though preparing for a deadlift and then strained against the bottom of the hatch.

The pen shattered, splattering ink everywhere. Frank winced as a stray shard of its casing nicked his forehead, but it stung only a second. The important thing was that the door swung up and out away from him, sending a gust of cold rain into his face as a yellow slide unfurled in front him.

"Thank you," Meryl breathed. "But I need the three of you to stay there and help the people off," she instructed. "Two at the top, one at the bottom. Tell them to jump out onto the slide with their hands up like this"—she threw her hands up as if he were pointing a gun at her—"and to run as far away from the plane as possible when they're on the ground." She leaned close to Frank, lowering her voice. "Push them down the slide if you have to. You understand?" Frank nodded. "Good man." She quickly pulled the scarf of her uniform up over the lower half of her face like a bandit and turned back to the main cabin.

"The rear exit doors are opened!" she bellowed into the chaos. "The rear doors—"

"Where do you want me, bro?" the college kid asked, offering Frank a handshake.

"Someone strong should be at the bottom," Frank said, nodding toward the slide.

The kid nodded in return. He stepped up, bent his knees and hopped onto the slide like it was a thrill ride. A moment later, he was on the ground, waving an "okay" as the downpour plastered his hoodie to the sculpted muscles of his chest.

Frank turned to find a line had already formed. The elderly lady who had sat in the seat ahead of them stepped up nervously, her eyes irritated and red.

"I—I—" she began tearfully, glancing at the slide uncertainly. "I don't know if I can—"

Jackie stepped into the space across from him and took the woman's hand.

"Frank and I will help you. Give him your other hand—" Plump fingers, the skin soft and well worn, found his. "Now just sit down—"

"Hurry up!" someone yelled from the darkness behind them. "We've got to get out of here!"

"Maybe the others should go," the lady said, tears rolling down her face as she backed away from the doorway. "I'll just—"

"Sit down," Jackie urged, her voice firm but kind. "Like it's a chair."

The elderly lady inhaled and nodded, bending her knees slightly. Frank felt the load of her weight as she sank slowly to the edge of the doorway, then its absence as her bottom hit the slide. "Now lift your arms," Jackie told her soothingly, but her eyes locked on Frank's.

Push her, they said. *For her own good, like the flight attendant said.*

"L-like this?" she stammered, releasing them and lifting her hands a few inches on either side of her face.

Frank didn't wait. *Forgive me*, he thought, and then shoved the center of her back hard enough to send her smoothly down the slide to the UCSD kid.

The next several passengers dove to safety without much assistance. Frank leaned out of the hatch and saw firefighters working the nose of the plane, but he couldn't see any flames. Inside the cabin, though, the pungent smog caught in his throat and stung his eyes. He heard Jackie coughing behind him, struggling to breathe as the aircraft emptied of people and filled with smoke.

"Jackie—" Frank began, determined to convince her it was time for her to go, just as the mother stood in front of him, her young son at her side. He was probably a little under two years old, with a mop of straight brown hair, red eyes and a runny nose. He was still crying, his little chest heaving in hiccups of distress as he coughed, his lungs sounding too full to gather enough oxygen. He rubbed his eyes and lifted his hands toward his mother, begging to be lifted.

"I—I can't hold him," the woman told Frank tearfully, bending toward the child with a wince. She staggered and then steadied herself with a deep breath. "My arm . . . I must have twisted it when we . . ." She lost the sentence in a fit of coughing. "H-he's . . . too little to go down alone—"

"Come here, sweetie." Jackie scooped up the little boy, leaning him toward the fresh air outside. "Hey there," she said in soothing voice. "It's okay. You wanna go down the big slide?"

The child stopped crying and reached out to touch her hair.

"Thank you," the mother said, weakly. "If you hold him in your lap when you go, he'll be . . . safe—"

"Oh, no," Jackie coughed, shaking her head. "I didn't mean—I'm not going down yet—"

"Yes, you are," Frank interrupted.

"But Frank—"

"They need to get off this plane," he murmured. "And he'll let you take him, Jackie." He put his hand on the toddler's head, ruffling his hair. "The little guy has good taste. He likes you. He wants to see you safe. And so do I."

Jackie hesitated. Frank read "stay" and "go" shifting in her eyes. "Wh-what about you?" she stammered at last.

"I'll be right behind you," Frank said, glancing around

the cabin. There were only a few dozen passengers left aboard—almost all lone male travelers like him reared with similar notions of chivalry—and thanks to the efforts of the firefighters on the ground below, the smoke, while dense, wasn't getting any worse. "I promise."

Resistance flared and then died on her face. The little boy stared at her with big solemn eyes, and then rested his head on her shoulder, curling a knot of her dark hair in his chubby fist. Jackie glanced at the child, then his mother and finally at Frank.

"All right," she sighed, stepping up to the opening. "But you'd better be right behind me. Promise me?"

Before his brain could stop him with reasons and rationales, he leaned over and kissed her again. Once again her free hand settled against his cheek, caressing the sensitive skin along his jaw, as she melted into him, surrounding him with the soft smell of her hair and the warm wetness of her mouth.

It probably lasted only a second—maybe less—but when he released her, her eyes locked on his in an expression he'd never seen before and didn't know how to interpret . . . except that it made his heart start pounding like music in his chest.

"I'll see you down there, Frank," she murmured, then wrapped her arms around the little boy and propelled herself into the rain, taking Frank's heart and hopes with her.

CHAPTER TWO

"You heard about that plane? The one that made the emergency landing yesterday?" Frank's boyhood friend Steve Hughes bellowed, attracting the attention of most of the room. He leaned close to Frank, dropped an arm around his shoulder and blew a blast of beer into his face. "This guy right here was on it, man! *On* it!"

Fifteen years ago—back in high school—people had joked that they looked like brothers, but these days Steve was the Philip Seymour Hoffman character in *Along Came Polly*, while Frank had largely maintained his *Scent of a Woman* Chris O'Donnell. Even in his "dressed up" clothes—a pair of dark slacks and a striped button-down topped by a dark blazer—Steve managed to look beefy, sloppy and disheveled.

Rutledge Hall's garden atrium sparkled with lights and

lively conversations. Frank remembered the space looking much different in his college days: a tangle of bare branches, often covered with snow, seen out of the corner of his eye as he hurried toward the Finance Office on the second floor to pay one bill or the other. But now, dressed in June's full green and with each branch wound with tiny white lights, the arbor was as elegant and vibrant as the company mingling beneath its boughs. Tables draped with white and dotted with little candles covered the grass, set strategically around a raised stage on which a band played pop hits in a jazzy style.

It was lovely, really . . . but as far as Frank could tell, the atmosphere was wasted on the attendees. Shouts of "Aren't you—" and "I'd know you anywhere!" clashed with bursts of laughter. From the amount of drinking and whooping and bragging and squealing he'd heard since he and Steve had arrived, the class of 2003 weren't stable members of society in their early thirties. They were drunken, foul-mouthed twenty-somethings—or in Steve's case, a loud, swaggering teenager recently escaped from the strict confines of his parental home.

"See, if he'd caught the flight Thursday with me like I told him to—"

"I had work to do, Steve," Frank reminded him.

"Rub it in," Steve chortled, nudging him hard in the rib cage with an elbow and activating the dull bruise in Frank's side the hard landing had left there. "The real estate market's still shit. I haven't had a decent listing in two years. Anyway, so he's on that fucking plane instead of sitting in the bar with me, like he was supposed to be!"

His audience—Mikey, John, Kevin and Dirk, whom

they'd always called "Dork"—laughed sympathetically. Frank hadn't seen them in years—not since their friend Al's wedding five or six years before—and he wouldn't have recognized most of them. Their trim, athletic builds had been replaced with softness at the arm and stomach. Hair seemed to be already making a retreat among those who hadn't anticipated its eventual demise by shaving their heads down to the scalp. They didn't look old exactly, but none of them was likely to be mistaken for twenty-one anymore.

"So, like I was saying about the plane—"

"Excuse me a minute," Frank said, glancing back at the atrium's entrance, where a table of women he didn't recognize had handed him his name badge. "I'm just going to..."

Steve grabbed him by the back of his blazer. "Whoa! It's fine, dude. At least let me tell them the story before you bolt—"

"I just want to check—"

"Hey, you paid for her. They made her a name badge—you saw them do it. If she comes, she can walk right in," Steve reassured him. He nodded at the guys. "He met some chick on the plane. Didn't even get her last name, but he still thinks she might drop by."

"She's more than 'some chick,'" Frank interrupted, making his annoyance plain. "And I told her about this reunion. If she's looking for me, she might—"

"Dude, I know you had a 'moment' with plane girl, but it's over! You'll probably never see her again," Steve said, grinning as if a smile would make the words less harsh. "Now let me tell them the story, okay?"

Frank shook his head. Like the scene of a movie he'd seen so many times he could repeat every word of dialogue by heart, the conversation with Jackie on the shuddering plane queued up in mind. He felt her arms around him after they had skidded to a heart-jarring stop on the tarmac and the softness of her lips when they kissed. He saw her slide down the yellow emergency ramp . . .

And then she had disappeared.

Because he was young, flying alone and in good shape, he'd been commandeered into helping the remaining passengers disembark, and couldn't follow her. But even though he descended only a few minutes—not even five—behind her, she had vanished. Gone, baby, gone. At the end of the slide, instead of the woman of his dreams, Frank found pouring rain, a paramedic with a blue blanket and a waiting ambulance.

"I'm fine," Frank told the EMT over and over again, but the young paramedic insisted on treating him as though he'd suffered some kind of shock or trauma.

"We're just going to check you out, sir." He was a kid—barely twenty—with a line of plump red zits running along his jawline. "Please try to relax—"

"I'm fine!" Frank shouted, throwing off the blanket and pushing away the oxygen mask. "The girl with the long dark hair—where did she go?"

"One of the area hospitals, probably. Everyone's being checked out. Just as a precaution—"

"Which one? How many hospitals are there in this town?"

The kid stopped trying to take his blood pressure long enough to look him in the face.

"Was she a family member, sir?"

"No, but—"

"We're trying to keep families in the same locations, but other than that . . ." He shrugged his shoulders. "Are you feeling any pain anywhere?"

"My ass," Frank muttered, rolling his eyes.

"Were you injured on the way down the slide?" the kid asked without a trace insult or irony.

"No," Frank sighed. "Never mind. Can I just—"

"You're bleeding, sir." The kid touched Frank's forehead with his gloved finger and showed him.

"It's just a scratch."

"We have to take you for evaluation, sir."

And that's how he'd ended up at Rhode Island Hospital. He saw several other passengers as he sat waiting until finally, three tiny stitches were administered to the little gash from the exploding pen—but no Jackie.

"She was right beside me. In seat 34E. Her first name is Jackie, I don't know her last name—" Frank told the airline representative who, he assumed, was on hand for some level of public relations damage control.

"Hmmm, I don't see that name on the manifest," she said, frowning at the cut on Frank's face.

"She was right next to me. Maybe Jackie is a nickname. Or her middle name. 34E—"

"We can't release information on passengers without their consent. But if you'll give me your name, I can let her know you're looking for her."

Frank sighed. Everything about it reminded him of the movie *Flightplan* and he was Jodie Foster's character. Everyone seemed determined to convince him that there hadn't been a woman named Jackie in the seat next to him—or that if she had been, he had no right to any information about her. He left his name, but he hadn't heard from her. Not yet.

"You know how chicks are, man," Steve had said when Frank related the experience to him. "Jackie might not be her name at all. They'll tell you anything, when they want you to go away."

I don't believe that.

Had he misread her? Was it just "a moment," like Steve said? Frank had turned it over in his mind, examining it from every possible angle—and still his thoughts kept returning to the way she looked at him just before she glided down the slide and into the night.

"See you down there?" she'd murmured, leaning close to him. "Promise me?"

Frank could still feel the connection of that moment, like an invisible cable stretched taut from his heart to hers. Either she'd meant every word and intended every gesture—or CZJ should hand over her *Chicago* Oscar if the doppelgangers' paths ever crossed.

"I know you all heard the news reports about how there were no serious injuries, but what you probably didn't hear about was how the rear exit door got stuck and my brother here figured out how to get it open—" Steve was saying when Frank tuned his attention back to the plane crash story. To his surprise, the tale had gathered a fairly decent crowd.

"Hold on a sec, Steve. I can't relive it empty." Frank lifted his beer and managed a smile. "You go ahead and tell it. I'll be right back."

"Aw, come on!" Steve snorted. "He's just modest, that's all. Won't toot his own horn—"

"No need," Frank joked, already in motion out of the tight circle of avid listeners. "Not when you're enjoying it so much." He shook a couple of hands, weathered a few slaps on the back and kept moving until he was clear of Steve's circle of listeners.

"Another," he told the bartender, showing the empty bottle. The older woman in her white shirt and black pants looked so familiar, Frank wondered if she had served him a soda the last time he was at one of these functions—nearly fifteen years ago, when he and his father had visited Broughton. Frank gulped down the beer and the painful memory of himself as a shy seventeen-year-old, more accustomed to brushing the dust from a fragment of bone than conversing with kids his own age.

There has to be something I'm missing! he thought. He'd tried Googling her name in combination with the words "speech" and "Boston," then again with the words "population control" and "poverty"—the two Ps, as she'd called them. But that was all he could remember about what she said she did for a living, and the results didn't seem to lead in the right direction. He'd tried adding the words "San Diego" and "nonprofit" to his search list. He typed her name over and over, spelling it differently each time. Jackie with an "ie." Jacqui with a "q." Jacky with a "y." If he could just be left alone for a few minutes, Frank knew he'd be able to—

"Frank? Frank Young?"

Frank recognized her instantly. She had abandoned her glasses for contacts and changed her hair, but the face was virtually the same. So was the figure. In a sudden erotic flash of memory, he saw her bare breasts, felt the weight of them as he cupped them in his hands. No one would guess this woman was possessed of such assets: she covered her God-given treasures with a demure black cocktail dress topped by a sequined jacket.

"You don't remember me?" she said with a smile. "I'm—"

"Meredith Lucas," Frank finished.

She blushed a little, but whether from embarrassment at the memory of that one frantic, drunken encounter or from the glass of wine in her hand, Frank couldn't be sure.

"Yes. Only it's Meredith Kolshack now. This is my husband, Mark." For the first time he noticed a man standing just over her shoulder.

"Nice to meet you," Frank said, shaking the hand of an average-looking guy, at least a half decade older, a little on the heavy side, crammed into a dark blue suit.

"You've hardly changed at all, Frank."

"And you haven't aged a day," Frank said earnestly. "You look great, Meredith."

"Thanks." Her cheeks crimsoned again and this time, Frank was certain it was the compliment.

"She really does," the husband chimed in. "Everyone's been commenting on it. Most of the gals who graduated when we did are starting to show a little wear," he chuckled. "I guess that moisturizing cream she slathers on every night really works!"

Frank focused on the guy again. "Did you graduate from Broughton, too, Mark?"

"Yeah. I'm a class behind you guys," He laughed again, seeing the surprise on Frank's face. "Yeah, I know. She's my older woman, but you'd never know it to look at us, right?"

"Wow—talk about good genes," Frank began as another woman stepped into the space beside him.

"Frank Young, I've been listening to the most amazing story about you!" she said enthusiastically.

A short brunette with her hair piled into some kind of elaborate updo and her ample figure poured into a strapless pink dress took his arm. Her face was round and youthful and familiar, but just beyond the border of Frank's memory. Another woman—thinner and plainer, as well as some years older—stood just behind her in a blue dress decked with a few too many sequins.

"Did you know Frank was on that plane? The one that crash landed in Providence last night?" she said, grabbing Frank's arm and leaning toward the Kolshacks eagerly. "Are you all right, Frank?" The woman presented a face crinkled with social concern. "Steve said you helped a bunch of people get off safe. I'm really not surprised though," she continued, without waiting for an answer to any of her questions. "Anyone who knows you knows there's more to you than there seems. It wouldn't have surprised me if they said you ran to the cockpit and landed the thing—"

"No, no nothing like that." Her name danced just beyond his reach. "You are . . ."

"You don't remember me?" She frowned, her lower lip protruding in a girlish pout. "We dated for most of our freshman year, Frank—and everyone's been telling me that I haven't aged a day!" She turned to the sequined woman. "Isn't that right, Jenny? Even Jenny said it. You remember Jenny—we were roommates. She said I hadn't changed a bit! Well, my hair is different. And I put on a few pounds, but that's because I haven't been able to work out like I used to in school. The women in my family tend toward just a little weight. I remember in school I used to eat only lettuce and work out three hours a day and it was a struggle not to gain—even then! And now that I'm working—I teach third grade at a private school in upstate New York—now that I'm working, well, I just don't have time for all that exercise these days! Who does? Well, apparently Frank does. Look at him. Still the same weight he was in high school, I bet, aren't you, Frank?" She squeezed his arm. "And still all muscle. Unlike me! But other than a few extra pounds, all night long, it's been 'You look just the same—'"

"Just the same," Jenny agreed, nodding vigorously. "It's amazing, really. I keep asking her what she's using—"

"Must be the same stuff as Meredith!" Mark Kolshack chuckled, but the woman barely registered his comment. Her attention was still fixed on Frank. Clearly, she thought the hints she'd given to be enough.

"Uh . . ." Frank stammered, praying for a rescue from his confusion—and from her merciless hold on his arm. "I'm not sure . . ."

"Grace! Grace Mitchell!" she cried, stamping her foot impatiently. "Really, Frank—"

"Of course," Frank said quickly. "It's been a long time, Grace. And I'm sorry. I . . . I don't remember a lot about my freshman year. There was just . . . a lot going on with me then."

Grace Mitchell's face softened again. "I remember. Your father had just passed. Just before school started, wasn't it? Of course. I remember now—"

"Yes," Frank interrupted as memories of the woman flooded his mind. Grace Mitchell was a talker—the kind who didn't require any participation from her conversation partners or even a listener. He remembered letting her never-ending stream of words surround him, cushioning the emptiness inside him. There were never awkward silences with Grace: she didn't seem to mind how little he said, and Frank had been grateful to her for that—and for the generous softness of her body as they explored each other on the narrow twin bed of her dorm when her roommate—this same woman, Jenny—was out.

And she was right: compared to Jenny, whose face registered the ten years since graduation plus a few more, Grace was the same fresh-faced co-ed he remembered.

It was weird. Unsettling almost. Frank looked from Grace to Meredith, expecting some recognition or comment about their youthfulness, but neither woman seemed to find it odd.

"Did you know him then?" Grace asked Meredith as her pale hand gave his jacket another ruthless, possessive squeeze.

"No," Meredith managed to interject. "We had a class together sophomore year, but—"

"Oh, he was a mess," Grace said as though she knew all about his interior life. "In shock, I think, but then I wouldn't know. Both my parents are still living. I can only imagine what it must have been like for you to be on your own so suddenly. Poor baby—"

"It's okay," Frank interjected, not wanting to send the subject down the path of his dead parents any further—not after all these years and everything else that had happened since then. It was one thing to talk about them seated next to a beautiful woman as their plane nosedived toward the ground. But here and now...

"I think he must have been better by sophomore year," Meredith replied as though Frank weren't standing there and they were discussing an unfortunate child. "Because I didn't even know—"

"I dated him in our senior year. Do I get a prize?" another female voice interrupted from the space just behind him.

Eva Cross angled herself into the space between Grace and the Kolshacks. She made the other women look demure in her low-cut, red cocktail dress, with her sandy blond hair spilling seductively over her shoulders. The energy shifted toward her, extinguishing the lights in Grace and Meredith like a black hole consuming a star. Compared to their girl-next-door looks, Eva belonged in another class altogether—and she knew it. Like the others, she looked remarkably youthful . . . uncannily so.

"Hello, Frank," Eva purred, leaning in to kiss his cheek. "You're looking well. Are you still an asshole?"

"Hello, Eva," Frank said calmly, resolved to let her insults bounce off him. "You haven't changed."

She rolled her eyes at him, registering the censure without comment. The last time they'd seen each other—the day he'd grown a backbone and stopped letting her take advantage of him—she'd chased him out of her bedroom, a naked warrior ready for the kill, throwing everything she could get her hands on as she screamed, "I can't believe you're leaving me like this, motherfucker! How am I supposed to pay my rent? How?"

Frank considered the three women and his place in this strange tableau. It was creepy: they looked like they'd been frozen at eighteen, nineteen and twenty.

"Well, this is an interesting little gathering, isn't it?" Eva said in her snobby sorority girl voice. "It looks like we've convened a meeting of the I Slept with Frank Young Club."

Meredith's cheeks flamed. She glanced at her husband. Grace's possessive fingers dropped from Frank's arm.

"Honestly, Eva. Haven't you learned to behave yourself yet?" Frank muttered.

"Well, I'm right, aren't I?" Eva insisted. "You've both slept with him, haven't you? And of course, *I've* slept with him. He's got a good body underneath these boring clothes he always wears, doesn't he? And, ladies, I'm sorry to tell you, Frank kisses and tells. I've heard all about you both." She turned to Grace. "He found you convenient, I think. And you . . ." She leveled a smile on Meredith. "He was just drunk—"

"Eva!" Frank barked. "Stop it! Now—"

"Or what, Frank?" Eva challenged. "What?"

"Excuse me," Meredith mumbled, turning on her heel and hurrying away from them. Her husband shot Frank a look of impotent jealousy and followed.

"It's nice to see you, Frank," Grace said quietly and slipped away, too, with Jenny in tow. It figured: only a force like Eva had the power to cease her endless stream of chatter.

Eva swung her blue eyes on Frank. "Gee, was it something I said?"

"Did you *have* to do that?" Frank hissed. "Did that make you feel better? Really, Eva, it's been ten years. Don't tell me you're not over—"

"I know how long it's been, Frank," Eva snapped back. "And no, I didn't have to do that. I *wanted* to do that. And yes, it made me feel better. Much better."

She leaned close. Frank thought she was going to whisper in his ear ... until he felt the cold wetness of the contents of her glass splash his face.

"That felt good, too," she said with a triumphant smile, then stalked away from him like a cougar with its prey's blood fresh on its lips, swinging her hips beneath the tight red fabric of her dress.

CHAPTER
Three

"I need a yearbook," Frank told Steve the next day as they strolled along the green grass of Broughton Quad. "Have you got one?"

"A what? Yearbook? What the fuck for, man?" The day was beautiful—a warm early June afternoon of sunshine and green—but Frank knew Steve cared little for the scenery. He was captivated by a different vista: the athletic, young college girls on bikes and skates, walking and jogging in sports bras, yoga pants and itsy-bitsy bottom-hugging shorts.

"I just . . ." Frank could hardly explain what he wanted. It sounded crazy, much too crazy to say aloud. "I just wanted to look up a few people."

"Who? Hey there . . ." Steve nodded at two girls in tank tops as they passed him, but neither of them altered her stride or paused in their conversation. Steve's head swiveled after them for a rear view. "Who did you want to look up?"

"I don't know," Frank lied. "I mean, I guess I wanted to look at Meredith's picture. It looked like she hadn't changed much—"

"Meredith?" Steve brayed his disdain. "Why would you want to do that? I mean, she's okay and everything. Nice woman. I liked her. I get why you did her: she was okay for a quick fuck on a lonely night. But now she's married. Why on earth would you waste your time with her now?"

"Did you see her? She looked as young as these girls. Almost exactly the same as she did when she was a student here! And that woman Grace. And Eva. They all looked so . . . *young*."

Steve lifted his baseball cap and wiped his hand across his sweaty forehead.

"Yeah, I saw Eva. And she did look great," he muttered. "But Eva always *looked* great. You have to *talk* to her to know she's crazy."

"She doesn't look great, Steve," Frank persisted. "She looks almost the *same*!"

Steve shook his head. "Man, I don't know what was in that drink she soaked you with, but you've lost it! I feel you: Eva is definitely still smoking hot. She puts most women her age to shame. But that's the end of it, man. What's with you?"

Frank inhaled. Steve was probably right, but he wasn't quite ready to let it go. What was it Eva had said? They were the *I Slept with Frank Young Club*? Was it possible he had something to do with it—or did they all just use Botox?

"I don't know. I just—"

"I know," Steve said wisely. "You're more shook up from that plane ride than you thought. Yesterday, it was all 'crash landing girl'—"

"Jackie."

"Whatever. You were up all night again, looking for her—don't even lie, man," Steve continued as Frank opened his mouth to protest. "But you didn't find her, did you?"

Frank sighed. "No." He'd searched for hours and had finally found one organization that sounded like it might be hers—a group cleverly named Life SPAAN: Sustainable Populating Aging and Endings. The website listed an address in a San Diego suburb, but Frank couldn't find her name anywhere and there weren't any pictures of her on the site. The best Life SPAAN offered him was a contact form, which he reluctantly filled out, writing what he hoped wasn't too ridiculous an explanation of the assistance he needed:

> *Met a woman named Jackie on the flight from San Diego to Boston that crash landed in Providence. She mentioned she worked for a nonprofit like yours. If there's a Jackie there who was on that flight, I'd very much like to see her again.*

It sounded like one of those "Missed Connections" ads that used to run in the Classifieds sections of alternative newspapers when he was in high school—but Frank sent it anyway, feeling like a desperate, lovelorn sap.

Now, another idea seized his mind, wrestling for supremacy with thoughts of Jackie.

"Look, you're right, okay?" Frank admitted to his friend. "I'm just a little . . . freaked . . . by how young those women looked. I just want to take a look at their pictures from school, okay? Come on, the library is right here," he said. "You don't have anything else to do before your plane leaves."

Steve sighed as if Frank were proposing a few hours of study instead of a frat party. "All right, bro. But only a few minutes, okay? I said I wanted to relive the old days . . . but there's a limit."

The cool of Foster Library was a welcome relief from the heat of the day. Frank took a deep breath, savoring the smell of old paper and wood, and the hum of the fluorescent lights above them. The building was old—built in the 1930s—and Frank had read in the Broughton *Alumni Flash* that soon the interior would enter the twenty-first century with a massive renovation. When construction ended in two years' time, the shelves of books would be replaced by docking stations for computers. Wireless networking throughout its six levels would allow students to access the three-million-volume collection almost entirely electronically. How much longer would yearbooks—or at least, anything like the hardcover *Centarian 2003* in Frank's hand—survive?

"I don't think I ever looked at this thing," Steve said in a voice that was soft for him, but loud for a library. "Am I in it?"

"Did you have your picture taken?"

Steve wrinkled his nose. "I don't even remember."

"We'll check in a minute. First . . ." Frank flipped the pages quickly until he found Meredith.

It was uncanny, really: a shy, intelligent face obscured slightly by thick glasses stared up at him. The thickness of her eyebrows, the unlined face, the fullness of the lips and the breasts were identical to those of the woman he'd reconnected with last night. Except for the clothes and the contacts, that ten-year-old picture of Meredith could have been taken yesterday.

"Wow." Steve whistled. "You're right. She hasn't changed much. Check the other one."

Frank flipped the pages again. Grace Mitchell's round face and curly brown hair leapt out at them, instantly familiar.

"She looks different."

"The hair," Frank agreed. "And she said she'd put on some weight."

"This is going to sound weird . . . but she looked even *younger* last night than she does in that picture," Steve muttered.

"I know."

"But how can that be possible, dude?"

"I don't know," Frank replied cautiously. "Now for Eva."

As soon as he found the right section, the flash of attitude in Eva's eyes arrested him.

"That is amazing." Steve voice went soft with awe. "There's almost no difference, man. Just the hair. But other than that . . ."

He was right. She was wearing her blond hair longer and straighter—but that was really the only difference. Her blue eyes seemed to glimmer at them out of a face that was supple and lineless, her lips pulled into a slight smile showing her white teeth. Her skin was dewy, unblemished perfection.

"It's a little weird, huh?" Steve said, grabbing the book for a closer look. "You think she had plastic surgery or something?"

Frank shrugged. "I guess she could have. Eva's the type for that stuff. But I don't think Meredith is. Or Grace."

"Yeah," Steve agreed absently. "Wait..."

He flipped the pages until he found himself, then surreptitiously flicked his phone out of his pocket and casually snapped his own picture. He held the newly taken image of himself against the one in the *Centarian*.

Of course, Steve's ball cap and T-shirt stood in such sharp contrast to the formal tux in the picture that neither man bothered to comment on it. There was no need anyway: his face fully showed the evolution of the years. Steve's face was fuller now—not fat or jowly, but just wider, even though Frank knew his friend to be only about twenty pounds heavier than he'd been ten years ago. Subtle puffy bags of flesh had settled on his cheeks and under his eyes, and his lips had thinned like something had been eating them from the inside. The changes were small, but noticeable enough to predict the future of his face. What struck Frank most of all were his friend's eyes: more serious, more weary, more worldly.

The two men stared at the images of Steve then and now, side-by-side in silence for a long moment, contemplating mortality.

"Well," Steve said at last with a sigh of resignation. "If it's Botox, sign me up—"

"Frank? Frank Young?"

A woman in a sundress in a busy fabric of vomited flowers approached them. Her hip-length blond hair hung in a single braid over one shoulder. A little boy about five years old stared up at Frank with piercing blue eyes in the same shade and shape as hers.

"Anne!" Frank took the hand she stretched toward him. "Anne . . ."

"It was Wainwright then. It's Vogel now. I *thought* that was you!" Her voice was still high-pitched and girly, and Frank instantly remembered how once she had rolled herself into a headstand and lisped, "Fuck me upside down, Frank!"

"This must be your son," Frank said quickly, to erase the image.

"His name his Josh. His father and I are divorced." She blinked her bright blue eyes and leaned toward him. "How about you, Frank? You married?" she asked sweetly.

"Uh . . ." Frank's brain screamed warning sirens like a scene out of *Pearl Harbor*. He glanced at Steve, but now that he needed him, his friend had suddenly decided that the yearbook was the most interesting thing he'd seen in a long, long time. "Look at you! You look great!" Frank said instead. "If I didn't know better, I'd swear you were a student here now!"

Anne laughed like one of those dolls that giggle when pressed. "I've been hearing that all weekend. Girls who wouldn't even speak to me when we were students here have been asking me my secret." She laughed again, winking. "I told them that it's yoga! That's what I do now. I own a chain of dance and yoga studios in the DC area."

"Wow." Frank felt himself nodding and smiling, nodding and smiling. There was a part of him that wanted to end the conversation as quickly as possible—and another that wanted her to keep standing there until he could make a grab for the yearbook and find her picture.

"Just about time to go, Frank. She'll be looking for you."

"She?" Anne and Frank said simultaneously.

"Frank's fiancée. Jackie. She's back at the hotel and we told her we'd meet her for a late lunch twenty minutes ago," Steve said with the earnest expression of a practiced liar.

"Oh." Anne's youthful features registered childish disappointment. "Well, congratulations on your engagement, Frank. She's a lucky girl. It's been really nice seeing you—"

"Hey, let's get a photo of you two," Steve suggested.

Thank you, man, Frank thought as Anne stepped closer to him. The smell of her hair as she slipped an arm around his waist triggered the sensory memory of it whipping around him as she rode him like a cowgirl. He was grateful when she moved away, waving him goodbye with her pinky finger like a bashful four-year-old.

"Did you find her picture? How does she look? Has she changed at all?" Frank asked urgently as soon as she was out of earshot.

"She's even more the same than the other ones," Steve muttered. "But wait a minute." Steve flipped toward the last letters of the alphabet. "There." Steve held the image on the phone beside Frank's yearbook picture. "What do you make of that?"

Frank studied his two pictures. Some of the same changes were evident on his face that he'd seen on Steve's—especially around the eyes—but on the whole, the ten-year difference seemed far less dramatic. "I don't know," he said at last. "I look . . ."

"Different," Steve finished. "Older, I guess . . . yes, a bit older. Just not . . ."

"Not as young as the girls," Frank offered.

"Not by a long shot," Steve agreed, with an edge of gratitude in his voice. "I don't know what's up with those chicks. Must be something in the water."

"Not the water," Frank muttered. That strange feeling of understanding that had been dogging the back of his mind was sharpening, gaining in clarity. It was like the plot of a movie—one of the Disney fantasies where a normal guy gets some kind of odd gift or curse. *A Thousand Words* or *Freaky Friday*, maybe. Or some superhero or science fiction pulp where a guy discovers he has strange powers, like *Spiderman*. It just seemed too ridiculous to actually say out loud.

"If not the water, then what? Botox?" Steve asked.

Frank hesitated.

"Look, if I tell you, you have to swear as my brother that you won't laugh and you won't tell anyone else. Do you swear?"

Steve's pale brows contracted in confusion. "What? What are you getting all serious for? What's the matter?"

"I don't know . . ." Frank began. "But you've gotta swear you won't laugh and you won't tell anyone."

"Dude . . . you're scaring me!"

"Swear!"

"Yeah, yeah! On my mom's life," Steve said solemnly.

"Okay. I know this is weird, but . . . what Meredith, Grace, Eva and Anne have in common is . . . me. I've slept with all of them." He paused. "I think I'm the reason they all look so young. I think . . . I think somehow sleeping with me . . . changed them, or something."

Steve stared at him, unblinking and unsmiling.

"Are you saying," he said at last, "you think your jizz is the fountain of youth?"

Frank nodded. "Yeah."

Five seconds stretched to ten seconds. Ten seconds stretched to twenty . . . then Steve's screech of laughter made every head in the library turn toward them.

"Magic jizz!" he said too loudly, his eyes moist from laughing. "Come on, man. When that plane crashed, you must have hit your head—"

"I'm serious, Steve—"

"No, you're not. You're stressed out about your company and that meeting with Lynch Capital tomorrow. Money's been tighter than a hooker's skirt lately and that wears a man down, believe me. And that plane shit?" Steve shook his head. "You've been through a lot the past couple of days. Let's face it, you're in good shape and all that, but you're not Superman. Come on, dude. I'll buy you a round or two before I gotta get to the airport. And promise me you'll stop chasing this Jackie girl and get some sleep tonight. Magic jizz . . ." Steve chuckled again, steering Frank out of the library and back into the warmth of the day.

CHAPTER
Four

Lynch Capital wasn't located in a downtown office tower, but in one of those classy old brownstones in Boston's Back Bay that stood for the kind of money and influence the wealthy of the town had had since the days of the Pilgrims.

Frank slid out of the cab and stood for a moment, drinking in the ambience of old money, hoping that at least the "money" part might be a part of his own future—and very soon. He offered up something like a prayer to whatever good spirits might be listening and immediately thought of Jackie and the way her lips had moved in silent prayer on that terrifying plane ride. *I believe in a life after this one. I believe enough for both of us.* Strangely, though, this time the memory of her—and the peace her faith had seemed to give her—eased his anxieties. He jogged confidently up the stone steps and pushed open the heavy wooden door.

"Mr. Young. Right this way." He couldn't have guessed the ethnic background of the young woman who greeted him—her mocha-brown skin, curly brown hair and hazel eyes offered far too many possibilities—but the bubble of her rounded behind beneath her slim black skirt made following her an interesting experience.

"May I get you something? Coffee? Water?"

"I'm fine. Thank you."

She left him alone in a large conference room with a massive oval table of dark wood polished so brightly that the elaborate chandelier over his head was reflected in its surface. Frank guessed the décor was calculated to be an intimidating show of wealth and position; it succeeded marvelously.

"Frank! You're early!" Jonathan Lynch strode into the room in a perfectly tailored charcoal-gray suit and impeccable steel-blue tie, commanding the room and everything in it. Frank didn't need to consult his files to recall how much money the man had made in his life: the clothes carried the water perfectly, along with the understated Patek Philippe watch that flashed briefly as he reached out to shake Frank's hand. He was nearly bald, but it was clear that he was a man in the vigor of his late middle age. According to Google, he'd run last year's Boston Marathon and finished with a perfectly respectable time of 4:24. He parachuted out of airplanes and collected increasingly younger wives for spare-time thrills.

"Nice to meet you, Mr. Lynch," Frank said. He couldn't compete with Lynch—or any of the men and women who followed him into the room—for sartorial splendor and he hadn't even tried. Instead, he opted for a look that complemented what he was selling them: a navy-blue golf shirt and another pair of khaki Dockers. The shirt showed his biceps without flaunting them, and he tucked it in and belted the slacks to emphasize his own lean physique. He hoped it conveyed the understated experience of a skilled and well-traveled guide.

"Call me Jonathan. There are no strangers here. Not when we're talking about making money together," Jonathan said, clapping him on the back.

Chase Lynch offered his hand next.

"Frank, old sport. Sorry I missed you at the reunion the other night. Work, you know?"

"Nice to see you, Chase," Frank said in as cordial a tone as he could muster. He tolerated Chase—always had—but had never really liked him. There was just too much silver spoon about him: the prep school lilt of his voice, the Brooks Brothers cut of his suits, the arch sophistication of his commentary. Chase was never the sort of guy who drank beer or tossed a football: he believed too much in the superiority granted him by his family's money for anything as plebeian as that. Of course, now that Chase was a partner at his father's venture capital firm—and Frank desperately needed $5 million—Chase could do and say whatever he pleased, and Frank was determined it would roll off his back like last night's rain.

"No more travel accidents, I hope," Chase said in his clenched-jaw prep school voice.

Jonathan Lynch's bright blue eyes twinkled with interest. "Oh, yes. You were on that plane."

"Yes, sir. I mean, Jonathan."

"But you're fine." Jonathan offered the words as a statement of fact. "None the worse for wear for the experience.

I would imagine it takes a lot to rattle a seasoned traveler like you."

"Absolutely fine," Frank agreed, but he couldn't stop the thought *except for the possibility that my semen is the fountain of youth,* and he could still hear Steve's laughter ringing loudly in his ears.

"Great. Grab a chair." Jonathan Lynch dismissed the plane, Frank's health and any other preliminaries. "Meet the team."

In a whirlwind of introductions, Frank shook hands with half a dozen men and one woman before taking his seat at the far end of a long conference table in front of a square white screen and a laptop set up for a PowerPoint demo.

"We've all seen your proposal and I think we're all fairly clear about what you're trying to do with XT—X-Treme Travel, that is," Jonathan said. "So unless you've got something new, we can dispense with the presentation. Even though this is our first meeting face to face, with all our emails and phone conversations, I see us as a little beyond the typical first-meeting protocols. Instead, we'd like to just talk with you about the business and hear your thoughts on its growth potential. Okay?"

"Sure," Frank said, glancing around the table. "Fire away."

Jonathan smiled and cut his eyes to the woman at his left hand. She wasn't anything special to look at: hair pulled into a severe ponytail, dark blue suit over pale blue blouse over boxy shoulders. Subtle makeup and no jewelry. Frank was embarrassed to admit it, but he'd already forgotten her name.

"Frank," she began, smiling a little. "We love the tours

XT puts together, and the research suggests that there is a market for greater and greater variety in the vacation experience. But it's decidedly a niche market right now. I'd like to ask you about the growth potential of your business when two-thirds of Americans are overweight, and the trends suggest that number is growing. For the average American, getting off the sofa is an extreme adventure!"

The table laughed appreciatively, and Frank smiled. It was a question he had anticipated.

"You're right, the most extreme travel tours appeal to a select group: those with the skills and fitness levels to attempt climbing Kilimanjaro, or a nomadic trek through the Sahara, or canoeing the Amazon—and sufficient affluence and leisure to pay for that kind of experience. We think we can attract those clients with both the quality of our tours and keep them by offering newer and better experiences. Right now, we're researching all kinds of interesting alternatives in China, in Africa and in South America—"

"You and your father did a lot of traveling there, didn't you, old sport? South America if I recall?" A blade of superiority sliced through Chase's words. "I seem to remember that from our school days."

There it was again—that twinge of discomfort at the memory of his father's death. *Why, after so many years, is this bothering me so much now?* Frank wondered. The whole weekend the subject of his parents' deaths had been like an ancient wound, deliberately aggravated and reopened for reasons Frank doubted anyone could justify. If only he hadn't started it, dredging up the past on the plane when Jackie—

I need this money.

"You're correct." Frank kept his voice steady and focused his thoughts on the business at hand. "I first visited South America when I was around six or seven, with my father—and first learned Spanish around that age. I've probably been half a dozen times as an adult. Different countries, different treks." He dismissed Chase casually and turned back to the woman. "And you are right: extreme vacations are relative. What's 'extreme' for one person might be tame—or at least not appealing—to another. With the right funding, I think we'll be able to serve not only the super-fit and über-adventurous, but create off-the-beaten-track experiences for those who are less fit and less adventurous—but still seeking something beyond the typical tourist-trap vacation experience."

"But once you start widening your market, what makes you different from any other travel agency?" asked a very young-looking man with a shock of curly hair and wire-rim glasses.

"Two things, I think. First, we'll always be searching for that 'X' factor in our tours, if you will. That signature edge that makes even the most pedestrian tour truly extreme. And second, our staff are among the most versatile and qualified you'll find anywhere. You've read my proposal so you know that between the three of us, we've traveled the entire world, climbed every peak, visited every continent. We have a world-class sailor and an Ironman triathlete, and all three of us climb and have some level of martial arts and weapons training. Each of us speaks at least one other language fluently—and all of us have some basic understanding of several others. We're all experienced in wilderness survival—"

"Sounds to me like we're back to point A." This time, Chase's interruption held a put-down. "It's a niche for athletes and wildman wannabes—"

"We're more than adventurers or extreme athletes," Frank continued, trying not to let his annoyance show. "One of my colleagues is a historian; the other is a nurse. My background is in archeology and anthropology—"

"Following in Daddy's footsteps, are we, old sport?" Chase murmured.

"You, too, I see," Frank fired back.

The energy in the room shifted uncomfortably. *Shit*, Frank thought, but he managed to find a smile again and say in the lightest voice he could, "I can't think of a better compliment to our fathers than being like them, can you, Chase?"

Chase's thin lips curled into the fakest smile Frank had ever seen. "Absolutely."

"Let's cut the bullshit," Jonathan interjected. "Your answers are good and I think you've got some creative, talented people involved with this thing. But the travel market still hasn't fully recovered from the recession and there's a lot of competition out there for the same dollars. Talk of expansion is nice but theoretical at best. So, let's just stick to the elite dollars. Niche market, boutique stuff. We'd be investing in your ability to expand on that limited market. With that said, we think five million is too much for a twenty-five percent share of your business. For that kind of money, we'd ask for fifty percent—"

"I'd never agree to that."

Jonathan smiled paternally at him. "I knew you'd say that, Frank. But you see, what I'm trying to tell you is from my perspective, your valuation is off. That changes the way I view the investment. I think for us a twenty-five percent share is worth two million dollars at best—"

"Two million dollars!" Frank exclaimed angrily. "But that's barely enough to cover the initial costs to expand the website and increase the marketing base. We can't research newer, better tours or hire scouts or—"

"Two million."

Frank's mind raced through his options. He should make a counteroffer, show himself willing to negotiate. But there was no counteroffer. It would take $5 million to accomplish what he needed for XT. Anything less would be giving away both his company and his chances for success.

There are other venture capital firms, he told himself.

But no one else has taken a meeting in nearly two months. Ask for $4 million, the other half of his brain argued back. *Maybe we can meet at three—*

Three won't be enough.

Three will keep us alive to raise the rest.

How? How? How will we raise the rest? And how much control will we have to give away? No. He's playing me. He knows we're onto something and he's trying to get a larger share.

"I'm sorry," Frank said at last. "You and I both know that XT can't succeed if it's undercapitalized. Five million for twenty-five percent is a fair valuation based on all the indicators and comparable start-ups. I can't accept less than that."

Jonathan Lynch's smile faded. He frowned in Chase's direction, then stood up and marched out of the room without saying another word. Like a line of ducklings waddling after their mother, his minions followed until only Frank and Chase were left in the room.

"Well, that went well," Chase murmured, beaming a condescending smile in Frank's direction.

"Yeah, great."

"No, I mean it, old sport. Good job."

"Your father just walked out of the meeting, Chase."

"I know!" He laughed like he was having the most fun he'd had in years. "You surprised me. I thought you'd cave! But I'm glad, actually. If you'd accepted the two he'd never have respected you." He stood up and stretched like a bored cat. "Good luck. For what it's worth, I still think you're onto something. I never would have forwarded your proposal to Pop if I didn't. Hope you can make a go of it." He paused at the conference room's heavy paneled door. "Oh—and if you're still in business next fall, sign me up for the Amazon. That's something I've always wanted to do. You know, bucket list and all that."

He offered Frank his hand and then disappeared, leaving him alone again in the ornate room. Defeated, Frank slung his laptop bag over his shoulder. It was heavy, but not as weighty as the realization that he would be returning to California empty-handed. There was nothing left to do now but move on. He glanced at his watch. He had an hour to kill before he was supposed to meet Darcy Hatfield . . . and nothing to do with the time but stew over his failure.

Steve had found Darcy on Facebook before catching his flight back to San Diego.

"You guys were a thing for a while. You slept her with her, right?"

Somehow, the *Centarian* had made it out of the library

without setting off the alarms as Frank hustled Steve, still howling with laughter, out of the place. Frank glanced at her picture and remembered a brunette with great legs and a weird laugh. "Yeah, a couple of times."

"Use a condom?"

"Of course I used condoms."

"Every time? 'Cause I'm thinking, if you were using condoms with some girls and not others it would be easier for me to believe your stuff's got magical properties, you know?"

Frank hesitated. "Well, not every time. Especially not with Grace and Eva. I dated them the longest, and—"

"What about Meredith? You only slept with her once. Condom?"

Frank closed his eyes with the effort of trying to remember. "It was so long ago, but . . . I think yes."

"Then it couldn't have been cum that did it, Frank," Steve insisted. "You never gave her any. Could it be something else? Swapping spit? Another bodily fluid?"

"You're beginning to gross me out, Steve—"

"Well, I don't know what else to call it."

"I couldn't tell you how many girls I've kissed. I wouldn't even remember them all."

"You didn't get freaky or anything. I mean Golden Showers or—"

"No!"

"It's a bodily fluid—"

Frank held up his hand, signaling the end of the subject. "Look, all I know is I've slept with all four of those women. Some always with a condom, some without. I didn't say I understood how it works or what exactly happened. I just said—" But Steve had already stopped listening, his eyes on his phone, his brow furrowed as fingers worked the digital keyboard. "What are you doing?"

"Getting you a date. You're having lunch with Darcy tomorrow," Steve answered. "See how she looks. And snap a picture of her, if you get the chance. A few more women and I might just have to take you seriously, dude."

Frank saw her before she saw him: a petite woman in a houndstooth-patterned skirt and white blouse, with her brown hair pinned at the nape of her neck like a sexy librarian, sitting at a corner table of the restaurant. She was studying the menu as if it were a final exam.

Darcy Hatfield didn't look a day over twenty.

"What the hell is happening?" Frank muttered aloud, slumping against the wall of the tiny Italian eatery, buried in a crack of the aging bricks of the city's North End. His knees felt weaker than they had after running the bulls at Fiesta de San Fermín in Pamplona. Darcy had just narrowed the likelihood of coincidence down to an even slimmer possibility.

"Am I the fucking fountain of youth?" Frank whispered to himself as he stared at the young woman waiting for him.

"Sir?" A nearby waiter paused to consider Frank skeptically. He held a huge pepperoni pie aloft like an offering.

"Nothing," Frank muttered. He took one last look at her . . . then backed quietly out of the restaurant, escaping to the dark cobbled streets of the North End, where he hailed a cab and threw himself inside.

It was wrong to stand her up—to leave her sitting there. But what could he have said to this woman? What *was* there to say? He certainly didn't want to be laughed at anymore. He didn't need anyone posting things about his theories on Facebook or circulating stories of a strange lunch with Frank Young all over the Internet. It was bad enough that he'd told Steve.

"Gimme a destination or get out!" the driver shrieked in exasperation, and Frank realized with a start that the man had been talking to him for several minutes. "You waste my time—"

"Okay, okay," Frank said quickly, recovering himself. "Logan Airport—no, wait." He opened his wallet and counted his remaining cash quickly. There wasn't much left—less than $100—and with no prospects for earning more in the immediate future, a cab ride was a luxury Frank couldn't afford. "Never mind," he muttered. "I'll take the T."

The driver cursed at him but Frank barely heard the words. He was broke, he'd met and lost the woman of his dreams, and every girl he'd ever slept with looked exactly like she did on the day he'd lain down beside her. There wasn't anything else to do here. It was time to go home.

CHAPTER
Five

"Shit. You didn't get the money, did you?"

Maxine Donovan stood in Frank's cluttered living room, her wife, Wendy, filling the space right behind her, her belly swollen in the last weeks of pregnancy.

Nothing about Max was feminine—by nature or design. She was stocky, with small breasts and a long, thick torso that didn't seem to curve at all from armpits to kneecaps—but who could tell under her baggy cargo shorts, masculine T-shirts and flannel jackets. She wore her hair razored short and no jewelry other than a black beveled watch in a mannish style. But Frank could have cared less: she was an experienced traveler and good friend. Wendy, on the other hand, was her exact opposite: a shapely, curvaceous wisp of a woman fond of perfume and nail polish whose figure and flirtatious manner, Frank was sure, had confused many a man before she came out. Still, like Max, she was a seasoned traveler and an amazing athlete. Frank guessed she'd finally stopped now that baby Conrad was due in a few weeks—but up until last week she was running six eight-minute miles every day.

The flight from Boston back to San Diego had been strangely unnerving. Leading tours for X-Treme and before that, in the years he spent travel writing, Frank had become inured to flight—but that was before crash landing. He hadn't wanted to think about what had happened in the meeting with the Lynches—or the cold, hard facts about what not getting the money would mean for the future of XT. And he hadn't wanted to think about Meredith, Grace and Anne, Darcy and especially Eva. He missed Jackie . . . and he hadn't wanted to think about her either. Even his trusty stash of DVDs betrayed him. He flipped past *Unbreakable*, *Limitless* and *Spiderman*—all stories about some average guy who had a special power. In the end, he'd busied himself with three double orders of Johnnie Walker Black . . . and even failed at getting drunk.

When the plane landed in San Diego, his ten-year-old Honda CR-V sat decrepit and abandoned-looking in the parking lot as if it had spent the weekend in a car nursing home, musing on its bygone youth. As he pulled up to 87 Armada Court, one of a quiet community of older homes with bright red Spanish tiled roofs, reality doused him again. The stucco of Frank's boyhood home was badly in need of painting, the square of browning grass in front required water, and Frank couldn't have parked in the garage because of all the boxes crammed inside it even if Steve and Wendy's cars hadn't been blocking the entrance. They must have planned to surprise him with a victory celebration—

Frank saw an open pizza box on the coffee table—only they were the ones getting the surprise.

"No. I didn't get the money," Frank sighed, shuffling into the house like a defeated old man. "I was going to wait until tomorrow to tell you—"

"We couldn't wait until tomorrow," Max interrupted. "You know how important this meeting was. For XT and for—" She didn't say "for us," but Frank knew that was what she was thinking.

"Max hasn't slept all weekend," Wendy murmured, rubbing her baby bump. "I haven't either . . . but that's because of this little guy," she said with a smile. "He's going to be a martial artist, I think. From all the kickboxing he's doing down there we should have named him Jet, after Jet Li, instead of Conrad . . ."

"I'm sorry," Frank murmured. "But I've got a plan to keep us afloat while we look for another source." He took Wendy's elbow and helped her waddle over to his father's old recliner, still stationed by the room's wide bay window, and turned to Steve. "I need your professional services. I'm going to have to sell the house."

"Sell the house?!" Steve's mouth dropped open.

"But Frank, you can't!" Wendy cried.

"Dude, can't we . . . sell some of this junk?"

The living room—like the rest of the house, except for Frank's bedroom upstairs—was almost unchanged from the day Frank's father died. Untidy while he was alive, his boxes and papers now cluttered every available space—not just in the living room and study, but the small formal dining area and the kitchen at the rear of the house, the master bedroom upstairs and the attic. Both the garage and the square of concrete that formed the back patio were so cluttered with broken lawn chairs, old grills and gardening equipment that Frank hardly used them anymore.

"Do you think anyone would buy it? It's just . . . papers and broken stuff. Worthless, probably."

"What about credit cards or—"

"Maxxed. I've leveraged everything I own already. There's nothing left. No credit cards. My bank account is down to the last few hundred bucks. There's no collateral of any kind. We're broke," Frank continued quietly. "I don't know what else to do. If you've got better ideas, now's the time."

The silence traveled the distance from long to uncomfortable to deafening as they each considered their finances—and still no one said a word.

"Well," Frank said at last, rubbing his temples. "It's the house. I'll start clearing it out . . ."

"We'll help you," Wendy murmured. "We would have helped you long ago, but—" She glanced at Max before giving him a sad smile. "We—we figured you . . . weren't ready."

I'm still not ready, he thought. Ignoring Wendy's comment and everything it suggested, he turned to Steve. "How's the market? Can you get me a decent price?" he asked.

"How many bedrooms upstairs again?"

"Three. Two baths. They're small, though."

"Yeah, I know," Steve muttered. "These houses were built for a different time. So we've got *this* room—"

"Living room, I guess," Frank clarified.

"Then the shotgun hallway to a paneled study, formal dining and kitchen." Steve sounded like he was writing an MLS description as he spoke. "Three beds, two baths, one-car garage and patio." He nodded his satisfaction. "I'll run some comps, but I think we can do okay. Of course, we'll have to clear it out and clean it up a bit. Maybe spend a weekend painting and a few other minor things. But, yeah. I think I could get you something acceptable." His eyes skewered Frank. "So where will you live?"

Frank shrugged. "I haven't gotten that far yet."

"Well, you're welcome to stay with me, dude. As long as you want."

"Thanks." Steve was sincere, but since he'd moved back with his parents almost two years ago, it also wasn't entirely his decision. The image of the two of them—grown men—sharing a bunk bed flashed in Frank's mind, laughable and pitiful at the same time.

"There's a cab outside," Wendy said, suddenly pointing from her seat by the window. "Were you expecting someone?"

Frank pushed aside the yellowed curtain and grimy blinds. A taxi idled in the driveway. He couldn't see the driver's face—it was turned toward the backseat—but from the way his hands jerked up and down a serious argument was in progress. The rear door flew open and a black stiletto heel scraped the concrete.

Frank peered through the window trying to make out the figure emerging from the cab until those unmistakable cougar hips caught his attention.

 Eva stood on Frank's driveway, decked in the red dress she'd worn to the reunion and carrying a plastic garbage bag like a purse.

"This place is a dump, Frank," she said when he stepped out into the yard. "You can do *wayyy* better. And you will.

The guy says he needs forty-three dollars. Seems high to me, but he's probably not going away until he gets it, and I'm tapped out. Take care of it for me, will you?"

"Eva, what are you—"

She strode toward the house.

"Hello, Steve. You have pizza sauce on your chin . . . as usual." She nodded at Maxine. "Well, I can tell you and Frank haven't been intimate! What are you, thirty-four or thirty-five?" She lowered her voice. "Sleep with him now, girl. Before those saggy lines around here"—she indicated the indentations around Max's nose and lips—"get any worse."

She swung on Wendy, her mouth curled for some additional critical commentary until she saw the baby bulge, straining against the fabric of the woman's maternity smock. Eva turned away from her without saying a word.

Maxine glared at her. "Who the hell is this chick, Frank?"

"You can call me the pimptress . . . and Frank is my man ho'," Eva laughed. "Ladies and gentleman, Frank and his pecker are about to make us some money, a shitload to be exact."

"She's kidding, right?" Max's eyes darted from Frank to Eva, then from Eva to Steve, her broad face registering the depth of her confusion. "I mean, this is some kind of joke, right? She's one of your friends' daughters or cousins or something. She's punking us!" She tried to laugh—and to get them to laugh, too—but when that failed she crossed her arms over her chest and began muttering under her breath, injecting her personal soliloquy into the conversation in furious commentary.

Eva whipped out her driver's license and thrust it in

Max's face. "Trust me, it's real. And if you don't believe me then maybe this will convince you." She reached into the garbage bag and pulled out the *Centarian*. Papers belched out of its binding, as though it had become the repository for every note, every bill and every scrap of writing Eva had touched in days. She dropped it onto the coffee table and sat down on the floor, kicking off her strappy black shoes.

"Steve and I already did this, Eva," Frank said with a sigh. "And yes, some of the women I was . . . involved with . . . do look really youthful, but that probably doesn't mean anything."

"Not *some*, sugar britches," Eva murmured, pulling a crushed pack of cigarettes out of the bag and lighting one absently. "All of us. Every single woman who has received your love juice has stopped the hands of time—"

"Eva, do you mind . . .?" Wendy asked, gesturing toward the unborn. "The cigarette?"

Eva locked eyes with Wendy for another long second before taking a last long drag and stubbing it out on the edge of Steve's pizza box. "Where was I?" she continued hastily. "Oh yeah. Frank's love juice—"

"Fucking unbelievable," Maxine muttered to herself, staring at the carpet as if she'd discovered something there. "Just fucking unbelievable . . ."

"Language," Wendy hissed, reaching for Maxine's hand. "You promised."

"Exactly," Eva agreed. "I couldn't have said it better myself, Marge—"

"Her name is Maxine," Frank corrected.

"Really?" Eva looked Maxine upside down. "She seems more like a Marge. Anyway. After that reunion, I started thinking. It really was weird how all of us standing there—me and Meredith and that chatty Cathy, Grace—all of us still looked so good, compared with the other women. And we *had* all slept with Frank. I didn't have anything else to do, so I did some research. I tracked down all of the chicks you diddled in college." She pulled a sheaf of papers from the back of the book and spread them out in front of them. At the top of each page she had written a name, and beneath that, glued the woman's yearbook picture and a series of more recent ones.

"Whoa . . ." Steve breathed, sinking down to the floor beside her to inspect the pictures. "How did you get these?"

"Facebook."

"How did you get them all to accept your friend requests so fast? I tried that and—"

"Easy. I'm not a slobbering, lecherous pig like you are, Hughes."

Steve guffawed. "Same old Eva."

"Crazy people," Maxine muttered, and Wendy stroked her hand again.

Frank leaned over the images. Sure enough, Eva had them all—all eight of the women he had been intimate with at Broughton and their current pictures, which she had taped beneath their yearbook images.

"How did you know about them?" Frank asked. "How did you know that these were the girls I—"

Eva laughed. "Like I said at the reunion, you kiss and tell. Years ago. When we were a couple. I asked you and you told me."

"And you remember that? After all these years?"

Eva smiled a toothy smile that felt about as warm as December in Canada. "I remember all kinds of things about you, Frank. You're the only guy who ever dumped me. Usually, I do the dumping."

"Insane!" Maxine sputtered at the carpet.

Frank squirmed. "Look, Eva—"

"Relax, Frank. I'm no stalker. I don't know what you've been up to since we called it quits—and trust me, I don't really care. But if you need more proof, I'd say look up some of those women. The earlier ones. I mean, whoever you slept with last week probably looks pretty much the same—"

"I didn't sleep with anyone last week, Eva," Frank muttered in exasperation.

"But if you go back a few years, you're going to see more of the same. Even better, go find the little girl you boinked in high school—"

"That's enough, Eva."

Eva shrugged. "Fuck whoever you want, Frank. For me this is strictly a business transaction. Marketed correctly, that tool of yours could make all of us a pile of cash . . . and you can have more pussy than an animal shelter."

"Language," Wendy murmured again, patting her belly as if soothing a child already born. "Children present, people—"

"Is this what you were doing in Boston?" Maxine exploded, wheeling on Frank in frustration. "Instead of getting the money for XT?"

"Hello?" Eva practically shouted. "Have you been listening? Money is easy now. Do you know how many women would pay top dollar—and I'm talking thousands of dollars, maybe even tens of thousands—to stop time? And they get to get laid in the process. Win-win—"

"That's ridiculous, you know that, Ella or Emma or

whatever the fuck your name is," Maxine said. "Everything you've said is just ludicrous—"

"Not so ridiculous," Steve interrupted. He hadn't said much so far—which, Frank realized, wasn't exactly like him.

"Aw, come on, Steve." Maxine whirled on him, her hands on her hips. "You're not falling for this crap, are you?"

"The pictures—"

"Pictures can be faked."

"True," Steve agreed. "But I was with Frank in Boston. I saw some of these women. And I've known Eva for almost fifteen years. She's hardly changed at all, Maxine. Besides." He stood up slowly and crossed the room to stand by Frank. "I don't want my buddy to have to sell his house. It's . . . it's all he has left of his dad, you know?" He dropped a hand on Frank's shoulder. "If there's another option, I think we should at least hear her out."

"Thank you, Steve," Eva said gratefully. She shot Maxine a gloating smile of victory, avoided looking at Wendy at all and pulled another piece of paper from the pages of the *Centarian*. "Okay, this isn't polished yet, but it's as far as I got on the plane—"

"Hey, bro?" Steve interrupted. "Maybe we could clear off the dining room table for her? Instead of making her sit on the floor?"

"It belonged to your mother's grandmother." Frank heard his father's voice in his brain as he and Steve surveyed the formal dining table that had sat in this room for as long as Frank could remember. *"Your mom loved it. She put it there . . . and as far I'm concerned, there it stays."*

But Frank couldn't remember the last time he'd used the

dining room for anything even close to its intended purpose. Even when he was a kid, the table had been claimed by books and papers, camping gear and dig equipment—and Frank had added to it with groceries that had never made their way into the pantry, sporting goods, even some laundry he wasn't sure was clean.

Shame burned Frank's ears when he saw Wendy and Max exchange a glance that seemed to have more than a little pity in its meaning, and when Eva's mouth fell open in shock at the mess. He steeled himself for her comments, but whatever she was thinking, she somehow managed to keep the words in her head. With Steve's help, he swept the junk off the table's surface and into piles on the floor, making room for the five of them.

Eva plopped herself down at the head of the table and reached for a cigarette.

"Nope," Steve said, seizing her lighter and nodding toward Wendy. "That's enough of that. It's no good for anybody. Including you."

"I could smoke all the cigarettes in North Carolina and it wouldn't matter. I'm forever young," Eva muttered. She shot a quick glance in Wendy's direction and Frank thought he read something like longing on her face. "All right," she said in the most dignified voice Frank had ever heard her use. "I don't have a laptop anymore, so I couldn't do a PowerPoint and all that—"

"Why not?"

Eva's expression made it clear she wished Steve would drop dead.

"Real estate isn't the only business where things are still tough," she muttered. "If you must know, it's busted. I haven't had the cash to fix it or buy a new one since I got laid off about four months ago—"

"From what? Last I heard you were sleeping with some famous architect. Least that's what was going around the rumor mill. What happened? His wife find out?"

Eva crimsoned angrily. "Screw you, Hughes," she muttered.

"Language—"

"Yeah, yeah," Eva waved the rebuke away. She slid a piece of paper across the table toward Frank. "Okay, so like I was saying. There's a business here. And it could go a few ways. The women who've had sex with Frank have all stopped the clock, myself included—right? So either there's something about the sex act or there's something in Frank that passes that along. So, on that sheet of paper, you see, I propose that we either find a way to sell Frank's cum—"

"No."

"Wait a minute, Frank," Steve said calmly. "Hear her out—"

"I'm not sitting in a room for the rest of my life, jerking off to pornos on RedTube, man!"

Steve shrugged. "Doesn't sound so bad to me."

"Well, there's another option," Eva continued. "And that's that we find a way to sell Frank—"

"No!"

"Just listen, okay, Frank?" She rolled her eyes. "Now's a fine time to become a choirboy," she muttered. "We sell time with you by the hour, or the act as it were, whichever comes first . . . excuse the pun—"

"That can't be legal," Maxine said. "I mean, you really are basically prostituting him—"

"It's a medical treatment, not prostitution!" Eva asserted. "And it's not like he's some abused fifteen-year-old. That's not what I'm not talking about." She pulled another piece of paper from her odd portfolio. "I'm talking about a super-select group of well-heeled women. Celebrities, models, power brokers and trophy wives. Like the names on the list—"

"Whoa!" Steve scanned the names, chuckling to himself. "How are you going to get A-listers like these to sleep with Frank?"

"I'm going to give them a personal invitation."

"And who are *you*?" Maxine read the list dubiously. "Why would these women listen to you? Do you know any of them?"

For the first time since he'd known her, Frank thought Eva looked a little nervous. "I know one," she said slowly. "I don't know if she'd do it. Her husband is very powerful and very possessive, so she might not be willing to risk it. But it's worth a shot."

"So what do you plan to do?" Maxine asked bluntly. "Call her up and say, 'Hi, wanna sleep with my friend Frank?'"

Eva rolled her eyes. "Of course not. It has to be classy. And super discreet. Confidential. Highly. We'll have to get them to sign something that they won't reveal anything they learn—and we'll promise to never tell anyone that they were there."

"Sounds like that movie *Hitch*—or the secret club in every movie ever written," Frank muttered.

"And of course, you'll have to go to the doctor," Eva continued as if he hadn't spoken. "Prove you've had all your shots and you're not riddled with STDs—"

"Okay, that's enough," Frank said. "I appreciate that you spent some time on this but I wished you'd have just called rather than flying all the way out here—"

"Would you have taken my call?" Eva asked pointedly and when Frank hesitated, she nodded. "Exactly."

"This is crazy, Eva! These women are going to expect immediate results and you know it doesn't work like that. You just said yourself that a woman I slept with recently wouldn't look any different—"

"That's why we give them a money-back guarantee—but we tell them they have to wait at least three years before they can claim it. Long enough for them to be able to tell the difference between themselves and the women around them—"

"Three years! You don't actually think you'll get anyone to do that, do you?" Maxine exclaimed. "Anything could happen in three years! They'll think you're just going to take their money and run away to—to—I don't know where. The Greek Islands. Switzerland. Grand Cayman—wherever it is that people hide their ill-gotten gains."

"I think it's Switzerland," Steve muttered.

"Might be Grand Cayman. Lots of corporations have accounts there, I've read," Max countered, "and the kite surfing is pretty awesome to boot."

"We're not going to be transferring their money to any offshore accounts!" Eva pounded her fists on the table, commanding their attention. "We're going to deliver! And we'll hold the money in escrow and give them access to the account so they can check to make sure it's still there or—or—something—"

"Eva, no one's going to go for this—"

"Look at me, Frank Young! Look at me, goddammit! Look at these other women—I'll recruit some of them to join me if I can, but even if I can't, this will work!" Eva pulled another picture from the *Centarian* and tossed it onto the table.

"First off, you're not recruiting anyone, Eva. No one, and I mean *no one*, outside this room can know about—"

"Who's that?" Steve asked before Frank could finish his sentence.

"Our first prospect. Her name is Carina and we grew up together. She's a few years older than me. She's married to a really wealthy older man now. Bigwig in banking or investment capital or something like that. I think you guys were in the same house as his son at Broughton. Lynch is the name—"

"You are shitting me!" Steve exclaimed, swinging wide eyes on Frank. "Well, that's one way to get the bastard back! Fuck his wife for cash—"

"Okay, this has all gone far enough," Frank interrupted as his jaw bounced off the floor at the sight of Carina Lynch. "Eva, I've heard you out, and while it's clear that you've put a lot of thought into this, it's all beside the point. I just can't do this." He shook his head. "I just can't."

"Why not?" Steve and Eva asked simultaneously. They eyed each other as if suspicious of finding themselves in agreement and then turned back to Frank.

"Because!" Frank exclaimed, looking to Maxine for support. But Maxine was studying all of Eva's handwritten marketing materials and wouldn't even look at him. "You guys can't be serious. I don't want to . . . to sell myself like that. It just seems . . . I don't know, wrong. Immoral—"

"What if I could get you one hundred thousand dollars per lady?" Eva said quietly. "And once people realize it really works, you'll be able to ask for even more than that."

"Yeah," Steve joined in. "And you could limit it to one or two a month—it's not like you'd have a stream of women to satisfy. Just one or two a month—"

"In a year that's between one and two million dollars, Frank," Maxine said softly. "It's a lot of money. It's enough to keep XT alive—"

"Minus my commission of course," Eva interjected quickly. "I think fifteen percent is fair—"

"You'll get ten percent and not a penny more, Eva," Steve said firmly. "And that'll be after expenses. And since I don't trust you any farther than I can throw you, you won't be talking to anyone about Frank without me standing right there—"

"You! What good are you?"

"I know sales. Better than you do, after a decade in real estate. And I'm protecting Frank's interests—"

"It's probably better if there are two of you," Maxine agreed. "More professional, if something like this can be 'professional'—"

"I can't believe what I'm hearing!" Frank shouted. "Do you realize what you're asking me to do?"

"Yeah, have sex with a hot chick whose husband screwed you out of five million dollars!"

"What makes you think she'd do it? And pay a hundred thousand dollars for it?"

"She might. And if she won't, there are plenty of women who will pay big bucks for just the *hope* of eternal youth. You know how much money is spent every year on creams and Botox and other crap by woman trying to look young? Try billions, with a capital fucking B..."

"This is ridiculous. We don't know if it's eternal youth. We don't *know* anything. It might be some freaky coincidence or—"

"'Eternal youth,'" Max sighed. "Makes me think of Ponce de León. Tramping through the Amazon looking for the fountain of youth..."

"And since Frank's actually *been* to the Amazon, that makes it easy," Steve added. "We can tell people he bathed in the fountain of youth on a remote jungle trail! It's the perfect backstory—"

Frank stood up so suddenly he banged his knee on the table's heavy wooden edge. A series of memories, suddenly sharp and vivid, crowded his brain, spinning dizzily around him.

Amazon... fountain of youth... not a fountain but a pool of crystal-clear water in the middle of the jungle, where he'd lost his virginity with a beautiful girl named Lucinda...

"Oh my God! Frank!" Maxine reached for him as Frank felt his knees buckle beneath him. "Are you all right?"

Amazon... fountain... youth...

Maxine's words were far away. The room felt hot and then cold, bright and then dark... and Frank felt himself sinking under a heavy black memory. His friends and the cluttered dining room disappeared and the past swallowed him whole as his head hit the floor.

CHAPTER Six

"It's your birthday present."

His old chair creaked as Francis Young, Sr. stood up and dropped the tickets into his son's lap.

"Peru?" Frank asked, studying them dubiously. "Are we going on another dig this summer?"

His father shook his head. His hair was shaggy and graying, but other than that there was a youthfulness about him that confounded his forty-eight years. Now, he bounced eagerly on the toes of his sneakers and grinned.

"Not us. *You.*"

"I'm going on a dig? By myself? But—"

"No, not a dig. Something much better—or at least, I think it will be. You're going on a hike. Into the Amazon."

"The Amazon?" Frank shrugged. "I've been to the Amazon before."

"Not this part. Not where I'm sending you." His father's voice dropped to an excited whisper and his blue eyes danced in his sunburnt face. "It's the place of my greatest discovery. My biggest find."

"Your biggest find? You mean that partial skeleton that dated back to—"

"No, no, not that," his father interrupted, waving the rest of the sentence away. "Something much bigger. Much more meaningful. Never mind—you'll see."

Frank sighed, knowing his father well enough to know that this "great find" could be something as small as a fragment of fossilized dinosaur or the remnants of some early medical implement. The prospect of the Amazon in July summoned such oppressive images of heat, bugs and wetness that Frank itched just thinking about it.

"Do I *have* to go?"

Frank, Sr. moved around his cluttered study. "I know I put it on one of these shelves . . ." he muttered to himself before replying, "Yes, son. You have to go."

"But Dad, it's my last summer," Frank whined. "Steve and the other guys are just hanging out at the beach. The only kid I know who's going anywhere is backpacking through Europe—"

"Europe!" his father scoffed at the bookshelves. "There's no adventure in Europe! This journey makes Machu Picchu, let alone Europe, seem like Disneyland."

"These last couple of years have been really tough on me, Dad," Frank said, switching tactics. "You know what a hard time I had adjusting to a regular school. And then all those AP exams and college visits and everything—most days since school got out I'm so tired, I just want to sleep."

He swallowed back the details about the heavy feeling in the center of his chest; it was as though a rock lay in the space where his heart should have been.

"I know, son. I've noticed." His father didn't turn. He stood still long enough for Frank to wonder if the older man had divined his omission. "That's one of the reasons I want you to go," he continued at last, yanking books out of their places and tossing them onto the floor. "Aha!" he yelled triumphantly, pulling a bottle from the darkness behind a thick tome and planting a kiss on its label. "There you are, my lovely. Now where are the glasses?" He turned to Frank with a smile, continuing as if he hadn't been interrupted. "That's one of the reasons I want you to go on this adventure, Frank—"

"I don't want to have an adventure, Dad. I want to be a normal kid."

His father set a glass in front of him and filled it with amber liquid. He poured himself a shot of the whiskey and drank it in a single gulp, frowning at the bitter burn at the back of his throat. When he spoke, his voice was firm and his expression serious.

"Let's get one thing straight, son," he said slowly. "You are *not* a normal kid. Never have been . . . never will be. You're going." He poured himself another shot and nodded for Frank to raise his own class. "And now, a toast. To my son as he approaches his eighteenth birthday."

Frank sniffed the contents. "What is this?"

"Only some of the finest scotch ever made," his father replied, knocking back another shot.

"You want me to drink it?" Frank asked.

"Well, what else?"

"But . . . the drinking age is twenty-one."

His father hooted a laugh. "Drink it, Frank. And then get upstairs and pack your rucksack. Lots of socks would be my advice. Can't hike with wet feet. It's an early flight . . ."

Frank stared at the tickets again. "It's *tomorrow*?"

"I think you're ready," his father said after a brief silence. "And I don't think we can wait much longer." He stopped Frank's questions before he could ask them, by standing up with his glass raised. "Now toast with me. To you, son. To you, as you embark on the mysteries of your life—of your calling, of loving and being loved." He paused a moment, then continued in a voice that trembled with emotion. "I'm very proud of you. I only wish your mother had lived to see this moment—" His voice broke and he wiped his eyes quickly. "Drink up and get busy, young man."

The next morning, he was off. Frank flew from San Diego to Mexico City to Lima, Peru, and finally from Lima to Iquitos, where at last, exhausted and disoriented, he emerged from the airplane to find a short, brown-skinned man in his mid-fifties waiting for him.

"Frank? Frank the junior?" the man asked, smiling broadly.

"José? José del Flores?"

The man nodded. He took Frank's outstretched hand and peered into Frank's face as if he were looking for something more than his resemblance to his namesake. "Yes," he murmured. "Yes."

"Is there something wrong?"

José's dark hair brushed his shoulders as he shook his

head. "You are your father. Very much." He paused, his grin widening. "I am sorry. My English . . . not so good. You speak Spanish? Like your father?"

"Yes," Frank said, switching to that language easily. "Not perfectly, but okay. I understand better than I can speak—"

"That is me in English," José replied, laughing. "Good. We will do well this way, I believe. Between you and me and Lucinda—"

"Lucinda? Who is that?"

"My daughter. She will be with us on this trip. Like me, she speaks Spanish. She speaks English, too. Better than I. You will meet her soon." He paused, surveying Frank again. "I had hoped to make our village tonight—the others on this tour have already arrived—but I see that you are tired from your long journey—"

"I'm fine," Frank assured him. "It would feel good to walk a bit."

José shook his head again. "It is more than a bit, son. My village is still several hours more to travel and the journey will be difficult. Tonight we will stay in Iquitos. Okay?" To his surprise, José reached over and lifted Frank's forty-pound hiking backpack off his shoulders and settled it on his own wiry frame.

"You travel heavy. What is in here?"

Frank grinned. "Lots of socks."

The older man chuckled. "Your father's advice. This way."

Outside, the air was heavy and humid in spite of the setting sun and the misting rain that swathed everything like a layer of thin gauze. The heat lapped at Frank's energy, drawing on reserves already depleted by travel, and he wished for the cool nights and temperate days of San Diego. Right now, Steve was probably lying on the couch of his parents' air-conditioned home, gaming *Resident Evil* on his PlayStation 2.

"We support our tribe members when we can," José said as he led Frank past a line of modern-looking taxis and pointed to an old jitney parked in a small lot across the street. He jammed his fingers into his mouth and let out a long, shrill whistle in signal. The ancient jalopy flashed its lights in reply and merged slowly into traffic toward them. "Your father would agree. He came to care very much about many in our village during the months he was here. That was long ago, of course. Before you were born."

Frank tried to imagine that—his father before he was born—but couldn't. "It's fine," he said instead, and it was true. He could have ridden in a wheelbarrow; he closed his eyes as soon as he was installed inside and saw nothing of the town—the last frontier of civilization before one entered the deepest and least explored wilds of the Peruvian Amazon—until the rusty vehicle stopped in front of a small wooden structure.

A single story of wood and thatch raised off the ground by an elaborate weave of crosshatched bamboo squatted cone-like in the dusk. As Frank contemplated its design, the door cut into the center of it swung wide. A girl around his own age emerged wearing a light-colored long-sleeved T-shirt tied above a pair of green cargo pants. For a long second, Frank was too captivated by the slice of flat brown stomach and seductively curved hip to notice that her long hair was tied up off her shoulders in a loose bun or that her feet were bare. But when he raised his eyes he found himself face to face with a kind of beauty he hadn't seen much of back home: exquisite black eyes in perfect symmetry to her nose and high cheekbones. He searched his memory, but there wasn't a film that he could compare her to. Backlit by the orange radiance of the fire inside, she seemed to be almost glowing. Looking at her, Frank's tongue beached itself in his mouth and speech was impossible.

"Papi!" the girl cried, leaping down the single step gracefully. A small knapsack dangled from her left hand. She continued speaking in a fast patois of which Frank understood none.

"In the morning," José replied in Spanish. "Lucinda, this is Frank. He can help you with your English. Frank, my daughter, Lucinda."

Lucinda's eyes swept over him, deepening his self-consciousness. For the first time, his father's birthday gift didn't seem like the most exquisite torture the man could have devised. He cleared his throat. "Hi."

Lucinda smiled at the ground. "Hello, Frank," she said in English. "Welcome."

The hut was more spacious inside than Frank would have guessed. He stepped into a wide circular room, its plank floors covered with bright woven rugs, its thatched walls bare except for the patterned curtains that separated passages leading to the sleeping areas. A few wooden chairs were scattered around an old stone hearth, where a low fire burned in spite of the heat of the evening. From somewhere out of Frank's sight, the spicy smell of something good to eat wafted toward him.

A plump woman with two long braids cascading to her waist emerged from behind one of the curtains. She offered Frank a gap-toothed smile of welcome and murmured something he didn't understand, gesturing toward one of the curtains.

"This is Swati. She runs this place. It is a guesthouse for many of the people who live in the interior but do business in Iquitos," José explained. "She wants to show you where you will sleep."

"*Gracias*," Frank said, following her behind the curtain.

She led him to an alcove with just enough room for the bamboo-framed cot inside. The floor was swept clean and a basin and ewer filled with clear water rested on a small table near the bed.

"Toilet . . . here . . ." Swati said in broken Spanish, pointing down the hall with another bright smile. "Eat soon."

"*Gracias*," Frank said again, leaning his rucksack in the corner. Swati dropped the curtain, giving him the illusion of privacy, and disappeared.

Frank sat on the cot, surveying the little room for a moment. The accommodation was comfortable enough—better than many he'd shared with his dad on some of their excursions together—and yet he still didn't understand.

Why am I here? he asked himself, pulling off his hiking boots. He splashed some water on his face and pulled off his T-shirt, using it to rub his neck and armpits. The cool water was like a blessing. He stepped out of his shorts and wiped the sweat from his legs and groin.

"Frank?" Lucinda sounded so near it was as if she were in the room. "I have a . . ." Her English failed and she switched to Spanish. "How do you say it in English?"

"Towel. *Toalla*. Towel. Thanks."

"They are close, yes? *Toalla* and towel," she said, giggling softly. Her hand appeared at the edge of the thin curtain. "Should I put them—"

"I'm good," Frank answered quickly. "Just leave it. I'll get it in a minute."

"Okay." She sounded so embarrassed, Frank suspected she could see him, crouched half-naked near the basin, rubbing his T-shirt between his legs. A rough brown square of fabric appeared near the curtain's hem. "When you are ready, Swati says we will eat," she said in a shy rush of words before retreating to the common room.

He emerged a few minutes later in a clean T-shirt and shorts, his neck and face still pink with embarrassment. Swati handed him a bowl of rich broth that smelled like heaven and gestured him into one of the chairs. Frank lifted the bowl to his lips and swallowed down a few mouthfuls, tasting vegetables he didn't recognize along with a bit of some stringy meat, steeped in a fragrant spice that tasted as good as it smelled.

"It's wonderful," he said in English and Spanish, smiling at Swati. "Thank you."

The woman grinned and then watched, beaming with pleasure as he finished his bowl. She refilled it twice before Frank couldn't eat any more.

"Tell me what it is like to travel in an airplane," Lucinda asked in English, her bright eyes sweeping over him shyly before resuming their consideration of the floor.

"Like riding in a car," Frank answered. "Only you see clouds instead of trees from the window."

She smiled. "I rode in a car once. What is it like where you live?"

He tried to tell her about the ocean, about his school in San Diego, about the life he'd lived traveling with his father, switching between English and Spanish when she did not understand. José added a word from time to time, but mostly he sat quietly, his eyes closed and his hands folded over his stomach like a much older man, dozing in his chair after the evening meal.

Frank asked Lucinda about her own life, and she told him about their village, several hours' walk deep in the jungle, and then about the years she went to school in Iquitos, learning Spanish and English, to help her father run tours into the heart of the Amazon.

"There are some in our tribe who have much more school. Who have traveled and seen more of Peru. More of the world. But not many. Compared to others my age, I am . . ." Her description failed as she searched for the words.

"Unique," Frank offered, thinking the word fit her perfectly. "It means one of a kind."

She blushed. "Yes."

José stood up and stretched.

"To bed, both of you," he said authoritatively. "We will start at dawn. The others are waiting and this will not be an easy trip."

"Yes, Papi," Lucinda murmured obediently. "Good night, Frank." For the first time, her eyes locked on his.

"Good night," Frank stammered, his heart pounding out his attraction, but she was already gone.

José stared after her for a moment. When his eyes found Frank again, they were grave. "A moment, Frank," he began as Frank turned toward his own room. "What did Professor Frank—your father—what did he tell you about our destination?"

Frank shrugged. "Something about seeing his greatest discovery."

"I see." José paused and Frank thought he might say something else, but he didn't. He gave Frank one last nod, and then yanked aside another curtain, stepping inside sleeping quarters almost identical to Frank's own. "*Buenos noches*, Frank," he said, and Frank was dismissed.

It was not a journey for the average tourist.

From Swati's guesthouse, they marched toward the river's edge, where they boarded a small motorboat and putted down the Amazon. An hour or two later, they abandoned the boat and hiked for several more hours until they reached a small village of thatched huts without any electricity or running water. Frank thought they might rest until morning, but they stopped only long enough to meet the rest of their party and to take a quick photograph to mark the start of the expedition. Less than half an hour later, they pressed on, headed along a narrow path that led them deeper and deeper into the massive jungle.

There were only three other tourists: a thickly built man named Jasper from Australia, an older Venezuelan man with an aggressive, roosterish manner and his quiet, slope-shouldered son.

"Oil money, mate," Jasper said of the Venezuelans in a conspiratorial whisper on the first day of the tour. "And lots of it. Not sure why he's here. God knows he can afford ritzier digs. I hear it's a dinky little temple, too. All grown over and the like." Jasper continued: "I'm just here for the survivalist aspects. You know: two weeks in the absence of civilization and all that. Good practice for the End Days. When Y2K hits, it's all over. Know what I mean?"

Frank nodded, not sure of what to say. Jasper spoke only a little Spanish and so he gravitated toward Frank and Lucinda when the urge to talk struck him, which wasn't very often. Most of the time, he contented himself with his own company—and with showing his skill with the machete as they sliced their way through the jungle.

At first, Frank found the experience exotic and interesting. The noise of the birds calling to each other from their homes in trees so tall they blocked the sun drowned out their conversations. The impossibly narrow trail was overgrown with lush, hanging green. The heaviness of the air, the thick smell of growing things, and the sense that if he stood still, the jungle would just grow over him, enmeshing him in itself, were all wondrous.

At first.

But after three days Frank just wished the whole experience were over. He hated to admit it, but the hiking exhausted him. His feet and legs ached. A dull, leaden feeling settled in the center of his chest, as though a circus elephant had decided to use his breastbone as its footstool and wouldn't go away—not even when they rested for the night. Every morning, Frank vowed he would keep up better than the day before . . . and every night, he straggled in farther and farther behind the group.

At least once a day—and sometimes more often—the hikers were bathed in a sudden soaking rain, then engulfed with relentless humidity. And the insects! Even in his long sleeves and pants, even after covering himself in the repellent he'd brought, mosquitos and other critters latched onto his flesh, sucking his blood and leaving him irritated and itchy. If it hadn't been for Lucinda, he might have turned around and headed back along the trail to civilization—even if he had to do it alone.

She had become more comfortable with him now, after hours of trekking at his side, often the two of them nearly alone in the jungle. More and more, her soft brown eyes met his. There were fewer and fewer silences between them, and she told him about her life, about her hopes to travel far beyond Iquitos and about the characters in her village. With every minute in her company Frank felt his initial attraction to her deepening.

"I didn't know I was this out of shape," he panted to Lucinda as, once again, the others disappeared ahead of them. It was embarrassing: here he was in the company of a gorgeous girl, sweating and stumbling like some awkward, pasty-faced nerd. *Never again*, he vowed, watching as Lucinda pretended she needed a full minute to lift her hair and twist it into a braid—just so he could catch his breath. *When I get back, I'm going to get into shape. This is never, ever going to happen to me again . . .*

"It is hard traveling," she said encouragingly. "You are not used to it."

"Neither are they," Frank muttered, nodding toward the others even though they could no longer see or hear the rest of their party—they were that far ahead. "They seem fine."

"Do not worry about them. They must make their own journeys. Tell me something. Anything. Something else about San Diego, your childhood."

Frank chuckled breathlessly. "Like what? I've told you everything."

"No. You've said nothing of your mother."

"That's because she died a long time ago," Frank replied. "I never knew her."

"So you are like me. It is just you and your father."

Frank nodded. "What happened to your mother?"

"Malaria."

"How old were you?"

Lucinda frowned. "Six or seven."

"Do you . . . miss her?"

"Sometimes. But my father, he is a good father. It is enough."

Frank nodded. He understood perfectly. It was hard to miss something you never had—especially when what you *did* have was so complete. He opened his mouth to try to convey that thought, but she changed the subject.

"My father and your father traveled this route together," she said in her soft, fragmented English. "Your father sends to us the people . . . to take this trip to the old temple."

Frank nodded. "Yeah, my dad told me about that. He did a dig here before I was born and found the temple. Jasper says it's not that much to look at."

"It is small. But very powerful. Many legends about the place. The old ones say—"

Frank was listening so intently he forgot his feet. He tripped, scrambling over a tree root raised in the center of the path. He would have landed flat on his face had Lucinda not grabbed him, shoring him up with the soft strength of her body.

"You okay?"

Frank nodded, his cheeks and his groin aflame at her touch. For a moment, they just stared at each other, alive with the sensation of being so close. Then she stumbled away from him, tripping over the same root and landing hard on her bottom.

"Ow!" she cried, tears springing to her eyes.

Frank rushed to her aid. She lifted the light cotton of her shirt and Frank saw the damage: the skin at her lower back was torn and the first faint shades of a large bruise colored her skin.

"You're bleeding." He slid his pack off his shoulders, grateful to be free of its weight if only for a few minutes. "Hold on a second."

Quickly, he unzipped one of the pouches at the front of his bag and pulled out a small plastic baggie stuffed with bandage strips and antibiotic creams. "Hold still," Frank murmured. "This might sting a little . . ."

With shaking fingers, he dabbed the cream onto the torn skin. Lucinda flinched but held still until after he'd affixed a brown adhesive over the wound. "Better?" he asked.

"Yes. Thank you." She hesitated. "You . . . are so different from the boys I know. So much . . . kinder."

"And you're different from the girls I know," Frank said sincerely. "You're so full of curiosity. You are so . . . yourself. I bet you'd be as comfortable in San Diego as you are here swinging a machete."

"I would love to go to San Diego. I would love to see America. But . . ." She sighed. "I do not know how I would get there. My father believes in the old ways. The money we make is shared with the tribe. He says it is time for me to marry and has chosen a husband for me—"

"Chosen? A husband?" Frank stared at her in disbelief. "Who? Do you at least get to—I mean— do you know him?"

"Yes. I know him," Lucinda laughed. "You've seen how small our village is. Everyone knows everyone! His name is Toro Quispe. He is a few years older. He is respected. He comes from a good family and he can provide for me."

"But . . . do you . . . *like* him?"

Lucinda shrugged. "He is okay. Much like the others. I know he is eager to work with us—leading the tours earns great respect—but my father says his Spanish is not good enough yet." She frowned. "I offered to help him, but he became angry and refused. He pushed me down and walked away. I did not like that."

Frank imagined a dark-haired young man with his face perpetually contorted into a scowl.

"I don't like it either," he muttered.

"It is what my father believes is for the best."

"But what if you told him that you wanted something else? Or someone else?" Frank felt his cheeks growing warm, but he pressed on with his questions. "Do you have to marry him?"

"I only know of one woman who left the tribe and went away—to America—to school. I do not know all of her story, only that she had friends who were able to help her—"

"Well, so do you," Frank said. "You have me. You'll come to visit me—just like I've come here to visit you—and we'll figure out the rest. I'm sure our fathers will agree."

"Oh, Frank. I could not—"

"Yes, you could. And you will. It's settled. I'll talk to my dad about it as soon as I get back. I know he'll help. It's a done deal." Frank offered her his hand.

"Okay. A 'done deal,' as you say." Lucinda laughed as her fingers closed around his; then, after a slight shy hesitation, she leaned close to him and breathed a gentle kiss onto his cheek. The unexpected touch sent a wave of longing through Frank's body. He turned himself away from her so she would not see the knot rising at his zipper.

"They're really far ahead of us," he said quickly. "Guess we'd better—"

"Yes." Lucinda lowered her eyes and stretched out her hand. "I am ready. We will catch up this time. You will see."

By the time they reached the others, the sun was setting. Frank had donned his headlamp to better see the path, but even with its aid, the way was difficult and torturously slow. They caught up in time to see the others dropping their packs around a small clearing where a pit had been dug for the fire they would use to prepare their meal and to deter the jaguars, wild boar and other nocturnal predators that might become interested in the smells of their food.

"We will not eat meat tonight," José said. "Tomorrow we go to temple. The gods will not receive us if we have eaten flesh."

The Venezuelan oilman rolled his eyes and spat out something in Spanish that Frank recognized as a curse word. He let out a torrent of words—all complaints.

"*Sí, sí.*" José's smile never faltered. "But mister, you paid for an authentic experience. This is it."

The oilman looked annoyed but helped himself to the jug of water José passed around. Lucinda released Frank's hand, suddenly guilty, and scuttled away from him to start the fire.

Frank eased himself onto the ground. His body hurt,

but he couldn't stop smiling as he watched her move. The spot on his cheek her lips had touched seemed to throb with fresh sensation and the hand that had held hers felt warmer than any other part of his body.

It was his turn at the camp stove, preparing their communal meal, and Frank started it happily—not even Jasper's loud complaints about a blister forming on his heel could impact his mood as he envisioned what the remainder of the evening would hold: in another hour, after the food was eaten and the leavings buried, she would sit beside him by the fire like she had every other night and they could talk quietly together. He would find a way to hold her hand again . . . and perhaps, when the others retired to their tents, there would be other kisses.

But as night fell, José became more watchful. He stationed himself between Frank and Lucinda and peppered Frank with questions—about his father's work, about Frank's own plans, about his hobbies and his habits—questions that seemed to serve no other purpose but to keep them apart.

"Lucinda!" he said at last. "Watch with me for a while. I wish to talk to you." He beamed his gracious smile on his party. "We sleep now. Tomorrow will be a long and difficult day. The temple is not far away, but there is no path. Good night, Frank," he said, nodding Frank toward his tent.

Frank obeyed reluctantly. He lay awake for the longest time, listening to their voices murmuring in the gathering darkness. He understood nothing—they spoke in their native language—but it seemed from the tone of José's voice that he was giving instructions. From time to time, Lucinda's voice rose in a soft question, and José's answers were long and thorough. Little by little, weariness claimed his limbs again and Frank drifted into a heavy and dreamless sleep.

"Frank! Frank!"

Frank jerked awake in confusion. For a moment, he didn't recognize the curved nylon walls of his tent or the girl leaning over him. Then it all came clear again.

"Lucinda? What's—"

She touched her finger to her lips and gestured for him to join her in the clearing outside. Frank emerged from his tent to find the fire still dancing in the pit, though not quite as brightly as earlier.

"Come," Lucinda whispered. "I want to show you something. Bring your flashlight."

Moving as quietly as he could, Frank grabbed his torch and tiptoed after her. At first they followed a narrow path, but then Lucinda turned, diving into the bush toward a massive kapok tree nearly the width of city bus.

"Here, I think," she said after they circled it. She pointed down a steep incline into a valley thick with trees.

Frank aimed his flashlight into the dark brush. It made such a tiny circle of light ahead of him that it seemed less than useless. Frank turned, but the campsite had been consumed by the darkness of the night.

"Come on," Lucinda urged, excitement bubbling her voice and she grabbed his hand. She parted the dense vines with the tip of her machete as she threw herself into them, dragging Frank along behind her as the path tumbled and dipped deeper and deeper into the inky forest. Leaves slapped at his face and something caught at as his boot before he shook himself free and kept going, sliding as much as walking with the steepness of the descent.

Then the ground suddenly leveled. Lucinda stopped, panting from the effort of their fall. The flashlight illuminated the smile of satisfaction that beamed on her face.

"Wh-where are we?" Frank asked.

Lucinda pointed.

They stood on the edge of a pond about the size of an Olympic pool—perfectly round, or so it looked lit up by the moon with the trees gathered around it. The water was so clear he could see their reflections in its surface and it was as still as glass. Pristine and silent in its loveliness, the place seemed as sacred as any European cathedral Frank had ever visited.

"God," Frank murmured. "It's beautiful."

"The old ones say there is power and protection in this place," Lucinda whispered.

"Protection? From what?"

Lucinda shook her head. "I don't know. My father told me of it for the first time tonight around the fire, after you and the others went to sleep. He says the place is special—but dangerous. He said it was important that someone of our tribe know where it is and that he has been the only one for many, many years. That is why he insisted that I come on this trek. That, and . . ." She lowered her eyes. "He thought you might be glad of someone closer to your own age."

"Did he and my father come here?"

She shrugged. "I don't know. Perhaps. My father said he will not bring outsiders here, but he speaks of your father differently. The others—he said they will destroy it."

"Destroy it?"

"Because they cannot accept what they do not understand. And to understand they must investigate, and in the investigation—"

"Destruction." Frank nodded. "I understand."

"I thought you would. From the way you walk in the forest."

Frank said nothing. He felt almost as though he were in a trance, captivated by the moon and the clear water and the silent trees. He'd even forgotten he was still holding Lucinda's hand until she stepped away from him and dropped her flashlight and knife.

"He told me to come and find it now—while the others are sleeping. It is not for them to know of it. But I did not believe he meant you. You are not like the others. Your father is my father's friend . . . and you are mine," she added softly.

Kiss her. Frank's brain was screaming the words, but before he could make his move Lucinda stepped away.

"Tonight, we swim," she said, shrugging out of her khaki shirt. Her breasts stood in high peaks under her gray tank top as she bent and tugged at the knots on her boots, kicking them aside. "Swim with me, Frank?"

Frank hesitated, thinking of caimans and anacondas and other water-loving killers. But the pool looked too placid and serene for that . . . and Lucinda was wriggling out of her pants.

"Sure . . ." Frank said, slipping off his shirt.

She giggled. "Turn around."

"Why?"

"Because I do not want to swim in my clothes, silly one.

When I am covered by the water I will tell you. And I will close my eyes, until you say you are as well."

"Oh . . . okay," Frank said. He could see the outlines of her slender body in the moonlight: her nipples stood erect beneath the thin fabric of her top, distracting him from everything but the desire to rub his fingertips over her skin.

When he didn't move, she laughed again and drew a circle in the air with her fingers. "Turn around."

He heard the sound of her zipper and imagined her pants hitting the soft ground behind him. The tank top made no sound as she slipped it over her head, but Frank imagined it anyway, and the idea of her naked behind him brought the erection so quickly he had to breathe deeply and think of something unpleasant—like the tough trek they would have up the ravine and back to the camp—to keep himself from an embarrassing mess of cum in his shorts. He heard her squeal and the sound of the water as she splashed to its center.

"It is very cold!" she said, her voice carrying in the stillness. "Come—my eyes are closed and my back is turned."

Frank stripped off his clothes in a flash. When he turned toward the pool, he saw her hair, wet from the water, and the outline of her naked shoulders. He raced toward the water, embracing its shocking coldness, ducking his head beneath the surface to swim to her more quickly.

"It's weird it's so cold," Frank sputtered, emerging at her side. "Everything else here is so hot."

"Y-y-es," Lucinda agreed. "It—it is unexpected, no?" Her teeth chattered as she spoke. "It—f-f-feels good—"

He reached for her, taking her hands.

"Maybe that's the secret right there. The power. Think

about how good it's going to feel to get out of here! It'll make the hot night seem nice."

"Yes," Lucinda agreed, forgetting herself and pulling closer to him for warmth.

Frank's arms went around her, pressing her bare breasts into the skin of his chest. His cock bongoed back to attention, pressing against her thigh, but Lucinda didn't pull away. Instead, she tilted her head toward his and captured his lips with her own. Even in the cold water, every nerve in Frank's body was on fire. His hands slid over her wet body, caressing the taut mounds of her breasts and the soft, slick hair at her thighs—and all the while her sweet mouth pulled at his lips and teased his tongue.

"L-Lucinda . . ." he stammered, disentangling himself from her before his desire consumed the last of his self-control. "I want to do this—more than anything. But we have to stop before—"

"No, Frank, no." Lucinda grabbed his face. In her eyes he read a determination that hadn't been there before. "Many things in life I cannot choose. But this—this I choose. I want you to be the one. The first."

"But what about—"

"I do not care," she whispered. "Please, Frank. Please do not say 'no.'"

"Are you sure, Lucinda? Because—"

"Yes," she answered, kissing him. With sudden boldness, her soft fingers tentatively encircled his cock, and Frank's resistance was over. He closed his eyes, surrendering to the sensation of fingers other than his own caressing the sensitive skin along the shaft and tip.

"Tell me what to do," she said softly.

I don't know either, he would have said if he hadn't been past the power of speech. Instead, he grabbed her thighs and lifted her astride his hips, his cock aimed at the tender skin in their center. His body moved almost of its own accord, slowly but relentlessly parting the gentle folds of her sex.

He heard her cry out and felt her fingers dig into his back as he thrust more deeply inside her tight, moist cleft, but she moved her hips against him, urging him on. Aided by the water's buoyancy, Frank ground her against him, bouncing her on the pole of his desire until he lost consciousness of anything other than the steady rhythm of his hips and the exploding sensation of his first time.

At last, breathless with the joy of release, he let go. Lucinda slid down his body and stood, locked in his arms in the still water, silent under the night sky. Frank could have stood there for hours had it not been for a sudden squall of rain, falling first in fat, slow drops, then accelerating. Wind gusted around them, stirring the water.

He looked up at the sky just as a bolt of lightning crackled high above the canopy of trees.

"It's going to storm!" Lucinda said, disentangling herself from his arms and splashing toward the banks and their discarded clothing. "Come! If my father finds me missing..."

She stopped, turning toward him, naked and perfect: high breasts topped with toffee-colored nipples, long flat stomach stretching down to a triangle of soft hair, and the perfect globes of her hips made him long to grab her again and press her down into the soft moss at the pool's edge. For a moment, she was utterly unself-conscious, smiling at him innocently. Then she remembered herself and quickly reached for her clothes, covering herself. Frank noticed a thin line of blood between her legs as she slowly worked her pants over her wet skin.

"I want your father to find out," Frank said, thrashing toward her. "I don't want to wait. I want you to come home with me when I go. I want to talk José about it now. Tonight," he continued quickly.

She kissed him. "I would like that, too, Frank. Very much. But tomorrow. He will be more at peace after we visit the temple."

Frank hopped into his jeans and his boots and slipped his T-shirt over his head. He reached for her hand, feeling stronger and more self-assured than he'd felt since leaving San Diego. "I'll lead the way."

By the time they'd struggled up the hill and back to camp, the rain had become a blinding gray sheet between them and the rest of the world. The fire was out, each of the tents was still zipped tight and every inhabitant was huddled snugly inside. José, however, was gone.

"Do you think he—" Lucinda whispered.

From the jungles behind him, Frank heard the sounds of movement and voices.

"Shh," he said. "Go to your tent."

"But—"

He kissed her quickly on the forehead. "Go. Hurry."

The voices drew close as Lucinda quickly unzipped the flaps of her tent and scooted inside.

Frank stood by his tent, breathing heavily as the humid rain pounded on him as if a sprinkler system had exploded.

It poured from the sky, dripped off the leaves and vines, then seemed to bounce back from the mossy ground. He closed his eyes, squaring his shoulders, preparing himself.

If José asks, I will tell him the truth. I love his daughter—and I will take care of her. If he wants and if she'll have me—a broke not-yet college student—I'll marry her. I'll find a way. He tightened his fingers into a fist. *I'll find a way . . .*

A light appeared on the path in front of him, and a few moments later, José's heavy form appeared under the dim glow of his headlamp. Two other men—strangers who had not been with their party—followed him. They were younger—perhaps only a little older than Frank himself—and had the same light-footed walk of the people who had grown up in the Peruvian Amazon. The rain didn't seem to have any impact on them; they stood comfortably, letting it douse their hair, clothes and skin as calmly as if the sun were shining.

"Frank!" he called out. "There you are!"

"Yes sir," Frank said.

"We have been looking for you, son." José's voice was gentle and the space between his eyes was creased with concern. "Are you all right?"

Frank nodded. He stood up straight, took a deep breath and began. "Sir, I was—"

"These young men have traveled nearly twenty-four hours without rest to reach us," José continued as though Frank hadn't spoken. "They bring grave news." He paused. "About your father."

For an instant, the forest faded away. Frank could no longer see the green canopy of the trees, or feel the rain. José's voice sputtered out of his consciousness as dread clutched at his heart with cold, grasping fingers. He saw his father's face wearing the same lopsided grin that Frank knew his own face could mirror, fingers lifted in a wave, his salt-and-pepper hair a messy, absentminded mop waving goodbye at the gate.

" ... collapsed ... " José's voice broke into his consciousness. " ... hospital ... very serious ... go immediately ... "

Frank nodded as though he understood, but in truth most of the words just washed over him. In a blink he was four years old, crying on his father's lap because he didn't have a mommy like the other kids; he was ten and spending the summer on a dig, working in the South American sun beside his dad; he was fourteen, talking man-to-man with his father about the birds and the bees. They'd never been separated until this trip: his father had taken him everywhere, included him in everything. Frank couldn't remember a time when he hadn't felt the certainty of his father's love.

Light-headed and blind, he reached out and found José's shoulder beneath his hand.

"You must go. Right now," José told him. "They say there is not a moment to lose. Pepe and Arnaldo will guide you. There is another route back—it will take you a day instead of three, but it is demanding." José inspected him a moment, a question he didn't ask in his eyes. "Take only what you need—money, passport, a dry shirt," he said instead. "Leave the rest. The boys have provisions enough for you. As for your belongings, Lucinda and I will pack the rest and send them to you."

Lucinda. Her name jolted Frank back to himself.

"C-can I tell her?" Frank stammered. "At least let me say—"

José shook his head.

"Your father needs you," he said softly. "I will tell Lucinda what has happened. Now go—and when you see my old friend, tell him we will be praying to the Holy Virgin for his quick recovery." He patted Frank on the arm. "Get your things and go. Every moment counts."

Frank dove into his tent and grabbed the small zippered bag that contained his travel documents and his wallet, which opened when he grabbed it to a photo of the two of them—himself and his father—two years before on Frank's sixteenth birthday, standing at the foot of the Sphinx with big, stupid grins on their faces. Looking at the picture made his eyes fill with tears, but he swallowed them down. Now wasn't the time. He needed to act. He needed to be strong. He needed to invoke all the things his father had taught him about carrying on under the weight of the pain of living.

As for Lucinda . . . after his father was well, he'd come back. He'd come back and take her away.

He stuffed a dry shirt, socks and underwear into a pouch on the inside of his rain jacket and emerged, determined.

"I'm ready," Frank told José.

José stared at him for just a moment.

"Yes," he said at last. "Yes, you are." To Frank's surprise the older man embraced him, kissing both his cheeks in the European style. "Goodbye, Francis Junior. Good luck."

José hadn't exaggerated: the terrain was rough and Frank was glad to be traveling unencumbered—except by the heaviness of his heart and the weight of time and space between where he was and where he wanted to be. Determination made him stronger and he pushed himself through it, remembering all the many travels he and his father had been on. If his muscles hurt, he ignored them. But then, for most of the trip he didn't remember feeling tired or sore at all.

They did not stop for food or rest. Almost exactly twenty-four hours later, they arrived on the banks of the Amazon, where a small boat waited to carry Frank into Iquitos for the flight to Lima, and then from Lima, home.

He arrived in San Diego forty-eight hours after José had delivered the bad news, smelling like sweat, wetness and weariness, but he didn't even stop for a fresh T-shirt from the airport gift shop. He begged his way to the front of the cab line and was at the hospital within thirty minutes of touching the ground.

The ICU was a web of curtained-off cubicles, each loaded with monitors and devices. Frank was directed to the space between two blue curtains by a nurse in pale pink scrubs.

He knew it had to be bad—he'd spent the entire plane ride preparing himself, and the doctor he'd met with had confirmed his worst fears.

"There's not a lot we can do." The older Indian woman had dark bags of fatigue under her eyes, but from the gentle way she'd touched Frank's arm and eased him to a chair, he knew he must look even worse. "He had a massive brain aneurism and severe bleeding in the brain. Most patients with that kind of rupture don't even make it to the hospital . . ." She gave him a small smile. "But he's been hanging on. I think your father was waiting for you."

And yet, even with that preparation, Frank had hoped . . . until he parted the curtain and peered down at the man on the bed.

He hardly recognized him.

The colors of life and health had drained from his dad's skin. White stubble covered his chin; his lips were flat gray lines. His robust frame seemed to have shrunk by half in just the six days since Frank had waved goodbye to him before heading down the jetway for his adventure. His eyes were closed and naked without his glasses. Frank understood immediately that if it weren't for the machines feeding their artifice into his veins, his father would be already gone.

"Dad," Frank murmured, his voice breaking with the fresh pain of the realization that José hadn't lied: there truly hadn't been a moment to spare. "I'm here."

He hadn't expected a response—the man lying before him looked beyond the ability to give one—but Frank slipped his hand into the older man's and squeezed his fingers anyway. The tears he'd forced back on the long ordeal home seeped out of his eyes and ran down his cheeks.

"Don't go," he whispered between sobs. "I'm not ready to be by myself. Please, Dad . . . don't go."

Later, he was sure he imagined it, but he thought he felt his father's fingers flutter in his own.

"Dad—" he began, but he never finished. As if cued by an unseen conductor, the machines began wailing and beeping simultaneously. An instant later, medical people filled the room, pushing him out into the cold corridor. Frank took a deep breath and forced down the panic rising inside him so he could bear to hear the words he knew he would:

"I'm sorry. He's gone."

CHAPTER Seven

"Get him some water or something, Max—"

"Sure."

Frank opened his eyes, surprised to find himself in a chair in the dining room of his house with Steve hovering over him, his face tense with concern.

"Wh-what happened?" he muttered.

"I was gonna ask *you*."

Eva's face appeared over Steve's shoulder. She looked impossibly young and terribly scared.

"Are you all right?" she asked just as Max appeared from the kitchen with a coffee mug full of water.

"Here ya go, buddy." Max rubbed his shoulder maternally. "Drink up."

Frank took the mug. His hands were shaking so badly,

he had to grasp it with both hands like a child handling his first glass.

"Take it easy there, big guy," Steve said gently. "Better?"

"Yeah, yeah," he muttered. "I just . . . it's been a long day. I guess I haven't eaten anything since yesterday and . . ." He stopped, frowning. "I just remembered . . ." He pushed himself out of the chair unsteadily and it toppled over behind him, knocking over a tower of papers.

"Whoa, there," Steve said. "Maybe you should—"

"I've been there. The Amazon . . . I've been there . . ."

"Of course you have, Frank. A few times—and those are just the ones I know—" Steve began.

"No . . ." Frank shook his head, but the fog memory was slow to clear. He stumbled out of the room, shrugging out of Steve's restraining grasp. "You don't understand. I've been there! To the fountain. Not a fountain . . . it's not a fountain. It's—it's—more like a pool . . ."

"Frank, please come back. Please . . ." Wendy sounded scared, but Frank ignored her plea and continued up the hall toward his father's study. "See, I think . . . I think I know what happened . . . but knowing him, he had to have written it down somewhere . . . probably in the study—"

"What are you talking about, Frank?" Steve asked, following a step behind him with the others at his heels. "Bud, you're not making much—"

"But where?" Frank asked himself. He attacked the desk, throwing papers aside, dumping them unceremoniously on the floor as quickly as he could determine their contents. "No . . . no . . . this is all just . . . old mail and junk. Junk, junk, junk—" He swept the desk clean in a matter of seconds, then turned around, surveying the bookshelves and the stacks of banker's boxes that held his father's work. "It's here somewhere. The explanation." Frank grabbed the nearest box and dumped it on the floor, sinking to his knees to begin sorting. "Oh my God . . . all these years I've wondered about that trip and now it makes sense . . . or at least sort of . . . or at least it will after we find his notes . . ." He glanced up at the four pairs of eyes peering at him anxiously from the doorway. "Somebody bring me a garbage bag. No, a box of garbage bags. And don't just stand there! Help me look!"

"I thought you said he wasn't hurt in the plane crash, Steve," Wendy said softly, blinking at Frank with worried eyes.

"Except that stuff with the girl, he seemed okay before."

"Not so much right now."

"Girl?" Eva demanded. "What girl?"

"Just some chick he sat next to. He's been convinced they're like soul mates or something—"

"Well, unless she's down with getting a little of Frank's magic salami, he'd better leave her alone. I wish I'd known beforehand. I'd never have let him into my secret garden no matter how cute his butt was, or much of his daddy's cash he spent—"

"Really, Eva. Can't you be quiet for once?" Maxine gave Steve a little shove. "Talk to him," she hissed. "Find out what he's going on about."

"She's the one with medical training," Steve muttered, jerking his head toward Wendy.

"You've known him the longest—"

"Oh fuck it," Eva muttered. "I'm calling nine-one-one—"

Steve grabbed her arm and pried her phone from her

fingers. He straightened himself to his full height, sucked in his gut and stepped into the study as though he were surrendering himself to a hungry monster.

"Dude," he said calmly. "I'll help you do anything you want. We all will. But first . . ." He shook his head. "You gotta tell us what the fuck you're talking about, okay?"

Frank stared into his friend's bewildered face.

"There *is* a fountain of youth, Steve. And I went there. My dad sent me just before I turned eighteen."

He filled their stunned silence with the story as quickly as he could, clarifying details as their questions required. When he reached the part about his last moments with his father, he stopped and glanced up at Steve. "You know the rest," he muttered quietly.

Steve nodded. "Yeah, I know the rest."

"But . . ." Maxine's gray eyes glittered with unshed tears. "I just don't get how you could forget something like that."

"He didn't forget," Steve snapped. "He just didn't want to remember! There's a difference!"

"What's the difference?" Max challenged. "And now that all this stuff about these women has come up, I'd think it would be the first memory to come to mind! The fountain of youth and all that—"

"Jesus Christ," Eva muttered. "What's wrong with you? Steve's right: sometimes forgetting is the only way you can move on. Besides, one look at this house and you don't have to be a shrink to know he's got some issues." She surveyed the cluttered room. "Okay, so what are you looking for here, Frank?"

"I don't know exactly. Something about that pool. Where it is. *What* it is. What it did to me."

"So we have work to do here. We need to find Frank's dad's notes or papers or whatever..."

"Do we know what it looks like?" Max asked, scanning the bookshelves hopefully.

Frank shook his head. "I know he used to keep his notes from digs in those red hardbound notebooks," he said, nodding toward a row of dusty crimson spines. "But I don't think it's in there."

"Why not?" Max pulled one of the volumes off the shelf and flipped its pages.

"I just don't think so. I can't believe he treated something like this the way he did all of his other digs. I mean, if that pool did what I think it did, it would be like—"

"The find of the century," Steve finished.

"Try the fucking millennium," countered Eva.

"Exactly. And Dad would have been famous. But that didn't happen. So he never published anything about it. He never even *said* anything about it. Not even to me. All he said was..." He stopped, not wanting to repeat any of his last conversation with his father again. "What I told you."

"But if he never said anything and never published anything," Wendy said softly, "maybe he never *wrote* anything."

Frank shook his head. "He was rigorous about methodology. He recorded everything—on every dig. No, it's here somewhere. It's here..." He grabbed a handful of paper off the floor. "In all this... junk. And if we can find it—"

"We can figure out what happened to you. Maybe we can find a way to turn *that* into cash instead of—" Max began.

"What's in that?" Eva interrupted, pointing to a small

wooden box tucked into the base of his father's old desk. It was about as long as a pencil, but at least six inches deep. The bands of rusted metal encircling it and the old-fashioned lock made Frank think of the treasure chests in every pirate movie he'd ever seen.

"I don't know. I've never seen it before." Frank reached for it, expecting the heavy weight of a container filled with gold coins. Instead it was so light it might have been empty, except for the faint thump of something hitting the interior walls. He tried the lid. "It's locked."

"Maybe we can find the key." Max hurried around the desk and began pulling open drawers.

"Don't bother, Max," Frank said. "It's a pretty box, but—" He turned it over so that the lock faced an edge of the ancient desk and finished the sentence by slamming the lock joint of the box against it. The fragile mechanism gave immediately.

Several sheaves of folded paper, tied with a frayed red ribbon, fell into his open palm.

"You think that's it?" Steve sounded excited in spite of himself.

"They look like . . . love letters," Max said in surprise.

"No shit," Eva agreed. "No one ties up their bills or dig notes with a red ribbon—even if that dig led to the fountain of youth."

"Well." Steve nudged Frank in the back. "Open them."

Frank's fingers trembled as he tugged at the little bow. As he unfolded the first few pages, his father's handwriting jumped out at him. Frank scanned the first paragraph quickly, then stopped, blinking rapidly to bring his emotions under control.

"What does it say, bro?"

"It . . . they . . . Eva's right. They're love letters," Frank told him, folding the letter again.

"Aren't you going to—"

"I-I think I'd like a little privacy."

"But what about—"

"Just—just go home. All of you. I appreciate your wanting to help, but this is something I have to do alone. Please. Go home."

Wounded. That was the look on his friends' faces, but Frank dropped the letters back into their box and waited.

"Frank, are you sure you're going to be all right by yourself?" Wendy asked gently. "You're pale as a sheet."

"I'm fine," Frank insisted. "I'll get some food in me, and I'll be one hundred percent, I promise."

Wendy cut her eyes at Max, unconvinced.

"So I guess this means you don't want me to call Carina Lynch?" Eva demanded, frowning.

"For the last time, I am not sleeping with Carina Lynch or any other woman. Not under any circumstances."

"But—"

"You heard the man," Steve said gruffly, taking Eva by the arm and leading her toward the front door. "It's time to go."

"Where? I can't go home. It was a one-way ticket. And I can't afford a hotel—"

"Well, you can't stay with us," Max groused. "Not smoking like a chimney the way you do—"

"I'll see if my parents can put you up," Steve interjected, heading off another girl fight. "But you'll have to smoke outside."

"And I'm starving," Eva said petulantly.

"Figures," Steve muttered.

When he was sure they were gone, he sat down heavily in his father's ancient leather chair and smoothed the creased pages of the first letter carefully.

February 26, 1980

Dear Helen,

> *Only two days since I left and I miss you dearly already. I don't know how I'll stand being away from you for three months! I know you don't like flying—and certainly I wouldn't want you to even attempt to accompany us on this dig—but I wish you would reconsider and come at least as far as Lima. I'd feel better knowing you weren't so far away. Please think about it, darling. Perhaps the doctors can give you something to make the flight easier?*
>
> *We are underway already. When we landed in Iquitos, José was there to greet me. If he were a fossil or scroll he would rank among my top five greatest finds (with you being in a category of your own, the Holy Grail of all discoveries!) for his knowledge and willingness. I hope we'll be joined by another scholar—someone familiar with the tribal legends—in a few days. If she is able to join us we will soon set off down the Amazon, heading north and east into some of the most treacherous and uncharted terrain of the rainforest. To make matters even more complicated, José tells me that The Shining Path guerillas have a stronghold deep in the jungle and we will have to alter our route to avoid them. José has*

brought extra men this time, so I feel safe for the moment. Those men will also make runs to some of the villages in the forest's interior—places that in many ways exist as they did hundreds, if not thousands, of years ago—for supplies. That is how my letters will reach you—slowly—delivered in supply runs back to Iquitos and posted by José's friends there. If you don't hear from me, don't worry. I'll be writing to you every day. You might go weeks without word and then get three dozen letters all at once!

I wish there were an easier way. But of course, there are no phones once we leave Iquitos. If you need me, call the number I left you and they will send a runner into the jungle, following José's map. Write me as often as you want. I will get your letters eventually—and they will be dearly welcomed whenever they come.

Promise me that you will behave yourself. Listen to the doctors and do what they tell you. If I find out you are overdoing it, you will leave me no choice but to come home immediately and abandon what could be the find of the century. Now, you don't want me to do that, do you?

With all my love,

Francis

March 5, 1980

My Darling Helen,

We have barely begun, and I confess, I'm already exhausted. We left José's village three days ago and the journey has been tense and difficult. Two of my colleagues have al-

ready become sick with the unceasing heat and had to go back. All of us are covered in insect bites. My arms ache from swinging the machete: there is no path but what we are able to hack for ourselves. José says that to the best of his recollection, we proceed due east toward the border of Brazil. He appears confident in our direction to the rest of our party, but privately,to me, he admits that he isn't sure.

I could regale you with a list of the flora and fauna of the jungle we have seen, but not today. Don't worry about me: I'm sure my spirits will lift soon, but this trip has already proved to be so much harder than the others—and we haven't even reached the dig site. I can see in the faces of the others, and even some of José's men, that we are all on edge.

But there is at least one piece of good news. The other scholar was able to join us before we left José's village. She is an indigenous woman who left her tribe as a girl and was educated both in Lima and in the United States. Dr. Amaru's expertise is anthropology. She has studied the legends of the aboriginal people extensively and it has been enlightening to listen to her. But even Dr. Amaru's stories don't help with the dark, oppressive heat of the jungle floor. The trees are so thick we rarely see the sun overhead. It's like walking through a humid, dark box littered with thick roots and vines. And sometimes, the vines aren't vines at all but snakes! Add to that the heavy rains that can fall without a moment's notice and the picture of my misery is complete. If it weren't for the feeling in my gut that this time we will find it, I think I'd join my colleagues and make a beeline back to Iquitos!

My longing for you grows by the day. I wish my work didn't take me away from you for such extended periods.

Maybe you're right: maybe I should take that position at UCSD when this trip is done. But please, please abandon this idea of trying to have a child. While I understand how much it means to you, you must understand what you mean to me. If I lost you in the effort, I don't know how I'd go on. The poor kid would have no mom—and a sorry excuse for a dad. Is that fair, my love? Of course not. If you force the issue, I promise—I'll never make love to you again. You'll have to cherish the memory of the night before I left forever— just as I cherish it when we camp at night.

Are you behaving yourself? While I look forward to seeing your decorating efforts in our humble abode, I hope you are taking care of yourself. It's just a house—and it doesn't matter to me if the walls are purple or green, if there are curtains or carpets—as long as you are in it.

I will write again soon, my love—and I promise to be in better spirits when I do.

Yours,

Francis

March 17, 1980

Dear Francis,

A packet of your letters came today—seven of them together. I read them one after the other—and then again, just because the words made it seem like you were right beside me, whispering in my ear. I was very glad to get them and to know that you are all right and to hear what you are doing. But the things I read scared me a little, too. I wor-

ry about you so much anyway—I swear you are the most absentminded man alive!—but this trek sounds dangerous. Between guerillas and snakes and diseases and heaven only knows what else, it seems to me that you should be worried more about your own health rather than mine! You can scoff if you want, but I pray for you every minute of every day. I know deep in my heart and soul that God is watching over you—but promise me you will help Him and stay safe, my love. Don't get so wrapped up in the dig that you take unnecessary risks.

I would love it if you would become a professor—but I can't imagine that you will ever do it! The digs are hard, I know, but you love what you do, Francis Young. You will never be happy just teaching. You'll always want to be out there, in some God-forsaken place, digging into the past. I'll just have to accept that as part of who you are—just as you have always accepted me.

I'm fine. Really. Okay, maybe I'm a little more tired than usual, but nothing to be concerned about. Don't worry about me. I am working on the house, yes, but just a little at a time. My friend Amy came over a few days ago and helped me hang new curtains in our bedroom and in the little room that ought to be a nursery one day (I'm sorry—but it's the perfect size for a child's room! Just an observation!). Then we went to dinner and hit the movies. The film was called **Apocalypse Now**. *I loved it—but even you'd probably find it slow (because we both know you can't sit still for more than ten minutes!). While I miss you so much I sometimes feel like I'm losing my mind, it's nice to go to the movies and sit beside someone who is actually watching . . . rather than wiggling and checking his watch like you always do!*

Oh, guess what? There was a preview for a film called Raiders of the Lost Ark *with Harrison Ford and it made me instantly think of you (except for the fact that you are far more handsome). It's about the adventures of an archeologist! Ha! It's supposed to come out next year.*

I don't know when this letter will reach you—or if you have received any of the others—but before I close, I have to tell you that if anything ever did happen to me, I have no doubt you'd be a wonderful father to our child . . . if God were ever to bless us with one.

Lovingly,

Helen

March 20, 1980

Dear Francis,

Don't be mad.

Please don't be mad. Even though you're thousands of miles away, I'm a little nervous about writing these words. If you were here, I'd put my hand on your cheek and stroke that little spot just at the corner of your temple to make sure you stay calm. I don't guess you could ask that Dr. Amaru to do that for you while you read these words (she'd better not! HA!)?

Okay, so here goes.

The truth is I sort of . . . minimized . . . how I've been feeling lately. Actually, I've been feeling pretty rotten. Just very, very tired—even worse than usual—and somewhat sick to my stomach. And the other day, when the handyman came over to paint the kitchen, well, I guess everything just came to a head. He says one minute I was standing there talking about shades of yellow . . . and the next minute he just barely caught me before I hit the linoleum.

Well, of course, he called 9-1-1 and of course we went to the hospital and of course, with my history, I was admitted. I'm writing this letter from room 213 in the Maternity ward.

Yes, you read that right, Francis. Maternity ward. I can only guess that it was the night before you left—remember we had trouble with the rubber? I take that as God's way of saying "HA!" to our care and preparation.

It's very early, Frank, very early. Four or five weeks, the doc says—so I'm guessing we conceived just before you left. The doc wants to keep me here for a while because this is not going to be easy. In fact, he argued that we should consider termination because of the risks to my own life! Can you believe that? I laughed at him. There's no way I'm going to terminate this pregnancy. If God decides I can't handle it, that's one thing. But I want to try. I can't imagine giving up our son—I know it's a boy, Frank—without trying to carry him to term.

Please, please, don't be angry. I'm going to take it easy—in fact, the doctor suggests bed rest. I'll do it. I promise. In a few more weeks, he says we can start with a drug that will help me. He says it might make me feel a little sick, but I don't care. I don't think I've ever wanted anything as much as I want this baby boy—except maybe to be your wife. If I thought the idea of our child displeased you, I don't think I could bear it.

Now at least I have a good excuse for not having to make the long trek down to Lima. HA! I hate flying—you know that. I never pray as much as I do on an airplane. By the time I reached Lima, I would probably have worn out my rosary!

I know you: you will want to abandon your quest and come home. There's no need. There's nothing you can do except hold my hand, which is nice but won't have any impact on God's will for me or our baby. But what you are doing down there is vitally important for you and for your research. Who knows? If you find it, there may be a way it can help me, too. Don't come home until you have found what you are looking for. Just promise me that you will be as careful with yourself as I plan to be. We are parents now, Francis.

Yours forever,

Helen

April 8, 1980

My dearest, dearest, Helen,

I hardly know where to begin. I scarcely know what to write or what to do.

I'm not angry—how could I be angry about our baby?—but I <u>am</u> scared. If I am angry at all, it's at myself for not being there. Despite your reassurances, I know how hard this will be on you. I know it will add stresses you don't need. I remember what the docs said the last time we asked about this. I'm sure nothing has changed in their prognosis—and I'm terrified.

Though you've urged me to stay, I can't. I'm coming home. I can't stay here now. As important as this dig is, you are far more important to me. José estimates it will take at least a week for us to reach the river. With luck, we will be able to get assistance from one of the fishing boats that tour the Amazon and get back to Iquitos within ten days or less. This letter and I may arrive around the same time.

I sense that the entire expedition is relieved at my decision to give up. It's been awful—by far the worst trip I've ever made. I've told you some of the hardships, but not all. I don't want to worry you, especially not now. Let's just say these entire six weeks, we've always been hot and rarely dry as the rains have been particularly constant, something that's unusual for this time of year. We've had trouble keeping adequate supplies. Two of José's men disappeared into the jungle one night and haven't come back. We suspect they grew weary of trekking in circles through this uninhabited part of the jungle and simply went home. Once, I felt certain that we were headed in the right direction, but now even I have my doubts. Dr. Amaru remains confident that we will find what we seek and has done yeoman service in keeping all of us—including me—from despairing. I am grateful for her optimism, but I confess I no longer share it. And, after receiving your letters, I wish we had been successful.

Perhaps it wasn't meant to be.

My place is at home with you and our little one. I can't wait to hold you in my arms again. Perhaps after the baby is born and I am sure you are well, I'll come back and try again. When little Frank (or little Helen—a daughter would be wonderful, especially if she looks just like you) is old enough, maybe the three of us will come back to Peru. I've never been a praying man—the notion of a wise old Man in the Sky has always struck me as ridiculous, sorry—but if He is there, I would only ask for one thing, Helen: that He watch over you.

Please, please, please stay in bed. Rest and wait for me. I'll be home soon.

Yours,

Francis

April 11, 1980

Dearest Helen,

They say it's darkest before the dawn . . . and that must be true because you will never believe what happened!

Yesterday, we surrendered to the will of the jungle. My colleagues turned toward the river, along with our guides, planning to give up and head for home. Though I had planned to go with them, I woke up this morning with the feeling that I should give it one more day—even if I went on alone. But when I spoke to José, he had had the same feeling . . . and so had Dr. Amaru. We shouldered our packs, said goodbye to the others and the three of us continued east.

I've never continued with a quest on sheer intuition— that is not my way. But I couldn't bear to turn back after nearly two months of searching with so little to show for it. If you can imagine me, walking along, arguing with myself in my mind: This is foolish, we should turn back and catch up with the others—no, keep going just a few hours. Turn back, keep going. Back and forth, over and over again. And then . . . we found it.

Quite by accident, in fact. I tripped over one of the many tree roots that have made our progress so slow and ended up tumbling down a 40-foot ravine—don't worry, other than some scrapes and bruises, I survived. Had I not tripped, I never would have found it. We could never have seen it from the path: it is shielded entirely by the jungle. It felt almost like the place didn't want to be found until the others had gone. Yes, I know: could it be that I have found some of the mysticism that governs your reality? You have always been such a good influence on me. I don't doubt that that's true even though thousands of miles separate us.

Of course, finding this place has revived our flagging morale. We're going to spend time here to see what we can unearth about the lives of the earliest people here. We can't stay much longer than that—we haven't food enough and though the jungle offers plenty, we have been too focused on reaching this destination to spend much energy on foraging or hunting. We need to get back. I suspect my return is now delayed by a week or so. Be patient—I'm on my way.

On another note, Dr. Amaru has told me of an intriguing legend associated with this place. I don't think I should write about it here, but I will tell you about it when I see you. Her input presents me with a bit of a dilemma. I'll resolve it—I must—but neither option is ideal.

I know, I'm being cryptic. I'm sorry.

Do you trust me, my love? Do you have any idea how much I love you—or how far I would go to see you healthy and happy and safe? There is no limit to what I would do for you, Helen—none at all. To see you well, I would do anything. To see you well, I would happily bear your anger with me for any transgression.

I love you, Helen. Promise you will take care of yourself—and I will be home within days.

Frank

Frank stopped, his heart fluttering against his ribs as if it needed to escape from his body in order for him to survive. The child his mother wrote about, he knew, was him. These letters were his parents' story, but they were *his*, too—the story of his birth and his mother's death—a story he knew only pieces of, and the pieces he knew were steeped in such sadness and loss that he had spent most of his life avoiding their pain. He glanced toward the photograph of his mother that had always stood in the midst of the clutter of his father's desk like a relic in a shrine. With her cascade of thick, dark hair and smiling brown eyes, she reminded Frank for all the world of Geena Davis in *Beetlejuice*.

Have these letters been here all along? Frank wondered. For fourteen years, he'd left his father's study untouched, rarely even entering it. For fourteen years had these letters—the only time he'd ever seen his mother's handwriting or heard her voice—sat in this little box, gathering dust, waiting for him to lift the lid and discover them? Now his parents leapt off these pages and conversed as though they were in the room—and he sensed from his father's vagueness about his destination that he had been seeking the very place that had changed Frank's life.

There were at least a dozen more letters, but he folded them, tied the ribbon carefully around them and put them back in the box, not yet ready to know any more of his parents' love story . . . especially since there was no happily ever after.

Instead, Frank glanced around the office. There were piles of unopened boxes, stacks of untouched mail, notebooks and journals on every single one of the bookshelves lining the walls—and more in the hallway, in the dining room, in the living room, the master bedroom, the attic and the garage. Frank sighed. He was surrounded by undisturbed memories and ghosts. What he needed to know about that mysterious Amazonian pool was in the house somewhere . . . and he certainly couldn't sell it until he found it.

He stood up, scanning his father's bookshelves from memory now, reaching behind an old hardbound atlas with a dusty black cover for the bottle. It was there, even dustier than the books, exactly in the spot his father had left it after Frank's birthday toast well over a decade before. As if this moment were part of some ultimate plan, there was just enough left for a single shot. Frank found the glass and poured, toasting the empty study and his father's accumulated work with an odd mix of excitement and fear. The scotch was strong and smooth and better than he remembered. Then, steeling himself against his own pain, Frank yanked opened the top drawer of the desk, lifted out the jumbled papers inside and began.

"You look worse than I do—and that's saying something!" Maxine said when Frank rolled into the office early the next morning. She looked rough: there were deep shadows under her eyes and her clothes were rumpled.

It was just after six in the morning—ridiculously early by anyone's standards—and yet here they both were. Frank headed straight for the little table that held their community coffeemaker and poured a cup into his mug before answering her.

"Couldn't sleep," he muttered.

"Were you . . . cleaning?" she asked delicately.

Frank nodded.

"Find anything useful?"

Frank shook his head. He'd spent most of the night sorting through his father's study—but the letters were still the only clue he had.

The letters. He pushed them from his mind. He couldn't get caught up in all that. He needed to work. He needed to find an investor. Fast.

"No one's sleeping at my house," Max said cheerfully, interpreting his silence accurately and steering the conversation in another direction. "Wendy's pretty uncomfortable now that we're just weeks away. Doesn't feel right to me to just roll over, you know?" She gulped a deep swig of coffee. "So . . . are you okay?" she asked carefully, focusing her attention on her computer screen so her questions wouldn't seem as intrusive. "Not giving any serious thought to that craziness Eva was talking, I hope? Preposterous, really. But then, I guess some women will do anything."

Frank sighed. "I can't imagine doing anything like that, Max. Even if it's for real, which I still can't completely wrap my head around, it's just—"

The phone rang, interrupting him. "I've got it," he told Max, grateful not to have to discuss the possibility of prostituting himself any further.

"My you're up early, Frank! I expected to get your voicemail! It's Michelle Doherty," chirped a cheerful female voice.

"Hello, Mrs. Doherty," Frank replied, relieved he'd already poured his coffee. He'd be on the phone for a while—but considering how much she and her husband were paying for their off-the-beaten-path safari in South Africa and Botswana, he'd talk to her as long as she wanted. He settled into his chair and got comfortable. "How are you? Are you excited about your safari? Just about a month away now."

"I'm great, thanks! Better than great, thanks to you. And that's why I'm calling. You remember those health forms you sent us?"

"Of course. We have to make sure you and your husband are fit enough for the excursion. Parts of it can be physically challenging—"

"I know. And since we're both runners and haven't had any injuries or health issues, I just sent the forms over to our doctor and didn't think anything of it." She paused dramatically, gearing up for the story to come. "Well, it turns out it's been a couple of years since either one of us had had a full physical and she wouldn't sign them until we came in. I go for mine and it's all good, no problems—well, except for the usual change-of-life stuff. I can't believe I'm actually perimenopausal! It seems like just yesterday that—"

Frank rubbed his temples. If he didn't say something, within seconds she'd be updating him on her hot flashes or the length of her menstrual cycle.

"What about David? How did his physical go? Everything okay?"

"Well, that was the surprise! The doc listened to his heart and she thought she heard a murmur. So she sent him for a stress test..."

Frank closed his eyes as a sickening premonition of disaster engulfed him.

"And they saw a blockage in the anterior left ventricle!"

She went on, narrating the procedures done and planned for in the near future while Frank felt his tenuous hold on his financial future slip from his fingers. "If it hadn't been for your health forms, they probably never would have caught it. David would have just—just dropped dead on one of his runs..."

By the time she finally said, "And so we're going to have to cancel. Will we be able to get our deposit back? Isn't this one of the exceptions in our contract?" Frank already knew he was in a deep, deep hole—one it might be impossible to climb out of.

"Of course, Mrs. Doherty," he managed to say—as though he actually still *had* their $30,000—as if it hadn't already been spent on the reservations for this tour or to pay the outstanding bills for the last one. "I'm so sorry you won't be joining us."

He managed a few more pleasantries before he finally disentangled himself from the web of her words and hung up, slumping forward in his chair.

"Please tell me that wasn't what it sounded like." Max was staring at him, her eyes round with anxiety. "Please tell me she didn't—"

"Cancel," Frank sighed. "Yep. Her husband's having heart surgery next week. Won't be cleared for any kind of travel for months. She wants a refund of her deposit."

"But Frank! We don't have it! Our cash flow is nonexistent—"

"I know—"

"We needed full payment from all ten of them just to break even—"

"I know—"

"And you haven't paid our rent yet this month—"

"I know!" Frank paced their tiny 20 x 20 space restlessly. "Even if I put the house on the market tomorrow, it'll take too long."

"There's got to be someone we can borrow from—"

"Who? Chase Lynch was the only rich 'friend' I had," Frank said. "And you see how *that* worked out. I guess I could take the two million—"

"And we lose control of the business. We'll end up employees in our own shop. It's a slower death, but . . ." She shook her head. "I don't want to go out like that." She scooted toward her computer. "I guess that's it, then. We gave it a good run, but we're done. I gotta start looking for a job, like *yesterday*. Wendy could probably find something fast—she's a nurse, they're always in demand—but she's not going to be able to job hunt until the baby's a few months old . . ." She buried her face in her thick, square hands. "Shit!" When she lifted her eyes to Frank, there were tears poised to make tracks down her cheeks. "What the hell are we going to do?"

What if I could get you one hundred thousand dollars per lady?

Eva's words ricocheted in his brain. $100,000—for a couple of hours, maybe less. Money he could have right now—or soon. Money to pay XT's debts and his own. Money to pay Wendy and Max and make sure baby Conrad had everything he needed when he arrived. If Eva could do it—if she could convince Jonathan Lynch's wife to pay—maybe Steve was right. Not only could it buy Frank some time to find another investor and keep control of XT, it would be the ultimate revenge.

What's the big deal? he asked himself. *I've had one-night stands before. That's all it is, really, only—*

He stopped himself before the words "gigolo" or "prostitute" could penetrate his consciousness and reached into his pocket for his cell phone. *Once,* he told himself. *Once.*

"Steve, where are you? Is Eva up? Because I need to talk to her. Things have changed. If she thinks she can convince Carina Lynch to do it, I'm in. But you have to promise me, Steve. No one, and I mean *no one*, finds out about this. I'm not worried about Max and Wendy, but you've got to keep those sweet lips of Eva's seriously shut, you got that?"

CHAPTER Eight

A week passed with little news. Frank took out a payday loan against his car and raised enough money for a couple of cheap tickets to Boston. Eva and Steve met with Carina Lynch, stayed two days and then returned without a decision. Frank went to work, came home and attacked the boxes that were his legacy faithfully—but was no closer to any answers than he had been when he first found the letters bound in their crimson string.

He had cleared the dining room and the hall, but on this morning, intuition sent him to the attic. Frank pulled the rung ladder down from the hatch cut into the second-floor ceiling and within minutes of climbing into the space, he was in the jungle—not a jungle of leaves and rain and mossy greenness, but a forest of rotting cardboard and forgotten toys, of dust and decay. The only thing it shared with his memories of the Amazon was stifling heat.

He emerged several hours later, slick with sweat and grime, his nose and eyes itching. In the end, there were eight heavy black garbage bags of trash—and more yet to be cleared still up there—but he'd also found two banker's boxes of his father's expedition notes, photographs and sketches that he dragged to his room to be perused later, after a shower and—

His phone vibrated. Eva's number shimmered and blinked, signaling the opening of a future Frank wasn't sure he wanted to embrace.

"I just saw her. Carina. She's here in San Diego," Eva said when he answered. "She's decided to do it. She gave me a cashier's check, but it's going to take a few days to clear. Can you hang in there? Because I've got a couple of things I could pawn—"

"The ATM says I've got nineteen dollars and seventy-three cents to my name. Which is as broke as I've ever been in my life." He tried to laugh it off, as if that would make it sound less pathetic. "But I've got gas and the refrigerator's full, so I should be okay. What's with the being nice to me? I thought you hated my guts?"

"Not right now. Right now, you're the boy with the golden nuts. Just protecting my investment. Now listen. Carina's only staying in town a day. She wants to meet you this afternoon. I'll text you the address. Steve said it's about forty-five minutes—"

"There's something I've been meaning to ask you," Frank interrupted, not ready to hear about it, not yet.

Already, he felt his stomach churning as he anticipated the encounter. What would he say to her? Would she know that he'd met with Jonathan and gone to school with Chase? "About something I thought I heard you say. About wishing we'd never slept together. Not because of . . . us . . . but because of this youth thing."

He heard a hard breath on the other end of the line like she'd taken a deep drag on her cigarette.

"Yeah?"

"Is that so?"

"Yeah."

"Why? I mean, isn't that what women want? To look young? To not age?"

"Maybe. Aging's a bitch. Or so I've heard. Guess I'll never know. But then there's lots of things I'll never know, thanks to you."

"What do you mean?"

"I mean, this whole youth thing has a downside, too," Eva said bitterly. "I'll probably never be a mom. I'll probably never really find a decent man who loves me. Never really get anywhere with my career—"

"I don't understand. You're a smart girl. A beautiful girl—"

"Yes," she spat, her anger crackling through the phone line. "And that's what I'll always be. A *girl*—I'll be twenty years old forever, thanks to you and your stupid dick! Think for just a second, Frank. Really think about it." Frank heard the pause of another inhale. "No man really wants a woman who doesn't age. They think they do—but they really don't. That much I know already. So before they even start to realize that they're changing and I'm not, I cut it off.

These days all I attract are dirty old men trying to recapture their lost youth with a twenty-year-old. They aren't serious and neither am I. I get what I can get out of it and move on." She paused. "It's probably just as well. If I ever fell in love—really in love—I don't think I could stand it. He'd get older and older—and I'll stay the same. People will think I'm his daughter, then his granddaughter. I'll get to watch him die, looking like I'm twenty while I lived my whole life at his side—"

She was right—and it sounded like torture. What could be worse than watching your loved ones slowly die . . . while you remained unchanged?

"You know why I was fired from my last job?" she continued quickly. "Yeah, they downsized, but they let me go because they thought I was 'too young' to make the leap to management—and I'd been there five years! All my experience didn't count. When they looked at me, they couldn't even see it. Not that I blame them. What client is going to take a designer seriously when she looks like she just got out of college? Who's going to report to someone who looks young enough to be their kid? And speaking of kids . . ." Her voice rose, veering onto the edge of hysteria. "Speaking of kids . . . how would you like it if your mother looked like *she* was twenty when *you* were twenty? Or if she looked like she was twenty when you were forty? Sure, it's fine when they're little, but children grow up. They get older and we're supposed to grow older with them! Yeah, it's nice to look young, but not forever. Not when you're someone's mother!" Her voice broke. Frank heard a small sound . . . just the softest moan of despair on the other end of the line.

"Shit," she muttered. "I—I don't want to talk about this

anymore, Frank. Just—now that you know about this power or gift or curse or whatever you want to call it—now that you *know*, if you really love a woman, do her a favor and keep your platinum pecker in your pants."

"Eva—"

"I said I don't want to talk about it!" she repeated, and he could hear the tears in her voice. "Besides, you've got somewhere to be. Carina's waiting. Don't fuck this up, Frank—and I'm not even thinking about a pun, here." She hung up.

If you really love a woman, do her a favor and keep your pecker in your pants.

He thought of Jackie, the girl from the airplane—not that she had ever strayed very far from his mind in the past couple of weeks. By now, if any of the efforts he'd made to find her or her nonprofit had been successful, he'd have heard from her. Or perhaps they'd been successful and Steve was right: it was just a moment, an artificial closeness created by the fear of imminent death. And maybe—much as it hurt to accept the idea—maybe after everything Eva had said, it was for the best.

An hour later, Frank confronted a new image of himself. Gone was his usual, average-guy look. Instead, a corporate version of himself met his reflection: tailored gray suit, clean-shaven face, freshly trimmed hair. He reminded himself of Ryan Gosling in *The Ides of March*—minus the millions of adoring female fans and the sneakers. The suit required dress shoes—and the closest thing Frank had was a pair of loafers that, when he looked at them closely, had seen better days.

He hurried out of his bedroom and moved through the hall toward the master bedroom, where he was pretty sure he could find his father's black dress shoes. They were practically new—what use were dress shoes on a dig site?—and only a little tight. For a couple of hours, they would suffice.

It was still 1980 in his parents' bedroom. The full-sized bed was covered with a wildly floral comforter and dust ruffle, with big matching pillow shams that Frank knew his mother had bought and his father had never changed, even though they were worn and old. There was a long dresser in dark wood, topped by a mirror nearly as long. Dusty knickknacks covered the dresser's surface: a comb and brush, still knotted with dark brown hair, and a paperback copy of Dr. Spock's *Baby and Child Care* captured Frank's attention before he hurried to the closet and pulled his father's black dress shoes from the rack on the closet floor.

If he hadn't seen the knob of the old combination safe, he might have forgotten all about it. Indeed, he hadn't had any reason to think of it. He'd opened it exactly once before—fourteen years ago on the day after his father died—to retrieve a will that barely seemed necessary since he was his father's only surviving relative. There had been precious little else in there: a life insurance policy, a few statements from his pension plan and the little jewelry box that held his mother's diamond engagement ring.

"She was buried in her wedding band." The memory of his father's voice was so clear Frank could feel him standing behind him, his voice hoarse with grief. "But I—I thought we should keep the ring. I think your mom would have liked the idea of you giving it to someone special one day."

Frank knelt and opened the small container. He didn't

know why—maybe it was just the letters and the woman he'd met through them. Or maybe in the back of his mind lurked the hope that he'd find some hidden clue there—something he'd overlooked in the past but that was now falling into his hands at the moment he needed it most, like in the movies.

Not a movie moment. The safe was empty except the small black box. Frank grabbed it and popped it open.

He really didn't know much about diamonds—except for whether they were big and expensive-looking or tiny chips of regard—but this one seemed to catch the light and refract it into rainbows around him as he twisted the ring in his fingers. The stone wasn't particularly large, but there was something about it that announced "I'm special," and immediately the girl from the plane filled his memory again.

If you really love a woman, do her a favor and keep your pecker in your pants.

Frank closed the box and dropped it into his suit jacket pocket. Then, as a talisman against the lovelessness of what he was about to do, he retrieved his parents' love letters and dropped them into the other pocket and set off to sell himself.

The directions Eva texted led Frank along the coastline to a sprawling compound of pristine grass and terra-cotta roofs nestled among the perfectly landscaped California palms. As the valets whisked his dirty Honda off to a lot filled with Bentleys and Rolls-Royces, Frank inhaled, filling his lungs with the cool sea breeze.

"Mabel Dawson," he told the foppish young man in a

suit nearly as nice as Frank's standing behind the reservation desk. That was the pseudonym his client was using.

Client.

Frank's stomach roiled nervously. In a few minutes, he'd be expected to produce a hard-on and satisfy a woman he'd never even spoken to. What if—?

"Your name, please?"

"Fr—"he began, before remembering that he was now a part of a hush-hush world of aliases, alibis and absolute discretion. "I mean, Michael. Michael Deere."

"But of course, Mr. Deere." The young man waved a thin, elegant hand and a small brown woman appeared as though conjured by magic. Like the man, she was impeccably and conservatively dressed in a dark suit and white blouse, her long, dark hair pinned off her collar with a tortoise-shell clip. "Anna is your personal concierge. She will escort you."

Frank half nodded with appreciation and half cringed as the thoughts of being escorted by "personal concierges" and *being* the escort did battle on his face.

"Right this way, sir." Anna flashed him a professional smile as warm as January and led him not to an elevator or along a corridor, but back outside. "It'll be just a moment," she said as they stood under the portico.

Thirty seconds later, the same valet who had reluctantly taken the keys to Frank's embarrassing ride pulled up in the fanciest golf cart Frank had ever seen. It was silver, with wide, comfortable leather seats for the driver and front passenger and a rear banquette long enough to comfortably seat at least three, equipped with a television monitor—in case the riders got bored on the short drive to their accommodations. Sparkling rims glittered on the wheels and the entire rig was shaded by a thick white awning. The Mercedes hood ornament on the vehicle's nose identified it as a member of an elite class.

"Thank you, David," Anna said as the valet jumped out. "Mr. Deere?"

Frank started at the name. "Thank you," he murmured, trying to sound unimpressed by the golf cart or anything else. He considered the rear banquette before rejecting it for the front passenger seat. Anna slid behind the luxury cart's steering wheel and they were off.

They followed a perfectly manicured, steeply descending trail from which he could only occasionally see a bungalow rooftop or the hint of a porch. Anna drove as quietly and intently as though she were a machine. Her silence was nerve-racking—and Frank was already so keyed up with anxiety that he could hardly sit still.

How am I going to do this? Am I supposed to just walk up to her and say, "Take your clothes off?" What if she's changed her mind . . .

Calm down, he told himself. *Eva said she's in. She's paid the money. There's nothing left to do but—*

He stretched a little, settling one hand in his jacket pocket, trying to appear as relaxed and cool as James Bond on his way to an assignation. But when he reached into his pocket, his fingers closed around the little black box that held his mother's engagement ring—and immediately he felt ashamed. His parents had clearly had the kind of bond Frank hoped he'd one day find—that he thought he'd found for a fleeting moment before Jackie slid down that damn slide and disappeared into the rain and wind—and here he was, their son, about to fuck a total stranger for a lot of cash.

He focused on Anna. Something about her reminded him of the girl in *Slumdog Millionaire*. He could imagine her in something colorful and sheer, her straight black hair in a long, thick braid, dancing in the streets of Mumbai—with the same grim expression on her face that she wore right now.

"Is there something wrong, sir?"

Frank shook his head. "No. Why?"

"You were ... staring," she said as delicately as possible. "I thought perhaps I was driving too fast."

"Oh, no. Not at all," Frank said hurriedly. *I'm just on my way to do my Magic Mike imitation and I'm scared to death. What if little Frankie doesn't want to play?* He'd raised that question to Steve the other night and been surprised when Steve reached into his pocket and produced a small bottle of little blue pills.

"There you go. Viagra. Take one an hour beforehand and if she so much as breathes on it, you'll be so stiff you won't be able to walk."

But he'd refused. Now Frank realized that might have been a huge mistake. Anna was definitely attractive—and even under that sober blue suit he could tell she had the kind of figure that normally, at least, made him think about what it would be like to have sex with her. But he felt nothing—except his own panic.

Finally, they turned off the drive onto a narrow, sheltered road. Frank measured about five hundred yards before they pulled up in front of an elegant hacienda with a wide porch. Three stone steps led to a red door the exact same color as its tiled roof. The Pacific Ocean lay behind it, tumbling with gray-capped waves.

Anna hit the brakes and threw the snazzy little cart into park.

"Enjoy your stay, Mr. Deere," she said in a tone that made it clear she was relieved to be free of him. *I'm not a bad guy*, he longed to tell her. *It's just that I've never slept with a woman for money before.* But since he doubted that explanation would help much, he simply slid out of the cart and turned toward the bungalow's white stucco exterior before his brain or his nerves sent him running back up the cliff to demand his car keys from the valet.

"This is probably just about the craziest thing I've ever done in my entire life," Carina Lynch murmured. "And if my husband finds out, it's also going to be the most *expensive* thing I've ever done in my life."

"Oh really? Why?" Frank tried to smile, but now that he was standing inside the lavishly furnished hacienda and looking into Carina Lynch's bright blue eyes, it was hard to think of anything but what he was supposed to do with her and to her.

She led him through the house and outside to a comfortable deck chair on the patio, and there he sat, regretting the suit under the warm sun and the gentle murmur of the waves. Carina wore some kind of sheer caftan in a brilliant turquoise that matched the clear water. He could see a tiny white string bikini beneath it, and a trim, tanned figure that spoke of hours of yoga, tennis lessons at the local club and carefully portioned low-fat meals.

"Because of the pre-nup. If Jonathan finds out I cheated on him, I get nothing. It's in the agreement." Carina reached for a silver cart loaded with premium liquor bottles. "Drink?"

"No, thank you," Frank began, but he reconsidered in the next instant. He couldn't just sit here, stiff and overdressed. "On second thought, yes." He stood up and stripped off the suit jacket and discarded it.

"What'll it be?"

Frank shrugged. He joined her at the cart, loosening his tie and jerking it off violently. "Make me what you're having."

"That's better," Carina said approvingly as he tossed the tie on top of the jacket. "You don't look like the suit kind."

"I'm not," Frank laughed. "Is it that obvious?"

She smiled. "No. You looked good. It's just . . . I don't know. Some men look most themselves in shorts and a T-shirt and some men look like they were born in a suit and tie, and you can't imagine them being comfortable in anything else." She quirked an eyebrow at him. "You look like a khakis and polo kind of guy."

"Cool trick. And you're right."

She nodded. "Jonathan's the opposite. To me, he looks funny in anything but a suit. It's what he was born to wear."

Jonathan. He didn't know why he was surprised that she said his name with genuine affection. For the first time, he really looked at her, taking in more than the obvious first-impression details of prettiness. Her blond hair dusted her shoulders, and from time to time, she lifted a slender hand to sweep a bit of it out of her eyes, which were blue and sparkling with self-deprecating intelligence. Her skin was tawny and smooth, showing age only in its thinness and in the smallest sag around the eyes and lips.

"Here you go," she said, handing him a martini with a pimento-less olive floating near the top and lifting her own glass in a toast. "To youth."

"Carina . . . can I ask you why you're doing this?" Frank ventured as the cocktail steadied his courage. "You're risking everything—"

"I know." She stirred her drink with a finger, flashing a diamond the size of an almond that put the little stone in Frank's pocket to shame. When she lifted her face, the tears glittering in her eyes outshone the stone. "You probably won't believe this," she began, "but I love my husband. People look at a couple like us—rich older man, attractive younger woman—and they write a story. A story that, in this case, isn't the reality. At least not for me. I worked for Lynch Capital. I admired Jonathan long before he knew who I was. I guess I had a crush on him for a long time and then one day . . ." She sighed. "You don't want to hear all of that. Let's just say that one day, he noticed me. And now, I'm his fourth wife. I loved him so much, I agreed to everything he wanted me to agree to, just to be with him. I thought that if I loved him well enough, that if I worked hard to keep him happy, it would be enough. That we'd be together forever."

She paced away from him. The sea breeze fanned her hair away from her shoulders like a halo. Frank watched her lithe body ripple under the sheer fabric as she leaned against the railing, staring out at the water.

"So I guess you were wrong?" he prompted quietly. "Love isn't enough?"

"Only partly wrong. Love's enough for *me* . . . but I guess I was a little over my head," she sighed. "I didn't see what I should have seen."

Frank waited.

"It's a double standard, Frank—I can call you, Frank, right? It doesn't matter how old a man is . . . but it matters how *young* the woman is. My husband likes to have a beautiful young woman on his arm. He feels he deserves that. A *young* woman. The younger the better. Do you know how old his first wife was when they divorced? Forty. You know how old his second wife was when they divorced? Thirty-eight. And the third? Thirty-nine. I am thirty-four years old. I'd have to be stupid not to realize there's a pattern here." She took a deep swallow of her martini and grimaced. "And though I'll admit I'm lots of things, I'm not stupid. I've already seen how he looks at some of the twenty-something girls Chase brings around. He stares at them like he was a starving man. He used to look at me that way," she finished in a low voice, turning back to the tumbling waves licking the beach. "At this point, I already feel like I'm living on borrowed time . . . and I'll do anything to keep my husband's love, Frank."

She shrugged out of the robe. In another blink the swimsuit lay between them and she stood naked before him, presenting him with her tanned, toned perfection: round high breasts that topped the flare where her hips abandoned the valley of her stomach. Her love triangle was shaved bare and looked pink and soft. Frank felt his own nether regions stirring.

She gulped down the last of her drink with a fierce determination and abandoned it. Wordlessly, she advanced on him and pressed herself into Frank's arms. Her mouth clamped onto his, desperate, insistent and almost wild.

"Whoa, whoa . . ." Frank murmured, pulling away from her. "Slow down, slow down—"

"Haven't you been listening?" Carina hissed. "I don't have any more *time*. I have to . . . I have to do this! I know it's wrong. I know I'm breaking my vows and risking everything, but—but—" Her face twisted as a sob racked her chest. "Oh God, what am I doing . . . what am I going to do?" She released him, sinking to the ground under the weight of her emotion, abandoning herself to her tears.

Frank wrapped his arms around her. "Hey, it's okay . . ." he murmured into her hair. "Really, it's going to be okay—"

"It's not," she sobbed. "It's probably already too late . . . and if Jonathan finds out—"

"He's not going to find out," Frank whispered, holding her soft body close to his. "And it's not too late."

She raised her tear-streaked face. "Are you sure?"

A funny feeling twisted in Frank's gut: sympathy mixed with attraction combined with desire. "If Jonathan Lynch can't tell you're a beautiful, smart, sincere woman who loves him, then he's a fool. He's a fool who doesn't deserve you—I don't care how much money he has or how young you look five years from now."

He read gratitude in her eyes. This time when their lips met, Frank's body was aflame, and when she wrapped those tennis-tanned legs around his hips there wasn't any doubt in Frank's mind: Viagra was the last thing he needed. Still, though, as they moved through the hacienda together, as he lay her down on the soft white sheets and closed his eyes, he wished he were making love to a girl who looked like Catherine Zeta-Jones.

He left her an hour later, her bare body wrapped once again in the sheer robe, her hair a wild mess around her face. But she was smiling.

"You're a nice man," she told him. "Thank you."

"Good luck, Carina."

"You, too."

Then she closed the door behind him.

He waited only a few short minutes before Anna, the personal concierge, appeared with her luxury golf cart. But with his mission accomplished, he felt like a different man—a man not in the mood for Anna's professional disinterest. This time, he climbed into the rear of the little conveyance and allowed himself to be chauffeured so he wouldn't even have to look at her. In spite of its Mercedes engine, the little cart ascended the steep hill slowly.

More out of impatience and boredom than anything else, Frank slipped his hands into his jacket pocket. His fingers curled around the little velvet box and he opened it again, inspecting the bright jewel. He could imagine his mother's diamond so clearly on Jackie's finger that it almost hurt to look at, especially knowing that with every day that went by, the probability of his ever seeing her again diminished exponentially. With a sigh of regret, Frank stuffed the box back in his pocket and distracted himself with flipping the channels on the little television built into the console.

The vision of two hyenas mating in Kenya prompted a quick channel change. A stage full of pregnant moms in each other's faces with Jerry Springer and presumably the women's lovers looking on . . . click. A young woman with a mane of thick, dark hair was talking urgently into the camera. Frank barely glanced at her. He was about to hit the remote once again when he heard her say, "Poverty and population—the two Ps, as we call them—"

Frank jerked forward, peering at the speaker.

"Jackie!" he said out loud.

"Excuse me, Mr. Deere?" Anna glanced over her shoulder.

"Population control is one of the keys to sustainability," Jackie was saying earnestly, gesturing with her hands. She wore a dark jacket and a blouse in a shade of purple that made her eyes sparkle like the night sky. "Lack of birth control is obviously a factor. But so are longer life spans and improved medical care. Those things are certainly blessings and I'm not arguing that we deprive anyone of them. But if we're going to live longer, we need to be responsible about how we live. That means birth control, euthanasia and responsible aging have to become real topics, not just in this country but worldwide—"

"So what does your organization suggest?" The camera shifted to the interviewer, an attractive black woman who wore her hair in thick strings of shoulder-length braids. "Would you implement policies like the one-child effort China imposed on its citizens?"

"Ours is a nonprofit organization—we're not here to impose anything on anyone," Jackie said firmly. The camera zeroed in on her, magnifying both her gravitas and her beauty. She kept talking—something about awareness and access and so on, but Frank wasn't listening. His attention was completely diverted by the words that appeared at the base of the screen.

"Jacqueline Noble, founder of Life SPAAN," Frank repeated out loud. He reached into his pants and then the pockets of his jacket. "Anna!" he called out, sounding for the first time like an executive used to having his needs met. "Paper!"

"Lower the bolster, sir," Anna replied. "And open the top. If you'd like, I can stop and—"

Frank was already scribbling. "Jacqueline Noble, Life

SPAAN." Life SPAAN? Wasn't that the organization he'd emailed that first weekend after the crash?

"Thank you," the interviewer concluded. "We've been talking with Jacqueline Noble, director of the San Diego–based nonprofit group—"

Frank started laughing.

"Sir?" Anna asked, glancing over her shoulder, her serious face puckered with concern. "Are you all right?"

"She's real. And she's here!" Frank answered, ignoring the confusion on his driver's face. "She was right here all along!"

CHAPTER
Nine

Later, he would count it as one of the craziest things he'd ever done—even crazier than "Frank Young, Fountain of Youth—Services for Sale"—but as soon as the valet brought his car and he'd stuffed his last few bills into the kid's hand, Frank drove straight to KYYR.

Somewhere in the interview, the call letters had been mentioned or appeared—Frank couldn't remember which—but the letters stuck in his brain. He could see the station clearly in his mind's eye—he'd driven by it hundreds of times—a low, flat square of concrete set back from the main thoroughfare and shielded by a giant satellite tower.

He drove straight and steadily, until he reached a parking lot crowded with cars and several big white vans imprinted with the station's call letters. Frank hopped out of his car and jogged to the glass doors of the front entrance.

The lobby was small—just a reception desk and a few black chairs lining the walls—and chilled to refrigeration temperatures by arctic blasts of air conditioning. An older woman with short, iron-gray hair looked up from her computer screen and wrapped her sweater more tightly around her shoulders.

"May I help you?"

"Yes . . . I hope so . . ." Frank began, pausing as he figured out how to ask what he needed to know. "I just saw—"

He heard her before he saw her—chatting to someone about the interview, expanding on a point that, apparently, she felt she hadn't made. "And really we could have spent another whole hour, just on that one issue—"

She appeared from the hallway behind the reception desk a second later, followed closely by a thin, effeminate-looking young man. All of the nervousness and self-doubt that should have restrained him—that should have kept him from showing up here with puppy-dog eagerness, hoping she might smile at him—settled on him with full force. Frank's mouth dried, his tongue shriveled and once again, he had the feeling of being over his head and out of his league. After all, Life SPAAN was the entity he'd contacted—two weeks ago now—and she'd never responded. Maybe Steve was right: maybe she hadn't wanted to see him again.

But her face was even lovelier than he remembered: pale skin, dark eyes fringed with thick black lashes, bow-shaped lips lined with a bright red lipstick—applied, he suspected, for the cameras. The television had misrepresented her: the dark jacket covered not a blouse but a dress in a shade of amethyst. Her black hair hung on her shoulders in loose waves.

"Jackie." Her name fell out of his mouth on its own; he couldn't have stopped himself from saying it if he tried. "Jackie."

She turned. Her brows contracted in bewilderment as her face rearranged itself. For the longest fraction of a second imaginable, Frank's worst fears took shape and pummeled him with his inadequacies. *What I am doing? Why am setting myself up for this rejection? Why couldn't I have just called her office like a normal person? This is going to be humiliating—*

His brain spun on failure, but his body insisted on hope. He opened his arms.

"Frank!" she cried, all the hesitation in her face dissolving into an expression of pure joy. "Oh, Frank!"

Her arms went around him hard, encircling him completely in a tight embrace, enveloping him with the sweet smell of her hair and the spicy aroma of her perfume.

"Oh, Frank," Jackie murmured over and over, clinging to him like she, too, was afraid to let go. "Frank. I thought I'd lost you. I thought it was—just one of those random things and you didn't want to be found—"

"Jackie." Her name was the only word left in his head. Everything in his world before that moment was erased from his consciousness: Steve could have walked up and he wouldn't have known him. He forgot XT; he forgot Lynch's wife's name. None of it mattered. He realized in a flash like the lightning that had first brought them into each other's arms that he'd missed her like a lost limb or an internal organ. It was miraculous that he'd been ambulatory without her.

There was no knowing how long they might have stood there had the thin young man not cleared his throat with sudden violence.

"Oh..." Jackie's cheeks bloomed embarrassment as she stepped out of Frank's arms and seized his hand instead. "I'm sorry. This is my assistant, Gregory Bernstein. Gregory, this is Frank..." The pink in her cheeks deepened. "I don't even know your last name."

"Young." Frank squeezed her hand and smiled. "It's okay. I didn't know yours either until about thirty minutes ago. When I saw you on TV."

"That stupid airline," Jackie muttered angrily, forgetting all about Gregory again. "I kept asking them to give me your information and they said—"

"They were only releasing passenger information to family members," Frank finished. "I know. I heard the same thing—"

"Frank was on the plane with me," she explained to her assistant. "The one that crash landed. I was scared to death. This guy kept me from completely losing my mind."

Gregory nodded, folding his thin lips over each other and looking Frank up and down critically.

"Hey, I was scared as well. You kept *me* from losing *my* mind, too."

"Now you're just being nice." She stroked his cheek as though she'd been touching him all her life. "All around us, people are going crazy... and *this* guy." She fixed Frank with an admiring stare. "Steady as a rock. Got me talking about—oh, I don't know what—" She laughed, but the look on her face told Frank she remembered every word as clearly as he did. "The next thing I knew, we were safe on the ground."

"I think the pilot had more to do with that part than I did," Frank said modestly.

"Nice to meet you," Gregory said, nodding at Frank. "I can't tell you how many phone calls I made trying to find out who you were. Every hospital in Providence and Boston. Twice. Turns out I'd have done better to have opened the San Diego phone book." He flipped his wrist to examine a watch. "I hate to cut you short, Jackie, but you know I've got that thing across town. If you're going to make your four o'clock staff meeting—"

"I know you have to go, Gregory. That mission is still critically important," she said, tearing her eyes off Frank to nod solemnly. "But can't we reschedule the staff meeting? I mean, I've been looking for this man for two weeks!"

"Reschedule it, Gregory," Frank said. "Please."

Gregory looked from Jackie to Frank, then back to Jackie. With an eye roll worthy of an Oscar, he muttered, "I'll see what I can do," and let himself out of the building with a sigh. He paced the sidewalk, murmuring into his phone and stealing an occasional glance at them like a twenty-first-century chaperone.

"I'm so very glad to see you. Very glad," she said, grinning at him. "So what's next?"

"I had the feeling you were about to ask me out just before—well, you know. Was that right?"

Red patches appeared on either side of her nose. "Yes."

"Then 'what's next' is dinner or lunch or whatever you have at this hour. I haven't eaten all day. Too nervous, I guess."

"Nervous? Why?"

"I had a meeting today."

"About your company?"

"Kinda," Frank replied evasively. "It's not important."

"Not important?" Jackie's eyes narrowed. "I don't believe that. Unless I'm a really bad judge of character, I'd say you're not the type to waste your time with things that aren't important. And of course, the fancy suit is a dead giveaway." She laid her hand on his cheek again and stared deeply into his eyes. "You just don't want to tell me. Which is fine. For now."

Busted.

Frank forced his lips into a smile. "So where to? What's your favorite restaurant?"

"You know what I'd love?" she said, her bright eyes gleaming with mischief. "A really good burger. How about the Burger Bistro in La Jolla?"

"A burger? Really? You don't seem like the burger type. I mean, how does beef fit in with sustainability?"

"Shh," she said quietly. "It doesn't. But it's a special occasion. You won't tell anyone?"

"Your secret is safe with me."

Once again, her eyes swept over him, reading him to his heart's core. Frank braced himself for the next penetrating question, but his phone rang, distracting them both.

"Go ahead. Take it. I need to speak with Gregory—and I need to make a call or two myself if I'm going to give you my undivided attention this afternoon." She hesitated, leaning close as though she were about to kiss him, then caught herself, flushing uncertainly. "I—I really am glad to see you, Frank. When you're ready, I'll be right outside," she said quickly and slipped away from him.

"Well, dude, it's official. You're a hit," Steve said as soon as Frank picked up. "She called Eva about an hour ago to sing your praises. Said you couldn't have been more . . . what was it? Kind and comforting."

"I'm glad. She's a nice woman."

"Yeah, nice. But savvy, too. See, there's a little problem with the money. Eva really should have told you this before you went to meet her, but she was afraid you might back out—"

"What kind of problem, Steve?"

"It's only half. Fifty thousand."

"Fifty thousand! But I owe nearly that to the Dohertys! With the rent and the health insurance premiums I'm just as broke as I was before—"

"I know, I know. But she asked for a hold-back. To be sure it works. Was going to pull the plug on the whole thing if we didn't agree. So . . . we agreed. Fifty K is better than no K, hear me? And we've already got you another client," Steve continued quickly. "Turns out Max has a candidate. That fitness model in all the ads for Master Class Gym? With the spiky hair and the perfect ass? You know the one? Max says she's in. Soon as you're ready. Tomorrow, even. We'll probably have to give her the same deal Carina got—fifty now, fifty later—"

"No."

"No to which part? No to tomorrow? Or no to the deal, because I think Max will have a shit fit if her friend pays different—"

"No to all of it. I'm out of business. No more women," Frank said firmly.

"What? Why? What happened?"

Through the TV station's glass door, he could see her,

her hair an ebony curtain over her face. As if aware of him, she lifted her head and smiled, waving a pinky finger at him, before her conversation reclaimed her attention and she turned away.

"I found her, that's what happened."

"Found who?"

"Her. Jackie. Airplane girl."

"You are fucking kidding me! How?"

"I'll explain later. But the other thing is over. No more."

"But what about Max's friend? We already—"

"I don't care what you already did. *Undo* it, Steve!" Frank hissed. "I gotta go."

"Wait, Frank, listen—"

Frank hung up. He might be broke, but there was one thing he was sure of: life was too short for hesitation.

She was standing a few feet away from the station's doors, sunlight crisscrossing through her glossy black hair. He had never seen anyone more beautiful and he had never felt more sure of anything in his life. Desire was there, but also something else. Something deeper, wrapped in a feeling of happiness that made almost every silly romantic comedy he'd ever watched have the weight of the Gospel. Without a word, Frank closed the distance between them and caressed her soft cheek, pulling her face closer to his. His lips brushed hers, gently at first, and then more aggressively. Her arms wound around his neck like jungle vines as she pressed herself into him, returning his kiss fervently and passionately, erasing any doubt in Frank's mind that what they'd shared was far more than "a moment": it was the stuff lifetimes are made of.

"I guess . . . we'd better get each other's phone numbers this time," she murmured.

"Yes, I think that would be a good idea, babe," Frank agreed. "Right after this . . ." Frank pressed his mouth against hers again. He felt her fingers at the base of his neck, twirling the hair just above the collar of his shirt. Her lips were soft and wet and she tasted like mint and something faintly nutty, as though she'd snacked on almonds or sunflower seeds. He wanted her, he wanted her with every fiber of his body and his soul, and yet he knew he could wait, content just to hold her in his arms forever, as long as he could be sure that he could hold her endlessly and never be parted from her again.

If you really love a woman, do her a favor and keep your pecker in your pants . . .

Frank pushed that problem to the back of his brain. *Later,* he told it. *I'll figure something out, later.* For now . . . he buried himself in the taste and smell and feel of her.

"Oh Frank . . . what . . . what are we doing?" she murmured softly into his ear when they finally came up for air.

"I don't know. I just know that I feel like I've found something that I didn't know I'd lost."

"Me, too," she whispered, slipping her hand in his. "Listen, Frank. There's something I have to tell you . . ." She paused, her forehead tightening in concentration. "I-I don't trust easily, Frank. I've had some experiences that . . . make it difficult." She sighed. "But you were so honest on the plane. So . . . raw. I feel like there's something about you, Frank. Something that I can put my faith in. Especially now." She seemed on the verge of saying more but stopped, biting her lip as if to keep it from tumbling out on its own accord. "Now, let's go. I'm hungry."

Trust. Frank ignored the guilt squirming in the pit of his stomach and obeyed her command.

He drove, she talked. She told him everything that had happened since she'd dived down that yellow evacuation slide and hit the tarmac in Providence. About the trip to the hospital ("Totally unnecessary—I was completely fine") and about her family arranging a car service for her to travel back to Boston ("I would have been fine with the shuttle bus the airline arranged, but I guess they were concerned"). About the speech she'd been in town to deliver ("I was more shook up than I realized. Totally bombed.") and the awful plane ride back home ("I missed you"), and her hand found his again.

"Now." She turned toward him, sweeping her dark mane over her shoulder. "Tell me what's happened to you since we last saw each other."

"Well . . ." *An hour ago, I was fucking this woman who paid $100,000 for my sperm so she can keep her husband.* "Not much, really." He kept his eyes on the road so she couldn't see his face and launched into the story about how Steve had taken a cab to Providence to pick him up, about the reunion and the meeting with the Lynches, about X-Treme and the troubles it was having. He answered every question and hid nothing—as long as the answers didn't require the use of the words "sex" or "youth"—and felt like the biggest jerk in Christendom while she laughed and asked questions and kept running her soft hand along the length of his bare forearm, like she couldn't bear being so close without touching him.

"And of course, I spent plenty of time looking for you. I even sent an email to Life SPAAN—a really stupid email probably—"

"You sent an email? I should have gotten that. It's supposed to be checked every day—"

Frank shrugged. "It doesn't matter. I found you. We're together. That's all that matters to me. That and finding a way to keep XT. You don't have any venture capitalists in your Rolodex, do you?"

An odd shadow clouded Jackie's features before she shook her head. "No. At least, none worth mentioning," she added cryptically. "So, this 'not much': you're leading a tour in South Africa and Botswana in less than a month," she continued briskly. "You've been to the Amazon and the Arctic Circle, climbed Kilimanjaro, earned your black belt at the Shaolin Temple and done an Ironman competition. You really have been on three hundred airplanes, haven't you?"

Frank nodded.

"And I hate airplanes. I fly because I have to. But I hate it. I never pray more than when I have to fly! In fact, it's fair to say I only pray when I fly. Unfortunately, I've worn out two rosaries in the last three years—"

I never pray as much as I do on an airplane. By the time I reached Lima, I would probably have worn out my rosary!

His mother's voice echoed in his ears, wraithlike and yet palpable. Frank jerked toward the sound, forgetting about the road in front of him.

"What did you say?"

"I said I hate to travel. I never pray more than when I have to board a plane—Frank! Look out!"

He tore his eyes from her face just as the traffic light turned red. He slammed on the brakes, throwing his arm out protectively as they both lurched against their seat-belt restraints.

"Are you okay, babe?" Frank asked.

"Y-yes." She sounded breathless and more than a little rattled. "What is it about near-death experiences when I'm with you?" She peered at him, studying his profile as Frank concentrated on the road ahead. "What's the matter?"

"Nothing. Hungry. Still in shock that you want a hamburger. I guess I was expecting something more . . . continental. French or Italian or—"

"Greek?" Jackie grinned. "My family is Greek."

"That explains a lot. Your looks, for one thing. Dark hair and eyes. There's just something very . . . European about you. Have you been there? Greece?"

"Many times. I even speak a tiny bit. Just don't ask me to read it. The difference in the alphabet completely confuses me."

"Then don't ever try Mandarin or Farsi," Frank muttered, shaking his head. "I've been working on them for years—and every time I'm in China or Iran—"

"Iran?" Jackie blinked at him in surprise. "You've been to Iran?"

Frank nodded. "Not lately, though. I went in 2000 on a tour that was called 'Revisiting Ancient Persia.' It was summer break before my sophomore year of college, so I guess I was about eighteen or nineteen. I'll never forget it. It was my first job in the extreme travel business and since I was the low man on the totem pole, I got the job of trying to learn enough Farsi to communicate."

"But surely you had a guide?"

"Yes, but that's not enough. You need to have a back-up plan. That's like the cardinal rule of extreme travel—any travel, really, but especially extreme travel. As it turned out, I needed my Farsi because our guide—at least the only one who spoke English—broke his leg while we were scaling the Zagros Mountains in the central part of the country. Understandably, he was pretty much useless after that. We had to carry him back down the mountain and into one of the little towns there. I had learned enough Farsi to find us some help once we were able to regroup."

"Oh my God," Jackie breathed. "So I guess that was the end of that trip."

"Nope. We hired another guide—who spoke even less English—and went right back up the mountain. Came down on the other side and bathed in the great salt lakes there. Then headed across the Persian Gulf to Kuwait."

Jackie's mouth parted in wonder. "Wow," she said at last. "You're like a modern-day Indiana Jones—except much better-looking."

> *There was a preview for a film called* Raiders of the Lost Ark *with Harrison Ford and it made me instantly think of you (except for the fact that you are far more handsome). It's about the adventures of an archeologist! Ha! It's supposed to come out next year.*

Once again the words of his mother's letters seemed to come effortlessly out of Jackie's mouth. Frank stared at her, searching her face as though there were clues hidden in the planes of her cheeks or the outline of her lips.

"What's the matter, Frank? Did I say something wrong?"

"No." Frank shook his head, trying to clear the strange feeling that something beyond his understanding was at work. "It's just . . . my mother called my father that. Indiana Jones. I told you he was an archeologist—always searching for some undiscovered civilization or . . ." He paused, not sure how much he wanted to reveal about what his father might have actually found. "As much as I traveled with him as a kid, I probably should have become one, too. But the academic life isn't for me. I think that might be because I saw how much he hated it. Not teaching—he loved teaching. Especially the graduate courses where he'd take the students out on digs to all kinds of cool places—mostly in South America, because he had a particular interest in the indigenous peoples of the Amazon. What he hated was the politics of being an academic. All the meetings and the pressure to publish . . . which he just refused to do. Don't get me wrong; he did write. Come to my house—you'll see how much he wrote. His papers are everywhere. But except for the very occasional article, he never wrote a major piece. And his reputation suffered for it." Frank paused, but she nodded, encouraging him to continue. "Lately, I've begun to think his greatest discovery is somewhere in all the boxes and piles of paper he left around our house."

"Why didn't he publish it? His great discovery?"

"I think he found something," Frank said slowly. "Something that he knew could be very dangerous in the wrong hands."

"Like what?"

"I—I'm not sure."

His phone buzzed in his pocket, but Frank ignored it and eventually, it stopped.

"In some hands, anything can be dangerous," Jackie murmured. She turned her face toward the window and fell silent. When Frank glanced over at her, her forehead was puckered and she looked as though she had slipped into a world that held only trouble.

He pulled his car into an available space behind a quaint old-style diner. "We're here."

"Great. But first . . ." She leaned across the car and kissed him gently on the cheek.

"What's that for?"

"Do I need a reason, Francis?"

Frank winced.

"You are a 'Francis,' right?"

"Yeah, but no one calls me that." He launched into his best imitation of a character from the movie *Stripes*. "'If you call me Francis, I'll kill ya.'"

Jackie frowned. "I'm guessing that's from some movie, but I don't know which one—and I don't care. No one calls you 'Francis'—no one but me, that is," she said and before he could further press his objections, she covered his lips with another long, luscious kiss that made his heart tumble down to his shoes. At that moment, she could have called him "Asshole" and he would have answered as eagerly as a loving dog, hoping for a game of fetch.

His phone vibrated in his pocket again with an audible hum that distracted them both.

"Do you need to take that?"

Frank fished the phone out of his pocket. Eva's number

flashed on his screen. He knew what she wanted—and he knew his answer.

"Nope," he said firmly. "It can wait."

They talked about everything: growing up, schools and friends, work and travel, loves and money. They held hands as if they were meant to be together; their meals sat on the table, half-eaten, forgotten in the volley of conversation—but every ten minutes or so the vibrations of Frank's phone interrupted them.

"Let's get the server to box these up and go down to the beach," Jackie said, nudging him. "Maybe the seals are out. But first I've got to powder my nose, as they say—and you need to answer whoever it is who keeps blowing up your phone."

He stood up and she slid out, shouldering her purse. It was an average gesture—repeated by women everywhere a million times a day—but as Jackie tossed her hair on her shoulders and strode away, it seemed to Frank that she turned the little diner into her own personal Paris runway. He half expected her to reach the bathroom door, swivel her hips to the left and come sauntering back toward him, but instead she disappeared into the back of the restaurant.

"Some boxes and the check," Frank said, reaching into his pocket and handing the server his credit card.

He sank back onto the black cushion, staring out of the window at the passing humanity, his mind circling. The feelings Jackie stirred in him were different from anything he'd ever known, and already she was as close or closer to him than anyone else in his life, including Steve. He wanted nothing more than to tell her everything—but he couldn't imagine how he'd tell her about Carina Lynch. It felt like cheating, even if technically it wasn't.

His phone buzzed. This time, it was an incoming text from Max that included the image of a familiar-looking woman in her early thirties with striking green eyes and a short pixie haircut. She wore a sports bra and a tiny pair of spandex shorts as she flexed a sexy, feminine bicep at the camera. "Roxy DeMournay, spokesmodel for Master Class Gyms—and your next client," Max had written.

No. He texted the word quickly and hit send.

Max called him almost immediately.

"Look, Frank, she needs your help. Master Class has been talking about replacing her—looking for a fresher face, they said. She's trying to keep her job!"

"Max, I'm sorry. I just can't—"

"This is different, Frank," she continued quickly. "Strictly business. You don't even have the right equipment to satisfy her, if you know what I mean."

"You mean she's—"

"A lesbian. Yeah. I had a hard time convincing her—I mean the whole thing sounds completely crazy—but she's desperate. I already told her you'd do it—"

"But I can't, Max," Frank insisted. His eyes strayed out the window toward a family in flip-flops and shorts making their way up the hill from the beach. They looked sun-kissed and connected, content with each other's company. Frank imagined himself in their shoes in a future he hoped might not be too far away.

"We need the money, Frank. *You* need the money. We're still on the verge of having to shutter XT—"

"If we have to shutter it, I'll find another way to make money, Max. I'll go back to travel writing or—"

"And what about me? What about Wendy and the baby?" Max demanded.

"I'll come up with something, Max. I promise. But I just don't want to do this anymore. It's just wrong—especially now that I found her again—"

"Found who?"

"Jackie. The woman from the plane. I'll tell you all about it later," Frank muttered. "Tell your friend I'm sorry. I've gotta go."

He hung up as the server approached the table again, his credit card held between a chubby thumb and forefinger like a rotten banana peel ready for the trash can.

"The credit card was declined, sir."

"Declined?" Frank frowned, calculating in his head. The bill wasn't much—just about $40. He added up his recent expenses in a flash. "Shit," he muttered. A nervous sweat prickled the back of his neck and ran down his dress shirt.

"There's an ATM across the street." The girl pointed toward the bank on the corner. "You can—"

$19.73—that was his bank balance yesterday. Not even enough for a quick withdrawal from a cash machine.

"No, that won't work either," Frank sighed. The financial realities of his life dumped cold water on the pixie dust being with Jackie had sprinkled over him.

"Have you got another one?" the girl asked. Worry creased her round face and Frank could tell she feared for her tip.

"Uh, no," Frank said, reaching for his wallet and counting out less than ten dollars in cash.

"Then maybe your wife—"

"No," Frank said quickly. "She's not my wife and—" What kind of loser would she think he was if he asked her to pay on their first dinner together? "No way," he repeated, shaking his head and searching his other pockets, hoping against hope to find a stray twenty stuffed in one of them. His fingers closed around the hard-topped jewelry box in his jacket.

"All I've got is this."

The waitress backed away from the sparkling little diamond, her expression a mix of awe and fear. "I think we'd better go see the manager."

In a tiny cubicle at the front of the kitchen, he was introduced to a dark-skinned black woman with suspicion permanently etched into the corners of her lips.

"I'm sorry," he began desperately. "It's an oversight, I promise. I'm sure you've heard it all before," he continued when the look on the woman's face didn't change. "But I'll come back and pay this check. In fact, I'll call my friend now and have him bring the money. And . . ." He pulled the ring from his pocket and opened the box. "And if necessary, I can give you this as security—"

The woman's eyes widened. For a long moment she stared at the precious stone. When her eyes found Frank's again, suspicion had relaxed into a smile.

"It's beautiful. From the way you two were sitting, I thought you were already married, but . . ." She winked at him. "I wish you the best of luck. As for the bill, let me write down your driver's license number and your phone number. Now, you gotta promise to come back." Her eyes narrowed slightly as she wrote his information down. "Don't make me track you down, Mr. Young. 'Cause I will if I have to."

"You won't have to," Frank promised, scuttling out of her office, his cheeks hot with shame.

I have nothing to offer her. The thought repeated in Frank's brain as, shaken and humiliated, he returned to their table. He was thirty-two years old, had met the woman of his dreams . . . and he was too poor to even cover a hamburger and cheesy fries.

Jackie stood beside the table with their burger boxes in her hands.

"What's the matter?" she asked immediately.

"Nothing, babe," he said as casually as he could, slipping his jacket on again so when she touched him, she wouldn't notice the puddle of sweat at the small of his back. "Are you ready to go down to the beach?"

You're lying, Frank.

She didn't say the words, but Frank read them in her eyes as she scanned his face. Frank tried to meet her gaze as though there were nothing unshared, nothing amiss, but in the end, he couldn't do it. He wasn't used to lying . . . and he didn't want to get used to it, either.

"Okay, there is something," he admitted. "But I don't want to talk about it here. Let's go down to the Cove and I'll tell you all—"

"No. The Cove is a bad idea. I had a boyfriend, Charles, who turned out to be a cheat and an alcoholic. He took me down to the Cove after months of lying to do his twelve step amends. That place is a bit tainted for me, and besides, I think I know what it is you're going to tell me—and it's cool. I understand. It makes sense that a great guy like you would have someone."

"Wait . . . you think I have a girlfriend?"

"Don't you? All day long you've seemed a little . . . guilty. And then there's the phone ringing constantly. And, well, you're not the only one. When we met on the plane I'd been seeing someone." Her eyes dropped from his face and she squirmed a little, as though she'd been telling a lie of her own. "For a while. But the relationship wasn't really going anywhere. Even if you and I hadn't found each other, I was ready to break it off. I probably would have done it already, but he's been out of the country. Or so he said. I still wonder . . ." She shook herself and for the first time, Frank caught a glimmer of her own secrets. "None of that matters right now," she said, dismissing her evasions with a shrug of her shoulders. "He's coming back the day after tomorrow. We've been seeing each other long enough that I think he deserves more than a phone call, you know?"

Frank forced his head into a slow nod, feeling an uncomfortable rumble of jealousy in the back of his mind. He wanted to ask questions, but given how he'd spent his afternoon, he didn't exactly have the right.

"I don't want there to be anything between us—not anything or anyone. I don't want to feel like I'm doing something I shouldn't be," Jackie continued passionately. "What I want—what I hope for—is something special. Something . . ." She paused, and another flush of color rose to her cheeks. "Something not even death can destroy," she said quickly as if the words were hokey. Frank opened his mouth to reassure her, but she shook her head. "Maybe we should chill out for a couple of days—just long enough for me to handle my situation." Her dark eyes bored into his. "And for you to handle yours. Go and do what you have to do so that phone of yours isn't constantly buzzing and we can start our . . . we can start whatever it is we're starting with a clear conscience."

Frank thought of his bank account, of the bill still sitting in the manager's office, of the places he could take her—if only he had a little more cash. *Go handle your business.* It was almost as though she was giving him permission.

"Yeah, you're right," Frank agreed. "There *is* something I need to do, too. And then we can start out together with a clean slate."

One more time, he thought. *One more and that's that. I can clear XT's debt and there'll be enough to pay everyone and market a new tour—and buy myself a few months to concentrate on raising the rest of the money legitimately.* And if he really set his mind to it, he could finish clearing out the garage before he saw Jackie again, too. He'd find what he was looking for in his father's papers and learn how to make the curse go away forever.

"Okay," he said. "But just two days. Now that I've found you, I don't think my heart can take being away from you much longer than that."

She stepped into his arms. "Two days—not a second more, Francis," she said, then gave him her lips to seal the bargain.

CHAPTER
Ten

"You want a drink?" Roxanne DeMournay asked as she retreated from the doorway of the bland downtown hotel room.

He'd seen her a million times. Her image was plastered on billboards and the sides of buses all over San Diego and of course, there were the TV commercials. But in person she looked completely different. Her dark hair was longer and the dark jeans and gray hoodie sweatshirt she wore hid the sculpted muscles flaunted in the advertisement. Her features had a harder edge in person, a clash of angles that was interesting more than conventionally pretty. She reminded Frank instantly of Rooney Mara in *The Girl with the Dragon Tattoo*.

"Uh . . . sure." Frank set out the "Do Not Disturb" sign and let the door click shut behind him.

It was a typical hotel room: bathroom to the right of the

exterior door and a few tall panes of shatterproof glass on the opposite wall. In the space between there was an armchair, a wall-mounted TV, a few nondescript pictures in frames on the walls, a desk and a side chair. And, of course, a king-sized bed. It dominated the space between them, an omnipresent reminder of the reason why they were there.

"Hope you like vodka." Roxy added two fingers of clear liquid into a glass that was a companion to her own. "It's all I brought. I don't really like it but it gets the job done." She gulped down the rest of what her own glass held before handing Frank his and returning to the desk to pour herself another. "I could never sleep with a man unless I was really drunk," she continued. "And now . . . I'm juuust . . . about . . . there," she told the bottle, slurring the words slightly. "I've been in training almost nonstop for the past three years—ever since I got the Master Class contract. Strict workout schedule. Really strict diet. No alcohol at all . . ." She shot Frank a mischievous grin. "Except maybe on my birthday. My tolerance isn't what it once was," she said as she gulped down another glass and winced. "Few minutes and I'll be ready for the fucking or screwing or whatever word for it you use in your business."

The words came together in a continuous jumbled thought and Frank guessed she'd been drinking for quite a while already. She poured another drink and kept talking.

"I guess you do this sort of thing all the time? Must be weird for you spending your days screwing different women. I mean, I can relate: the world is full of beautiful women I'd *love* to do. But even for a guy that's gotta get tough after a while."

She drained the last of her glass and then turned toward

him, looking into his face for the first time. Even addled by alcohol she had bright and inquisitive eyes that shone like emeralds in the planes of her face.

"Or are you the same as me: tuning out the sex. Thinking about the reward afterwards." She blinked at him. "I guess we're both just doing this for the money. You get cash, and I get to keep making bank, doing what I love. Is that what it is?"

"Actually, I—"

"'Cause if that's it, I get it. If it had been anyone other than Max I would have never believed a word. You know, when she first told me about this—" She hiccupped, pressing her hand against her mouth. "When Max first told me about this, I thought, I mean even if you can stop a woman from aging with your . . . thing . . . what kind of person builds a business around it?"

"Well, I really don't—"

"Don't be offended," she continued, rambling on in spite of Frank's best effort to change the subject. She hiccupped again and knocked back her third glass, pounding down the drinks so rapidly Frank started to feel nervous. The last thing he needed was to have to call an ambulance because his "Jane" had alcohol poisoning. "We're all whores in one way or the other," she was saying now. "I sold my body and soul to Master Class Gyms, contorted myself into every position they asked, and for what? Fresher face," she muttered. "Whatever. Okay." She stopped abruptly and set her glass down so heavily the clear liquid splashed onto the dark desktop. "I think I'm drunk enough. Let's do this before I change my mind. And if this doesn't work you can tell Max that payback is a motherfucker. I haven't slept with a man since college—and I haven't missed it. If I weren't desperate, you can bet we wouldn't be here right now . . ."

She staggered around the bed, pulling off the thick beige duvet and tossing the matching throw pillows onto the floor while Frank stared at her uncertainly.

"Now?" he asked. "Don't you want to talk a little more or—"

But she was already pulling the thick gray sweatshirt over her head and wriggling out of the faded jeans. Underneath she wore nothing at all, and immediately Frank's senses were overcome by one of the most perfect bodies he'd ever seen. Every muscle, from her shoulders and arms to the six-pack of her abdomen and the curve of her behind, was beautifully and femininely sculpted. She was both hard and soft at the same time. Her skin was the perfect shade of tan—a color that suggested health and vitality and sunshine, and that probably took hours to perfect. In spite of himself, Frank felt the stirring of desire—coupled with an awful feeling of guilt.

It's what I'm here for, he told himself. *And this is the last time. Besides, for all I know, Jackie might be sleeping with her boyfriend or—*

No. He knew that wasn't so. It was terrible to even suspect her of such a thing. Just because he was about to do something faithless and wrong didn't mean she would. But he *was* going to do something faithless and wrong—or at least it felt that way, even though technically they weren't committed to each other.

His drunken client climbed onto the bed and spread herself out in front of him.

"So what's your favorite position?" she asked. She

opened her knees and showed him a tidy landing strip of hair and the smooth labia where he was expected to make a deposit. "Are you a missionary kind of guy?" She rolled over on her belly and thrust her behind in the air. "Or maybe you prefer doggy style?" She looked over her shoulder at him. "Why are you still standing there with your pants on for? Are you freaked out about screwing a lesbian? Because trust me, dude, you've done it before. You just didn't know it."

"No . . . No . . . I . . ." Frank reached for his belt and loosened his pants. The smooth, round globes of her perfect round ass winked at him, waiting for him to lay hold and claim them, but his erection had completely evaporated with the thought of Jackie and his guilt. "I just need a minute," he mumbled, stepping out of his pants and backing away toward the bathroom. "Give me just a second. Just a few seconds!"

He turned on the water and splashed his face quickly, grabbing a towel from the rack, considering his own reflection in the mirror. A well-built guy in his underwear and polo shirt stared back at him with a terrified expression on his thirty-something face.

What have I gotten myself into?

The experience was so different from the connection he'd shared with Carina. Panic tangoed with the vodka in the pit of his stomach and for a few seconds, Frank feared he was going to throw up.

I can't do this—I can't —

You have to. Just this one last time, replied a calmer, more rational-sounding voice in his brain. *And the sooner the better. The sooner we do this, the sooner we can put it all behind us.*

You need the money. Badly. You had to borrow forty dollars from Steve's dad just to pay for a hamburger! Get over yourself and get back out there before she changes her mind!

Frank took a deep breath and closed his eyes. When he opened them, the man looking back at him in the mirror seemed calm and purposeful . . . but his penis was calm, too. Too calm.

Great, Frank thought. He sat down on the toilet. There was a small television mounted on the wall across from him and Frank considered ordering an erotic movie to help set the mood. Would that be rude? Was there a professional code about these things? His own imagination would have to suffice. Frank reached into his briefs and grabbed Frank the Third firmly. He closed his eyes and tried to conjure the usual masturbatory fantasy, but for some reason none of his "best of" reel of playmates would show themselves. Instead, only one figure appeared in his mind.

Jackie.

He massaged himself gently and imagined the night they would be together. It wouldn't be sex—body parts rubbing mindlessly against each other. No, he imagined himself taking it slow, making love to her gently and consciously, more determined to give her pleasure than to take it for himself. He imagined himself kissing her breasts, then tasting the sweetness between her legs. He imagined the feeling of her calves locked around his back as their two became one in a fulfilling caress. In a matter of moments, his desire had flared to life and he held the hardness of passion in his hand. He was ready.

Renewed, Frank emerged from the bathroom, prepared to provide good service.

"Sorry about that, but—"

Roxy lay in the exact same position he'd left her in—with her butt in the air and her face pressed into the mattress. Her hands rested at her sides while her chest rose and fell evenly.

"Roxy?" Frank touched her gently on the back and shook her shoulder. "Roxy?"

She murmured something incoherent, blowing acrid vodka breath in his face.

"Roxy, it's me, Frank. We're supposed to . . ."

"Yeah, yeah," she agreed. Her eyes rolled open for just a moment and then closed again. "I'm not doing flips for a dude. I lubed up earlier so just stick it in. Get . . . this . . . over . . ." The sentence ended in a snore.

It was humiliating, but he took his place behind her and eased himself into the appropriate spot. Her slit was warm and tight, and he closed his eyes so he could almost forget how shameful and ridiculous it felt to be banging a woman who wanted nothing more from him than the power of his sperm. It seemed like it took forever to bring himself to a climax but at last, he squirted something down her canal and pulled out with a choked groan.

"Roxy?" Frank asked as he stepped into his pants. He peered at the woman on the bed but if she was awake, there was no evident sign. She lay still except for this steady lift of her chest. Her face was still squashed against the mattress and her rear end was still high in the air like a little kid who had fallen asleep at play.

Frank considered waking her and then thought better of it. Instead, he dropped the duvet over her nakedness and crept out of the room like the high-priced call boy he was.

By the time he reached his car, an incredible sensation of relief vanquished his shame.

I'll do a little work, go home and start on the garage. And tomorrow night, I'll see Jackie again.

The thought was a bubble of happiness that danced before him, erasing everything but its own promise. He imagined them, sitting together in a nice restaurant—the kind of place with white tablecloths and candlelight. Her dark eyes would shine in the guttering flame. He could hear her calling him "Francis" with a little giggle of pride that she could get away with it. He could feel their fingers intertwined across the table, connected like something meant to be.

He longed to call her, but resisted. Tomorrow. Like they'd planned. Instead, he texted his friends, "It's done," and then drove to XT's tiny office, whistling along with the radio.

He had been working for about an hour, deep in the pursuit of an investor for XT, when the door to the office suddenly opened.

X-Treme rarely had walk-in visitors—most of its business was done on the Internet—and Frank was so sure it was the mail carrier dropping the day's correspondence on the table near the door that he didn't even look up until a female voice said, "Hello?"

A striking redhead stood in the narrow corridor between Frank's workstation and the door. She was dressed in a dark blue suit that stopped just above a pair of pale but shapely legs. She held a leather satchel in her hand—something that looked too large to be a handbag but too small to be a suitcase. From the gold buckle on the clasp, Frank guessed that the bag cost more than all of his clothes put together. In fact, there was something about every detail of this woman that said "money" even more obviously than Carina Lynch.

What on earth is a woman like this doing here? Frank wondered, rising.

"Can I help you?" he asked, crossing the distance between them. As he drew closer, he saw porcelain-pale skin, eyes the icy blue color of a late October sky and ruby-red lips. She looked to be in her early thirties, but there was something about the way she held her body that made him wonder if perhaps she was quite a bit older and wonderfully well-preserved.

"I'm looking for Francis Young," she said in a sultry, confident and completely businesslike tone.

Frank hesitated, taking in her attire and the leather satchel again. The voice and the clothes together said "lawyer" or "process-server" or some kind of pricey bounty hunter. For a second, he seriously considered introducing himself as "Steve Hughes."

"I'm Frank Young."

Her eyes swept over him, taking in his khaki pants, cross-trainers and blue polo.

"I see," she said after this inspection. She thrust out her hand, offering him five immaculately manicured nails. "I'm Pandora Constantine."

"Hello." Frank shook her hand. "I'm sorry. Do I know you?"

"No." She glanced around them. "Are we alone?"

Frank nodded.

Pandora glanced behind her. "Is it possible to lock that door from the inside?"

"Yes, but—"

She strutted toward the door, her hips moving precisely under the fabric of the dark suit.

"There," she said, smiling efficiently when she returned to him. "That should give us a measure of privacy."

Frank stared at her. "Excuse me. I don't mean to be rude, but what do you want?"

Pandora laughed like the situation wasn't funny at all. "Well, I would hope that it would be obvious, but since that appears not to be the case, I'm here to retain your . . . services."

Services? Frank was pretty sure she wasn't talking about X-Treme Travel.

"May I sit down?"

Frank quickly retrieved the chair from Wendy's workstation—it was the most comfortable—and slid it into the space next to his own desk.

"Do you operate your business here?" Pandora inquired, resting the satchel on the floor. She crossed one thin leg over the other and leaned forward like a bird of prey.

"Um . . . yes . . ." Frank said, still trying to recover from the surprise of her arrival and the unsettling certainty in this woman's bright blue eyes. "At least, I operate my travel business from here. If you're talking about . . . the other thing, well . . ." He shook his head. "If you don't mind me asking, how did you find out about that?" He hesitated to use either Roxy or Carina's names. "Were you . . . referred by someone?"

"Not exactly," she replied vaguely.

"Then how?"

"Let's just say on a recent plane trip to Boston, I had the pleasure of being seated near a man and young woman who had a mission there . . . which they discussed somewhat more loudly and more argumentatively than would be considered discreet or wise."

Steve and Eva. He could imagine them on the flight to Boston, arguing like a cat and a dog . . . but in the economy section. There was no way this woman flew steerage. Frank quirked a suspicious eyebrow at her and she flashed him another icy smile.

"From what I heard, I deduced that you have a very unusual gift. One that I am intrigued by. You see, Frank—may I call you Frank?—without revealing too much of my personal situation, I can tell you that I'm fascinated by the lengths that women will go to—and the billions of dollars they spend—seeking a youthful look. Indeed, I'm one of them. In the last decade, I've made it my business to search out all kinds of anti-aging remedies and solutions with varying degrees of success, I'll admit. But never have I heard anything like what your friends were discussing. And if you are able to do what they seemed to believe you could do, then it's worth any price." She slid the satchel across the floor toward him with the toe of one stilettoed foot. "Go ahead, Frank. It's only money. It won't bite."

Frank opened the bag and found it stuffed with banded hundred-dollar bills.

"I understood one hundred thousand to be the fee but if you've increased your rate, please let me know. There are also some documents in there that I'll need your signature on. Secrecy is of paramount importance to me. I would prefer you not discuss our . . . encounter . . . with *anyone*. Your friends have shown themselves to be something less than discreet. I'm sure you understand."

Frank lowered the bag to the floor.

"I still don't understand. How did you find me?"

"I overheard your friends—"

"Bullshit," Frank said abruptly.

"I see. Well, does it matter?" Pandora said after a long pause, in which she seemed to measure him down to the number of seconds between breaths. "I'm here. I have money and I'd like to engage you—literally and figuratively—as soon as possible. Do we have a deal or not?"

She was hiding something and Frank knew it. The money, on the other hand, was very real. So *much* money. And in cash—ready to be put to use. She watched him, those October eyes fixed on his face, her expression blank as a seasoned poker player's.

"Yes, but on two—no, three—conditions."

"Name them."

"I'm getting out of this business. I want you to sign something that says that you're not going to ever discuss this with anyone—no referrals, no hints, no nothing. I don't want any more unsolicited women showing up like you just did."

"Easy enough. From the looks of this place you are out of business entirely, but in any case, I'm not the sort of woman who likes to kiss and tell—it's just not in my basic instinct," she said coolly. "Next?"

"We do it as soon as possible. Either tonight or tomorrow afternoon. If the sun goes down tomorrow and we haven't done it, the deal is off."

"You'd find me prepared to perform immediately, Frank," Pandora replied with a mirthless chuckle. "But I suspect that tomorrow afternoon would be best. It will give us both the opportunity to prepare." She quirked an eyebrow at him. "And third?"

Frank took a deep breath. "The price has gone up. It'll be two hundred fifty thousand dollars—or it's no deal."

Pandora Constantine gazed at him flatly for several silent seconds.

"Done," she said at last, rising and offering him her hand. "You surprise me, Frank. There's a bit more to you than there appears to be. Keep the money as a deposit. I'll give you the rest after we . . . consummate. Will that be sufficient?"

Frank nodded.

"I'll send a car for you here tomorrow. Two o'clock." She strode toward the door, the thick red hair swinging bountifully on her shoulders, the suit clinging to her body like a corporate glove. Frank tried to imagine her naked but couldn't. "And sign the papers in the bag," she added as she turned the lock to let herself out. "You'll find your concerns about confidentiality have already been addressed."

She slipped out of the office. Frank heard her high heels echo on the marble of the building's foyer and then she was gone.

CHAPTER
Eleven

Right on the button of two o'clock, a young Latino in black chauffeur's livery stood on the threshold of XT's little office. He smiled pleasantly and escorted Frank into his waiting sedan.

"My instructions are to raise the partition until we reach our destination."

"And where is that?" Frank asked. "Where are we going?"

"I am not at liberty to say. Now sit back and relax, sir."

"Hey—" Frank began, but with the touch of a button, soundproof glass was raised between them and Frank was silenced. He was going for a ride, whether he wanted to or not.

They headed east out of San Diego. Cacti, acres of brown flatlands and the occasional jackrabbit sped past him as Frank sat by the window, cursing himself for following his greed over his intuition.

After about an hour, brown signs announced that they were approaching Cuyamaca State Park and a small village appeared like a mirage out of the nothingness, indicating a return to civilization, even if on a much more rustic and smaller scale than the city they'd left.

The car pulled up in front of an old-fashioned-looking building that seemed to have jumped right out of the movie set of a spaghetti western: an old-time saloon on wooden planks with rooms on the upper level. A painted sign hung out front announcing his arrival at "The Last Trail Hotel."

"We're here, sir." The chauffeur opened the door with such a friendly smile, Frank almost forgave him for the cloak-and-dagger routine. "Please go right inside."

Frank approached the hotel's entrance cautiously, his internal alarms already on high alert. Through the ornate beveled glass set into the wood, the interior was so distorted he could see little more than the colors of the objects inside—but not their exact structure or location. What he didn't see at all was people. Not a single one. He grabbed the hotel's thick black wrought-iron handle and pulled, stepping over the threshold and into another century.

Except for the updated lighting and the air conditioning, the place was clearly a careful replica of a nineteenth-century frontier hotel. Polished plank floors led to a small L-shaped registration desk. On the wall behind it hung a shelf of cubbyholes in which old-fashioned room keys hung on pegs. On the other end of the room, a spiral staircase circled toward the upper floor. At the rear, behind a pair of swinging wooden cattle doors, he spied a tiny bar populated with a few small tables that looked like survivors of the Indian Wars. He could imagine Clint Eastwood in a Mexican serape and smoking a cheroot cigar pushing those doors open and demanding a whiskey.

"You're right on time. Come on up."

She stood on the old curved staircase, dressed in a pale pink peignoir that looked like something Joan Crawford would have worn in the 1940s: a satin gown and robe with wide fur-trimmed sleeves and a fur-trimmed hem. She had piled her lustrous red hair atop her head in a hairdo that reminded Frank of Connie Nielsen in *The Devil's Advocate*.

"You could have told me you planned for me to have to come out to East Butt Fuck yesterday."

"Why? Do you have something against the glories of nature? Do you perform better in a smoggy old city or with a view of the ocean? If so, you should have stipulated that when we made our agreement. You did not, and so . . ." She gestured around them. "I suited myself. Besides, I thought you would find this place charming. It is, in its way, a kind of archeological treasure. Or a movie set. I understand you enjoy both. The entire hotel is at our disposal for the next several hours."

"The entire hotel? Is that necessary?"

"It is for me," Pandora replied, leading the way to the upper level. "I prefer to remain as anonymous as possible. It makes it far easier for me to do my work. An empty hotel means there will be no interruptions—and no questions."

"And what do you do exactly? You never said."

"No, I didn't."

Frank waited, but she didn't say more. She climbed the stairs slowly and deliberately, her hips swaying in front of him.

"Is Pandora Constantine your real name?"

"It may be . . . and it may not be." She glanced over her shoulder at him. "But whatever my name is, you'll have your money. That should be sufficient, shouldn't it? This is our room."

Frank stepped into a sitting room, complete with a Victorian settee facing a large wood-burning fireplace. An open bottle of champagne rested in a stand in the center of the room, with two glasses on a table beside it. Heavy brocaded draperies in a dark mustard color covered the windows and matching hand-woven rugs were spread over the burnished wood floors. Frank glanced through the open doorway into the nearby bedroom, where a massive four-poster bed complete with a canopy hunkered against one wall. It looked like it hadn't been moved in over a hundred years.

Frank hesitated. There was still a part of him—a large part of him—that wanted to back out of the whole deal, but before he could verbalize his misgivings, Pandora crossed the room with the two champagne flutes in her hands.

"Don't just stand there!" Pandora's laughter splashed over him like ice water. "Come in and have a drink. This is going to be fun."

Sure. Fun, Frank thought, taking the champagne reluctantly.

Pandora eased closer to him, so close Frank could smell the scent of a heavy, spicy perfume along the side of her neck. His heart began to pound uncertainly as the first stirrings of desire coursed through his body. He didn't want to be attracted to this woman. He tried to think of Jackie, but when she released her hair from her its height and shook her head until it swung voluptuously on her shoulders, Frank felt the beginnings of an erection.

"To us!" Pandora murmured, lifting her glass to her lips.

"Yeah," Frank muttered. He was going to need a drink to get through this one, even more than the others—he was sure of it. Carina he'd genuinely liked, and even Roxy had had a certain soused charm—at least while she was conscious. This woman . . .

The moment the alcohol hit his tongue he knew something was wrong. Really wrong. It tasted too bitter, too . . .

His vision dimmed and swam. Pandora's face went out of focus, snapped back and then disappeared completely. He felt himself falling and then smelled the carpet jammed against his nose.

"Good night, Frank. Sweet dreams," he thought he heard her say before the darkness engulfed him.

CHAPTER
Twelve

He was in a jungle . . . a jungle of boxes piled to the ceiling, crowding in on him like the flora of the Amazon, brown instead of green and trailing cobwebs instead of vines. He stepped carefully along a narrow path, searching for something, reaching out from time to time to steady himself as the way became more and more crowded.

"Where is it, Dad?" Frank said aloud.

"It's here, but you'll have to look differently."

His father stood in front of him on the narrow path. He was dressed exactly as Frank remembered from that last day, the day he'd dropped Frank at the airport: rumpled khaki pants held onto his hips with a thin brown belt, frayed white shirt rolled up to his elbows, pens stuffed into the breast pocket. His face was brown and lined from hours of work in the sun at various digs, but his hair, though graying, was still thick and in need of a trim against his collar.

"Dad!" Frank's heart leapt. Instantly, fourteen years fell away. It was all a bad dream. He was a teenager again—and his father was alive. He rushed forward, eager to get closer, but somehow the distance between them didn't change. "You wouldn't believe the dream I had—"

"I know all about it, Frank," his father said sadly. "That's why I'm here."

"I don't understand."

"You do, Francis. You know everything. Think about it."

Frank concentrated.

"You knew all about that pool in the Amazon."

"Knew about it?" Frank Senior's laughter made the walls of boxes shiver dangerously. "It was my greatest discovery."

"Then why didn't you—"

"Please, Frank," his father interrupted, raising his eyebrows. "I raised you to *think*. Much better than this."

Frank stopped talking. Instead, he considered the boxes around him. Suddenly, he understood he wasn't in the Amazon at all. He was in his own house, standing in his bedroom. As if by magic, the boxes vanished.

"The junk . . . the boxes. It's all to cover what you found in the Amazon."

"*Now* you're thinking!" his father said, nodding his approval. "That's better."

"And you knew what would happen to me when I went down there?"

"Not exactly. I wasn't certain that José's daughter would be on the quest. Or that you would explore your desire in the water. If I had known that . . . well, I would have warned you. But I hoped *something* would happen. Yes. And I hoped that you would have better luck with the powers of that pool than your mother and I did." He sighed. "Foolish. I confused eternal youth with eternal life. I see it now."

"Then—"

"Yes." His father nodded.

"But in the letters, Mom wrote that she didn't get to go to the Amazon."

"That is correct. Your mother never swam in the pool. Whatever she might have gained, it would have been passed along to her by me."

"Then you had . . . sex . . . with someone else? In the pool?" Frank managed.

"Yes," Frank Senior admitted. "It was wrong . . . but sometimes you have to do something that seems wrong to make something right. Or at least, that's what I hoped. I don't know if it would have worked. There were so many legends, so much uncertainty . . ." He shrugged a thin shoulder. "I took a chance. In the end, that's all we can do."

Frank frowned. "I don't understand."

"All the pieces are right in front of you, Frank. All you have to do is stop trying so hard. You'll see. It's right in front of you."

"You mean a way out of this? For Jackie?"

"Ah, Jackie. We like her very much, your mom and I."

"Mom is there?" Frank's pulse quickened. "Where? Can I see her—"

"Of course she's here. She's always near you. So am I."

"But . . . I never dream of her, Dad. I never . . . feel her."

"She knows that. But maybe when you're able to see things differently that will change, son. Your mom likes

Jackie a lot. She thinks she will be very good for you, if—"

His father turned suddenly as if he'd heard something.

"If?" Frank prompted.

"Well." His father turned back to him with a benign smile. "It looks like you'll have to figure that out on your own, son. It's time for you to wake up."

"Wake up?"

"Yes."

"But—"

"Wake up, Frank!" his father said sharply. "Wake up!"

Frank blinked, groggily. "Huh?"

"Frank!" Fingers made contact with his face, harder than a caress but a little short of a slap.

Frank started, his eyes flying fully open. Instinctively, his fists went up in preparation for defense as he looked warily around him.

"Hey . . . take it easy, sweetheart. Take it easy."

Jackie stood beside him, leaning into the open window of his car, her features creased with concern. She wore a cocktail dress in a shade of burgundy that perfectly complemented her hair and skin, with a beaded shawl draped over her shoulders. The darkening sky told him it was evening, but other than Jackie and the onset of night, Frank had no clue where he was or what had happened to him. He glanced around quickly: he was wearing the same clothes and this was his car, but the last thing he remembered was taking that champagne from Pandora Constantine and—

He sat up and opened the car door, easing himself out of the vehicle. His legs felt strange, as if they belonged to someone else. A dull pain throbbed in the back of his head like a serious hangover. He slumped against the body of the car, struggling against dizziness and nausea.

"Are you okay?"

"Oh man . . . I had the weirdest dream . . ." he muttered, rubbing his forehead. "Where am I?" he asked.

Jackie looked at him curiously. "You're outside my condo building. We have a date tonight, remember? Only . . ." She looked at his sneakers and jeans dubiously. "I thought you said we were going to La Perla." She stepped close to him, peering into his face. "You haven't been drinking, have you? Or . . ." Jackie hesitated. "Using something else? Because you look kind of like—"

"I'm okay. I had . . . I had a drink—just one," he said, quickly erasing the details. "Guess it hit me harder than I thought . . ." Frank grabbed her hand and held it tightly as he searched for an acceptable lie. "I—I've missed you. I've been thinking about you all day. I—I came by just to see you before dinner tonight. I guess I fell asleep."

Her face softened. "I missed you too. You don't know how many times I almost called you today. I actually dialed a few times—but when it started to ring, I hung up!"

Frank reached for his cell phone. He always kept it in the front right pocket of his khakis, but this time, his fingers curved around nothing but a few stray coins. It wasn't there.

Pandora.

Who was she? And what exactly did she want with him? And why would she have her driver go to the trouble of driving him here—and in his own car? Where was his phone? What was going on? There were so many unanswered questions about what had happened to him over the afternoon that he wouldn't have been surprised if Pandora herself had walked right up to them.

"Our reservation was for seven; it's nearly that now," Jackie was saying. "You can't go like that. I've been there a few times and they are absolutely fanatical about proper attire."

"I'm sorry, babe." Frank rubbed his head. His stomach felt queasy and he pressed back the urge to vomit. "I—"

"No, don't be sorry! I'm glad. I have much better idea anyway—if you're up to it," she said, grinning mischievously at him. "You're probably the only person adventurous enough to try it with me. Didn't you tell me that in your many travels you've learned to always carry your passport? You've got it now, right?"

Frank felt for his wallet and found his passport wedged into the leather as usual. "Why? What do you have in mind?"

"A run for the border," she said, taking him by the arm. "Leave your car. This time, I'll drive."

He stumbled as he followed her and Jackie's brow furrowed. "Are you sure you're okay?"

"Yeah," he managed. "Fine. Let's go."

Half an hour later, they were in Mexico. Jackie handled the stick shift of her bright yellow VW beetle confidently, surprising Frank with the skillful way she eased from gear to gear as they maneuvered through the tourist areas crowded with people. She turned off Tijuana's Avenida Revolución with its shops and restaurants and drunk American teenagers for the quieter streets of a residential neighborhood.

"Where are we going?" Frank asked. He'd rolled down the windows for the benefits of the night air, and the fog in his head had lifted. Now exotic smells and Latin music wafted through the breeze toward them.

"A little place called Blanco y Negro. It's a club I've heard a lot about but never been to. More of a local place—and my Spanish isn't so good, but they say it has some of the best salsa in town."

"By salsa, I'm hoping you mean the dip and not the dance."

Jackie laughed. "Sorry. I love salsa—and I do mean the dance. Some girlfriends and I used to go out almost every weekend, but things change, I guess. Two got married, one moved away. I don't even see them much anymore."

"And your ex? Didn't he ever take you dancing?"

Jackie shook her head. "No. Jacob doesn't dance. I think he'd find it less than dignified. He's a very staid person. That's one of the reasons I wanted to end it. He's nice enough—just no fun. And your ex? What's she like? What does she do other than maybe drug you?"

Frank shook his head. "Let's not go there," he said evasively. "Not while I'm still trying to wrap my head around the salsa part."

"Get over it, Francis. We're here, and I'm expecting to see some moves! Knowing you, you were probably the California junior salsa champion," Jackie said with a wink. "Only . . . I don't see anywhere to park," she said, sighing. "Looks like we're going to have to walk a bit."

In the end, they parked several blocks away and trekked through the darkened neighborhood until they reached a red adobe building belching Latin music. A large banner hung from the eaves that Frank translated quickly in his mind. "Live Music Tonight, featuring Hector Chavez and the Tomorrow Boys."

"Come on," Jackie said, beaming with excitement and picking up speed, even in her strappy high heels. "This is going to be so much fun!"

The place was jammed. They found a small table in a corner a little too close to the stage for Frank's taste, but Jackie seemed thrilled to be near the musicians and the dance floor. He watched her foot swinging in time to the trumpets as the band blared out a cha-cha rhythm.

When a cocktail waitress approached, he ordered off the little menu in Spanish.

"I knew I was traveling with the right man," Jackie shouted over the music.

"Huh?"

"I knew I was traveling with the right man!"

Frank shook his head, deaf from the music.

Jackie stood up, stretching her arms toward him. Her hips swayed as she shimmied from side to side. She leaned over him. "The only way you're going to be able to hear me is to dance with me, Francis—don't roll your eyes like that!" She pulled his arms, her feet crisscrossing back and forth. "Don't be a stick-in-the-mud—"

Frank allowed her to glide him onto the floor. He two-stepped self-consciously for a measure or two, then let her go, watching as she rocked and undulated away from him. She tossed her hair and wriggled her shoulders seductively, kicking out a leg as a smile of pure joy played on her face.

A young man with a mop of thick black hair and a mustache stepped up to her.

"Beautiful lady," he said, taking her hand and twirling her around the dance floor. He matched her steps, wiggling his hips.

Frank stepped up to him, smiling but making his ownership clear. The young man's eyes flashed angrily, but he stepped aside and Frank pulled Jackie close to him.

"Looks like I'm learning the salsa. Show me the steps," he murmured.

"It's simple. One two three, pause. One, two, three, pause. The music tells you what to do."

Frank thought of the kata forms he had practiced at the Shaolin Temple and the complicated footwork they required. Salsa couldn't be as hard as that, right?

He was just beginning to relax into it when the music crescendoed and stopped, except for the drums and the maracas. Jackie lifted her hands with the others around them, clapping out a syncopated rhythm that matched the driving beat. Frank committed to the steps in his head, and when the clapping stopped and Jackie started to move, he pulled her into his arms and moved with her.

"You got it!" she cried excitedly. "Now front and back." She demonstrated and Frank followed. He glanced around, watching the men in the other couples spinning and dipping their ladies—ladies who were pretty enough, but nothing compared to his Jackie in her sexy magenta dress and heels, her dark hair swirling as she shimmied toward him. He pulled her tight, then spun her over his arm so quickly he nearly dropped her before lifting her upright again.

When the song ended, they were both out of breath. The mustached young man was still glaring, but he made no further move in their direction.

"You continue to amaze me, Francis Young," Jackie murmured, slipping her arms around him. "Is there anything you don't know how to do?"

"Cut it out, Jackie. I suck. But I'm willing to learn. There's nothing I wouldn't learn for you, babe," he answered, kissing her. "What's this one?" he asked as the musicians transitioned into a different beat. "Not another salsa?"

"Merengue. I'll teach you that later. First let's eat. Our food is here and I'm starving."

Hours passed before they finally lurched out of the building, laughing and exhausted, the drums and the horns still echoing in their ears. Frank's shirt was wet and Jackie had long ago abandoned the heels for her bare feet. He cha-cha-ed her along the street for a step or two, then executed a much smoother and more polished dip before they began walking slowly, arm in arm, toward the car. They turned away from the main street, leaving the streetlights behind them.

"Thank you for that."

"Hey, I wasn't about to let you keep dancing like that without a partner. I'm just jealous enough to want to make sure every man in the place knows you're spoken for."

"Am I spoken for, Francis?"

"What do you think?"

The lopsided grin split her face and they walked together quietly for a while, enjoying the silence and the bright company of the starry night sky.

"So . . ." he said casually as if they were playing a round of Truth or Dare. "If you could take a pill and freeze time so that you'd never age, would you do it? Would you like to look just like you look right now—for as long as you lived?"

"That's a strange question!"

"Yeah. But would you?"

"Absolutely not!" Jackie replied fervently. "How shallow would I have to be to want to be twenty-nine or thirty forever? Not to mention the kind of impact a decision like that would have on population control. 'Forever thirty' probably means 'forever fertile.' That could be serious. And 'forever thirty' also means that the chances are pretty good that, barring accident, substance abuse or some kind of genetic failure, you'd live a really, really long life. I mean, thirty is the prime of life, right? Can you imagine what would happen if there were no more aging, no more disease—and we kept breeding like rabbits? Not a world I'd want to live in. No one's thrilled about the prospect of aging—or dying—but I'll take my chances, thank you very much. Anything less would be socially irresponsible." She quirked an eyebrow at him. "Why do you ask?"

"No reason—"

A shadow moved in the darkness. A moment later, a kid jumped from the nearby trees onto the dark sidewalk in front of them. His switchblade gleamed menacingly in the moonlight.

"Your money," the kid said in Spanish, thrusting the blade toward Frank's abdomen. "Her bag. Now!"

Frank stepped between Jackie and their attacker, his hands raised. "Okay, okay," he said in English, reaching for his back pocket. "Just don't hurt us—" He stopped short, fixing his eyes on space behind the kid. It was a trick he'd seen in so many movie fight scenes that he was a little surprised it actually worked—the kid turned his head to see what Frank was staring at.

Frank took advantage of the moment of distraction, delivering a quick roundhouse to the kid's wrist that sent the blade sailing out of his hand. It landed in the dirt several yards away. The kid lunged toward it, but Frank caught him with a front push kick and sent him down hard.

"Jackie—" he began just as he heard a rush of air behind him and two more young men emerged from the darkness. "Run!"

They were teenagers—just boys, really. In another situation, he might have tried to talk to them—to discourage them from a life of waylaying Americans on dark roads—but this wasn't that moment. Frank registered T-shirts—one white and one yellow—before they dove on him, intending harm. He raised his fists, the many years of mixed martial arts training flooding through his muscle memory, but the kids had no intention of fighting fair. From out of the darkness, something hard and heavy—a rock, he guessed later—connected with the back of Frank's neck and a moment later another crashed into the side of his face. He dropped to the ground in the dust, stunned.

"Leave him alone!" Jackie screamed in English from somewhere behind him.

The boys stopped.

"Look at the pretty lady," one of them said in Spanish. "Very pretty. Very scary!"

"She watches too much American television," the other answered, and all three of them chuckled.

"Leave him alone or I—I—I'll cut you," Jackie stammered. "I will."

Frank pulled himself off the ground to the accompaniment of the boys' laughter. His head hurt and when he touched the side of his face he felt the sticky warmth of blood, but he focused his eyes on the scene unfolding in front of him.

Jackie held the switchblade out in front of her—overhand like a knife instead of underhand, where it would have been more useful—as the three teens advanced on her. The strap of her dress had slipped down her shoulder and her shoes lay behind her on the ground, but her face was set with the same frightened determination he'd seen on the airplane. There was so much fight in her expression that Frank fell for her all over again. He pulled himself soundlessly out of the dust and waited for the right moment to strike.

"What are you doing with that knife, pretty lady?" the tallest of the boys asked her, his voice threatening. He was probably the eldest, but not more than seventeen, and clearly the leader. He sidled toward her while the others laughed and made catcalls. "You are going to cut yourself."

"She will not cut anything holding it like that!" the kid who owned the blade joked.

"Remember what he told us," the smallest one said cautiously. His voice was high, youthful. Frank pegged him as not more than fourteen. "Not to hurt them. Just to scare them—"

"A few kisses will hurt no one, eh?" the leader leered. "A few kisses for a pretty lady—"

Frank lunged for the leader, grabbing him by the throat from behind and delivering two quick punches to his face before he even realized he was beat. He sank to the ground, motionless, while the other two stared.

"*Vamanos*," Frank said, making his voice as menacing as he could. He crouched, assuming his fighting stance. "*Quien es el siguiente?* Who's next?"

"*Ayee!*" The little kid came running at him, swinging wildly—showing more courage than skill. Frank moved quickly and lightly aside, and, tangled by his own momentum, the kid fell face first on the ground. He scrambled up quickly and charged again, but Frank blocked his punch and delivered a solid upper cut to his rib cage. The boy dropped to his knees, breathless, holding his gut, then rolled to his side, whimpering.

Frank turned to the last one—the kid who'd started the whole thing with his switchblade—but he needn't have worried. The kid took off running without a single word.

Jackie dropped the switchblade like it was poison and was in his arms a moment later.

"Oh my God, Frank! Are you okay?" she breathed into his ear, and he could feel her trembling against him.

"Yeah, thanks to you. If you hadn't grabbed that blade and distracted them, I'd have gotten my ass kicked." He glanced around him warily. The two kids on the ground didn't seem as though they wanted any more to do with either one of them, but he didn't want to take the chance that the one who'd run might come back with reinforcements. "Let's get out of here," Frank said, scooping up her shoes.

They sprinted hand in hand for Jackie's little car and threw themselves inside. As Jackie sped through the streets and the danger diminished, Frank exhaled.

"We make a pretty good team, huh? We keep surviving stuff together," she said.

Her eyes locked on his face and the flutter in Frank's

heart deepened once again, from that first infatuation to the connection on the plane, from rediscovery and into another level of depth and maturity. This time, there was no need for embrace or for the sensation of her lips. It was enough just to feel her fingers laced tightly in his own, and to read similar feelings shining out of her black eyes.

"My Spanish is pretty bad, but they were saying something about someone else—"

"Yeah. Apparently someone hired them. To scare us. Probably that guy from the club that I cut in on. He was glaring at us all night."

Jackie frowned. "Maybe."

"You don't think so? Then who else could it be?"

"I'm sure you're right," Jackie agreed, flashing him a quick smile before turning her eyes back to the road, but the worry creased the center of her forehead again.

"What is it, Jackie?" Frank asked.

"You're bleeding, Frank," she replied.

Frank touched the side of his face and the back of his neck. Blood stained his fingers, but neither wound hurt much.

"I think it's okay—"

"It's not okay," Jackie said sharply. "This whole thing is my fault."

"Your fault? How is it your fault?"

Jackie shook her head. "It's . . . I . . . I don't know. I just know I need to get you home."

She led him into a forgettable lobby and an empty elevator, but when they reached her condo, with the flick of the light switch, Frank was transported to Europe. He entered a room that was a beautiful collection of colors and regions that came together to create a space that seemed to reflect everything he knew about her. The sofa was a heavy baroque-looking thing in red damask that, to his surprise, was as soft and comfortable as the ratty old thing at his own house. The patterned throw rug beneath it said "Old World" even though Frank was sure it was some kind of imitation. At first he thought the end tables were inlaid with expensive Italian mosaics—until he realized that the furniture wasn't wood at all, but some kind of pasteboard.

"You did this?" he asked, touching the bits of colored glass.

"Yeah," Jackie called from somewhere out of his sight.

"You are absolutely never, ever coming to my place," Frank called. "If you saw the state it's in, you'd probably decide I'm some kind of sociopath and I'd never see you again."

She didn't answer, appearing a moment later with a tube of antibiotic cream and a wet cloth. "Let's get that cleaned up," she said, settling herself on the couch beside him.

"It's okay, Jackie." Frank squirmed away from her probing fingers. "It's just a couple of scratches. It's fine."

Jackie set her implements on table. "Well, maybe you'd prefer the *Raiders of the Lost Ark* cure. I know you've seen that movie, Francis. The scene where Indy and Marian are on the train and he's all banged up . . ." She leaned closer. "But instead of iodine, she does this"—she kissed his forehead—"and this"—another butterfly kiss grazed his cheek—"and this"—she kissed the corner of his mouth and waited, her eyes aflame with desire. "Just don't pull an Indy and fall asleep on me."

If you really love a woman, keep your pecker in your pants. Eva's words circled in Frank's brain. *I should go. I should go now before—*

Her lips brushed against his and Frank exhaled, his resistance defeated. Little Frank woke up and stood at attention almost instantly just from the pressure of her lips on his and her body flush against his. Frank tightened his arms around her.

Leave now, leave now, his mind urged, but Frank was too lost in the curves of her body and the sweetness of her mouth to take heed. She straddled him, pressing him back against the softness of the ornate couch as she tugged his shirt away from his body and dropped it to the floor. Her hands caressed the knotted muscles of his arms and chest as her tongue teased him out of all logic and sense.

"Oh, Frank," she murmured. "I never do this. Not this soon, but . . ." She stood up and slid her dress off her body. Beneath it, she wore a tiny lace bra and matching panties that revealed the luscious mounds of her breasts and firm behind. She stretched out her hands to him, waiting.

Frank hesitated, debating with himself. Leaving now would be like a slap in the face—but if he didn't leave now . . .

It'll be fine, he told himself. *It'll be fine as long as I keep my pants on and she doesn't touch me. I'll make her feel good . . . I want to do that.*

He let her lead him to her bedroom but once there, he pressed her down on the bed and held her there, pinning her hands above her head while he explored every inch of her perfect body—the pink tips of her breasts, the rounded curve of her triceps—determined only to give pleasure, not to receive it. He wished he'd worn a tie, or she a scarf—he would have used it to keep her wrists secure and hope that she took it for a love game—but instead, he had only his own strength and resolve, and some killer jiu jitsu moves, to keep her hands trapped behind her back.

"Frank . . ." she moaned, resisting him, struggling to wrap her arms around him, but Frank released her only long enough to pinion her hands firmly at her hips as he worked his way in kisses down her body until she wriggled in ecstasy beneath him. She shuddered as he buried himself at the softness between her thighs. He continued, working her furiously, feeling the waves of her pleasure as she strained beneath him.

And everything was great . . . until in his determination to bring her to complete climax, he forgot and released her hands.

In a flash, she grabbed him, rolling atop him in the heat of her own desire. Her mouth crushed down on his, demanding all he could give, and her hair tumbled around him, brushing his shoulders and abdomen as she ran her hands along the tight muscles of his body. He was hard—but he was still in control of himself until Jackie unzipped his pants and started rubbing him gently with her small, soft hand.

A furnace of desire exploded inside him, obliterating his rational mind with the force of its heat. He groaned as that little hand manipulated him steadily, drumming restraint out of his mind.

"Jackie—" he grunted with last of his self-control. "Don't—"

"I want you, Frank," she whispered, her voice urgent

with passion as she guided him toward complete union. "I need you inside me—"

"No, Jackie," Frank panted. "We can't . . . I can't . . ."

"Don't worry," she said, pulling his face toward hers with one hand while the other aimed his cock toward heaven. "I'm on the pill . . ."

The tip of his shaft eased into the hot wetness between her thighs. Frank exhaled, his body preparing to thrust deeply and be enveloped, surrendering to his passion and desire, so different than what he'd felt for Roxy or Carina or any other woman he'd ever—

Shit.

He jerked away from her, scrambling backwards on the bed as if he'd been scalded.

"What?" Jackie sat up. He couldn't see her face in the darkness, but her tone was heavy with concern. "Frank, what is it?"

Frank bounced off the bed and stood up. His erection tent-poled his trousers, but there was nothing he could do about it. She reached for the lights.

"What is it, Frank? What's wrong—"

Her hair was a wild, bed-tousled cloud that cascaded over her shoulders and partially covered her cherry-topped breasts, the nipples still pert from the attentions of Frank's tongue. Concern had etched a frown line into her forehead, but even with that she was so lovely, Frank wanted nothing more than to lie back down beside her and pick up where they left off. He turned his head and focused on yanking his zipper over his boner.

"I can't do this, Jackie," he told her. "It's . . . wrong . . ."

"I don't understand," she said in a small voice. "Did I do something?"

"No, of course not," Frank said quickly. If he didn't get out of there soon, he could tell he wouldn't be able to resist her. His desire would override everything. "It's just—" He stopped, wondering if he could tell her, wondering if he should. "It's me."

Her face contorted and he saw tears shimmering in her eyes. "Oh . . ." she said softly.

He longed to touch her, to reassure her, but he didn't trust himself.

"I—I have to go," Frank muttered, grabbing his shirt and pulling it over his shoulders. "I'll explain all this but not now. Right now, I have to—I—I want you so much, Jackie," he told her just as the first tear rolled down her cheek, and his heart twisted with the knowledge that she was reaching the wrong conclusion. "But I can't do this."

He grabbed his socks and shoes and hurried out of her bedroom, moving quickly through the condo and heading back down in the elevator. It wasn't until he was in his car that he realized that he was shaking. He drove, heading home on automatic pilot as he tried to force his brain to some kind of solution.

Go back to the Amazon. Try to find Lucinda . . . The words echoed in his brain. Could it be as simple as that? He squeezed his eyes shut, trying to remember every detail of the trip there, fifteen years before. He hadn't seen a phone the entire voyage . . . but there must have been one. There must have been some way of getting in touch with the people there. And now, when people all over the world had cell phones, perhaps—

And tell Jackie the truth. Right now, before you lose her.

He turned onto Armada Court intending to circle at the end of the cul-de-sac and return immediately to Jackie's place to confess—until he saw the long, black limousine parked at the curb in front of his house.

CHAPTER
Thirteen

Every fiber of Frank's consciousness instantly snapped into high alert.

Pandora, he thought. *She's back—but if she thinks she's going to catch me off guard this time she's wrong. I'm going to get some answers, even if I have to choke them out of her.*

He killed his headlights and parked far enough from his house to conceal his arrival, but close enough to see. He waited for several minutes, but there was no movement from the limo. Frank slid out of his car and approached slowly. The car appeared to be empty and the engine wasn't running . . . but the lights were on in his house and a shadow moved near the bay window.

Frank crept toward the front door. It was open—the lock was intact and however she'd gotten in, it hadn't been forced. Frank gave it a slight shove. Through the slice of the opening, he saw his guest wasn't Pandora Constantine.

A lone man stood in his living room, his attention apparently absorbed by the contents of a box Frank had left on the old couch.

He was older—probably in his late fifties or even early sixties—stocky and barrel-chested. He wore a pair of dark jeans, a white shirt open at the chest and a black vest. A black leather messenger bag stretched full rested on his hip. His complexion was as deeply tanned as a sportsman's and a mane of salt-and-pepper hair was slicked off his forehead in a loose ponytail. He looked like a vigorous, aging hippie. Harmless seeming... except for the fact that it was two o'clock in the morning and he had let himself into Frank's house. He seemed to be alone ... only Frank doubted that he'd driven himself over in that sleek black limo. There was at least one other person with him—the driver—and there could be more.

Frank opened the door an inch wider and eased himself through the opening. Silent as sunrise, he covered the distance between himself and his unexpected visitor. Before the old hippie could process what was happening to him, Frank had him in a headlock.

"Who are you?" he demanded.

"I-I'm ... *Arrrrgh*—"

"Who are you?" Frank shouted, shaking him.

But the man had recovered from the surprise of Frank's assault. He bent his neck and his knees like an aging wrestler and grabbed Frank's legs. An instant later, Frank was airborne and in another, he was on his back on the living room floor.

A man in a dark suit burst in from Frank's kitchen, holding a container of yogurt Frank recognized as from his refrigerator in one hand and a spoon in the other. He was dark-haired and nearly as wide as he was tall, but Frank could tell by how fast he crossed the room and the thickness of the fist that he aimed at Frank's face that the man was an athlete, not a fatso.

"It's okay, Tony! It's okay!" the older man chuckled breathlessly, staying the muscleman before he smashed his knuckles into Frank's nose. "I didn't know I could still do that. Been many years since I wrestled."

"Who are you?" Frank demanded. "What are you doing here? How did you get in my house?"

"Right, right," the man said with the faint lilt of an accent Frank couldn't place in his voice. "Sure. You are angry. You come home and find someone in your home and you are right to defend it." He waved the heavy man back and Frank scrambled to his feet. "These are crazy times." He wiped his hand on his jeans and stuck it toward Frank. "Me, I am Ari Kousakas. You have heard of me, perhaps?"

Frank ignored the hand. "What are you doing here?"

Ari nodded toward the bodyguard, signaling that he should leave them alone. The man glared at Frank but edged past him toward the door, closing it gently behind him.

"Tony—my driver," Ari offered as an explanation. "He also does some security for me when I'm out and about. But I think we should speak privately, yes?"

"What do you want?"

Ari Kousakas studied him with an amused smile.

"I have heard some very interesting things about you, Frank Young—but in this moment, I think they underestimate you. You have a good deal more spirit—more fight both literally and figuratively—than we imagined."

"'We'?"

"My associate Pandora Constantine." The stocky hippie lifted a half-full garbage bag off the sofa and sat down as though he'd been invited. "You will remember her?"

Frank dropped his fists as confusion overtook his instinct for self-defense. "Pandora? You work for Pandora?"

"Not exactly. Pandora works for *me*. In fact, she's chief general counsel for one of my companies—there are several, you know—ReGenesis. Ah. ReGenesis you have heard of."

"It's one of those genetic testing companies, right?"

"She sends you this. I believe it was owed." He upended the contents of the black bag on the low coffee table and sent a stream of bills out over the wood. Frank's cell phone bounced out and rested atop the pile.

"My phone! She took—"

"You left it. Now, it is returned," Ari said, nodding his head gallantly.

"How kind," Frank muttered sarcastically. "Almost as kind as drugging me in the first place."

Ari crossed one leg over the other, showing Frank a tanned bare ankle over an expensive black leather moccasin. "She believed it necessary, I am sure. Now, back to ReGenesis. My baby. My pride. As I said, I have other businesses, of course, but ReGenesis is . . . the most exciting, shall we say? And Pandora is a most intriguing woman. A woman of many talents. To make the story brief, she brought me something yesterday afternoon. Something from your . . . uh . . . experience together. And what she brought to me has brought *me* to *you*." He leaned forward, lacing his fingers together. "You see, Frank, I'm about to change your life. Forever. And you? All you have to do is say 'yes.'"

Frank gaped at him.

"Forgive me, son, but your expression—it is priceless," the man chuckled. "Just priceless!"

"I don't see anything funny here," Frank said harshly. "In fact, given my experience with your employee yesterday, I'm seriously considering calling the police. I don't care who you are or how many businesses you say you have or what you're offering—"

"Calm down, calm down," Ari said, waving his hands at Frank. He leaned forward, fingering the cash that still lay on the coffee table, then tossed it aside, unimpressed. "This? It is peanuts," he said with shrug. "How do they say it? 'Chicken scratch,' yes? I can offer you a whole lot more. A real partnership. The chance to be rich—richer than you have ever dreamed." Ari's dark eyes gleamed. "But you've got to stop glaring at me like that!" he finished with another hearty burst of laughter. He gestured toward the old recliner near the bay window. "Sit down and let me explain—"

"Don't tell me what to do in my own house!" Frank bellowed as fury and frustration exploded simultaneously inside him. "Who do you think you are? I don't want to hear anything you have to say until I find out exactly who that Pandora woman is—and just what she did to me! Do you understand? And if you don't tell me what I want to know—"

"Yes, yes, I know. You'll either beat me to a pulp with those rather impressive fighting skills that Pandora documented in her excellent bio of you or you'll call the police to have me removed from your humble abode, yes?" He smiled. "All right. But you will allow an old man to unwind his story in his own way?"

Frank waited, offering neither encouragement nor denial.

"Thank you, Frank." Ari rubbed his hands together, as though he were excited to have the opportunity. "As I said, Pandora is the general counsel of ReGenesis. The company has one mission: the search for immortality—"

Immortality? Frank tried to hold his face completely still, but Ari's smile indicated he'd seen a reaction.

"Yes, immortality. Our research is aimed primarily at developing products and procedures that will extend human life. We have had some successes in creating some anti-aging concoctions sold to cosmetic brands. But the vision is much bigger and broader. Our scientists work to stop time." Ari studied his broad fingers. "I admit to a rather personal interest in the subject. It seems only yesterday I had a physique like yours. I had . . . what do they call it now? The six-pack. In my prime, yes. In my prime, a Greek god." He sighed. "Ah, time."

"What does this have to do with me?" Frank demanded. "I asked you about this Pandora woman. I asked you why she drugged me—"

"I'm coming to that, Frank. Be patient. In my country, we have a saying: 'One minute's patience is ten years' peace'—"

"I've got a saying, too, Mr. Kourakas—or Kousakas or whatever your name is. It's 'All trespassers will be prosecuted.'"

Ari's sharkish smile widened. "I like you, Frank Young. You are tough. I respect that. Now, to answer your question, she drugged you to better enable us to get a sample of your unique genetic matter."

"Then why didn't she just ask for one?"

"Would you have consented to—forgive the crude expression—'jerking off' in a cup? And then there were a few other medical tests."

"So instead of getting my consent, she just knocked me out and took it—is that what you're telling me?"

"She took nothing. You signed this consent form." Ari pulled a carefully folded piece of paper from his jeans pocket. "And here we are."

Frank inspected the paper carefully. "I don't remember signing this."

"And yet, that's your signature." Ari stowed the document in his pocket again. "And it's a good thing, too, because my scientists have done a preliminary analysis and . . . let's just say they've never seen anything like it. Your genetic structure differs substantially from that of the average man of your age—and your semen?" Ari leered unpleasantly. "They are still completing the full analysis, but Dr. Garajan said he'd never seen anything similar. And of course, I was so excited to learn of this, I decided I couldn't wait until business hours to seek you out." He gestured to himself with an elaborate flourish. "And so, here I am. Frank Young, you are a miracle man."

Even though he'd known it, hearing that science had confirmed it was like seeing his last window of hope snap shut. "Oh, man," Frank sighed, feeling the weight of his exhaustion and despair settle like a bag of rocks around his neck. "Man . . ."

"A heavy responsibility, yes." Ari rubbed his hands together. "So we talk terms. I am prepared to offer you a generous salary and of course, stock options, as well as bonuses based on the success of any product generated as a result of your 'contribution,' shall we say?"

"What are you talking about?"

"Of course, it will take some time—perhaps years—even after they isolate the correct genetic sequences and begin to replicate them. There will be clinical trials and FDA approval and all of that . . ." He sighed at the burden of the process. "In the interim, however, I expect there to be brisk interest on the black market. Enough, I would guess, to keep you motivated."

"Replicate my genetic sequences? Black market?" Frank shook his head. "I don't have any idea what—"

"I'm talking about you coming on board with us, Frank."

"No. I *have* a job."

"Ah, yes. The little travel company. Putting together tours to climb mountains and sail the world and other fantastic, once-in-a-lifetime opportunities. Not doing very well, is it? It's a worthy idea, certainly, but even you must realize its inherent problem: the market that has the money, inclination and physical prowess to participate in your offerings is . . ." He pinched his thumb and forefinger together so that hardly any light shone between them. "On the other hand, eternal youth is something everyone wants and something a great many people are willing to pay a great deal of money for." He bared his teeth at Frank again. "It is a 'no brains' decision, I think the expression goes." He shrugged. "But if you wish, by all means, continue with your little venture. I don't require you to punch a clock at ReGenesis. Only that you make yourself available to us from time to time—"

Available. It was a simple word that Frank had heard—and spoken himself—thousands of times before. But in Ari

Kousakas's mouth it sounded suddenly sinister. The memory of sinking helplessly into blackness, locked in a strange, empty hotel miles from friends and help, rose in Frank's mind like a warning.

"No," he said firmly. "I'm not interested."

"You haven't heard the offer—"

"It doesn't matter. Not interested."

"And yet, you very much need the money," Ari said softly. "Enough to be willing to sell yourself like a common prostitute."

"I'm out of that business now," Frank said angrily. "Didn't your 'associate' tell you that—"

"Two million dollars," Ari interrupted. "A year. With annual bonuses that will more than likely be many multiples of that salary, Frank. All in exchange for the occasional sample, an occasional meeting and perhaps a little study here and there."

"No."

"Three million."

"No."

"Five million. Think of it, Frank. Five million a year. You can take care of your friends. Mr. Hughes and his parents have been very good to you, I understand. Ms. Cross can be rather difficult, but you care for her in your way. And then there's Maxine Donovan and her little family. Imagine the good you could do baby Conrad with that kind of money. Uncle Frank could make sure he never wants for anything. The best schools. College—"

"No."

"You can buy a new house," Ari said, gesturing to the wreck around him. "Upgrade."

"No."

"Then keep it forever—and still buy something new. A place in Boston. Or New York. Or Bangkok. Or in Antarctica if it is your pleasure. Build something for yourself and that special lady. The one you danced with in Tijuana tonight, perhaps. Jackie is what you call her, I believe."

Frank's stomach tensed. "What do you know about her?" he asked warily.

Ari showed his sharklike teeth. "You are far too valuable for us to simply let you wander around unchaperoned, Frank. And may I say, your Jackie is a lovely girl. Quite lovely—"

Frank's fingers curled in on themselves. The idea of Jackie mixed up with the likes of Ari or Pandora made him want to start swinging—and right now, before the threat hissing beneath the man's words could blossom into action. "Let's just leave her out of it," he said with venom in his voice.

The older man's toothy smile spread even wider across his browned skin. "Ah. She is very dear to you. Well, of course. Yes. Let's leave her out of this. You could invest every penny in your little company, then. Instead of endlessly searching for capital, *you* could be the investor you seek. You could develop X-Treme Travel in any direction you choose, without any strings."

Frank hesitated.

"And of course, you'd be among the first beneficiaries of whatever ReGenesis develops with your input. As I understand it, it appears you are not . . . ah, shall we say, forever young. Only the young ladies who have been so fortunate as to be the recipients of your . . ." Ari gestured toward the nether regions of Frank's body. "You will age, but the young lady—whoever she is—will not. With your help, we can change this. We will work to develop the right product and of course, you will have immediate access. With that serum, you both will be forever young, you and your young lady." Ari stepped closer to him. "Can you imagine it, Frank? Frozen forever in your prime? Imagine the things a man could do, knowing that his experience and understanding will grow, but his body will never show the accumulation of the years! Imagine avoiding decay and decline, loss of strength. Imagine eternal vigor! What price would a man pay for that?"

In spite of himself, Frank imagined it: himself and Jackie, both forever young, frozen in their thirties together, full of energy and life. But . . . she'd never agree to it. Her image filled his mind, exactly as he'd left her last—her eyes filled with tears of shame and regret—and his heart twisted with anxiety.

"Or . . ." Ari continued softly. "Perhaps you would prefer the opposite. To, as they say, 'turn it off'—"

Frank's eyes locked on Ari's face.

"Yes. An antidote. We will ask the scientists, but, yes, it's probably possible. In fact, if you'd like, I'll arrange for you to meet with Dr. Garajan—after you've joined us, of course. He should be able to answer your questions about that. In the meantime, allow me the opportunity to demonstrate my good faith. Why don't you come to my house tonight? I dabble in some venture capital myself and I can introduce you to the kind of people who might just be interested in your little travel company—"

"No," Frank interrupted, shaking his head as hope

for a future with Jackie sputtered to life inside him again. "There's something I have to do."

"Ah yes. Your lovely lady friend. Bring her with you, of course!"

"No."

"Ah," Ari said after considering him for a long moment. "She does not know. Not yet. But I am sure she will be very happy to learn of your gift. What woman would not be? Forever desirable. Forever beautiful—"

"I'd like to bring another friend," Frank decided. "Someone to keep an eye on my drinks and make sure no one drives me off into the desert somewhere. Someone to make sure I don't sign something I don't remember signing. And's that's not negotiable."

Ari chuckled, lifting his hands in surrender. "All right, all right. Bring your friend. And we meet on your schedule. Name the day."

"Wednesday."

"Wednesday. Hump day, they call it, yes?" Ari said, nodding. "Strangely appropriate. I'll send a car for you Wednesday at seven p.m.—"

"You're not listening, Aristotle—or whatever your name is. I don't trust you. No car. Write the address. I'll drive myself."

Ari sighed, shaking his head as though he were being gravely misjudged. He pulled an expensive black pen from his shirt pocket and scribbled something on the topmost hundred-dollar bill in the pile closest to him. "I am aware you have many debts, but don't spend this one, Frank Young. At least, not until Wednesday." He stood, rubbing his knees as though they ached. "Good night."

He let himself out of the house. Frank watched as his driver hustled to open the car door. The man glanced in Frank's direction before sliding into the driver's seat and whisking the car and its occupant into the dawning day.

She does not know. Not yet.

Ari Kousakas's words had the flavor a threat—and instinct told Frank that this was exactly the kind of man who would press any advantage he had.

I've got to tell her. Right now, Frank thought. But he headed up the stairs to his room first.

His parents' letters rested on the edge of the old cherrywood chest of drawers, the little ribbon that held them fraying with age and Frank's constant tying and retying as he read them over and over again. They'd begun to feel like a talisman: something he needed to have with him. He grabbed them and dove back down the stairs to his car.

CHAPTER

Fourteen

He looked into her eyes . . . and hated himself.

They were red-rimmed and sad above deep hollows of fatigue. She had changed into a faded gray sweatshirt and a pair of loose black shorts that looked several sizes too big. With her hair in tangled black whorls around her face, Frank caught a glimpse of what she must have looked like at fourteen: all legs and hair and bright black eyes. But the way she held her mouth and jaw tight with the determination to hold herself together was all woman.

"Jackie," he began, reaching for her, but she evaded him.

"Let's not start that again, Frank. Please. I-I can't—" She blinked fast at him, trying to keep more tears from sliding down her cheeks. "I know what you came to say. You're married, aren't you?"

"No, Jackie—"

"It's like I said: I knew a guy like you couldn't be single. I just wish you'd told me. Or worn a ring or something, Frank. Please—"

"I'm not, babe, I swear—"

"I know you didn't mean to keep it from me. I can tell you're not the kind of man who just . . . lies because he can . . . I know why it was so hard for you to tell me. God knows there I things I can't seem to say—things I probably should. It's hard to say some things because . . . after the plane crash . . . I don't know. We just connected and—" She shook her head. "I'm mad at myself. I don't know if you'll believe me, but I'm not usually like this. I don't just throw myself at guys like—like—"

"But you didn't—"

"I did. I've been looking for someone who'd make me feel the way you do for so very long that I guess I just wanted to believe . . ." Her voice broke, but she inhaled and pushed through it. "I wanted to believe I'd finally found the one." She sank onto her sofa and covered her face with her hands. Frank saw her shoulders shaking with sobs, but when he touched her, she jerked away from him. "I don't know why this hurts so much. I mean, it's not like we—like you owe me, but—but—I guess I just—I thought you felt like I did, Frank. And that's why I acted like such a—such a *slut*—"

"Stop it, Jackie. You *didn't*—"

"I did! I'm so ashamed of myself," she sobbed.

"Don't be. You haven't done anything wrong. It's *me*, Jackie—"

"Then I was right," she said dully. "You're married."

"No, I'm not married, Jackie. There's no one else. I'm not even dating anyone . . ." He moved slowly toward the empty spot beside her on the sofa and sat down hesitantly. "It's just . . . we can't have sex. Not yet."

Her hands slid away from her face.

"I don't understand."

Frank sighed. "I hope it's just temporary . . ." he began with difficulty.

"Oh my God, there's something wrong, isn't there? Down there." Her eyes shifted toward his crotch. "There is, isn't there?"

"Would it matter?" He knew his face was aflame—he could feel the heat in his cheeks—but he ignored the embarrassment and made himself look at her.

"I—I don't know. If it's some kind of STD—"

"No. Nothing like that."

Her eyes held a thousand questions. "Are you telling me—are you saying—it doesn't work? Because from what I saw and felt, I would never have guessed—"

"No. It works fine. But . . ." Frank continued carefully. "Suppose it didn't. Would that make a difference?"

"What are you trying to tell me, Frank? What's wrong? Why—"

Frank took a deep breath. "Jackie, I know this is going to sound crazy. Really crazy, but . . . I'm afraid that if we sleep together, you'll change," he began. "Or rather, that I'll change, and you won't—"

"I don't understand. Of course sex changes relationships, but that's not necessarily a *bad* thing. And it's not crazy to want to take things slow, Frank, if that's what you're trying to say. *Is* that what you're trying to say?"

"Not exactly." Frank sighed. Now that he was here, looking into her trusting soft eyes, explaining the whole thing about the pool and his power or curse was infinitely more difficult. *Thanks a lot, Dad,* he thought, while frustration and anger sparred with the desire to do the right thing. *What were you thinking, sending me to that place? Why on earth would you do this to me? What am I supposed to do now?*

"Is that yours?" Jackie asked, bending suddenly to retrieve something from the floor near Frank's shoe. A moment later, she showed him the little bundle that had been in his pocket. "They look like . . . love letters."

"They are. They were my parents'," Frank said, touching his pocket. "I guess they fell out when I sat down—"

"Your parents' love letters? You carry them with you?"

"I just found them, not too long ago," Frank explained. Uncomfortable emotions coursed through him and he almost demanded the little packet back, but he couldn't bear to keep another thing from her. "They were in a locked box under my father's desk. I guess I would have found them a long time ago . . . if I'd ever cleaned up in there." He told her quickly about the house and the years since he'd disturbed anything inside it, following the example of his father's grief.

Jackie turned Frank's archeological relic gently in her fingers, handling the letters as though they were something sacred.

"They'd been there all that time? And you never—"

Frank shook his head. "I don't know why. I just . . ." He sighed. "You probably think I'm some kind of nut."

"I think . . . I think there's a lot going on in *there*." Her forefinger grazed his chest. She offered him the bundle, but as soon as his fingers closed over the fragile paper, he understood why he'd brought them there. They weren't just his anymore. Nothing was. He pressed them back into her hands.

"Read them."

Surprise, pleasure and finally reticence each took a turn on her face.

"Oh, Frank, no," she protested at last. "I couldn't. It's so very . . . personal. Intimate. You don't have to—"

"I want you to." He slid the ribbon off the letters and rearranged them quickly. "When I found them they were in date order—but lately, I keep rereading the last few ones. They must have overlapped—it had to have taken at least a couple of weeks and maybe longer for them to reach each other, if they ever did. And there are some missing, too. You'll see."

"Are you sure?"

"Yeah . . . I'm sure. No one's seen them but me, and maybe . . . maybe it's time for another pair of eyes, you know?"

Her smile shouldered the weight of his trust. As she read, Frank stood up and moved around the room, avoiding her face, afraid of what he might find in her expression. But when she reached the last few letters, he hung over the back of the sofa, rereading the words over her shoulder.

April 13, 1980

Dearest Francis,

Are you getting my letters? I write most days. Some days it's harder than others, though. Some days it seems like the pen weighs a thousand pounds and I can't put my thoughts together no matter how hard I try. Thankfully that passes.

KYLE & FOLAN

I hate to tell you this, my love—I hate to worry you when everything came out okay in the end—but I suppose you should know. Yesterday was a really bad time. I woke up to the most terrible cramping pain. I called the nurse for some help—sadly I don't seem to be able to get out of this hospital—and of course, within minutes the doctor was there. There wasn't any bleeding—thank God—but the doc said I was probably having a miscarriage. He said they could give me something for the pain but that there wasn't anything he could do to keep it from happening because little Frank is too small.

I started praying to the Holy Mother right then. I don't think I've ever prayed so hard. I begged her to intercede for me. She is a mother; I knew she understood. I tried to stay as still as possible and I just prayed. It hurt so much, Frank. So much that I almost took the drugs to dull the pain. But when the doctor admitted that the painkillers might harm the baby, I didn't do it. I guess he thought I would lose the baby anyway—and that's why he didn't see the harm. I don't quite trust him. He consulted with Dr. Strahn—and you know how she feels about my trying to have a baby. She completely persuaded you that it was a bad idea. Now, this OB-GYN is acting just like her. Everyone seems to be more interested in saving my life than this child's.

I'm sorry, Francis, but I see it differently. I'm going to carry this child—at least until his body is strong enough to survive without me. I will. I don't care what I have to do.

I know this will worry you, so let me quickly tell you the good news. Little by little, I started to feel better. I guess I fell asleep and when I woke up, I was very weak, but the pain was gone. They ran some tests and God heard me. As far as they can tell, our little boy is still alive inside me—and I am so very, very thankful. When Father Ramirez dropped by to see me this morning, he said he thought it was a sign of how strong little Frank is. Our child is special, Francis. I know he is.

There is more I want to share with you, but it have to wait until tomorrow. My thoughts flutter and flit and my hand can no longer hold this pen. I'm going to rest now.

Lovingly,

Helen

April 20, 1980

Dearest Frank,

Amy dropped by and I enlisted her help to write you as I've been so very tired. I keep starting letters to you and then running out of steam! I've heard that the first trimester is very hard for many women and thankfully, in just a few weeks, it will be over. I'm hopeful that I'll soon start to feel much better, though I suppose it will never be easy for me. By the time you get home, I plan to be well enough to leave the hospital. I am eager to sleep in our bed and see my own things around me.

The ultrasound tests show our Little Francis is hanging in there—as am I. My only worry is for you: I haven't had a letter in several weeks now. You warned me this might happen, so I tell myself that you are fine—that you are deep in the jungle uncovering the mysteries of the past. Sometimes I dream of you wrestling jaguars and boa constrictors. Or walking through the jungle with a macaw on your shoulder like some kind of pirate! Ha!

Still, I will be glad when you come home. Very, very, very glad.

You should see your "honey do" list. It grows by the minute! You have a lot of work to do, mister. You'll need to get to work painting the nursery. I want a nice rocking chair, too. One of those ones with the footstool? And I think we should fence the backyard so junior will have a safe place to run around and play.

Speaking of play, do you remember the Hugheses—that nice couple we met shortly after we moved in? They live a few streets over on Galleon Drive. Remember we went walking one day and their dog startled me? They were so apologetic and kind. Since then I've seen her—Irene is her name—here and there. Well, to my surprise, she stopped in yesterday—and her belly is huge! Turns out she is pregnant, too—due in a month. She was at the hospital for a tour of the maternity unit. She knew I was here—I don't know how—so she came in and sat and chatted with me for a bit. She looks marvelous—so glowing and happy—I almost felt jealous. But mostly I'm thrilled for them. After all, their child might be a playmate for little Frank!

Okay, they want me to stop now. I pray for you every moment. Don't worry—all will be well.

Lovingly,

Helen

April 20, 1980

Frank,

I don't know if you will get this letter but after writing

Helen's letter to you, I feel I must include a note of my own.

You need to come home.

She isn't doing nearly as well as she says she is. Twice already she has nearly died and every day she grows weaker. She seems to be slipping away little by little. She is determined to have this child and to be a mother, but the doctors have grave doubts that either of them will survive.

I'm scared for her, Frank.

If you get this, drop everything and come NOW.

Amy

April 23, 1980

Dearest Helen,

I know you won't get this letter until probably after I am home—or perhaps I will place it in your hands!

We've had no runners from here, of course—we are quite lost to the world at this point. By now, the rest of our team have probably returned to the United States and given us up for lost! But we are not. If anything, we are jubilant and invigorated by our discoveries here.

I had thought we would remain here only a week or so—but we discovered some nearby food sources and were able to stretch our provisions. We have been working night and day and what I have found here is nothing short of amazing—but I won't write of it here. I'll tell you about it when I see you—which will be very soon now. For now, I'll simply say that the legends that Dr. Amaru has shared and what we have recovered in this expedition are too precious to share with an avaricious world and yet too wondrous to be allowed to be forgotten. In short, they present me with a dilemma, one that I know my sweet Helen's good judgment will help me to solve.

There is more to Creation than Science easily explains—which will not surprise you, my love, but for me, it comes as something of a revelation. I leave here feeling that all will be well. You will be well. You and our son. I can't wait to meet him—and I can't wait to get home.

Lovingly,

Francis

"That's the last one," Frank said when she lay the pages in her lap and raised eyes that glistened with tears to his face.

"And when he got home?"

Frank shrugged. "I don't know. I never asked. He . . . he couldn't talk about her. But I was born in September. A couple months early. But . . ." He spread his hands wide. "Here I am. She died that day. The day I was born."

"Poor man," Jackie muttered. "You can tell how much they loved each other. And that's a lot of guilt for a man to carry."

"Yeah," Frank said, suddenly wanting more than anything to be talking about mysterious Amazonian pools or the power of the penis—anything but death and loss. "But he wasn't getting the letters. He didn't know."

"I'm talking about *you*, Francis," Jackie said quietly. "Thank you for letting me read these. I think I understand better now."

"Understand?"

"Why you hesitate to take our relationship to the next level. It's hard to believe in hearts and flowers and happily ever after when . . ." She nodded at the nest of paper in her lap. "And it's a lot of guilt to carry, knowing that it was your life or hers . . . and she chose yours—"

"No, it's not like that," Frank interrupted. "I never even think about that. I never—I don't—" He stuttered, stumbling for the words to stop a conversation as anger and futility mounted inside him. "I don't know how to talk about this stuff, Jackie. It's like . . . there's a rock there. Where these feelings are supposed to be. I'd rather *not* talk about any of this. It's just . . . useless. Useless to go there when there are so many other more important questions I need to answer. About his discovery. Where it was and how I can get there and why we can't have sex yet—"

"I know," Jackie said softly, taking his hand in her own and pulling him onto the sofa beside her. "But you *did* tell me. These letters tell me. I understand completely."

Frank raced through the contents of the letters in his memory. Had he missed something? Were they more explicit than he remembered? "You do? But how—"

"I understand that you have to deal with the past before you can face the future, Frank. And you're doing that. You're doing that as hard as you can. So, we'll wait. Until the time is right for anything more between us."

"Jackie—"

"What was it he found? Do you know?"

Frank exhaled, trying to calm himself, but the anger and frustration were too strong for mere breath to ease, especially now when he knew he would have to tell her. He couldn't do it, not sitting so close to her, staring into the midnight of her eyes. He jackknifed off the couch, pacing restlessly. "I don't know how to say this, so I'm just going to say it. I think he found—"

Her phone jangled loudly, startling them both.

"It's awfully early," she muttered. "Hold on a sec," she said, jumping off the couch to retrieve it. "I may have forgotten a call with one of our program reps in Uganda. It's—"

"Around noon. Eight hours ahead," Frank finished, sinking onto the couch in defeat.

What? he asked as though his father's spirit were beside him. *You don't want me to tell her? Then help me find the answer! Show me where it is—*

"How did you get this number?" Jackie said sharply into the phone. "Oh," she said quietly. "Yeah . . . I guess that's okay. Yeah, I did say that." She glanced toward Frank, then turned away, speaking in a low soft voice. "This really isn't a good time. Wednesday? I suppose I could do that. No. I'll drive myself. Because I don't trust you. Just give me the address. Hold on—" She paced into the kitchen and he heard a drawer open and close. "Okay, I'm ready." There was another pause.

She returned a few moments later holding a piece of paper in her hands.

"This is the weirdest night ever," she murmured, collapsing onto the couch. "You'll never guess who that was." She cut her eyes at Frank. "My father. He says he's in San Diego. He wants to meet."

"That's good, isn't it?"

"No. And no, I don't want to talk about it. This conversation is about you, not me." She yawned suddenly, then shook her head as though to clear fatigue from her brain. "Back to what we were talking about before. About you. You were about to tell me what your father found—"

"Are you going to go? Meet with your father?"

"I don't know. I'm too tired to think about it right now." And suddenly, she looked it. Her skin was gray with fatigue and tight lines of exhaustion crinkled the corners of her eyes. She rubbed her forehead wearily.

"I think you should."

"Will you go with me?"

"I'll go next time. Besides, I heard you say Wednesday. I've got something Wednesday evening."

"Another meeting for XT?"

"Yeah." *Sort of*, he added in his mind.

"I don't know. Maybe . . ." she said after another long yawn. She sighed, her shoulders drooping with the effort of focusing her attention. "There was something you were going to tell me?"

He opened his mouth . . . and shut it again. He'd been certain he needed to confess but now, watching her blink at him through weak, teary eyes, it felt wrong. Selfish, even.

"Later." Frank took her hand and led her down the condo's narrow hall to the bedroom. The bed was still a rumpled mess from their interrupted coitus, but Frank pushed that to the back of his mind as he pulled back the sheets.

"What are you doing?"

"Text your assistant and tell him you'll be in a little late today. You're exhausted. You're going to bed."

"If I'm going, you're going," she said. "You look like hell, Frank. Come lie down with me—I won't touch you, I swear." She smiled wearily. "Now *those* are words I never thought I'd be saying to a man—ever."

"No, I don't think—"

"Frank . . . I don't want you to do anything you're not ready to do. I don't mean to sound like some kind of nymphomaniac here, but I'm not a nun, either. I'll admit that sex is important to me. I think a healthy sexual relationship is crucial—and I know we'll have that when the time is right. I mean, you don't plan on keeping me waiting forever, right?"

Frank swallowed hard. A thought—sort of like a prayer—soared out of his heart to an unlikely god. *Ari, I hope your scientists have some ideas because I can't go on like this. I won't go on like this. I'll let her go before I tell one more lie, so help me.*

But all he said was, "No, babe. Not forever."

"Sit down. Take off your shoes."

"Jackie, I—"

"Do it. Please."

Reluctantly, Frank obeyed. She slid into bed beside him and lay her head on his broad shoulder. "I'm in my spot now. Go to sleep, Frank," she murmured into his ear.

"But I really—"

"No talking."

I'll stay until she falls asleep, he told himself as he lay beside her, staring into her eyes and watching her lashes rise slower and slower after every blink. It was something he'd never done—watch someone surrender to sleep—and the intimacy of it struck him. Face to face, eye to eye, feeling each slow puff of breath in his face while his senses registered each slight shift of expression. He felt protective in the gentlest of ways, wanting nothing more than for her to know that he was there and would be, content to feel her breathing, content to be wakeful while she was vulnerable. But when she reached up and lay her hand on his cheek, his eyelids dropped heavily over his eyes as though she'd cast a spell on him.

"It's okay, Francis," she breathed in a voice as soft as a sigh. "Sleep now."

He did.

CHAPTER
Fifteen

"You've done a lot," Steve said, stepping into Frank's living room. "I hardly recognize the place."

Steve was right: he'd accomplished a great deal. The house felt like a stranger's now that he'd cleared all of the papers and junk, and Frank felt like an alien in it. He'd been through everything now—every room—and in the small box of relevant materials now stored by his bed there was nothing that answered his dilemma. He'd stripped every room, studied every piece of junk, crawled through attics and garages, sifted through Dumpsters—and no matter how hard he tried, he couldn't seem to see what his father had been trying to tell him. It was as if the whole "message from beyond" had been little more than a drug-induced hallucination.

"Lately, I've been thinking I need to go back to the

Amazon and—" He stopped, focusing his attention on his friend. "You cut your hair!"

Steve ran his fingers over his shorn head. Gone was the straggling mop of gold that had always rested on his collar and curled over his ears as if to make up for the fact that it was pulling slowly away from his hairline. In its place was a high and tight almost military-looking cut.

"Yeah," he muttered, trying to sound nonchalant. "It was time for a change."

Frank eyed his friend from head to toe. The jeans were new, too—the denim looked fresh—and his shirt looked like it had been ironed. Uncomfortable with Frank's inspection, Steve backed toward the front door. "You want me to drive, or—"

"What's up with you?" Frank asked suspiciously, following him out of the house. He answered his friend's question by heading to his own CR-V, keys in hand. Steve slid into the passenger seat carefully, as though he didn't want to mess up his look.

"Nothing's wrong with me!" Steve's voice rose defensively. "Can't a guy change it up a bit?"

"Eva still at your house?"

Steve nodded. "It's actually working out okay. All that hard-ass attitude? It's a bunch of bullshit. Most of the time, she's scared to death."

"Of what?"

"Same as most of us: being hurt. Rejected. Unloved."

"You understand Eva?" Frank said quietly. "I've officially entered the Twilight Zone—and I'm not talking about those dumb vampire movies."

"So you're thinking of going back to the Amazon?"

Steve said, changing the subject. "You haven't found anything in all your dad's stuff?"

Frank shook his head. "Lots of notes, lots of dry journal entries. Nothing about the pool. Nothing about why he went there—or why he sent me. Not a map or a contact phone number. I can't even find anything in his papers with the name of his guide, José del Flores."

"Yeah, but can't you find the guide just by his name? On Google?"

"There's nothing, Steve."

"But you've known people down there. Can't you—"

"I tried that. No one's ever heard of him. Which leads me to believe he's either no longer in the business or dead."

"So why go down there?"

"Because of Jackie. Because I have to find a way to undo it. For her. That's the only reason I'm bothering to talk to this guy from ReGenesis. I'd make a deal with the Devil himself if it meant Jackie and I could have a normal life."

"You're that serious about Airplane Girl?"

"She's the one," Frank said quietly.

Steve absorbed this information silently.

"Well, I guess I can understand that. The right woman . . . changes things," he said at last. Frank turned toward his friend, the follow-up questions already on his lips, but Steve deflected him. "What about the other girl? The one in the Amazon," Steve asked at last. "What's her name?"

"Lucinda." Frank sighed. "I haven't found her either. I'm pretty sure she's married now—she told me she was about to get hitched when I was down there. I don't remember the guy's name. And—" Guilt knotted in the pit of Frank's stomach. "Even if I found her, I'm not sure she'd help me. I broke a promise to her. I told her I'd come back for her . . . and I never did. I forgot all about her, Steve."

"You had your reasons, man."

"Somehow I doubt she's going to see it that way."

"Still, if you go there, to what's the place—"

"Iquitos."

"Yeah, Iquitos. Maybe someone knows them. Or maybe you can find someone who can guide you to their village."

"I don't even remember the name of it. The Amazon is huge, man. There are dozens of little tribes living in the interior. Without a name or a map or some coordinates, it's a wild goose chase. But I'm beginning to think I may have to chase that goose—"

"Whoa. Is that the house?"

To call it a house—or even a mansion—was an understatement. "Palace" would have been closer, but even that didn't seem adequate to Frank's mind.

The address had been his first clue—it was in one of the tonier suburbs north of San Diego. The kind of place where a "cheap" house would cost several millions of dollars. But Ari Kousakas's place was something else altogether. It was set far back from the road, with grounds that were more carefully maintained than a nature preserve. They parked along the circular drive lined with expensive automobiles and walked the paved driveway to an entrance so grand it seemed like it should have uniformed sentries in front of it.

When they reached the door, the light and noise of the activity inside spilled out into the twilight. Frank could hear laughter and music and see people moving around through the cathedral-style windows that lined the front of the house.

Inside, a palatial ceiling vaulted over a cool stone floor that reminded Frank of the churches he'd visited in Italy, except for the bright chandelier that filled the space with dazzling light. A grand piano occupied a far corner—complete with a young woman in a black strapless dress who worked the keys with graceful fingers—and the bar was set up in the other. The space in between was filled with at least fifty people who stood around talking and laughing with drinks in their hands, occasionally grabbing snacks from the trays of waiters in white coats who circulated the room. Just beyond the piano, a huge arched doorway of paned glass led to a verandah, also crowded with people. And beyond that, Frank saw the glimmer of an impressive swimming pool with its own view of the Pacific Ocean.

"Drink, sir?" asked a waiter bearing a silver tray of champagne flutes.

Frank frowned. Champagne had never been a favorite, and after the experience with Pandora, it now ranked definitively at the bottom of his preferences. "No thanks," he muttered, but to his surprise, Steve grabbed a glass and chugged it like a beer.

"What are you doing?" Frank hissed. "I thought you were here to back me up."

"I am!" Steve insisted. "But you don't honestly think all these people are drinking poison champagne, do you?" He snagged a few snacks from another circulating white coat and popped one into his mouth. "Mmm. That's good," he muttered. "So . . . where's Darth Vader? You see him?"

Frank peered around the room. He didn't recognize any faces and couldn't have named any names, but it was clear he was the poorest person in the room. Even though most of the men were dressed in jeans, they all had the bearing of people who knew that money was power—and who were used to having plenty of both. In one corner Frank saw a group of men who could have easily been mistaken for half of the San Diego Chargers' starting front line, but who were probably Ari's muscle.

"No," he said, shaking his head. "But maybe he's outside."

They maneuvered through the room, avoiding elbows cocked by arms holding every kind of drink imaginable and the movements of people circulating from one conversation to the next, until they reached the archway and stepped out onto the verandah.

White tables and bar stools dotted the expanse of the open gallery as well as strategically placed heat lamps to keep the guests insulated from the chill of the sharp ocean breeze. The ceiling twinkled with white lights, and the tones from the piano complemented the hum of laughter and repartee.

"See him? See him yet?" Steve repeated the words like a kid on a long car drive. "See him?"

"No," Frank answered over and over as they moved from one end of the verandah to the other. Frank estimated another hundred people outside enjoying the evening and the atmosphere—but Ari Kousakas didn't seem to be among them.

A hand on his arm stopped him. "Hello, Frank."

Pandora Constantine stood behind him. She looked exactly like she had the first time he met her: dark suit clinging to her body like a glove, spike-heeled pumps, long red hair caressing her shoulders.

"Nice to see you," she said.

"I wish I could say the same."

She smiled, seeming pleased by his irritation. "Ari told me you were a bit annoyed by how I chose to conduct our . . . transaction," she said, toasting him with her champagne flute. "But you signed the papers. I did nothing that wasn't permitted by the contract."

Frank offered her a chilly smile. "I don't recall there being a provision about drugging me, Pandora."

"Oh? Perhaps you should read it again. I'm fairly sure that it's covered by the language there. You do have a copy, you know. It was somewhere mixed in with all that money Ari delivered the other night."

"Speaking of Ari . . . where is he?"

"Oh, he's around. Probably giving a tour of the house. This is a new place, you see. He just bought it last month. It's a bit closer to the city. Not as big as some of the others, but with some nice amenities. Private movie theater. Bowling alley. Three separate guesthouses on the property. Private golf course. And of course the beach." She nodded over her shoulder toward the ocean. "Naturally, most of these people aren't impressed by those little extras. The house tour is just a tactic he uses when he wants to speak to someone more privately." Her eyes flicked over Steve, measuring him from hairline to sole. "I see you've brought backup. Would this be Mr. Hughes?" she asked.

Steve nodded at her, his face flat except for his eyes, which darted all over her face, then down to her breasts, then lower before returning searchingly to her face.

"Nice to meet you, too." Pandora's voice was silky as a spider's web. She dismissed Steve as completely as if he were invisible. "I'm sure Ari will be with you soon. In the meantime, enjoy the party. Plan for your own house—or houses. Get some decorating ideas, perhaps. There's no virtue in poverty, Mr. Young. Ari's offering you the opportunity to use your . . . talent . . . in a much less demeaning way. Even better, you'll be helping people. There's no limit to the breakthroughs a genetic variation like yours might lead to. The aging issues are really just the beginning. We could slow the progress of debilitating diseases, dwindle the growth of cancer cells so dramatically that it will be like they don't exist. Can you imagine that? The impact that would have? The number of lives you can save—simply by saying 'yes'? Simply for making yourself available for relatively minor medical interventions? And if, in the meantime, you become incredibly rich, what's the harm in that?"

Steve snorted. Pandora pivoted toward him.

"Is something wrong?"

Steve shrugged. "I guess not. Just curious, though. Is Pandora your real name?"

Pandora's eyes narrowed. "Excuse me?"

"I'd lay money you were born a 'David' or 'John' or 'William'—and this is one of the best jobs I've ever seen."

"I'm sure I don't know what you mean," Pandora murmured. "Enjoy the party, gentlemen—"

"Because that would explain a lot." Steve's voice rose over the music to a few decibels short of a shout. "Like why you had to knock my friend out the other day. You knew there was no way he was going to do it with a dude—even if the dude looks really good in a dress."

"Steve," Frank hissed as heads turned toward them. "Lay off—"

"Look at her, Frank. Or him. Or her," Steve said calmly.

"I don't think he's had the surgery, but I could be wrong. Either way, the hands don't lie." He addressed himself to Pandora. "It doesn't matter to me—it's your business. I'm not prejudiced. Live and let live, that's what I always say. I just don't like that you're misrepresenting yourself to my buddy here. And if you're not upfront about something like this, makes me wonder what else you're hiding."

As usual, his voice was loud. Conversations within a five-foot radius stopped.

"I assure you, Mr. Hughes, I'm not hiding anything," Pandora said calmly. She gestured over her slender body in her tight blue suit. "And I'll offer you no further proof than what you see."

Frank couldn't stop himself from staring at the hand that curled around the champagne flute. The nails were long and perfectly manicured into red talons . . . but Steve was right: the fingers were a little thicker and more masculine than many women's hands. His eyes swept over the rest of her. If this woman was really born a man, she was the most polished transgendered person he'd ever seen.

Steve laughed. "Well, if you're counting on my being too much of a dude to make a grab for 'em, you might be in trouble. Normally, I try keep my distance from other guys' nuts, but if it'll help my buddy Frank, I'm willing to take one for the team—"

Pandora lurched away from Steve's outstretched paw. If she was aware that the exchange had attracted an audience, nothing in her expression betrayed her: it remained as flat and icy as always. "Let me see if I can find Ari," she said. "It was nice seeing you, Mr. Young. But next time, I suggest you leave your pet gorilla at home."

The crowd parted like the Red Sea as she strode toward a door that must have led to the private parts of the house. Once she was out of sight, soft speculative noises rose around them. Frank's cheeks felt hot with the glare of dozens of inquisitive eyes.

"What was that about?" Frank hustled Steve off the verandah and down toward the pool. There were people here, too, scattered on comfortable patio furniture that circled a fire pit. More lights twinkled around them as the moon met the water in the distance.

"Calling it like I see it," Steve answered simply.

"But here? Now?"

"Why not?" Steve took another gulp of champagne. "Look, I know that was bad—"

"Yeah, Steve, that was bad. Very bad," Frank muttered. "And what if you're wrong?"

"Nah. I'm not wrong. I'm sure of that. One of the guys in our real estate office made the transition. From male to female. This was a few years ago, when the market was white hot and we were all making money hand over fist. It's an expensive thing, you know?" Steve stared at the water. "And it takes years. It was weird watching him go through it. The stages and all that. But by the time it was done, if you hadn't known he was a man before, you wouldn't have. He had that same slight, feminine build—just like your friend Pandora over there—and a high voice. The only thing that gave him away at the end was his hands and his feet—both just a little big for a woman." He paused. "He ended up quitting and moving to New York. He said he wanted to start over where no one knew anything. His name was Martin. Changed it to Marci and that was that. Wild, huh?"

"Okay, Steve, but even if you're right, why did you have to do that? What good do you think it did to humiliate her like that—"

"I know these kinds of people, Frank," Steve said quietly. "Trust me. I know them. They're sharks. Any kind of weakness they can find, they'll exploit. See, your problem is you think everyone's like you: basically honorable. Basically honest. But I'm telling you, that is not this game. In this game, you have to throw them off balance. You have to let them know you know how to play. And then play hard, like your life depends on it. Because in a way, it does."

"I don't know, Steve—"

"She went off to get her boss man, didn't she? You think she would have done that if I hadn't shaken her up a bit?" He shook his head. "Nah. They'd leave you sitting here until they got good and ready. Wear you down. Trust me, Frank. It's High Pressure Sales 101. It's a game."

"So what do I do now?"

Steve shrugged. "Nothing. Let him do his dance. Make no commitments and no promises. Wait him out."

They sat together staring off at the immensity of the ocean until Frank spoke.

"Steve, if you were me—if you had this 'power,' for lack of a better word—what would you do?"

Steve sighed. "I don't know, man," he told the moon. "I've been asking myself that since it first happened. At first, I thought it was cool. I was even a little jealous. But the deeper we get into this thing . . ." He shook his head. "Just seems like it might be better if it'd just go away. But if that can't happen, I guess there's nothing wrong with making some money on it. I just don't know if these are the right people," he said in a softer voice. "I mean if this ReGenesis is interested, chances are good others would be. Maybe we could—" He stopped, and a wide smile spread across his face. "Well, look at this. Is that him?"

Frank turned. Ari Kousakas stood on the verandah stairs, his head tilted to better hear whatever Pandora was saying. He was dressed in another pair of perfectly tailored jeans and a crisp white shirt with a skull and a sword sketched on the lower right panel in rich black ink. The youthfulness of the shirt and the long gray ponytail swinging at the old man's back created an odd contrast.

"Yeah, that's him."

"He's pretty hip for an old guy," Steve observed.

Pandora stood just behind him, her arms folded over her chest, her trim hip cocked to one side. Her lips were moving but other than that, her manner retained its frigid calm. If anything Steve said had shaken her, she had very quickly recovered. When she finished speaking, she turned and walked back into the house without even glancing in their direction. Ari, on the other hand, jogged toward them with a wide, wolfish smile pasted on his tanned face.

"Frank!" he said happily, stretching out his hand as though Frank were a long-lost son. "I did not know you had arrived already!" He offered the same cheerful expression and glad hand to Steve. "And this must be your friend, Mister . . . ?"

"Hughes. Steven."

"Very nice to meet you, Steven. May I call you Steven?"

Steve nodded and crossed his arms over his chest, taking his feet wide apart like a soldier at rest. With his buzz-cut hair and broad frame, he almost looked like he could have been Frank's security personnel. Ari cut his eyes between them, calculating for a silent second.

"I didn't realize there were going to be so many people here—"

"Not so many," Ari said, drawing up one of the chaise lounges. "These are just a few people I pulled together at the last minute I thought you'd like to meet. You brought some business cards, yes? They are the people who'd love Xtra Travel—"

"X-Treme Travel," Frank corrected. "But I thought we were going to talk some more about ReGenesis and the offer you made me the other night."

"Sure, sure. There's plenty of time to talk—and much to talk about. But not tonight. Tonight's just for getting to know each other a little better." He squeezed Frank's shoulder as if they were old buddies. "Have some drinks. Chat a bit in a more relaxed setting. Get a feel for the circles you will be moving in when you join us. Just relax and enjoy—"

"Sure," Steve interjected. "Frank doesn't mind a little schmooze. But just to let you know, we'll be talking to the folks at Dynagentex on Thursday."

"Steve—"

"No, Frank. It's only right to let Ari—you don't mind if I call you Ari—let Ari know that we're talking to the competition."

"I see," Ari said. "I understood us to be operating more . . . exclusively. I believe that might have been in our contract—"

"Signed under duress," Steve said calmly.

"Are you a lawyer, Mr. Hughes?"

"No. But I know plenty of them."

Ari measured Steve in silence. "Well," he said at last with determined bonhomie. "How very interesting. Come with me. There are people you should meet. Arnie Melchedesh is here. You know of him, Frank, yes?"

"Real estate developer, right?"

"He did the Sandy Beach Amusement Park and the Point Grove Shopping Complex." Steve sounded impressed in spite of himself.

"And he owns a couple of sports teams," Ari added vaguely, as though he couldn't be bothered with remembering which ones. "But most importantly, the Amazon is on his . . . what do you call it? Kick-the-bucket list. I told him earlier that I knew just the person who could help him." He stood and Frank and Steve rose with him, following his lead back to the verandah.

"Arnie! Arnie!" he called. "Come here!"

It went on like that for another hour, moving through the clumps of guests, being introduced to one power player after the other, with Ari at Frank's side. "Any experience in the world you want to have—this is the man," Ari repeated again and again, thrusting Frank into the spotlight like his own personal project.

Steve followed them, saying little and watching everything as Frank's pants pockets filled with the business cards of the rich and powerful. Once, when Frank glanced at his friend's face, he read just the hint of the conversation they would have in the car. Steve was impressed . . . and still very much on his guard.

But as the evening went on, Frank found himself enjoying it more and more. In the center of a circle of people who could buy and sell him—and XT—many times over, he found himself telling the story about his trip to the Arctic, then reliving his botched attempt at Mt. Everest. He was urged to relate the story about the boa constrictor that had nearly capsized his raft on the Amazon and the difficulties of navigating the Yangtze in China. He barely noticed when Ari slipped away from them.

Finally the conversation shifted and his audience began to drift away. Frank looked around him. "I've had enough."

Steve nodded. "Hey, I've heard these stories before. I had enough an hour ago."

"I guess we should bid our host good night. Where'd he go?"

Steve shrugged and fell into step with Frank as he headed for the exit. "Did you really call Dynagentex?" Frank asked.

"No, but you can bet I will. First thing tomorrow morning."

"Yeah, that's probably smart," Frank agreed. "Thanks, man."

"No thanks needed, brother. There's your host. By the door with that hot brunette—"

Her back was to him, so all Frank saw was a slender figure in sapphire blue and a mane of long dark hair. But it looked familiar; that body . . . that hair. He recognized the curve of her hips and the slope of her shoulders . . .

"Jackie?" he murmured to himself as confusion filled his features.

She turned, her eyes blazing with the joy of welcome surprise. "Frank! What are you doing here?" she asked as she stepped into his arms and kissed his cheek.

"I—" Frank began, but Ari interrupted.

"You know each other, I see."

Jackie shot the older man a wary look and nodded. "Yes, Ari. I know Frank. The question is how do *you* two—"

"I'm considering investing in Mr. Young's travel company," Ari said, lying as quickly and as easily as if the words were true. "You remember. My venture capital business? Always looking for the next big moneymaker. What do you think, Athena?"

Athena? Frank's head swiveled between them in confusion. Jackie grimaced at the name but did not correct him. Instead, she frowned warily. "What are you up to?"

"What do you mean?"

"You know what I mean! This isn't going to work, Ari. I don't like it and I won't let you use Frank like this—"

Use me? For just an instant, Frank thought she knew about the deal on the table between himself and the older man, and the strange power that lived in his loins. But in the next instant, he was sure she was talking about something else.

"Use him?" Ari exploded indignantly.

"What else would you call it?" Jacqueline's voice was hard and angry and this time, when she glanced at Frank, he thought he saw an undercurrent of fear in her eyes.

"I don't understand," Ari and Frank said simultaneously.

"Frank is the man I was telling you about earlier. The one I wanted to bring with me but he couldn't make it tonight?" She sighed. "But you already knew that, didn't you? What, are you having someone follow me again? Have you bribed another one of my employees at Life SPAAN? Or are you tapping phones again—"

"Athena—"

"My name is Jacqueline—"

"Ridiculous," Ari spat, shaking his head vehemently. "You were named for a Greek goddess, not some French whore—"

"I'd rather be named for a French whore—"

"And as for these accusations," Ari shouted over her, "I promise you, I have done nothing. I would never—"

"Well, you've certainly done it before. And you'll do it again. You don't know how to do anything else—"

As Frank looked from Jackie to Ari and back to Jackie, he saw the hint of something familiar in the shape of the eyes and the curve of the chin. *Oh shit*, he thought, just as Jackie reached for his hand.

"Frank, I don't know what he's told you, but Ari Kousakas is my father—at least in name. And Ari, Frank is the man I've been seeing. The man I met on that plane."

Frank felt cold—as though someone had dunked him in water and hauled him out of it in the middle of snowstorm. When he raised his eyes to Ari's face, the older man was showing every one of his sharp white teeth, and Frank had the sick feeling that Jackie had just given the man the very thing he'd needed to lock him into a deal with ReGenesis for the rest of his life.

Jackie yanked his arm. "Come on, Frank. Let's get out of here."

"I can't believe him. I just can't believe him!" Jackie seethed to the night air.

"That guy's your father?" Frank couldn't process it. What was coincidence? What was design? Nothing felt real or sure, not even Jackie herself. He shook his head, trying to clear it, trying to make his brain compute what to say next, what to do. "That guy's your *father*?"

"Yes. That's my father." Even in her heels, Jackie was walking fast, striding down the driveway as though she couldn't put distance between herself and the occupant of the house fast enough.

"B-but . . . your last name is Noble," Frank stammered. "And why was he calling you Athena?"

"I took my mother's maiden name after they divorced—and I use my middle name—Jacqueline—not my Christian name, Athena. I was fifteen and I already knew I didn't want to go through life being known as 'Ari Kousakas's daughter' or saddled with some name out of Greek mythology. I wanted to stand on my own. And—and—I needed to distance myself from him. Even then I knew I had to."

"But—"

"I could tell you so many horror stories. So many stories of how he's interfered in my life. In my relationships. Corrupted things that started out so good. And that's not even the worst thing . . ." Her voice broke. Frank reached for her but she pulled away from him. "There's more . . . and you should know it all. I should have told you before, but I hoped—I *hoped*—oh, never mind what I hoped. It doesn't matter now," she said, as more tears slid down her cheeks. "I—I can't talk about this now. I—I just—can't. Can you meet me tomorrow? At Life SPAN? Three o'clock?"

"Yes, but—"

"I'm sorry, Francis. I-I just can't be here anymore—"

And before he could stop her, she ran down the driveway. He heard an engine and then nothing, except the occasional plink of distant piano music and the sporadic burst of laughter from the house behind him.

Steve lay a heavy hand on his shoulder.

"Guess you'll be telling Kousakas to go to hell and booking a ticket to the Amazon tomorrow," he said softly. "And I'll call Dynagentex. Gimme the keys, Frank. I'll drive."

CHAPTER

Sixteen

The flight to Lima departed at six p.m.

Frank tried to sleep, but gave up as the first light of gray dawn lit his window. He rose, grateful to trade the relentless circle of thoughts of Jackie, Ari and the nasty nest of coincidence and design in which he was enmeshed for more practical concerns.

He stumbled down the stairs to his father's study, seated himself in the cracked leather chair and grabbed his cell phone. He Googled "Iquitos" and quickly jotted down the numbers for every tourist business, every government office and every guesthouse.

"Do you know José del Flores? He used to run Amazon tours for foreigners? With his daughter, Lucinda? I'm a friend."

By the time he finally abandoned the effort, it was after one p.m. in San Diego and other than being even more deeply frustrated than before, Frank had accomplished little. He'd reached the mayor's office, the police, a small newspaper and several of the shops in Iquitos. No one had been willing to answer his questions. He gained only one piece of useful information.

"It was a rooming house. A place for the jungle tribes," Frank explained. "The woman's name was Swati—"

"Ah, I recall that place. She put up quite a fight."

"A fight? Why?"

"They moved her out—nine or ten years ago. There is a Holiday Inn there now."

"Where did she go?"

"To the jungle," was the nonchalant reply.

All roads led to the same conclusion. He had no choice: he had to go.

In the hall closet he found his rucksack, soft nylon with wide straps, a metal frame and dozens of zippered pockets. Ideal for carrying as much gear as possible on a long hike. Frank set to work quickly packing boots, extra socks, rain gear, his headlamp and everything else he could think of that might be needed on an extended trek through the rainforest.

His phone buzzed. Frank reached for it absently.

"Frank, Frank, Frank . . ." Ari chided him. "What are you doing?"

"What are you talking about?"

"You think you can just leave town now? Without so much as a word of 'goodbye' to me?"

"How did you know about that?"

"I make it my business to know about the people who are important to me. And you are very important to me. Call it off, Frank."

"What are you talking about?"

"You just a made an airline reservation. To Lima. I don't know what or who is in Lima, Frank, but I do not want you to go. Not when we were just getting to know each other—"

"You can't stop me from going."

"Oh, but I think I can." His voice dripped with menace. "Call it off, Frank. All of it."

"Just what are we talking about, Ari?" Frank demanded. "The trip? Jackie?"

"You are not going to Lima, Frank. And I'm very interested in what your friend Steve is up to. I really think you should tell him it's ReGenesis or no one, do you understand me? You will stay here and work with me. In time, I believe you will tell me just what it is that is in Lima that you are so desperate to reach. Yes, I think with the right . . . shall we say 'inducements,' you will tell me all about it. For now, put down your backpack—"

"You can't stop me from going, Ari—"

There was a short pause on the other end of the line before Ari said softly, "Yes, Frank . . . I think I can. In fact, I'm certain that I can. I think now it is *you* who underestimates *me*, Frank Young. Pandora will drop by tomorrow morning. Early. Let us say eight a.m.? She will bring the contract and you will sign it."

"I won't be here, Ari. I'm leaving tonight."

"You will be here. And you will sign, do you understand me? Soon, you will realize there really isn't any other option

... unless you're willing for the people you love to suffer for your mistakes. See you soon, Frank."

The people you love ...

Jackie.

Frank dropped the rucksack and ran.

"Are you all right?"

Her eyes were haunted, worried shadows set in the pale skin of her face, but she nodded, confusion puckering her brow. "Yes, why wouldn't I be? You're early, Frank. Something's wrong. What is it?"

It was the first time he'd been in her office. Somehow, he'd been expecting something larger and more lavish—not the cramped and cluttered rooms he found himself in right now. In fact, it closely resembled his own space—except it had windows. Filing cabinets and banker's boxes lined the narrow halls and there was a large whiteboard on which someone had drawn a red thermometer under the words "Population Sustainability 2013 Fundraising Initiative." Only the bulb of the thermometer had been colored in. There was a clock on the wall just behind it—one of those big black industrial ones that Frank always associated with high school classrooms. It read 2:25 p.m.

"Ari called me. He said something ... cryptic about making the people I love suffer—" He pulled her into his arms. "After last night, I thought he meant you. But you're okay."

"He threatened to do something to drive me out of your life if you didn't sign your company over to him, didn't he? I know he did, so don't bother to lie."

"He made some noises to that effect, yes. But it won't work because—"

"No, it won't work, Frank. I don't care what he does, or what he says or what he thinks! He's not going to break us up! He can't just move people around like chess pieces! He can't just buy whoever and whatever he wants—"

"Jackie," Frank interrupted. "First let me tell you—"

"No," Jackie continued angrily. "Let me tell *you*. I hadn't spoken to him in years. You know why? It wasn't just how happily he was willing to crush any competition he had in business—and I mean *crush*. I've seen him shut down entire companies, putting hundreds of people out of work. I've watched him fire loyal employees without so much as a 'thank you' because it served his purposes. And maybe that's just how business works; I don't know. I just know I never liked how happy it made him, almost as though he enjoyed it. And I could even overlook the things he's done to me—following me, hiring people to infiltrate this foundation to spy on me, paying guys to date me so he'd have information on what I was doing and where I was—"

"He did *that*?"

Bitterness laced her laughter. "Yes. Yes, more than once. In fact . . ." She paused, seeming to debate with herself before continuing. "I always suspected that Jacob—the guy I just broke up with—was one of my father's spies. And, I'm almost certain he had someone follow us to Tijuana after I broke up with him. I'd bet money that those thugs who jumped us were hired by whoever he sent to keep an eye on us—"

"Come on, babe. That sounds crazy. You don't really think—"

"You think I don't know how ridiculous that sounds? But there's a pattern, Frank. Every time I've dated a man who wasn't on Ari's payroll, something strange happens. Almost like . . . like he's trying to test them. Or scare them away. I know, it sounds crazy. Paranoid. If I were listening to me, I'd probably think that I was some kind of nutcase."

The image of the three teens on that dark Tijuana street replayed in Frank's mind.

He said not to hurt them, just scare them, the youngest had said like a warning. At the time, Frank had been sure he was speaking of his rival in the club that evening—the mustached man who had wanted to dance with Jackie. But now, he wasn't sure. After all, just hours before, he'd been with Pandora—and he didn't even know how he'd gotten from there to Jackie's building or what had happened to him in the interim.

"You don't sound like a nutcase, Jackie," he said slowly. "Unfortunately, it's starting to make sense."

She quirked an eyebrow at him, but Frank shook his head, signaling her to go on.

"But he's just done so much, so many things that—I stopped calling him 'Dad' when I was a teenager. We've had as little to do with each other as possible for years—especially after I started this foundation four years ago. He hates it. He thinks it's stupid. A waste of energy, time and money. Tried to blackball us with a bunch of powerful donors—"

"He did that?" Frank asked incredulously. "To his own daughter?"

"Daughter? Frank, I was *embarrassing* him. Again. Like I did when . . ." She stopped, evasion creeping into her tone again. "This—this is all a really long story, Frank, and . . .

parts of it are just really hard for me. Even after all these years..." She paused again. "Last night he said things have changed, but I'm afraid to believe it."

"What did he say?"

"He said—a bunch of crazy stuff." Jackie recited the words emotionlessly like the computerized voice on Frank's cell phone. "He said he's on the path to immortality. That he won't get any older and that if was I waiting for him to die, to forget it. He said it was my last chance to earn his forgiveness, before he stopped the hands of time, or some other such nonsense. He said that he would like to reconcile with me because he has no other children. At least no others who are still alive."

Still alive? Frank frowned.

"I told you: I had a little brother once," Jackie continued quietly. "Half brother, really. Zander. His mom was Ari's second wife, Vanessa. He was born when I was nine. He would be twenty now if..."

For a moment, she stared at the top of her desk as though she'd never seen it before. Frank longed to reach for her, but he sat still, waiting, letting her unwind the story in her own way.

"Zander had Down syndrome. It was pretty clear from the time he was a baby that he wasn't going to be running the Kousakas empire. Ari didn't want to have anything to do with him. He sued the obstetrician who delivered him, shut down the group practice and ruined all the doctors. He divorced Vanessa and did his best to pretend as if Zander had never been born at first. But Zander had a way of making people love him. He wore Ari down with his unquestioning love for him. I never saw Ari look at any of us with as much genuine affection as that kid. Such a sweet spirit . . ." She paused. "Anyway, about eight years ago when he started ReGenesis, I don't know how he got it into his head, but he decided that the work the scientists were beginning to do with genetics could 'fix' Zander and so—"

Frank understood in a sudden blinding flash of horror. "No," he muttered. "He didn't—"

"Of course he did," Jackie said softly. "He wanted his son . . . he wanted his son to be a scientific guinea pig. He sued for custody, but Vanessa resisted. She hired lawyers, but by then she knew that the law probably couldn't protect her. She was planning to take Zander and run—as far away as possible. But before she could finalize her plans, Zander disappeared. The police said he was just another teenaged run away. But he wasn't and we all knew it. Zander was chronologically twelve—but more like a five-year-old mentally. He wouldn't have run away. It just wasn't in his mind to do something like that—even if he knew how. But—but—he would have gone with Ari. If Ari had asked him to go anywhere, anywhere at all, he would have gone. He loved him. He didn't understand why the rest of us were so suspicious of him."

A few tears wet her lashes, but she blinked them back and continued quickly, hurrying the tale along to its conclusion. "I was there the day Ari took him. I just didn't know there was a problem. I—I had just gotten home from a trip abroad. I was working with another nonprofit then, doing outreach at a school for young girls in Mali. I literally had just arrived and was on my way home when I noticed the time and I thought of Zander. He loved surprises. He loved coming out of his program at the end of the day and finding one of us there to greet him. See, usually he took a bus that dropped him right in front of Vanessa's. I knew he'd be thrilled and since they knew me there, it would be all right. So I drove over to the school—and I *saw* him, Frank. I *saw* him—"

"Saw who, Jackie? What did you see?"

"Ari. I saw Ari leading Zander away from the bus. I saw him. I didn't think anything of it—I didn't know about ReGenesis or the lawsuit. I also didn't know that Ari hadn't followed the rules and signed Zander out. I just saw them walking together and I remember thinking that it was good. That even if I couldn't seem to connect with him, maybe Ari finally found a way to let himself love Zander for who he was. I mean, Frank . . . they looked *happy* . . ." A tear rolled slowly down her cheek. "And that was the last time I saw Zander—the last time any of us saw Zander—alive. He was with Ari."

"But Jackie. Surely, the police—"

"I told the police!" Her eyes flashed with anger. "That I'd seen Ari there, though he denied it. He said he was nowhere near the school. Had an alibi—he was at his attorney's office signing the papers for the incorporation of ReGenesis! An alibi! Your son goes missing and you call your daughter a liar and produce your alibi and you let the kid's mother believe for years and *years*—and—and—"

"It's okay, Jackie," Frank interrupted. The ragged sound of her voice and the way she couldn't seem to stop shaking frightened him. "You need to take a deep breath now, okay? Please. I'll listen as long as you want—to anything you want to say. Just take it easy."

She nodded, swallowing hard as she forced a deep inhale down, then blew it out in a loud exhale.

"I—I—I'm okay. Besides, there's only a little more. Three years ago, Zander's body was 'discovered' in Los Angeles. There were needle marks all over him and the police thought he was a drug addict who overdosed . . . at least until the autopsy contradicted them. It didn't reveal the presence of any known drug. When I think about what he must have suffered . . ." She covered her face in her hands. "I haven't spoken to Ari since. I know he took Zander to ReGenesis. I know he died there. And a couple of months ago, I finally got the proof. A file. Zander's file from ReGenesis. Since then . . ." She swallowed hard. "Since then, I've been trying to work up the courage to send my father to jail."

"You're sure about this, Jackie? I mean, couldn't he have—"

"I'm sure," Jackie said firmly, her eyes finding Frank's at last. "If you see this file . . ." She sighed. "I don't know why I've hesitated. And there are so many other incidents. Things he did to my mother and her friends. He cheated on her, divorced her, found some loophole to keep from giving her more than the minimum of child support so she was always struggling financially—and all of that would have been fine, but it wasn't enough. He didn't want her anymore, but he didn't want her to be happy with anyone else, either. Somehow, every man who ever got close to her ended up in the hospital. Car accidents. Violent robberies. One guy 'fell' off a two-story balcony—or so he said. That was the last one. A guy named Nelson who worked with Mom and really only just came over a couple of times to help her with some repairs around her house. He recovered, thank God, but after that . . ." Jackie shook her head. "Mom got the message. She doesn't date anymore. She . . . she doesn't do much of *anything* anymore. She's too afraid of what Ari might do. She says she doesn't want to see anyone else get hurt. Of course, if you ask him about it, he'll deny it. He'll say he never did anything to anyone—and there's nothing wrong with his checking from time to time to 'see what Mom is up to.' That's how he puts it: 'I'm interested in what your mother is up to.' But there was no way all those 'accidents' were a coincidence—"

I'm interested in what your friend Steve is up to.

"Wait," Frank interrupted. "He said he was interested in what your mother was up to?"

"Yes." Jackie frowned at him in confusion. "I confronted him about it every time one of my mother's friends got hurt and he always denied any involvement. But he always knew about them. He'd always say that. That he took an interest in what she was up to. It's like the code phrase for—"

I'm interested in what your friend Steve is up to.

Frank grabbed his phone.

"Frank, what's wrong—" Jackie began.

Frank shook his head while the phone rang and rang and rang . . .

"Shit," Frank cursed, considering his next call. He could try Steve's parents—but his gut told him differently.

Eva answered on the first ring.

"Oh Frank!" It was obvious she was crying. "You have to come. You have to get here now!"

"What happened to Steve, Eva?" Frank demanded, even though with a part of his brain he already knew. He could see Ari's face in his mind and with everything Jackie had just said, there really was only one piece of the puzzle left to drop into place.

He stood up, reaching for his keys as Eva choked out the words.

"I'll be right there," he told her.

"What is it?" Jackie asked again.

"My friend Steve was in an accident. He's in the ICU at San Diego Holy Cross," Frank told her. "Your father called me an hour ago. He told me he had 'taken an interest' in what Steve was doing—Steve was setting up some meetings for me with some other companies—and that it was important for me to sign on with him and ReGenesis now. Or else."

Jackie frowned. "He wants you to sign on with ReGenesis—his genetics firm? Why? I thought you were talking to him about venture capital."

Frank took both her hands in his. "Look, babe. I have something, something Ari wants very much. Enough to hurt Steve for, just to get me to sign with him—"

"What? What is it, Frank?" Jackie demanded. "We're not talking about a travel business anymore, are we?"

Frank shook his head. "No. I just hope . . . I hope . . ." He smoothed her hair and kissed her. "I hope you'll understand. I've wanted to tell you but there just didn't seem to be a good time to do it—and I want more than anything to be with you, but I don't know how this can ever work. I can't ask you to wait for something that might not ever happen. But right now, right now before I say another word, there's one thing you've got to know: I love you, Jackie. I love you and I'll do anything to be with you—"

"Frank, what is it?"

"Eternal youth," Frank answered, and watched her face shift from concern to confusion.

"Eternal *wh-what*?" Jackie sputtered.

"I have a unique... power," he sighed. "It's a long story, Jackie, and I swear I'll tell you every word of it. But right now I've got to get to the hospital—"

"I'll go with you. You can tell me in the car."

"It started the day we met—on that trip to Boston," Frank began.

He drove as fast as he dared from her office on Coral Street through the city streets toward the hospital. More than once when he glanced in his rearview mirror he saw a small blue car either right behind him or a couple of cars back, keeping pace with them as they maneuvered through the city.

"There weren't that many girls in college—and not all of them were there. But the ones who were..."

He told her about Eva and the appearance of certain of his female classmates—the ones he'd had sex with. He told her about remembering the trip to the Amazon and the understanding that something had happened to him when he was around eighteen years old—something he might have comprehended more had he not suddenly been called home because his father lay dying.

"My father must have had an idea—I think he sent me there for that purpose—but I can't find anything in his papers, nothing in his letters that explains it even though I've turned the house inside out looking. And meanwhile... X-Treme was going under."

He paused again and again, waiting for her to interrupt him, to ask a question or express hurt or outrage, but she was silent. Her eyes never left his face—he could feel them even when he was focused on the road.

He pushed on, telling her about the crazy idea to sell his services to try to save XT and his friends. He sketched in the encounters with Carina and Roxy—omitting the most embarrassing details but leaving her with no doubts about what he'd done.

"That night outside your apartment?" he told her as he slowed to stop at a red light. The blue car was right behind him, but the driver was wearing sunglasses and a baseball cap and Frank couldn't make out his features—not even whether his pursuer was male or female. "I have no idea how I got there," he continued. "She—he—whatever Pandora is—drugged me. I guess that's how your father found out about me—"

"My father found you because of me," Jackie said softly. "Because Jacob was one of his spies . . . and when we broke up Ari wanted to know why."

Frank wanted to disagree, but he couldn't. She was probably right; they both knew it. "He came to see me the in the middle of the night and . . . well, the rest you know," he finished.

"So . . . you slept with these women, after we . . ." she began, then let the sentence drop.

"With Roxy, yes. I don't know what happened with Pandora. There wasn't any emotion involved; it was strictly business—"

"Does that make it better or worse, Francis?" she asked in a low voice.

Frank stopped talking. She turned toward the window and he couldn't read her expression at all when she said, "Go on."

"There's really not that much more," Frank muttered. "Just that I was going to turn Ari down and he knew it. And now Steve . . ." He couldn't finish the sentence. He folded his lips together and felt her slipping away from him in her silence, growing more distant with every breath she took.

"Eva is here? At the hospital?" she asked as they turned onto the grounds, the little blue car in hot pursuit.

"Yes," Frank said.

"And you said . . . you said you slept with her when you were twenty? You both were twenty?"

"Yes."

"And now . . . she's twenty . . . forever?"

Frank nodded, parking quickly. He glanced into the rearview mirror, but for the first time, the blue car was nowhere in sight.

"And if you and I had sex . . . then I'd be . . ."

"Unless we never . . . unless we weren't—"

"But what about condoms or—"

"I used them with most of these women," Frank muttered. "It didn't seem to matter." He sighed. "You hate me, don't you? You think I'm—"

She opened the car door suddenly. "I don't hate you," she told the parking lot's black asphalt. "And I think your friends need you."

"Frank!" Steve's mother, Irene, popped out of a black chair made of hard plastic in a dull gray alcove outside the hospital's ICU and threw herself into his arms. "I'm so glad you're here," she sobbed into his neck. "I'm so glad . . ."

Steve's father, Arthur, stood up slowly, leaning hard on

a wooden cane he'd been using since a recent hip replacement. He looked haggard, the skin on his cheeks sagging in deep jowls on his face. He took a shuffling step toward Frank like an old man—far older than his sixty years—then pulled both Frank and his wife into his arms with a surprisingly firm embrace.

"He's tough. He's going to pull through this," Steve's father murmured into the hug.

"What happened?" Frank asked, shepherding Irene and Arthur back into their seats.

Irene pressed a wad of tissue to her eyes. "We don't know. Some man—a guy just passing by—"

"Good Samaritan, if you ask me," Arthur mumbled, interrupting.

Frank knew well the tag-team way Steve's parents had of speaking. As though it were a natural by-product of thirty-five years of marriage, they finished each other's sentences as a matter of course. Every conversation he'd had with them for decades was split between the two of them. "If he hadn't stopped, God only knows—"

"He found him just lying there all . . ." Steve's mother's voice broke. "Banged up and bleeding. The police thought someone jumped him—"

"More than one person, likely," his father added in the same low mutter.

"For his wallet—"

"It was gone."

"Phone, too."

"Poor boy was finally making some money again. Been a hard few years for him on the business side." Steve's father blinked rapidly, but a tear rolled down his face in spite of his effort. He flicked it away and continued, shaking his head. "Might have been a robbery, but . . . seems so vicious. Like it was personal, you know?"

Frank's gut constricted in a fresh wave of guilt.

"But who would do such a thing?" Irene moaned, burying her face in her hands. "And why?"

"He's hurt real bad, Frank. Real bad . . ."

"It'll be okay, Irene." Frank hugged her shoulder, hoping he was right. They'd been like his own parents in many ways, and he wanted nothing more than to be as much comfort to them as a real son. "Like Art said, he's tough." He glanced at Jackie, but she was studying her hands, intense pain marking her features. He wanted her near him—he *needed* her near him—so badly his body hurt. But she wasn't ready. Frank closed his eyes and squeezed Irene tighter. "You know Steve. He's not going out like this. It's not his style."

"I know, I know . . ." Irene tried to laugh, but her voice choked and broke, crumbling into sobs again. "Steve's too—too—too much of a c-c-character for this kind of thing, isn't he?"

"I guess it could happen to anybody. That's the kind of crazy world we're living in. What doesn't make sense is where," Arthur said.

The hairs on the back Frank's neck lifted with premonition. "Where?"

"Way out in Bel Mar. Not far from where that DNA place is. What's it called—"

"Dynagentex." Jackie's voice was hollow and faint and there were tears in her eyes. His own pain and guilt rose relentlessly in his throat.

"Dynagentex," he whispered.

"This is my fault . . . I should have sent him to jail. A long time ago—"

"No, it's mine, Jackie. It's my fault—" He reached for her, but she shook her head and turned away.

"You know it?" Arthur asked, looking from Frank to Jackie in surprise.

"Steve was doing some research for me," Frank explained in a low voice that shook in spite of his best efforts to control it. "It's a long story. Not for right now. This is Jackie Noble," he began as the Hugheses' eyes strayed in her direction. "She's my . . ." He stopped.

My love, my life, my future . . .

Those were the words he wanted to use but he was no longer sure he had any right to them. Frank lowered his head as emotion overtook him, too powerful to suppress. Arthur rubbed his shoulder, the gesture filling the gap more eloquently than any words the man might have said.

"I'm very, very sorry." Jackie crept closer to them and took Irene's hand.

"I don't know what you and Frank think you've done, but as far as we're concerned, you've got nothing to be sorry for—either one of you," Arthur said gruffly. "Unless you belong to the gang of thugs that roughed my boy up, it's not your fault—"

"Of course it's not their fault! Neither of you would ever—"

"Can I see him?" Frank's voice was loud and rude, but he couldn't help it. Their forgiveness and trust was worse than anything Ari might have planned for him and Frank couldn't bear another second of it.

"Only one visitor at a time. Eva's with him again now, poor girl," Arthur said. "She's the one who called us. She got worried when he didn't answer his phone. Started calling the hospitals."

"He must have told her where he was going because—" Irene began.

"She knew something was wrong," Arthur finished. "Those two are closer than peas in a pod. Never saw him change so much so fast for any other girl before—and all for the good, too—"

Frank's head whipped toward him.

"Steve . . . and Eva?"

"Don't you like her?" Irene asked. "She *is* a little young for him—I'll give you that—but she's gotten Steve to do something I wasn't sure anyone could."

"What's that?" Frank asked in amazement.

"Got him to grow up," Arthur replied.

"Surely you noticed?" Irene continued. "When he cut his hair and started tucking in his shirts I said to Papa, 'This girl's the one,'" Irene said.

"She sure did." Arthur's eyes strayed to Jackie and then back to Irene, and Frank understood that whatever sign they'd seen in Steve, they'd found in Frank as well.

"And now, right when he finally found the right woman, to have something like this happen!" Irene began to cry again. "And poor Eva! That little girl is just—just—"

"I'm all right."

Eva was dressed sloppily and haphazardly in a pair of faded jeans and a sweatshirt that had seen better days. Her hair was pulled up into a high ponytail and rings of black mascara pooled around her red eyes. She wasn't all right:

she looked worn and scared, impossibly young, vulnerable and strangely beautiful all at the same time.

"Frank," she said, stepping into his arms and pressing her face into his shoulder. "You're here. Thank God."

There wasn't anything he could do but hold her and for a long moment, he did just that, rocking her gently in his arms as her slender shoulders shook with sobs.

"How is he?" he asked when she'd calmed down a little.

"About the same. Unconscious. They say there's head trauma. The next twenty-four hours are critical. He'll either wake up or . . ." She raised her eyes to Frank's face and tried to smile. "I bet you're surprised that I care so much . . . I guess *I'm* surprised that I care so much," she added. "But I guess it's not the first time I said one thing and felt another . . . Is this Jackie?" Eva asked, stepping out of his arms and nodding toward her. Jackie let go of Irene's hand and stood up.

Frank nodded. "She knows everything. I told her on the drive here—"

The women studied each other silently, one blond and slight, the other tall and dark-haired. Seconds ticked by, heavy and weighted with significance.

"Twenty . . ." Jackie whispered at last. "Forever?"

Eva nodded once, a slow, sad tilt of her head that was more eloquent than any words she'd ever spoken.

Jackie's shoulders sagged. Defeat, complete and entire, registered in her eyes. She staggered backwards, reaching for the wall like a crutch. Instinctively, Frank moved toward her, but Eva stepped between.

"You should go see him," she said abruptly. "We'll wait for you—"

"Yes, Frank," Jackie said. "You should go. Your friends need you." She pulled her handbag higher on her shoulder. "And I need to go. There's something I need to do. It won't make this right, but maybe I can stop it from happening again."

"Jackie..." he began.

"Please, Frank. Don't—"

"What about us...?"

"I can't do it, Frank. I just can't... do this. Please... take care of yourself, okay? Don't let—don't let him corrupt you. Goodbye," she murmured.

CHAPTER

Seventeen

"Frank."

He squinted at the bright fluorescent hospital light in a moment of confusion. He didn't remember falling asleep, but his body insisted on a victory in the ongoing battle between it and his mind.

"Is there news? Did he wake up?" he croaked, his voice hoarse with fatigue.

Eva stood over him, clutching a Styrofoam cup of coffee. She looked like he felt—something beyond exhausted—but there was also a glint of firm determination in her face.

"Not yet, but he will. The docs kicked me out. They're running some more tests. Said it would take a couple of hours."

Frank nodded. He stood up slowly, his limbs feeling like they had been pinned into contortions after hours in the hard plastic waiting-room chairs. Eva stretched the coffee cup toward him.

"Want some?"

Frank accepted the cup and gratefully took a long draught. It was hot, bitter and black, more like hot tar than coffee, but the acrid taste tasered sleep to the farthest corner of his mind.

"Thanks," he muttered.

"No, thank *you*. For being here," Eva said quietly. "And for helping me get Irene and Arthur to go home. Even after he wakes up, it's going to be a long recovery. Neither of them is particularly strong—"

"I know," Frank murmured, remembering how vital Irene and Arthur had been when they first welcomed him as grief-stricken teenager into their home. Somehow, as the days had slipped into months and the months into years, they had gotten grayer and slower. It seemed like it was taking Arthur forever to recover from his hip replacement; Irene sometimes lost focus these days. Frank suspected that was one of the reasons Steve had been happy to have Eva in his parents' home. She was another set of eyes, ears and helping hands.

"Frank," Eva said seriously. "I need you to do something for me."

"Anything."

"Go home." Eva's voice was firm and steady. "Please."

Frank shook his head. "No, it's okay," he muttered. "I'll stay. I don't want to leave you alone."

"I'm okay," Eva insisted. She chuckled sadly. "After all, I'm young. I'll bounce back faster than any of you. Besides, I'd kind of like to be alone for a while."

"I'll take a walk, then. Let you have some space—"

"No. Go home," she repeated. "After he wakes up I'm going to need you—I'm going to need all of you. But . . . I promise I'll call you as soon as anything happens. Now go."

"I can't." Frank paced away from her, hoping to hide the emotions cascading inside him. "Don't you see, Eva? This is *my* fault. If it hadn't been for me and this stupid curse—"

"Stop it."

Steve's bruised and swollen face and thickly bandaged skull appeared in Frank's memory like an ugly image from a war zone.

"We both know it's the truth!" he exploded. "He wouldn't be lying in there all banged up if it weren't for *me*. None of this would have happened if it weren't for *me*!" The look on Jackie's face just before she disappeared flared in his mind, extinguishing his anger with the heaviness of his defeat and despair. "I wouldn't blame you if you hated me," he muttered.

"Oh, come off it, Frank. Hate you?'" Eva's eyes were hard and wild. It was a look Frank recognized—he'd seen it in her face many times in the past and it was only in recent weeks that it had softened into something gentler. Now, her expression struck Frank as hard as a slap. "Do you really think that little of me?" Eva bit her lip, bringing herself under control with a few deep breaths. "Look," she continued in a low voice. "You know how I feel about your . . . power. It's definitely not everything it's cracked up to be—and it's got as many drawbacks as it does advantages—but let's get something straight, Frank Young. Whatever I think about your *power* has nothing to do with what I think of *you*. And you and I both know that Steve doesn't blame you. No matter what happens . . ." She swallowed hard, then continued with the same forceful determination. "No matter what happens, you have to know that Steve wouldn't have blamed you either. He'd blame whoever did this—"

"Eva. I *know* who did it." Frank lowered his voice as though the walls of the empty room had eyes and there were bugs built into the metal legs of the chairs. "I know who did it and you do, too. Ari Kousakas wants me. He wants me to be his eternal youth experiment and he wants to make sure that I know he's not going to take no for answer. He all but admitted he'd do something like this if I didn't sign an agreement to supply him with my . . . stuff . . . until he's made every kind of drug and procedure he can make a dollar on. He'd think nothing of killing Steve—or you—or anyone who stood in his way—if I don't agree to do exactly what he wants."

Eva sank into the nearest chair. The coffee sloshed a bit, wetting her hand, and she hissed as the hot liquid made contact with her skin.

"So what are you going to do?"

"I don't know. Ari's dangerous. I don't want to have a thing to do with him. I was planning to leave for the Amazon tonight—try to see if I can find someone there who can help me undo this. Track down Lucinda. But he already knew all about it. He called me to say I wasn't leaving and then made sure I didn't." Frank glanced at his watch and sighed. "The flight left hours ago."

"Get another one. Go. Run, Frank. Run as far and as fast—"

"How far am I going to get? He's got someone following me. Somehow he knows about everything I do—the minute

I do it. I don't know if he's bugged the house or the car or—"

"Your cell phone," Eva said. "Remember how you lost it after that afternoon with that woman? And he brought it back to you with the money. I bet—"

As soon as he lifted the battery, Frank saw it: a slim disc of metal sprouting a couple of wires that disappeared into the inner works of the device.

"Shit," he cursed, smashing the phone on the chair's edge, then dropping it into a nearby trashcan. "Why didn't I think to check this sooner? *Fuck!*"

A nurse—or he might have been a doctor, Frank wasn't sure—appeared from around the corner.

"I'm going to have to ask you to keep it down or to move this conversation elsewhere," he said sternly, frowning at them.

"Sorry," Frank muttered. "I just . . . I'm sorry."

The man returned to the ICU. Frank paced back in forth, trying to dissipate his anger with the movement, but it wasn't working. His fist ached to connect with Ari's face, hard enough to draw blood.

"Frank." Eva's voice cut through the miasma of red emotion. "Look at me."

He couldn't. He didn't want to look into her eyes and see her forgiveness—not right now, not knowing that Steve might not recover, that Jackie was gone and the Ari would be looking for him in a matter of hours with his nasty contracts in hand and even more threats if he failed to sign.

"I've got to go, Eva," he told the floor. "I shouldn't be here. The longer I stay, the more danger I put you in. All of you. I've got to go back. To the Amazon. It's the only way. Goodbye, Eva."

He strode past her, walking fast but not running, too determined to stop, ignoring the soft wail of her voice as she called after him like a lost little girl.

He peeled out of the hospital parking lot, his tires spinning in the dark silence of the early morning hours. The deserted, bleak streets echoed Frank's state of mind. He sped through them with his windows down, letting the cold air slap his face as he tried to cool the fiery anger and searing pain burning inside him.

He had almost forgotten about the blue car, but there were so few cars on the road, it wasn't long before he noticed it again: the same little blue compact that had been on his tail what felt like a lifetime ago as he and Jackie drove to the hospital was there again. This time, the driver didn't bother to try to conceal that he was following, since there were so few cars on the road in the first place. He stayed a respectful distance behind him, but turned when Frank turned and stopped when Frank stopped.

Lose him.

Using what he remembered from a travel-writing gig a few years back on stunt driving, Frank jumped the red light, accelerating beyond the speed limit. The car kept pace. Frank punched the gas pedal harder, squealing around a corner, almost wishing for a police officer to pull him over. He imagined himself swinging on the cop, releasing some of the mounting fury building inside him.

"Take me to jail!" he heard himself screaming. "Take me to fucking jail!"

At least in jail he'd be out of Ari's reach. At least in jail he'd have the peace to think over his options, if he had any left.

But there wasn't a police officer. Frank careened through the streets, steadily increasing his speed, but the car kept pace: a distance behind him but always in sight, even as he peeled into his own neighborhood and slammed on the brakes in his own driveway. He tumbled out of the car, belligerent and ready for battle, but the driver hung back several driveways away from the house.

"What?" Frank bellowed up the cul-de-sac. "What? Now you're scared? Come and face me, motherfucker! You can only do your dirt in the dark? Come and face me! Even better, go tell your boss I said to go fuck himself. Tell Ari to come and face me and leave my friends alone!"

A window opened at one of the neighboring houses.

"Shut the fuck up, man!" a man bellowed into the night. "Or I'll call the cops!"

"Call them!" Frank hollered. "Fucking call them!"

But after a few more muttered curses and the words "drunk" and "loser," the window closed. Frank's pursuer's dark car backed slowly out of the cul-de-sac and disappeared, leaving Frank standing alone in his driveway, still ready to fight but completely without a foe.

Frank barreled furiously into the house, expecting the home he'd always known. But it, like everything else in his life, was irreparably altered.

It was clean.

Nothing was left of his father's clutter. The wood floors were bare and smooth and every surface was blank and sparse. The old curtains were long gone, leaving only the ancient blinds; the rug had been removed and discarded in

last week's trash. No dust, no papers, just the sad old furniture and the faint smell of disinfectant.
Ready to sell.

The irony of it might have been funny at any other time. But now with Steve's life in the balance, the situation aggravated the long suppressed rage in the pit of Frank's stomach. He raced up the stairs to grab his rucksack and go.

The sturdy blue hiker's pack rested against a neat row of banker's boxes—the only few remnants of the mountains of paper Frank had cleared that seemed to have anything to do with the Amazon. He'd been through them a thousand times already—shaken every book, paged through every notebook—and found nothing. Frank tossed the rucksack aside and grabbed them.

"Useless!" he screamed, dumping first one box and then another onto the floor. "My legacy! Fucking useless! You could have told me *something*, Dad!" he shouted, kicking the papers as if he could somehow hurt them. "Given me a clue, you know? I can't find that place again on my own! Or was that your grand plan: to die—"

His foot connected with the black plastic edge of his father's heavy circular Rolodex. The thing was a behemoth: a relic of a time before everyone kept their data in a cell phone or on a cloud in cyberspace—and more than once he'd almost thrown it away, then decided at the last minute to store it with the notebooks and papers. Time after time, he'd turned the wheel, lifting the rows of white cards attached to it: first *F* for *Flores*, then *J* for *José* and *L* for *Lucinda*, and then finally *D* for *del*—in a last-ditch hope that he'd missed something. And each time, his search had revealed nothing.

"Why did you have to make this so hard?" he shouted at the Rolodex, grabbing it. "You saved everything else. Where is the stuff I *need*?" he bellowed. "Where is it? Where?" he screamed as he sent it flying across the room. As it hit the wall, its black plastic frame shattered into shards and the white cards scattered around his room like snow.

He barreled out of the room and up the hall like a crazy bull, flinging open the door to his parents' bedroom. With a single furious sweep, he sent everything on the dresser onto the floor: the pictures, the hairbrushes and perfume bottles—everything his father had saved so meticulously. He opened the drawers, pulling out sweaters and skirts and slips that hadn't seen daylight since 1980. "Useless! Useless!" he screamed, tossing them aside like so much trash.

It wasn't enough.

He whirled toward the closet, grabbing racks of hangers and sending them and the clothes they held to the floor in heaps. "Junk! Nothing but junk!" he shouted. "Why did you leave me nothing but junk? Why—why—*why* did you leave me—"

Suddenly, he couldn't stand any more. The anger that had hurled him like a missile through the night evaporated, leaving in its place a deep, unbearable pain that shook the breath from his body. He sank to his knees, overcome by guilt, fear and a monumental, insupportable sense of loss. A dam of emotion burst inside him and he wept, his shoulders shaking with sobs.

"Why did you do this to me, Dad?" he wailed to the mountain of his parents' clothes. "Why? What am I supposed to do? How do I stop it? What was the point of sending me down there if you knew—you *had* to know—something like this would happen? What am I supposed to do *now*?"

Frank squeezed his eyes shut tight. If his father's ghost had floated into the room at that moment—if his mother had appeared before him as a wraith of light—Frank would have greeted the apparition with joy and not an ounce of fear. But nothing happened. The stillness and silence—the complete lack of anything like his father's presence—broke him down, and Frank surrendered to a grief so black and deep he doubted he would ever find its end.

He didn't know how long he sat there, weeping until his body couldn't produce another tear and his throat was raw. But little by little, the emptiness inside him was replaced by an urgent need to act. Before too long, it would be morning—and Pandora would come for him.

He inhaled, closing his eyes, summoning his determination, and then stood. His limbs shook, exhausted from the outpouring of emotion, but he wiped his face with the tail of his shirt and forced himself to think.

"All right," he muttered to the pile of clothes at his feet. "The Amazon. I have money—and now, I have nothing to lose. I might not find José or Lucinda—I might die in the jungle—but he won't get what he wants, Dad. I just want you to know that."

As he left the bedroom, he caught his reflection in the mirror. He'd seen himself after some pretty harrowing trips: after twenty-four sleepless hours on an airplane, after wild alcohol-fueled evenings, after a nasty bought of Avian flu—but to his own eyes at least, he'd never looked more depleted, more hopeless and more alone.

He needed one more thing, so he lurched down the stairs to the garage.

His revolver was in its usual position, hidden in a little case behind a panel that also held the circuit breaker box. He opened it quickly, inspecting the .44 Magnum sidearm he'd bought for self-defense on remote hikes where bears and other predators were factors.

Just in case, he thought, then grabbed the case and hurried back inside.

He tried not to think of Steve or Eva or of Jackie and the look on her face just before she ran away from him—probably forever. He even pushed down the desperation that motivated his every step. The important thing now was action. He had to find a way to the Amazon—a way that Ari couldn't track. Everything—every trip he'd ever taken and every story he'd ever written about travel—flipped through his brain like a computer accessing a database. Commercial airlines weren't the only way to reach South America. Little by little, a new plan formed in his brain.

His rucksack lay on the floor of his room among the litter of his father's notebooks and papers. The remains of the ancient Rolodex lay in a corner, the little white cards crumpled like dying butterflies on the dark blue rug. A deep dent in the old plaster the size of a dinner plate marked the place where the object had made contact with the wall, scraping paint away in its descent.

Frank had bent to stuff the gun into the rucksack when it struck him—a slender fragment of a movie image. A movie starring a French actress and Tom Hanks. When he'd first met Jackie, he'd thought they looked something alike . . .

He glanced back at the marks the Rolodex had left on the wall.

Odd dark marks shone beneath the chipped pale paint. Frank dropped the backpack and moved closer, scratching at the wall with a fingernail. Several more chips fell into his hand—enough for him to see that the marks were letters. Frank bent so close his nose nearly touched the wall's surface. In his father's tiny, spiky handwriting he read the words "legend of the eternal pool."

"Oh my God..." Frank muttered, barely able to contain his excitement as he scratched desperately at the wall, shaking away more paint—and found more words, but out of context and unfamiliar.

Right in front of you. See it differently...

His father's notes were written beneath the paint, right on the very walls of his room! It was straight out of *The Da Vinci Code*—and Frank marveled that he hadn't thought of it sooner.

"Thank you," he whispered, digging at the wall with his nails. Finding his hands insufficient to the task, he hurried back to the garage for tools—a chisel, a screwdriver and even a can of old paint stripper—and set to work.

Hours ticked by, his muscles cramped and tired, but Frank ignored time and discomfort. He stripped off his sweaty shirt and kept working until at last, he sank onto his bed and surveyed his work.

Beneath the paint, the details of the eternal pool were written in his father's script in indelible ink. The writing was small—as though he'd been writing on a piece of paper and not on walls—but there were words everywhere, some of it too small to read, in other places large enough to decipher, but all of it making it clear his father had written a full treatise on his find, then painted over it, making it impossible for any of the information to fall into the wrong hands. From what Frank had read as he removed the paint, his father had laboriously outlined the legends associated with the pool, carefully sketched maps and other drawings plotting its location, and laid out the stories of the indigenous people about its sacred power and its uses, giving credit to a "Dr. C. Amaru" for her contributions. More than once, José del Flores's name was mentioned.

He found only one passage that referred to a return to the pool:

> *The legends say that one can only take the waters once. To approach the pool twice angers the gods and any gifts bestowed upon the supplicant will be reversed. Depending on the benefits conferred—which, as we have stated, vary with the healing required by the supplicant—occasionally a second approach to the waters has resulted in death.*

It read like a warning, but Frank's fevered mind locked onto "any gifts will be reversed" and relief coursed through his body, cooling and warming him at the same time.

It can be done, he thought eagerly. *Thank God, it can be done.*

There was more—much more—and Frank knew he would read it all, but it was only that paragraph, the coordinates for the pool's location and digits of the phone number his father had recorded as being the best way to reach José del Flores, that he committed to memory.

His phone was gone—in a trashcan at the hospital—so Frank grabbed his camera and quickly documented everything he'd uncovered with the same careful detail his father had taught him on archeological digs. Pandora would be here soon—Frank was as certain of that as he was of the sun beginning to rise in the street outside. And while he had a plan to handle her, he knew it was just as important that his father's greatest discoveries remain secrets.

When he finished taking the pictures, he reached for a thick black marker. He drew heavy black blocks around the most critical details—the latitude and longitude of the pool's location, mentions of Iquitos and of José—and blotted out as much as he could of the legends of the pool's powers. But he was out of time. He gathered up his tools and hurried back out to the garage.

Two weeks ago, the garage had held gallon after gallon of old paint, dried up and making rust circles on the concrete floor. Now, there were only two half-full gallons—remnants from when Frank had repainted his boyhood room a few years ago. They'd have to be enough.

He rolled the paint on as quickly and neatly as he could, covering the ink easily enough, blending the paint into the nearby walls to keep from emphasizing one wall over the others. Another hour later, the only evidence of Frank's discovery was the smell of fresh paint.

Frank stashed his painting tools and hit the shower, removing his mother's ring and the packet of letters from the pockets of his khakis before tossing them on top of a pile of dirty clothes in his closet. It might be hours—possibly even days—before he would stand under clean, warm water again, so he took just a few minutes longer, letting the pulsing shower head wash away not only sweat and paint dust, but uncertainty and doubt as well.

This is going to work, he declared to himself. *I'm going to make it down there. I'm going to find the pool again. I'm going to reverse this thing and Jackie and I are going to start over,* he told himself as he slipped on his oldest pair of jeans and a lightweight long-sleeved shirt, and then wrapped his windbreaker around his hips. Like talismans against evil, he stuffed his mother's ring and the little cache into his pockets before grabbing his rucksack.

Downstairs, as the first light of morning was filling the room, he heard the phone begin to ring. At first, he instinctively reached for his cell, but of course it was in pieces and no longer operational. Frank grabbed the landline phone in the kitchen.

"Frank!" Irene's voice was excited and happy. "Steve woke up! He's got a long road, but the doctors think he's going to be okay!"

"I'm so glad," Frank said, a lump of gratitude rising in his throat as he blinked back the stinging wet relief that temporarily blinded him. "Tell him . . . tell him and Eva that I'll be over to see him as soon as I can. I have something I have to take care of first. I'm not sure how long it will take, but as soon as it's done, I'll be there, Irene. I promise."

He hung up and lifted the blinds, peering out into the cul-de-sac. The little blue car that had followed him home was parked a few houses up, but if there was a driver inside he was doing an excellent job of concealing himself.

It doesn't matter, Frank thought as scenes from *Home Alone* cued up in his mind. Thanks to all his recent efforts to clear the house, he knew exactly where to find the old fishing nets he and his father had once used on a trip to the Mediterranean. All of the pulleys and ropes that formed his mountain-climbing gear were neatly coiled like thick snakes on the wall, and he knew he had enough wire and motor oil to set up the mother of all tripwires.

None of it took very long. There was only one last thing to do and he was ready.

He let himself into his father's study. The bookshelves were almost completely empty, and except for his father's old desk and chair, the room could have belonged to anyone, but it was almost as if Frank could feel the man beside him. He grabbed his laptop and its carry bag, took a few sheets of white computer paper off the stack near the printer, then turned to survey the room one last time.

"Thanks, Dad," he murmured, feeling as awkward and ashamed as any kid called on the carpet for his misbehavior. "Sorry about the stuff I said before. I didn't mean it." Then he left the room, closing the door respectfully behind him just as he'd always done when the man was alive.

He paced back to the living room. Slowly, he pulled the old chain and widened the opening in the timeworn Venetian blinds—just enough for him to be able to see the street outside. Then, satisfied, he crouched down by the window just out of sight of anyone peering in, and using the backpack as a chair and the laptop bag as a table, spread out the paper and a pen and began to write.

Dearest Jackie,

By the time you read this—if you read this at all—I'll be far away. It's probably better if I don't tell you exactly where I'm going—but I can't keep this power or gift or curse or whatever it is any longer. It's a long shot and I know it, but while there's still a chance I can undo what was done, I have to try. Not just for you and me, but for my friends. For all of us. My effort may very well fail and if it does, you might not hear from me again.

This isn't your fault. It's mine.

After everything you told me—and what I have seen for myself now with what happened to Steve—I know Ari will stop at nothing to get what he wants. What he wants is me. I have to make sure that he doesn't get a thing. I'll do everything I can to keep him from following me but if he does, I'll protect my father's research with my life if necessary. If I can't reverse the power, I'll have to disappear.

The sound of an engine interrupted him and Frank glanced cautiously through the slats of the blinds in time to see a black sedan roll slowly up in front of his house. A moment later, two dark-suited men the size of linebackers emerged from the front of the vehicle, but the back doors stayed closed. The two men approached his front door and rang the bell like expected guests.

Frank looped his arms through the straps of his backpack as quietly as possible and slipped his laptop bag over his neck, stuffing Jackie's letter into the front pocket. He flattened himself against the wall like a piece of furniture, making himself completely still, soundless and invisible to the men outside.

The ring was followed by a knock and then after a few long seconds, a louder one. He heard the muffled sounds of voices as the two "muscles" sought further instructions from the brains inside the back of the limo. *Who is it?* Frank wondered. *Pandora, as Ari had promised? Or Ari himself? Both of them?*

Minutes ticked by. Frank's hamstrings protested, but he ignored them, staying focused and ready to spring. He'd have only a few seconds after the traps were released to sprint out the garage doors to his car.

Then he heard it—the thud of force against the back door and the groan of old wood giving up its resistance. With their third assault, the old door shattered, bursting off its hinges.

Frank held his breath. If they took the time to look, they might notice the wetness on the floor or the thin wire placed an inch above the threshold . . .

But in the next moment he heard the crash of bodies as the oil sent them skittering to the floor and the rattle of the old paint cans as the tripwire rocketed upward. Curses echoed from the kitchen as the netting dropped over his unwelcome guests, snaring them like fish.

Frank sprang across the room toward the garage entrance. In a moment he was in the sunlight and only a few feet from his car door.

"Hello, Frank."

He froze.

Pandora stood on the front lawn, her auburn hair loose on her shoulders and pair of sunglasses on her nose.

"You've laid a few traps, I see. I'll admit you are very resourceful, but—"

Frank didn't give her time to finish. He rushed at her at full speed, tackling the slender woman at full force. They hit the ground hard together, Pandora crushed beneath Frank's weight. She lay limp beneath him, stunned and winded.

"That's for Steve," Frank muttered through clenched teeth as he quickly pulled himself up off the ground.

The soft purr of the limo's running engine carried in the still of the early morning. An idea struck him and he sprinted toward the vehicle.

It was empty. Tony—or whoever had been the driver—was inside the house, covered in paint and struggling in fishing net. Frank opened the door quickly and removed the keys, pocketing them as he trotted away from his house with the rucksack on his shoulders and the laptop bag banging against his thigh.

The blue compact still sat where he'd last seen it: two doors up, hidden among the many cars on the street. Frank ducked, concealing himself among the minivans and sedans as he crept closer and closer.

The driver wore a baseball cap and baggy sweatshirt to cloak his body and big-framed sunglasses to hide his features. He was talking on a cell phone and apparently became more agitated as Frank, keeping low—lower than the car doors and out of sight—snuck around the rear of the vehicle and approached the driver's side door.

"He did what?" the driver said into his phone, reaching for the keys to turn the ignition. "On my way—"

Frank yanked at the car door with a roar an Army Ranger would have been proud of. He grabbed the driver by the front of his sweatshirt and slugged him as hard as he could—a sucker punch that landed solidly along the man's jaw and made Frank's knuckles ache from the impact. The man crumpled to the ground, unconscious—and his hat and sunglasses fell off his face.

Gregory—Jackie's hovering assistant—lay on the ground in front of him.

Another piece of the puzzle snaps into place, Frank thought as he dragged the kid out of the way and tossed his rucksack into the passenger seat of the blue compact. In another second, he'd turned the car's wheels and U-turned out of the cul-de-sac.

He kept his eyes on the mirror. He didn't seem to have a tail—at least not yet. But the car was too familiar to Ari and his minions for Frank to hold on to it long, so as soon as he had the opportunity, he abandoned it in an underground parking garage in Balboa Park and hurried up to the street. Another minute later, he'd hailed a cab and slid inside, stowing the awkward rucksack beside him like a traveling companion.

"Draper Airfield," Frank told the driver, sliding low in the backseat.

Once, before he started X-Treme, he'd done a piece on chartered air travel, interviewing the pilots at an outfit called Brightseat Flights whose base of operation was a hangar at Draper Field. That was at least five years ago, but Frank gambled they were still in business and that, for the right price, he could convince them to help him out.

"What's the matter? Cops after you?" The cabbie was a youngish-looking black man with his dreadlocks tucked into a knitted cap.

"No, my girlfriend," Frank lied, sliding still lower as the traffic whisked by them. "I want to duck out of town with my boys..."

"But if she finds out, she'll either be mad or want to go, too." The cabbie laughed. "I got you, bro. Don't worry about a thing."

CHAPTER
Eighteen

"Can't do it. At least not that fast." The pilot—Frank guessed that was who she was from her powder-blue flight suit and the confident way she spoke—shook her head. "Maybe before 9/11—but now. Even if I didn't already have a booking this afternoon, the soonest I could get international clearance..." She squinted her clear gray eyes—almost the exact same shade as the color of her hair—at him. "Maybe tomorrow morning?"

It was just after eight in the morning. Brightseat Flights was closed and although there were several charter companies based out of Draper Field, the only hangar open was one with the highly descriptive name "Elite Air Services" written in elegant black script outside on a gigantic sign over the door. If the name hadn't been clue enough, walking into the small lobby of comfortable couches, soft rugs, lamps and scented candles made it clear that the place catered to an upscale clientele. He wasn't surprised when the gray-eyed woman appeared. The place clearly had benefited from a woman's touch.

"Tomorrow morning is too late," Frank said with a sigh. Exhaustion gathered around him like a tight mask, pressing against his eyes and making it harder for him to breathe. It had been over a day since he'd slept well and adrenaline couldn't carry him much farther. He needed to rest . . . but he also needed to get out of San Diego and as close to Peru as possible. He closed his eyes, trying to decide the best thing to do, but now that he felt safer, both his body and his brain seemed to be saying *no más*.

"You okay?"

Frank nodded. He eased his rucksack off his shoulders and let it slide to the ground with a groan of relief. "I'm just trying to think. I need to get there as soon as possible."

The woman studied him maternally, taking in his backpack and hiking boots, the stubble ghosting his chin and the shadows under his eyes. "Hold it a second," she said, turning away from him to type a few strokes on a keyboard. "I'm checking Last Minute Charters."

"What's that?"

"It's a group of charter companies that share passengers and destinations. Say I've got a run to New York and a couple of extra seats," she explained, her eyes still on the computer screen. "And another pilot's going to Hawaii, but he's got a client who needs to get to New York—"

"Gotcha," Frank, said nodding.

"But no one's going to Lima," she said a moment later. "The closest South American locale is Panama City—"

"I'll take it," Frank sighed. "Thank you. Thank you very much."

Yes, he thought. *This might even be better than flying direct.* When Pandora and Ari came looking for him—and he was certain they would—the last thing they would expect was for Frank to take such a circuitous route. "Thank you—"

"Don't thank me yet. The charter company isn't flying out of San Diego. They're flying out of Miami in about five hours." She glanced at a large black chronograph on her wrist. "I can get you there, but we've got to leave as soon as I can get approval of the flight plan . . . maybe twenty minutes—and we'll have to take the Challenger 300. It's a heavier jet, big enough for ten people, but none of the smaller planes can make the distance without having to stop and refuel." She eyed Frank's average-Joe khakis, nylon laptop case and backpack. "It runs five thousand dollars an hour, so it's going to be about twenty-five thousand."

"Fine," Frank agreed. He opened the laptop case and counted out two stacks of hundred-dollar bills. "This should be enough, I think."

The woman eyed the money for a moment in silence. When she looked at Frank again, there was suspicion in her face.

"Do you always carry around that kind of money?" she asked warily.

"No," Frank said bluntly. "In fact, if you'd told me three weeks ago I'd be carrying this much cash, I would have laughed at you. Told you you were crazy. Told you if I ever got my hands on that kind of money, I'd be using it to charter a trip for my clients, not for myself." He shook his head.

"Just goes to show you how quickly things can change . . . and not always for the better."

Her clear gray eyes blinked at him, considering his words, parsing them for truth and meaning. When she spoke, her voice was soft.

"Are you in some kind of trouble, Jeff? I'm sorry. You look so much like my son, Jeff. He's a Marine. In Afghanistan right now and he's—" She folded her lips, shutting down the topic with a slight wince of pain. "What I mean is, do you need some help?"

"Just get me to Miami in time," Frank replied, looking around the small reception area. "And if you don't mind, is there a phone I can use?"

There was a buzz, followed by a click as the door separating the reception area from the office opened.

"Come on back," she said, pointing him to an empty desk on the other end of the room where an old-fashioned black multiline sat nestled in a pile of papers. "There's fresh coffee in the pot. Make yourself at home. Oh, I'm Lilly," she said, offering Frank a smile and a surprisingly soft hand.

"Thank you, Lilly. You're a lifesaver."

First, he booked a ticket on a flight out of Panama City to Lima, Peru, on a commercial airline. Then he tried Eva's cell. He got no answer, but since cell phones weren't allowed in the ICU, Frank knew she was at Steve's bedside. He left her a quick message, telling her not to worry and to look out for Irene and Art. Then he pulled his camera and his laptop out of the bag and quickly plugged them in.

The pictures uploaded quickly. Frank scrolled through

them in a hurry, increasing the magnification so that he could read his father's cramped script more easily.

"Come on, come on . . ." he murmured, looking for the section about his father's guide. "Where is it?"

At last, in a footnote, he found what he was looking for: José's name and a thirteen-digit number that included the country code for Peru. It was a long shot, but Frank grabbed the phone and dialed.

It rang for what felt like a lifetime while Frank's heart pounded with anticipation. Then at last, a recorded voice—a woman's—narrated a greeting in a barrage of Spanish so rapid that Frank caught very little of it, not even a name, if she'd even given one.

"Uh, hello . . ." he began in English when the beep encouraged him to speak. "I don't know if I have the right number. But I'm looking for José del Flores or his daughter, Lucinda. My name is Frank Young . . . and, well . . . I'll be arriving in Lima around five p.m. I have to get back to the pool. I have to get back there and . . . and I'm hoping you can help me," Frank concluded. "If I have the wrong number and you know José or Lucinda, please—*please*. Tell them Frank Young is on his way to Iquitos and that I need their help."

He hesitated for a moment, repeated the critical facts of the message in Spanish and then hung up. He wasn't sure the message was adequate any more than he was sure it had reached the right person, but it was all he could do.

"We're all set," Lilly said, appearing beside him with several sheets of paper rolled up in her hands and a pair of sleek steel-framed aviators on her face. A younger Asian woman stood next to her wearing a matching blue aviator suit. "This Eun," Lilly added. "She'll be my co-pilot."

Eun smiled, then flipped her sunglasses down over her bright black eyes. "Welcome to Elite, Mr. Young. I think you'll enjoy this."

"Wow," Frank said.

He would have hardly known he was on airplane—it looked more like he'd walked into someone's living room, and a very nice one at that. Eight deep captain's chairs in an elegant shade of cream leather sat near spacious windows, each with an accompanying side table in some rich dark wood. The floor was covered with thick carpeting in a modern geometric design. Artwork lined the walls.

"Yeah, nice, huh?" Lilly said proudly. "Wait until you see the bathroom. It's nicer than the one in my house. This one gets a lot of use by celebrities and some of the high-roller business types around here. Or at least the ones who don't have their own planes. But that's not the best feature." She slid back a partition and nodded for Frank to go inside.

He'd been expecting a tour of the cockpit, but he was way off. Behind the door was a bedroom—a comfortable-looking full-sized bed covered with a plush burgundy comforter, a flat-screen TV mounted on the wall in front of it and another captain's chair secluded from the main body of the plane.

"I thought maybe you'd like to hang out in here," Lilly said thoughtfully. "It's gonna be a little over four hours. Long enough for a good nap. You look like you could use it."

"Yeah," Frank agreed. Once he arrived in Peru there might not be much time for rest. If despite his best efforts, Ari figured out what was behind that fresh coat of paint—

"FAA regulations don't require flight attendants for less than nineteen passengers. Eun or I will check on you from time to time, though. Any questions?"

Frank shook his head. "Don't worry about me. I won't be any trouble."

Lilly nodded. "The galley's here. I'll tell you when it's clear for you to get up and make yourself a snack. For now, though, pick a seat and buckle up. We'll be underway in five minutes or less."

The bedroom was enticing, but Frank returned to the main cabin. He stowed the rucksack in the closet Lilly indicated, then took a seat, the laptop bag joining him like a companion in a nearby seat. Lilly was as good as her word. Within a few minutes, the plane was rolling down the runway and then jumped smoothly into the air.

Frank reached for the laptop bag. He needed sleep and he knew it, but before he could rest, there was one more thing he had to do.

It felt as though he had started the letter years ago—not an hour or so before, crouched on the floor of his home waiting for danger to arrive. The sheet of paper was now crumpled and ripped at the corner from all it had been through pressed in the front of his laptop bag. Frank reread the words he'd written, his heart twisting with regret.

Dearest Jackie,

By the time you read this—if you read this at all—I'll be far away. It's probably better if I don't tell you exactly where I'm going—but I can't keep this power or gift or curse or whatever it is any longer. It's a long shot and I know it, but while there's still a chance I can undo what was done, I have

> to try. Not just for you and me, but for my friends. For all of us. My effort may very well fail and if it does, you might not hear from me again.
>
> This isn't your fault. It's mine.
>
> After everything you told me—and what I have seen for myself now with what happened to Steve—I know Ari will stop at nothing to get what he wants. What he wants is me. I have to make sure that he doesn't get a thing. I'll do everything I can to keep him from following me but if he does, I'll protect my father's research with my life if necessary. If I can't reverse the power, I'll have to disappear.

Frank fished a pen out of the bottom of the bag and continued.

> I'll have to disappear forever. I don't dare contact you or Steve or Eva or return to X-Treme. The less any of you know, the safer you will be.
>
> In case I don't get to look into your eyes and say these words, I want you to know what you mean to me. I've probably seen a hundred romantic comedies, love stories, movies where people connect in a chance encounter and fall in love. I always thought it was a clever plot twist, but not reality. At least not a reality for me. Before we met, I didn't believe in love at first sight. I guess I was just drifting through my life. I thought I had goals, I thought I knew what I wanted—but I was wrong. From the moment we held hands together on that plane, I've known that my life before you was missing something. It was missing purpose. It was missing heart.
>
> You are my purpose. You are my Babe. You are my heart. I've loved you from the first moment I saw you. If I can't

reverse this thing then it's just as well that I disappear. I cannot live without my heart—and I love you far too much to ask you to make this choice. I'm sorry for every tear I've made you cry and for any pain I've caused you. My whole reason for being on this earth is to take care of you and make you happy, and hurting you is the last thing I ever wanted to do.

Writing that makes me think of my parents. They loved each other, but my father knew that my mother wouldn't be strong enough to survive childbirth. He made some mistakes trying to keep her alive—and was thwarted by fate. I know he loved me too. I guess he thought that this power would help me—would make my life longer and easier. That it would protect me. He was wrong about that, too. I wish he hadn't made those choices, but I know he made them out of love for me and for my mother.

I won't judge him. I've made too many bad decisions of my own, Jackie. I made them because I hoped to help my friends. I hoped to find a way to provide for you. I hoped that I could use this thing to build my business and become a big success so I could take care of you. Because that's all I ever want to do.

I love you so much, Jackie. If I can undo this, I hope you'll find it in your heart to forgive me and we can start over again, together.

Yours,

Francis

P.S. Gregory is working for your dad. He's the leak. Whatever you do, don't let him see this letter. In fact, it's probably best if you destroy it.

Frank reread the words and, satisfied there wasn't anything more he could say, lay the pen aside. His head ached and his muscles felt stiff from the long squat back at the house. He was rubbing his thighs, hoping to ease the strain, when he remembered.

He reached into first his right pocket and then his left, pulling out first his parents' letters and then his mother's ring.

Frank held them both in his hands. He wanted nothing more than to keep them with him, and yet . . .

Jackie's letter was open on the little table in front of him, ready to be slipped into its envelope, yet now that he held the letters and the ring in his hands, Frank hesitated. He had planned to keep them with him, but now he wondered if once again, he'd brought them for a very different reason than he originally thought.

He dropped them both in the envelope and grabbed the letter again.

> *P.P.S. I'm sending you my parents' letters and my mother's ring for safekeeping—with all of my love. As I look back on it, I've had them with me almost every time we've been together—except for the very first time on the plane before I knew you and the very last when I lost you. I feel like that means something but I don't know what. I just know that something in my heart tells me they have served their purpose and don't belong with me anymore. I want you to keep them. The hope that I can slide this ring on your finger and hear you say "yes" will be in my mind at every step of this journey.*

He scribbled Jackie's name and address across the front and finally at peace, closed his eyes.

When we're on the ground in Miami I'll find a FedEx box . . . or something, he thought, settling back in the oversized chair. Scattered thoughts—barely coherent—in which Ari tampered with mailboxes or robbed postal workers at gunpoint filled his mind before weariness rolled over him like a warm blanket and he drifted into sleep.

When he awoke, Lilly stood over him, her sunglasses pushed back from her face and his rucksack in her hand. "We're here," she said, smiling at him. "We just made it. They're holding the plane for you. But no worries." She leaned toward the window and pointed. "It's right there."

A jet slightly larger than the one he was on sat on the tarmac less than a hundred yards away.

"That's great, Lilly. Thank you."

Lilly handed him his pack. "Sure. Anytime." But just as Frank turned toward the exit, she lay a gentle hand on his shoulder. "Look, I know it's none of my business, but you seem like a decent guy and it's pretty clear you're in trouble. You might as well just admit it."

Frank shook his head. "I can't get you involved with this, Lilly—"

"Okay. But if you need a plane, call me. I've got friends with planes all over the world." She handed him a card. "Say the word and I'll do what I can."

"Thanks." Frank pocketed the card. He stared into her plain face for a long moment; then, on an instinct he couldn't justify with logic, thrust the envelope into her hand. "Would you mail this for me?"

Lilly glanced at the name and address. "I'll do better than

that. I'll deliver it myself, this afternoon when I get back."

"You really don't have to—"

"My pleasure, Jeff—I mean . . ." She blushed, then nodded at the waiting plane. "You'd better *get*, Mr. Young. Your charter awaits."

The charter from Miami to Panama City was comfortable, but not nearly as ritzy as the experience on Elite. Frank filled an extra seat on a booking made by a group of men around his own age traveling to Panama for a wild weekend of the *Hangover* variety. They were loud, boisterous and more than a little tipsy already—and Frank felt himself to be as far removed from their carefree excitement as Pluto was from the sun. He slipped on his noise-cancelling headphones and opened his laptop, not for a DVD this time, but for his own private movie created by the photographs he'd taken of his father's research.

He studied the map and then signed on to the WiFi, trying to relate the coordinates to the current topography. They seemed to point him toward a remote region nearly a hundred miles from Iquitos—and that was assuming he could walk it in a straight line, which Frank knew was highly unlikely given the density of the forest. Even with his father's maps, he'd need help. He'd need José or Lucinda, or someone else intimately familiar with the jungle.

Please, please, let that number be good, he thought, refusing the flight attendant's offer of a beverage. Alcohol was the last thing he needed.

Please, let them get my message. Please let them be willing to help me . . .

Lucinda.

A different brand of guilt joined the weights he was already carrying. Had she found happiness and forgiven him for his youthful betrayal? Would she help him or would she refuse? If she refused, would he be able to continue alone, or would they have to return together? What if she had long ago left Iquitos, or worse—was dead? Where would that leave him?

Frank's mind swirled with questions—and while his father's notes about the legends and stories surrounding that cold, clear water offered more hope than he'd had in weeks, there was still plenty left unknown.

"Do you have anything to declare, *señor*?" The customs officer's English was so heavily accented that at first Frank wasn't sure what he'd said.

The charter jet had landed on a small runway adjacent to the Tocumen International Airport in Panama City. Frank had already learned he could take a shuttle bus to the main airport to pick up his Copa Airlines flight to Lima, but the schedule was tight. He had barely half an hour to get to the gate.

"You'll make it, no problem," the flight attendant had assured him. "Customs is the big headache and we have a special line here just for our passengers. You'll be out in a heartbeat."

And sure enough, he was third in line and in a matter of minutes, standing before the officer.

"No, I have nothing to declare," Frank said, shaking his head as he presented his passport and set his laptop bag and rucksack on the conveyor.

The man wore a blue uniform with a gold badge affixed to his right breast pocket bearing the name "Garza." The airport was warm, already testifying to the tropical temperatures that Panama was known for, and there were dark stains of sweat at the man's armpits.

"And your reason for visiting Panama?" he asked, squinting at Frank's picture.

"Just getting a connecting flight to Peru," Frank answered, switching to Spanish. "It leaves in less than half an hour, so—"

Another officer approached Garza and murmured something in his ear. Garza's eyes snapped to Frank's face.

"You will come with me, *señor*."

It was a command, not a question. Confused, Frank stepped out of the line, following the man out of the concourse and into a small white room that housed a table, a couple of chairs and a not-at-all discreetly placed surveillance camera in a corner angled toward the seat Frank was directed to take. Another officer followed behind him, rolling his backpack on a cart like a patient on the way to critical surgery.

"Is this your bag?" Garza demanded, shutting Frank inside the room with the two customs officers.

Frank nodded. "Yes. Is there a problem?"

Garza's companion opened it and pulled Frank's gun case out.

"Is this your weapon?"

Frank sighed at his own stupidity. "Yes. I'm sorry. Yes, I forgot it was in there—"

"Are you aware that it is illegal to bring firearms into Panama?"

"Yes . . . I mean, if I'd thought about it, I'm sure I would have realized that—"

"What is the purpose for your traveling with such a weapon, *señor*?"

"I'm visiting a remote section of the Amazon," Frank said without hesitation. "You'll see from the rest of my gear that I'm packed for hiking. It's become a habit of mine to pack a sidearm for remote hikes in the United States and—"

"That is within the United States!" the man snapped. "You cannot assume that you may bring a weapon to the sovereign nation of Panama!"

The man would be appeased by nothing less than abject contrition—and Frank knew it. "I'm sorry, sir," he said, hanging his head. "I don't know what I was thinking."

"Bah!" Officer Garza spat at him, gesturing to the other officer to take the gun away. "Was there anything else?" Garza asked the man quietly.

The man glanced at Frank, then leaned close to Garza's ear, murmuring something that Frank couldn't hear.

Garza's thick black brows shot up. "Interesting. Check everything," Garza ordered, indicating the backpack. "Very carefully."

The more junior officer disappeared with the gun case and Frank's backpack, leaving Frank and Garza alone in the white room.

He muttered something under his breath, then opened Frank's laptop bag, pulling out his computer, his camera and three thick stacks of cash.

"Yours also?"

Frank's chest tightened and he realized he'd violated another of his own travel rules: carry cash, but not too much—especially when traveling in the Third World.

"Yes."

"Why do you travel with so much money, *señor*?"

Frank searched his brain for a plausible answer, but the only thing that came to his mind was the lame but truthful reply: "There wasn't time to go to the bank for traveler's checks."

Garza laughed at him, shaking his head.

"Okay," he said, smiling, fingering the stack of bills. "We'll begin again. What is your business in Panama, Mr. Young?"

"I told you, officer. I have no business in Panama. I just want to catch the flight to Lima—"

"What is your business in Lima?"

"I told you that, too, sir. Hiking the Amazon. I run a travel company offering extreme tours. I'm exploring new trails for trips and I don't have much time. I have to get back to California in a couple of days, so . . ." Frank stood up and smiled, hoping to signal that the interview was over without making the man angry. "I understand you have to confiscate the weapon. It was a mistake on my part. I was in a hurry and I forgot. But I don't want to miss my flight, so—"

"No, no, of course not, *señor*," Garza said, matching Frank's smile with one of his own. "But you understand that the combination of the sidearm and this much cash requires me to make inquiries. Make certain you are who you say you are and that your business is as you say it is. I would not be doing my job if I just accepted your story and let you go—not in these troubled times, yes?" He rose, scooping up the cash and Frank's passport. "And of course, there is a fine for attempting to bring the weapon into this country." The man locked eyes with Frank. "You understand."

Frank understood—his money was as good as gone. He tried not to let his disappointment show while his mind processed the inevitability of this fact. He'd had the presence of mind to stuff some cash in his wallet—there was enough to get to Iquitos and hire a guide. But if he missed the flight—

"I understand," he said slowly. "But that presents something of a problem for me, officer. I'll have nothing to offer my guide in Iquitos—"

"Ah, but you are American. You will think of something. Your people always do," he said casually, reaching for the door. A moment later, Frank was alone.

"Shit!" he cursed, shaking his head at his own stupidity. He glanced at his watch and sank back into the metal chair. The flight to Lima would depart in less than fifteen minutes . . . and unless he'd completely misread his conversation with Officer Garza, there was absolutely no way Frank would be on it.

He sat in the white room, waiting, becoming more anxious with every passing second. Had it not been for the camera staring unwaveringly down at him, Frank might have thrown the rickety metal chair at the walls in frustration.

"Good news, Mr. Young," Garza said when he returned at last—an hour later. "You appear to be who you say you are and we found no further items of contraband in your belongings." He handed Frank his passport and his laptop bag. "You can retrieve your backpack from Officer Mendez before you enter the terminal." He nodded officially and when spoke again he switched back from Spanish to English. "Thank you for visiting Panama, Mr. Young. Have a nice day."

His flight to Lima was long gone.

"Two hours. That will be five hundred sixty-four dollars," was all the ticket agent had to say.

Frank forked over the cash with a sigh of defeat. Ari already knew he wanted to get to Lima—and by now Pandora and her friends had torn Frank's house apart trying to figure out why. As much as Frank hoped that they wouldn't discover the writing on the walls, he didn't dare count on that. For all Frank knew, Ari had already hopped on his private plane and had landed in Iquitos by now. Once there, it only took finding the right person—or bribing the right villager—and he might discover the location of the pool, no matter what Frank had done to hide it.

Time had been the only thing Frank had in his favor . . . and now he had lost that advantage completely.

CHAPTER
Nineteen

When his flight finally landed in Lima, Frank wished for the gun Officer Garza had confiscated even more than the money. The feeling that the unexpected and the unwelcome awaited him just outside the aircraft made him lag behind the other passengers, waiting until the aisles were clear and the cleaning services came aboard before finally, reluctantly, he strapped his laptop over his shoulder and hauled his backpack down from the overhead bin. He set his face to "wary" and stepped off the airplane, half expecting to see a line of police ready to haul him away to some foreign jail where he would never be heard from again—and half expecting to see Ari himself, gray ponytail swinging on his back and that sharklike smile on his face.

But no. Nothing more awaited him than the tail end of a very long customs line. He cleared the inspection station and joined the passenger traffic of Jorge Chávez Airport within twenty minutes, following the signs for the ticket counter. His destination was set: LAN Perú airlines to purchase a ticket on the next flight to Iquitos.

He walked quickly through the busy terminal, weaving his way among pedestrians, navigating awkwardly under the weight of the backpack that felt like a sign on his shoulders announcing "Here I am! Headed to the Amazon! Come and get me!" True, there were others carrying hiking gear—his plane had included a touring party of young American backpackers—but they were long gone, far ahead of him in the airport traffic. He paused from time to time to glance behind him, but there were so many people moving about that it was impossible to tell for sure if he was being followed.

"You just made it, *señor*," the ticket agent told him. "The last flight of the day leaves in forty minutes."

Frank thanked her, gave a nod of gratitude to the travel gods and hurried on to the gate. Too nervous to sit down and wait in one of the few seats left available in the small waiting area, Frank took a spot against the window where he could see all the activity of the airport. He left the backpack high on his shoulders—just in case he had to run.

"Excuse me."

A young woman approached him, speaking cautious formal Spanish that carried the lilt of an unfamiliar dialect. "May I . . . ?" She gestured, indicating her effort to pass.

"*Sí*," Frank answered, nodding at her.

She scooted past him, considered the limited seating options at that end of the waiting area and sighed before occupying the space beside him against the window. From time to time, she glanced at him, as though she wanted something.

Any other time, being checked out by an attractive young woman would have flattered him, but her scrutiny made Frank nervous. She could have been Lucinda's sister: her big, dark eyes were framed by thick, black lashes and she had a swath of heavy, straight black hair. With her smooth brown skin and lithe, athletic figure, he guessed she couldn't have been older than her late twenties, but there was a certain maturity in the way she dressed—in a light cotton button-down blouse and a pair of jeans, accessorized by a matronly brown carryall—which suggested she hoped to pass for older.

She glanced at Frank again, from the messy mop of his hair to the soles of his shoes.

"Why are you staring at me?" Frank demanded, turning toward her. If she were an enemy, he could see no reason to play footsie about it.

"I am sorry . . . it is only . . ." she replied in English. "I was sent to meet someone coming from Panama City, going to Iquitos. He was to arrive hours ago, but he was not on the flight. I must leave now to return to my home and I do not wish to have to say that I did not find him." She paused. "He was coming from the United States. You are an American, yes?"

"Who are you? Is this one of Ari's tricks?" Frank hissed, scanning the waiting area for the familiar bulk of Ari's security; but if Ari's people were here, they weren't following the usual movie-script bad-guy dress code of black suits and sinister expressions.

"I do not know of this 'Ari.'" The girl's soft brow contracted in confusion. "But I must be careful. Very careful. But you are so like him . . . more than any other I have seen."

"I don't understand."

For a long moment, they stared at each other, searching each other's faces for something to trust. Finally, the girl reached into her heavy purse and pulled out what looked like a scrap of paper. She slipped it into Frank's hand as if she were passing a note in social studies, staring innocently out at the concourse while her hand touched his. Frank matched her stealth. He felt the square of paper in his hand but didn't look at it. Instead, he hefted his pack off his shoulders and set it on the floor between them, then bent as though he were tightening the laces on his boots to read it.

But it wasn't a paper at all, rather a piece of a photograph. Frank recognized it instantly: it was his own young face that smiled up at him. It had been carefully torn away from the rest of the faces that had surrounded him when the picture was snapped—on the first day of the expedition he'd taken into the Amazon, when he was eighteen. The Australian had been standing beside him on the left and Lucinda had been standing to his right . . .

"Where did you get this?" he muttered, struggling to keep his voice low.

"That is you, yes?" the girl asked. "You are mostly the same . . . but, yes, a little different. Very like your father. Yes, very like." She sighed. "But it has been so very many years. I hesitate to trust memory."

"Where did you get it?" Frank repeated.

"She gave it to me. She said you would be older, of course—"

"She?"

"She said to tell you her children's names. Francis and Helen."

Frank started. "Th-those were my parents' names," he stammered before he could stop himself.

The girl sighed, her eyes closing in relief. "Then it is you, Frank Young. I am Charmaine Amaru. Lucinda sent me to lead you to our village."

"Then she got the message. She's willing to help me." Frank suddenly felt like laughing. *It really is going to be okay*, he thought. *Maybe it will even be easy. Maybe I can reverse the curse and be home by tomorrow. I'll go straight to Jackie and—*

"Yes. She has been waiting many years for you to return. She wanted to come herself, but . . ." She shook her head. "It is impossible."

"Why? Is she all right?"

The girl shook her head sadly. "She is married to a very jealous man. If he has heard the message you left, he will probably kill her." She lowered her voice.

"But I didn't say anything on that message that should make him jealous—"

"He knows what you did together all those years ago. He believes that, as she was promised to him, you stole something it was not your right to steal."

Frank sighed. Of all the obstacles he had imagined he'd face in trying to reach Lucinda and the pool, a jealous husband had never made the list. "Then she still looks nineteen."

Charmaine nodded. "Yes. And he is tormented by it. A wife who looks as though she is your daughter and then your granddaughter is not—"

"Wait—" Frank interrupted as her words took full hold

in his mind. "Didn't you say your surname was Amaru? You knew my father!"

A sad smile flitted across Charmaine's face. "Yes."

Frank peered at her closely. His father's letters dated their trip together as 1980—over three decades ago—and yet he was sure this woman wasn't more than thirty.

"Then you and my father . . ." Frank began. "You . . . were there. Together."

"Yes," Charmaine said quietly. "I am fifty-eight years old, Frank. But these are not things to be spoken of here," she said softly. "I am glad I found you. I may not be able to change my own fate, but if I can free Lucinda, that will be something. But it will be difficult. For many reasons, which you will soon understand." She glanced at the gate. "They are calling our flight. Take a taxi to the marina and ask for Indigo Pier. I will find you again there."

Iquitos had changed.

He remembered it as a sleepy backwater centuries removed from his modern life. But that time and place was gone. Frank stepped out of the airport terminal and was greeted by a cab line of metropolis length—a sight he couldn't have imagined when he was there fifteen years before. Across the street, instead of the lot where José's battered jitney had parked, there was a sleek modern-looking hotel that would have more at home in San Diego than only miles from the Amazon rainforest. On the brief cab ride to the marina, McDonald's and Pizza Hut stood shoulder to shoulder with local eateries, their walls painted in festive colors.

When he reached the pier, he hardly recognized the Amazon itself. He remembered an unimportant pier populated with small motorboats not unlike the one that sent them down the river in the direction of José and Lucinda's village. But now there was a new and modern terminal where boats of all sizes and speeds queued up to take tourists to their various destinations up and down the river. Signs in English and Spanish screamed "River Boat Cruises," "See the Amazon!" and "Authentic Amazon Experience" as though the rainforest were an amusement park.

"Where is Indigo Pier?" Frank asked a short young man who stood just outside the marina's entrance handing out flyers to anyone who would take one. Between his Mohawk-styled hair and the muscles rippling beneath the white T-shirt he wore, he looked like he could have been an extra in *Apocalypto*.

The kid looked him up and down. "*You* want Indigo Pier?"

Frank nodded.

Once again the kid did a once-over, then shrugged. "It's that way," he said, pointing to the right. "Keep walking. Walk until there's no place left to walk. Indigo Pier."

Frank thanked him and set off. The humidity assaulted him like a fist in the face. The plane had been cold, but now he stripped off his jacket and tied it around his hips. He wished he could wear his shorts, but he knew better: in the jungle the insects would eat his bare skin alive. He didn't dare take the risk.

He walked for what felt like half an hour, traveling farther and farther from tourist boats, then past a dock of smaller ones; then for a long stretch there were no boats at all and the paved sidewalk turned into a strip of dirt road. In the distance, Frank thought he saw a small collection of battered boats tethered to a worn wooden post sticking up out of the water. As he drew closer, he saw Charmaine at last. She had taken off her shoes and rolled up her pant legs, revealing a set of calves a teenage triathlete in San Diego would be proud to sport. As he approached, she waded out to a small motorboat and hoisted herself inside.

"Come," she said, gesturing for Frank to follow her lead. "The sooner we are on the river, the sooner we can talk."

"This is Indigo Pier?" he asked, looking at the sad collection of boats.

Charmaine nodded. "It is the name for the place where the tribes who live in the forest leave their boats—those that interact with outsiders. Many still refrain, though that gets harder with each year."

Frank waded into the water, feeling the silt and mud between his toes before he hoisted himself into the small boat. It sat low in the water, with four stake-like poles set into each corner and a slightly longer one dead in the center like a flagpole. The seats were little more than bare planks of wood.

Charmaine started the motor and grabbed the tiller, piloting them into the river, nearer to the overhanging vines and trees at the banks than to its center. As a seasoned sailor, Frank immediately sensed the strong current carrying them quickly into the jungle as Iquitos receded into the distance.

"José del Flores—Lucinda's father—bought this boat many years ago from the profits of guiding foreigners through the jungles. It was for the tribe to use, though mostly now it stays here, at the pier in Iquitos," Charmaine murmured. "There are no more tours, though some of the tribe do find work as guides. The lady who now has the phone number you called is one of these. She sent a messenger to say that you called and Lucinda sent him back, to me."

"Then José is dead."

Charmaine nodded. "Yes."

"How long?"

"Ten years, I think. He died the year Lucinda's daughter, Helen, was born."

"What happened?"

Charmaine didn't answer. Instead, she steered the boat toward a narrow channel branching off from the river's wide expanse, avoiding the periodic tree or rock breaking the surface of the water. For a while, they puttered along with the ancient engine as a soundtrack. She stared out at the slow brown water for so long that Frank began to doubt she had heard him.

"We turn again." She pointed downstream. "Up ahead. When this finger of the river ends—maybe an hour from now—we walk. There is a path of sorts, if you look for the mark of the machete."

Frank nodded. He opened his mouth to repeat his question, but she preempted him.

"What happened to José is as good a place to begin as any," she said. "You did not know that he had swum in the pool when he was a young man—a teenager. He did not know what it was. He became lost—separated from the others during a hunt. A sudden storm washed away his path and he had wandered for days, trying to find his way back to his village. When he swam there it was not because he was searching for healing, or for powers or for immortality. He saw cool, clear water, only. He swam. He drank. He rested on its banks. He did not realize the place was forbidden—"

"Forbidden? Why?"

Charmaine smiled sadly. "Years ago, I would have said that it was superstition. But now, I say it was for our own good. The waters extend life in one way or the other—and this is power not meant for men and women. Such a thing is only for the gods—if they exist. The ancient priests knew how to use the pool for healing, but that knowledge was lost—or abandoned—long ago. I don't know. Indeed, it was all just stories when I was child. Many stories—I wrote some of them down, but they were confused. Contradictory. Even the way to the place was long forgotten, buried deep in the heart of the jungle—until José stumbled upon it."

"And he didn't tell anyone?"

"He did not know there was anything to tell. He aged, though slowly. He buried one wife, then another. Then his children. When he outlived his grandchildren, he began to understand that—"

"Wait," Frank interrupted. "Outlived his grandchildren? What are you saying?"

"It is my best guess that José drank from the pool in the late 1800s. When you knew him, he may have looked like a man in his fifties—but he was probably over 120 years old."

"That's just not possible," Frank muttered. "If he lived that long while looking so young, surely everyone wanted to know why! Why didn't he just . . . I don't know, take his whole family on a swimming trip?"

"He did not connect his long life with that experience. For many years, he did not realize that he had found the legendary waters. He might not have ever understood it, had it not been for your father . . . and me."

She paused as if expecting a question, but Frank simply studied the muddy brown water as it churned beneath the rotors and waited. They had been on the river for half an hour and he already felt as though any hint of civilization had disappeared. Trees and vines hung dense and thick, swiping his face from time to time as the little boat chugged along. The sun was very low in the sky now—maybe within an hour or two of setting—but the air was still heavy and hot. Frank wiped his forehead with the palm of his hand.

"The man who knew most about the mystical pool and the people who lived on its banks long ago was your father," she began at last. "More than me—and more than José. I do not how it began, but José was hired as a guide by one of the touring companies that began bringing foreigners to the rainforest. He learned Spanish, and then English. They liked him because he was native—and he knew the forest well. Eventually, he was asked to lead tours on his own—deep into the jungle. Around the same time, your father had begun to research here. He had found evidence of the tribe that lived near the waters in some of the Quechuan texts discovered at Machu Picchu. He was looking for the remnants of that civilization and he believed it was here. Near Iquitos."

"And he needed a guide. Someone who knew the rainforest."

Charmaine nodded. "Your father wanted to find the mystical waters—not for fame or for money but for love. To save the woman he loved. You understand?"

"My mother," Frank murmured softly. "I found their letters."

"Yes... the letters," Charmaine repeated softly, and sadness overtook the symmetry of her features. "He wrote to her often. At any moment that he could." She sighed, then continued as if Frank had never mentioned the letters or his mother. "José knew of a pool of water that sounded like the place your father sought, but he had not been there in some time and wasn't sure he could find it again. Still, they set out into the jungle. Your father and a few of his colleagues. José and eight others from the village, to serve as runners and to help carry the supplies. And me. Although I grew up in that same remote village, I had attended San Cristóbal University and studied Quechua. I had been working on a paper about the stories of the interior tribes—and had interviewed many of the old ones from various villages. I had heard many versions of a tale about mystical waters that healed and changed people. I had recorded stories about extended youth and exceptionally long life. Your father sought me out in Lima when he arrived here and asked me if I would accompany him on his dig."

She paused. Frank watched as her face softened. "I was twenty-six, a new professor at Universidad de Piura. A teacher for whom television and toilets were still miracles. Awkward in the modern world, awkward in the jungle. I agreed to go because his project complemented my own work... but also because I had never met a man like your father before. He was... brilliant. Everything interested him and he knew about many things. He was forever sketching. Forever writing things in his little notebooks—"

"The ones with the maroon covers? There must have been a hundred of them scattered around his study and in the garage."

Charmaine laughed. "He recorded everything. Like a good scientist. He never seemed to notice the hardship. You have been here before. You recall the difficulties of traveling in this place, beyond the careful trails prepared for the tourists?"

"I would never have been able to find my way without Lucinda and José."

"When your father and I—and the others—made our trek, it seemed even more so. The rains were heavy and we were often very wet. The jungle challenged even José's skills. We were lost. It took us weeks to find the ruins of the temple and several weeks more to find the pool . . . and through it all," she smiled, "your father was often like an excited little boy, even though by the time we found the pool most of the others had abandoned the trip due to the hardships we faced."

Frank thought of the way his father always looked in the photographs he had seen of him from the late 1970s: sloppy khakis and thick-soled shoes, his T-shirt clinging to his back and his glasses sliding down his nose.

"While we searched, I told him the stories I had heard and he confided to me his hope: that the waters might heal your mother. Often when we were alone, he talked about her. At first, he hoped that after we found the pool, she would come. And then, after he received a letter telling him that she was pregnant, he hoped he could take something back that would make her stronger after she delivered the child. But there was no record of such a thing being possible—that one could take the water to another. All of the legends—every story—told of the seeker coming to the pool. I told him I doubted the water would have any power beyond this place."

She paused. Frank glanced at the sun sinking into the muddy water ahead of them and the darkening shore passing by with surprising speed. The heat hung heavily in the twilight and he could almost smell the coming rain. From time to time a tamarin or howler would screech out a welcome—or warning. As if reading his mind, Charmaine said, "Frank, put up the tarp. Beneath your seat."

Frank lifted the flap of wood that formed his chair and pulled out a patched piece of drab plastic.

"It hooks there and there." Charmaine pointed and Frank secured it to the poles along the sides of the boat as she continued. "I was the one who told him of the stories of the power men had received when they shared love with a woman in the pool. By then, of course, I was in love with him. I knew he did not love me—his heart was ever true to your mother. But . . ." She sighed. "I persuaded him that it was his best hope—to experience the pool with me. Then he could take back the power and perhaps it would be enough."

As the rain began, it quickly made droopy puddles in the aging fabric of the tarp. Charmaine kept her eyes focused on the river ahead of them.

"My part in your story ends. I heard from José that you were born . . . and that Helen died. Your father never returned to this part of the Amazon and though I followed his career, he did not write about his experience. Neither did I. It seemed . . ." She glanced at Frank. "A betrayal. Of something sacred. Years later, I heard that you were coming. There was a part of me then that longed to meet you . . . and another that could not bear to see you. His child. His son. You could have been mine, Frank. My son. Mine and his . . . In the end, I decided to leave the village. I went to Lima to visit friends from the university who marveled at my young face and slender figure after all those years!" She laughed wryly. "You know what I told them? I told them it was the blessing of life in a place without toilets or electricity! I was right to go. I knew how like him you would be . . . but she is there, too. Your mother is in your face. I know how he must have felt. How terrible and wonderful it must have been for him . . . looking at you."

Frank studied her, seeing her the way his father must have: an exquisitely beautiful woman for whom he felt professional respect and academic kinship—but not love. Nothing he could think of to say would have been the right response to this woman's sacrifice and longing, so Frank did the only thing a deeply uncomfortable man could do under the circumstances: he changed the subject.

"Do you know why my father wanted me to come here?"

"Perhaps he wanted to share this place with you. Or maybe he hoped you would receive a gift from the pool. He had no way of knowing that you and Lucinda would share love there as we did. Any more than José knew. I do not believe either of them would have condoned it, had they known. José only wanted his daughter to know where the waters were. He did not wish the knowledge to become lost again. I am sure he discouraged her from touching the water. By then, he knew from hard experience that a price would be paid—"

"I've already paid a price." The anger Frank had tamped down to a low simmer while she spoke erupted again. "I've lost the woman I love. I've got a greedy billionaire on my ass and he nearly killed my best friend. All I want to know is, can this be reversed? Is there a way to just go back to being normal?"

"Perhaps there is a way. The effects of the water are never known with certainty. But to even try, you and Lucinda must return together. You must repeat the act that gave you the power in the first place," Charmaine said, staring seriously into his eyes. "But Frank, you need to understand . . . if you return to the waters—"

"Charmaine, look out!" Frank shouted.

In front of them a large tree threw its branches up to the sky. Charmaine leaned hard on the tiller, but it was too late.

The little boat struck the tree and splintered with a tremendous rush of force and sound, throwing Frank, Charmaine and their belongings deep below the surface of the dark river. Stunned by the impact, Frank inhaled, choking on muddy water. Water and silt weighed down his boots and jeans as Frank fought his way to surface, his lungs burning. When his head broke the surface, the current caught him and set him spinning, sweeping him along according to its will until a long fragment of wood drifted within arm's reach. Frank grabbed for it, kicking his feet as he steered himself toward the bank.

"Charmaine!" he yelled over the rush of the water and pounding rain. "Charmaine!"

Hugging the strip of the craft, he slowly traversed the current toward the shore and pulled himself out of the water. His wet clothes felt like a hundred extra pounds of weight, but Frank scrambled to his feet and immediately turned back to the turgid water. "Charmaine!"

The only answer was the rain splashing against the broad leaves of the trees and the bubbling river.

"Charmaine!" He hurried down the bank, searching the brown waters. "Charmaine!"

At first he thought it was his backpack turning in aimless

little circles in the shallows a few yards away, but as he grew closer, he realized he was looking at a torso, floating helplessly in a tangle of rushes. Charmaine. He dove into the water again, grabbing her by the arms and half pulling, half dragging her toward land. Her chest rose and fell as she coughed out blood and water. A shard of the boat stuck out of her abdomen, surrounded by a spreading patch of dark blood.

"Charmaine," Frank murmured, staring at the wound. Even if he had it, the first-aid kit in his rucksack was inadequate for such a serious injury. Frank swallowed, glancing around him for something—anything—he could use to try to stop the bleeding.

She coughed, and another trickle of blood oozed from her mouth.

"Be still," he murmured. "It's going to be okay . . ."

She shook her head. "Follow Tinka Tributary. Meet . . ." she croaked. "Lucinda. Kapok . . . outside village. Wait for her . . ."

"Save your strength, Charmaine," Frank told her. "There were so many boats back at the marina. Someone has to come along here soon. We'll get you some help—"

Her bruised and scratched face twitched into a smile and she lifted her hand toward his face.

"So like . . . your father . . ." she murmured as her last breath rattled in her throat. He watched her eyes stiffen on a spot over his shoulder, glassy and unseeing, and knew that she was dead and he was alone in the jungle.

CHAPTER
Twenty

He hated leaving her, but there wasn't any choice. The boat was nothing more than firewood; the tarp that had sheltered them from the rain was gone. Even his rucksack and laptop bag were invisible, submerged or drifted farther downstream. Still, it felt wrong just leaving her there—a woman who had tried to help him—alone in the jungle rain.

"I'm sorry," he murmured, covering her with a makeshift shelter he was able to craft from a few broken piece of bamboo. "I'll come back and make this right. I promise."

The rain slacked off, leaving the air hotter and heavier than it had been before the downpour. Frank glanced at the horizon. The sun sank lower and lower, seeming to have only a few measly minutes left above the rim of the river. Frank held his breath, listening for the sound of a boat's engine even if far in the distance. But the only sounds were the continual drip of the rain and the occasional shrieking call of a parrot or African gray somewhere in the nearby trees.

Great, Frank thought. *Night in the jungle without fire or weapon, food or even company.* It wasn't an experience he was looking forward to adding to his travel résumé.

"Follow Tinka Tributary," Charmaine's last words echoed in his brain. It wasn't much hope, but it was the best of his options, as turning back was not even a consideration. If he could make it before it was completely dark—and if Lucinda were somewhere near to meet him—he might just survive.

He set off walking, staying as close to the river's edge as the terrain would allow, but the banks were marshy and more than once, he took a step and sank knee high in a thick brown muck that had looked solid a moment before. As he scrambled toward sturdier ground, he kept his eyes carefully trained at the surface of the water. It looked placid and calm, but Frank had traveled here enough to fear it. This weedy terrain was home to the river's most deadly creatures, predators who knew how to conceal themselves as the most innocent-looking of sticks floating in the water, or how to be so still and silent that when he saw them it would be too late.

He struggled along for nearly an hour, watching every step as the sun set like a tangerine rind over the water. He reached into the pocket of his old jeans and was glad when his fingers closed on an old lighter that had probably been there since his last hike. He flicked it once, searching the shore for something he might use as a torch—and saw it: something tangled in some tall grasses at the foot of a submerged tree. A hundred feet away, his rucksack, half submerged in the muddy water, bobbed a faded blue nylon welcome.

He was about to scramble toward it when something rippled in the brackish water a few yards ahead of him. Frank froze, listening and waiting, not daring to move. The sound did not repeat—and the water ahead of him did not change—but he stood still, barely daring to breathe, his eyes focused on the space between him and the rucksack.

At last, two reptilian eyes broke the surface of the water. A moment later, a long, cracked snout of powerful jaws lined with jagged teeth bobbed up. Frank recognized it instantly: a caiman—an alligator that made its home almost exclusively in the Amazon rainforest. He couldn't be certain of its size—not with only its head showing—but chances were good that it was at least as long as he was tall, and it probably outweighed him by two or three times. The caiman sat still in the water, its eyes focused in Frank's direction, waiting like the ancient Amazonian chess player for Frank to make the first move.

Hoping to appear not to be moving at all, Frank turned his head very slowly, scanning his surroundings for anything that might be used in self-defense. A thicket of guava trees grew in a knotty clump less than ten feet away, but Frank didn't like his odds. A caiman on the hunt could run twice as fast as he could—especially since the terrain was as much water as it was solid ground—and even if he reached a tree the thing would have his foot or even his whole leg in its mouth before he could climb it. There was nothing within easy grab that he could use as a weapon, either.

In slow motion, he loosened the jacket around his waist and wrapped it around his right hand like a thick mitt. The caiman studied his preparations dispassionately. It made no move toward him but it didn't move away, either. Frank's backpack bobbed a bit in the brown reeds behind the reptile, teasingly close and yet completely unobtainable.

You want it? Come and get it! the caiman seemed to be saying. It was almost as if it knew that it didn't have to expend any effort to get its dinner tonight; its meal would come on its own accord.

Can I wait it out? Frank wondered. Was there any possibility the thing would eventually just swim away and leave him to retrieve his belongings without a conflict? Maybe it wasn't hungry. Maybe—

With a sudden swift flick of its massive tail, the reptile lunged and was on him. He stumbled, falling into the water, three hundred pounds of ancient alligator flesh on top of him. Frank lifted his right arm and the thing's powerful jaws wrapped around the jacket, biting through the wadded cloth and clamping down to bone while another claw raked across his chest.

"Yah!" Frank cried, flexing his foot to kick at the thing's soft underbelly as though it were a heavier opponent in a mixed martial arts ring who had gained an unfair advantage. "Yah! Yah! Yah!"

The caiman released its hold on his arm and rolled off of him, but Frank's rest was short. With another flick of its tail the reptile knocked him back again, and then its jaw snapped shut on his ankle just at the spot where his hiking boot ended and his flesh began. Searing pain consumed Frank's reason as the creature's teeth penetrated muscle.

"*Get off me!*" Frank screamed, pummeling the thing with both of his fists in the eyes and snout. He heard a popping sound as his knuckles connected with the eye joint, breeching the critical orifice. Black blood squirted from the reptile's eye. *"Get off—"*

The caiman made an awful yowling sound and released him, disappearing under the water's surface.

Frank sprang up as fast as he could. His ankle and arm throbbed painfully, but he pushed himself through the water toward his pack and grabbed it, then scrambled back onto the bank as quickly as possible. For several minutes, he hobbled along as fast as he could move, scanning the space behind him, expecting the caiman to reappear. But eventually, he slowed and then finally stopped.

For the first time he dared to look at his foot. Deep lacerations circled his ankle like a bracelet of tooth wounds. His sock was crimson and soggy with blood.

He unfurled the jacket from his right hand and arm, noticing that, too, was soaked with blood. Two semicircles of deep gashes raced across his forearm from where the caiman had sunk its teeth. And now that the desperate adrenaline of escape had ceased to course through him, both wounds burned like fire.

Frank collapsed onto the ground, unzipping the top pocket of the rucksack awkwardly with his left hand and pulling out a large baggie of self-adhesive bandages. He grabbed one and ripped it open with his teeth, wrapping it around his ankle with his good hand. It was just large enough to touch its other end and, thanks to the sticky adhesive of the underside, relieved Frank of the need to hold it in place. He grabbed two more and pressed them onto the tooth marks in his arm, then reached into the plastic bag for a tube of antibiotic cream, gauze and tape.

Five minutes later, having bandaged the wounds as

best he could, Frank unzipped the larger compartment of his rucksack. Thanks to its waterproof material, some of the contents were only slightly damp in a few places and others were dry. He rummaged through the clothing, found a pair of dry socks and slowly eased them onto his throbbing foot. He inspected himself carefully: like the socks and the jacket, there was blood on his shirt and on the cuff of his jeans. He took them off, too, slipped on a dry shirt and lightweight khaki cargo pants and then rolled the bloody clothing into an empty plastic bag, zipping it firmly before returning it and the other items to his rucksack. Caimans were attracted to the smell of blood—as were other jungle predators—so he hoped the plastic would blunt the odor. Without a weapon and as banged up as he was, if he was accosted by another predator, he'd have no chance.

Meet Lucinda near the kapok tree outside the village.

Those were Charmaine's last directions, but he wasn't sure he could find Lucinda's village in the darkness without a guide. His father's map was printed in his memory, but his camera and laptop were now resting somewhere at the bottom of the Amazon River and any other directions his father might have written were with them. Even if he found the village, there were so many kapoks in the jungle—how on earth would he know which one? Frank sighed. His foot and arm throbbed, begging him to stay put and wait for help.

And he might have, had he not been certain that to do so would mean his death.

He palmed a few aspirin, took a long drink from his canteen and settled his headlamp on his forehead. Then he loosened his hiking poles from inside the backpack and used them to haul himself to his feet.

The sun set abruptly like a window shade pulled over the sky as Frank took his first steps into the jungle. Trees towered over him, blotting out the sky. Frank kept moving, leaning hard on his hiking pole every time he came down on the bitten left foot as the jungle came alive with sound around him. Capuchins, tamarins and billions of insects with names Frank knew he'd never bother to learn called to each other in the darkness.

It wasn't long before Frank realized that he was following some kind of path, worn into the jungle by frequent use. It wasn't marked exactly—and it was certainly no wider than the shoulders of a single man walking alone—but the leaves and vines were bent back away from it as though recently cut by a machete's blade. Except for an occasional tree frog jumping from one branch to the next and a flock of bats screeching overhead, he met no more animals.

For Jackie, he thought with every step, his heart filled with darkness. He relived it all: the terror on her face the first time he saw her, the feeling of her soft lips as they grazed his own. He watched her samba and cha-cha and spin, and remembered the ecstasy of his moments of passion with her, longing for consummation. He saw the tears on her face just before she ran away from him at the hospital. He imagined her reading her letter and slipping his mother's ring on her slender finger.

For Jackie.

He limped on, deeper and deeper in the forest, following the swath of parted greenery.

He'd been walking for over an hour, taking occasional sips of water but as few breaks as his body would allow, when he saw it. Twenty yards ahead of him a massive kapok tree divided the path. It was as wide as a house—two dozen men could have stood shoulder to shoulder at its trunk—and disappeared into the sky like a desperate giant reaching for heaven.

"Frank . . . is it you?" a voice whispered from the edge of the jungle. A moment later, she stepped into the clearing by the tree.

Lucinda was almost exactly as Frank remembered: glistening black eyes set in smooth brown skin, a pair of perfect pink lips that seemed to say "kiss me" every time they moved, a curtain of soft black hair hanging in a braid over her shoulder and down to her waist. She wore a shapeless green T-shirt, but even the dull fabric couldn't hide the points of her breasts or the curve of her waist and hips. For an instant, Frank was a dumbstruck eighteen-year-old again, overcome by her exotic beauty.

But then, he noticed the differences. There was a bump in her nose that crooked it to one side, disrupting the harmony of her face in a way that reminded Frank of a young boxer on a bad losing streak. A deep scar showed white in the brown skin over her left eye and another just in the crease of her lips. When she smiled, Frank saw that one of her teeth was chipped. She was still young—still nineteen—but her beauty was being destroyed by force.

"Frank! At last!"

The voice was the same—soft and gentle, English spoken with a lilt that betrayed her native tongue. She threw herself into his arms and he felt her joyful kisses on his neck.

"Lucinda. Thank God, I found you," Frank murmured. "You got my message—"

She stepped out his arms, her smile evaporating. "I

have been waiting so long I feared something bad had happened." She glanced over her shoulder. "Now, I can stay no longer—" Her eyes swept over him. "You are hurt! Where's Charmaine? What has happened?"

Frank put his hand against the bark of the massive kapok. Its solidity steadied him for the news he'd have to deliver about Charmaine.

"No . . . oh, poor Charmaine," she said softly. "Her love for your father was unchanging as my . . ." She lowered her eyes and a virginal touch of color lit her cheeks. "But at last she is at peace. That boat! It was only a matter of time before something like that happened. It was nearly forty years old! It was showing age when I rode in it as a child—"

"You look like a child still, Lucinda. That's why I'm here. I have to—"

"No." Lucinda glanced into the darkness behind them again. "We will not speak of this now. He—my husband—will be looking for me soon. I have to go home—to the village—and it is best if you stay out of sight for now. Besides, you are tired and hurt. You need rest. If the men in the village heard the story of how you fought the caiman you would be retelling it all night. The only thing they love more are tales of the great boar that lives in the jungle—the thing they call the 'Devil,'" she said, laughing as she helped him slide his pack off his shoulders and settled it on her own. "My father said the Devil was old when he was a boy—that it must have drunk from the waters. Come. There is a hut not far from here that we use when hunting, but there is no hunt tonight. You will be safe and there is a small store of food and water kept there. I will come back as soon as I can. Perhaps tonight. If not, tomorrow," she said, moving as quickly as she spoke toward a narrow path to the right of the giant tree. "It has been years since I tried to find it, but my memory is that the pool is three days' hike deeper into the center of the forest from here. Charmaine had crafted a plan to explain my absence to my husband, but . . ." She sighed sadly. "We will need a new plan."

"Charmaine said your husband was jealous—"

"*Shh*," Lucinda hissed, turning a fearful face toward him. "Lower your voice, please. This part of the forest has many eyes."

She seemed so scared that Frank's questions died in his throat. He nodded and concentrated his energy toward following her down the dark path.

The hut was a circle of thatched palm raised a foot above the forest floor on long poles of bamboo. An open space cut into the side served as the door. Lucinda hopped up the single step and then reached back to help Frank stumble up and inside.

It was very small, but a fire pit had been dug in the center and benches lined the walls like a row of shelves. Frank limped over to one of these and sat, reaching for the bandage at his ankle. It was soaked with blood again.

"Crap," he muttered, unwinding the dressing and reaching for his makeshift medical kit to start again. Not only had it bled, but now his ankle had swollen to fill his boot and the leather chafed his skin as he removed it. When he touched the bite marks, the torn skin felt hot and inflamed.

"It is bad, Frank. I will ask the healer what to do. She has treated caiman bites before," Lucinda murmured, turning from the small fire to inspect him.

"Has she got some penicillin?" Frank quipped.

"No, clavillia," Lucinda answered. "It helps . . ." She paused, searching for the word, and in the end, just pointed to the inflamed skin.

"We definitely need that, then."

Lucinda pulled two bamboo baskets across the room toward him. One was heaped with nuts and dried fruit, the other with some kind of cake wrapped in banana leaves. "The jug is filled with water," she said, indicating a tall vessel in the corner. "And now I must go. It is two miles to the village, and even if I run—" She shook her head. "This is not much welcome for an old friend, but I am glad to see you, Frank. I have thought of you often. Very often." To Frank's surprise, she leaned close to him and kissed him, covering his lips with her own. When she stepped away from him, Frank read in her eyes an expectation he hadn't prepared for. "You are many years late, but it doesn't matter. You are here."

Then, before he could reply, she darted out the door and was gone, her footsteps soundless in the depth of the jungle night.

Frank dressed his ankle again, this time leaving the boot aside. He reached for the food baskets ravenously, but after only a few handfuls, lost interest. Instead, he took a long drink of water, swallowed a few more aspirin and pulled out his Mylar blanket. He situated himself on the floor, with his eyes on the opening to the little shack, the fire between him and any unexpected visitor, and settled in to watch and wait.

His thoughts filled the empty benches with images: Charmaine and his father and the triangle of love and pain they'd shared; the look of rekindled love on Lucinda's face and his own youthful promise to take her away; Eva and Steve in a hospital in San Diego and the long recovery ahead. He thought of Ari and the feeling that even now, deep in the jungle and hidden by the darkness of the rainforest floor, he was steadily being pursued.

But mostly, he thought of Jackie. By now, if his trust in Lilly was justified, she surely had his letter. And now that he had found Lucinda he was even closer to undoing his strange power, even closer to getting back home, and even closer to begging her to give him—and their future together—another chance.

Though his eyes grew heavy, he fought the urge to sleep, shifting his position so that his arm and foot burned and the pain jolted him awake. But it was a short-lived revival, and within a few minutes, his head lolled forward on his chest. As he drifted into sleep, he thought he heard the distant thumping rotors of a helicopter overhead.

"Frank . . . Frank . . . wake up . . . wake up, please!"

He snapped awake with a start. The fire was dead and Lucinda was crouched over him in the low light.

"What's the matter?" he asked immediately, registering the urgency of her tone. "What's wrong?"

"Strangers are here. Asking questions about the mysterious waters. They are looking for someone to guide them to it—"

"What do they look like?" Frank demanded, hoisting himself up from the floor to the bench and reaching for his boots.

"I did not see them. I only heard that they had come,"

Lucinda answered, moving quickly away from him so that he couldn't see her face. Frank noticed she wore a heavy-looking knapsack on her back and had her machete in a loop at her waist. "They landed a helicopter right in the center of the village. Americans, I think. They asked about you—"

"Me?" Frank forced his foot into the boot and stood up, testing it gingerly.

"They asked if there had been another foreigner. They described you so well that I knew who they meant. They said you were their friend and they were looking for you—but I knew that could not be true. They are offering a great deal of money—enough for a new boat." Her hair was free from its braid and hung loose and wild around her face. Frank noticed fresh bruises on her wrists and arms. "My husband wanted me to guide them—I am the only one who knows where the waters are—but I refused and he—"

"Beat the shit out of you," Frank murmured softly. "Isn't that right?"

She raised her face to him and even in the low light, Frank could see the swelling beneath her eyes and along her jawline before she shook her hair back over the side of her face with the practice of a proud woman who had spent years concealing abuse.

"It is better than being confused for your ten-year-old daughter's sister." Anger laced the words together. She took a deep breath and then continued in her usual soft voice. "He told them I would guide them at first light. But when he fell asleep, I got my gear and came straight here." Her eyes locked on Frank's face. "What do they want with you, Frank?" she asked.

"I don't think they want me anymore at all. They want the pool, Lucinda. We can't let them find it." His arm burned. The wounds needed to be re-dressed, but there wasn't time. He shouldered his backpack and grabbed his hiking pole. "Let's go."

His ankle was worse—he knew it as soon as he put weight on it—but he did his best to keep up as Lucinda abandoned the path and darted headlong into the dense thicket of trees, slicing through the heavier vines with determination. Frank longed to talk to her, to ask her where they were going and about the strangers who had descended on the village, but she was too far ahead and it took nearly all of his breath to keep within a few paces behind her. Besides, it was more important that they keep moving than that his questions be answered right now—and they both knew it.

They continued. A glance at his watch marked the coming of dawn, but the light in the jungle seemed to grow darker, not lighter, as the heavy canopy of trees blotted out the sun. The air was close and humid, and Frank was soon bathed with the slick wetness of his own sweat.

Finally, Lucinda stopped. Wetness matted her dark hair to her forehead and plastered her clothes to her slender frame. Now Frank could clearly see her eyes: both were swollen and turning an ugly shade of purple as the wounds aged.

"Water," she panted, reaching out her hand for the canteen slung at Frank's hip. She drank long and then handed it back to him. "Sit. I have something for the bite."

Frank found the ground with the palms of his hands before sticking his legs out and letting his bottom rest against the spongy softness of the earth. Lucinda crouched over him, unlacing his boot. As she unwound the bandages, something moved behind on the dark path behind them.

"Do you think we're being followed?" Frank whispered.

Lucinda shook her head. "You hear how much noise we make? Others would make as much or more." She tried to smile. "Probably just a capybara or a brush pig or—" She caught her breath at the bright red marks lining his ankle. "It must be painful, Frank," she murmured, brushing her fingers gently against the damaged skin. "How are you able to walk?"

"We have to walk, so I'm able to walk," Frank answered, grimacing. "And we really should keep moving. It's three days at least—"

Lucinda shook her head. "It would be three days if we followed the path José marked—and even that does not take one directly to the water's edge," she explained, reaching inside her knapsack. She pulled out a flat package of dried leaves and carefully pressed them against Frank's skin. "We create our own path now. It will be more difficult, but it will cut the time in half."

"Are you sure?"

She nodded. "Yes. Pretty sure."

"Then why didn't we go that way when I was here before?"

She sprinkled a little water on his ankle, softening the leaves into a cool balm, then rewrapping the bandages, and repeated the procedure on his forearm. "You did. When you returned," she said softly. "There is no fresh water on this route, Frank. Only what we can carry and capture from the rains, if we are lucky. And because there is no path and we must exert ourselves so heavily just to make our way—"

"We run the risk of dehydration—or worse," Frank said.

"Yes." Lucinda wriggled his boot back on his foot. "But if we reach the pool quickly we will have plenty of cool water to drink." Her face changed as she stood up. "And I will drink. I don't care what the price. I *will* drink and I will share love again with you."

Frank frowned. "Charmaine told me José was well over 100 years old when he went back to the pool. What happened?" he asked.

Lucinda stretched a hand toward him. "How does it feel now?"

Frank stood up. The wound still throbbed, but the cool salve of the leaves eased the pain enough for him to reply, "Better."

"Good," she said, handing him the machete. "You swing for a while. I'm out of practice and my arms are tired. I will tell you about my father while you work." She pointed. "We head into the sun."

She followed slowly behind him as Frank settled into a rhythm, slashing their way through the low-hanging vines and maneuvering carefully over the thick roots of trees.

"My father returned to the mystical pool," Lucinda told him. "He left the village as a healthy man in the prime of life and returned looking much the same." She paused. "Three days later, he was dead—a wizened, ancient man." She shook her head. "Not a man. More like a mummy. Something preserved but not alive. The waters not only took back the years they gave him but added more."

"But that just means it works, doesn't it?" Frank asked eagerly. "It means that we can undo what was done. Your father drank from the pool and it stopped time for him—or at least slowed it down so that he aged gradually. We didn't drink it, we just had sex, and now you're young and every woman I've been with since is young. I don't want to be able to do that anymore. I need to be able to live with a woman and not pass that along, Lucinda. It's not a power, it's a curse—and it's caused me a lot of trouble. Other than that, everything else about me is unchanged—"

"Unchanged, Frank? You are unchanged?"

"Of course," Frank muttered, shifting the machete from his left hand to his right. The effort of swinging made the caiman bite on his right forearm burn, but he swallowed down the pain and kept at it. "I don't look eighteen—"

"You don't look thirty-two, either."

Frank laughed. "Sure I do—"

Lucinda frowned. "So, when you stand together with the other men, your friends, you look like they do?"

"Yes—well. I guess I'm in better shape . . ." he began and then stopped.

He thought of the yearbook picture and then of Steve—but then rejected the thought. After all, Steve was in terrible shape—a college athlete gone to seed as his lifestyle changed. It didn't seem fair to compare them, since Steve hadn't so much as lifted a weight since they graduated from college and Frank was still active. But then again . . .

He thought back to guys he'd seen at his college reunion, comparing himself to each of them in his mind's eye. Some were in better shape than others—with Chase Lynch probably looking the most like he had in school—but all of them were beginning to show the signs of approaching middle age. Receding hairlines, thickening waistlines . . .

Frank wiped the sweat off his brow. His hair was wet

on his forehead, as long and thick as it had been fifteen years before and still cut in the same way. He looked down at his dirty cargo pants—he'd had them since he was twenty and they fit exactly the same. He'd always chalked his youthful appearance up to good habits and lots of outdoor exercise . . . but now he wasn't so sure.

"I remember you, in this forest, years ago before we swam together. You struggled to keep up."

"I was in terrible shape then," Frank chuckled. "I've worked on myself a lot since then—"

"Any other man would be unable to continue with a wound like that," she said, nodding toward his ankle. "How many days have you been sick since we parted, Frank? How long can you go without sleep? How fast can you run? How hard can you hit?" She lowered her voice. "How fast do you heal? How well do you bear pain?"

Frank stopped, the machete hanging suspended in mid-stroke as he thought about it.

"I . . . I don't know."

A snippet from his father's journal floated into his mind. Something about the waters being forbidden to all but the highest priests—who made the sacrifice of remaining forever young for the good of the tribe. Their long lives served as the institutional memory of the people and helped to secure their survival. For everyone else, the sacrifice was too great.

"But what about my father? He aged. I watched him—"

"There was a time when José took great pains to appear older. Whitened his hair with ash. Dressed and moved differently." She shrugged. "Perhaps your father used makeup."

The image of his father as he lay dying filled Frank's

brain, his inner zoom lens tight on the man's face. "I don't think—"

"I do not know how he managed it. I only know that he *was* changed." Lucinda took the machete from his hand and stepped close to him, searching his face with her eyes. "As *you* were changed, Frank Young," she whispered.

"I didn't ask to be changed," Frank muttered.

"No. I did not mean for what happened to us to happen. I did not know, Frank. That night, when you and I went to the waters, Papi—José—told me for the first time of the place. He said it had powers, but he did not say what they were—only that they could be dangerous. He said he did not wish the location to become lost to us—as it had been for many, many years. Much as your father wanted to share his greatest find with you, he told me where it was—and he asked me to show it to you. He thought your father had told you about its powers. But when we got there, and I saw how beautiful it was, my curiosity overwhelmed his many warnings to me. What happened between you and me . . . happened. I do not regret it. Only that it happened in the water." She sighed. "If I could go back to that moment, I would never have touched the pool. I would have discouraged you from so much as dipping your fingers in it. But I did not know." She touched his cheek, gently, like a mother comforting a child. "When you step out of that pool, you may lose more than the power you give to women."

"Fine. If I look a little older—or even a lot older—if I move a little slower, don't heal as fast—so what? I don't care. If I can't run as fast, or hit as hard—I don't care. I'd rather that than *this*. I don't want my wife to look like my daughter—or my granddaughter. I want to be able to tell

Jackie that it's over. It's reversed. I want the chance for a normal life—"

"Is Jackie your wife?" Lucinda asked softly. "You are married now, Frank?"

He heard the hurt in her voice before he saw the sudden wetness in her eyes. She turned away from him.

"Of course you are," she said thickly. "I am foolish to think..."

"I'm not married, Lucinda," Frank answered as gently as he could. "But I hope to be. She's..."

"I understand. She is the reason you are here," Lucinda said, grabbing the machete from his hand. She attacked the jungle in silence, refusing to show Frank her face or to say another word.

CHAPTER
Twenty-One

For hours, they marched on without speaking, lost in their own thoughts. Except for the occasional brief breaks for water or to switch places chopping through thickly overhanging vines and heavy leaves, they did not stop, either. Birds—parrots and macaws of every color, toucans, African grays—screamed and cawed at them, and the insects serenaded them with a steady reminder of their presence. But other than an occasional colony of bats, rousted from their homes by the machete, they saw no animals. Every now and then, though, Frank—who was most often at the rear of their procession—thought he heard something shuffle in the dark thickets behind them, but when he turned, the sound did not repeat and the leaves were still.

Frank's foot and arm still ached, but the swelling and redness seemed to have subsided, leaving him with the same dull discomfort he had felt while recovering from a bad sprain or a deep cut. The real torment, however, was in his mind.

With every step, he felt Lucinda's disappointment and hurt. More than once, he caught up to her, determined to try to explain—but the words died in his throat every time she turned her sad eyes to his face.

Will she still go through with it? he worried. *Will she still help me to undo the pool's effects—even knowing that I didn't come to take her away, but to go home to another woman?*

And he couldn't think of Jackie without an agony of heart worse than the throbbing pain of his foot. What if she didn't forgive him? What if, after everything, his deceit outweighed the risks he'd run to try to correct it? What if, in her mind, he was a liar—or worse, an unfaithful cheat? After all, here he was, hoping to once again sleep with another woman. In his own mind, the act was justified, but Jackie—who had put so much of her fragile trust in him—might very well see it as just another betrayal.

He tried not to think about the pool itself or what might happen if Ari Kousakas found someone to lead him to it. That outcome spelled disaster—for all of them.

"Frank!" Lucinda called from somewhere just out of his sight line. Frank quickened his pace a bit, closing the distance between them.

"I am tired," she murmured, wiping her sweaty face with the bottom of her T-shirt and handing him the machete. Angry red blisters marched across her palms.

"Maybe we should rest a while." Frank glanced at his watch. "It'll be night soon."

She shook her head. "I think it's better if we keep going—"

Once again, something set the leaves behind them aflutter. Frank and Lucinda startled, staring warily into the narrow open space they had just emerged from until a pair of tamarins darted across the path and up a nearby tree, chattering loudly as they chased each other through the leaves high over their heads.

Lucinda exhaled, then laughed. "Maybe you are right. Maybe we *should* take a break. We are both . . . what is the word for it?" She imitated their jerky, nervous movements with an expression of exaggerated fear on her face.

"The word is 'jumpy,' and you're right. We are," Frank agreed. He reached for his canteen, but it was empty. Reluctantly, he pulled the second one from his pack.

"It's okay," Lucinda said, reading his face. "I have one here, too." She patted her own bag. "You first."

The water slid down his throat as smooth and fortifying as any alcoholic drink he could ever remember having in his life. He longed to dump the entire container over his head and let its refreshing power cool his face and neck. Instead, he handed the canteen to Lucinda.

"There's something I want to ask you," Frank said as she tilted back her head to drink. "About the strangers who are looking for the pool."

"Without a guide they are unlikely to find it," Lucinda said, shaking her head. "It is not on any path. Remember? It is invisible to the eye . . ."

"I know, but let's say they find a guide—"

Lucinda shook her head even more violently. "Not possible. It is deep in the jungle, Frank, down a dangerous ravine—"

"Listen to me, Lucinda," Frank interrupted. "I know the

pool is remote and well hidden. But you don't know these people. They are ruthless and determined. They'll do anything to find it. When we get back to the village, they'll be there waiting for you. They'll threaten your children, hurt your friends—they'll do anything to *make* you take them to it. They'll stop at nothing to get what they want." He told her quickly about what had happened to Steve and then how he'd fled San Diego to avoid being coerced into a business relationship with ReGenesis. "They'll find a way, Lucinda," he concluded. "I'm sure they found the drawings my father made in our house. That's how they got this far. I concealed his exact coordinates for the pool's location, but it's only a matter of time before—"

"But this man must not find the pool!" Lucinda exclaimed, her dark eyes flashing resistance. "It's sacred to my people, even if to most it exists as a story and not as a reality! It must not be defiled by—by—such a man."

"I agree," Frank said grimly. "Which means that after we've . . . finished . . ." He felt a bit of blush come into his cheeks when he thought about what they would have to do when they reached the water. "Then we have to figure out a way to conceal it or—"

"How can you conceal it? It is must be a hundred meters deep!"

Frank sighed. One of the largest mosquitoes he'd ever seen circled his head several times until he slapped it away. "If we can't conceal it, we'll have to destroy it," he muttered.

"Destroy it!" Lucinda stared at him as though he'd just suggested they set fire to the forest around them.

"The only way to protect it is to destroy it."

"And how will we do that?"

Frank shook his head. "I was hoping you'd have some ideas—"

"Ideas! It is not possible! How could we destroy something that large? It is not a cup full of water that you can smash like—"

"I don't mean like that," Frank said softly. "I mean, make it unusable. I mean destroy its ability to do what it does."

Lucinda studied his face, understanding slowly lighting her own. "You mean . . ." Her voice dropped to a whisper. "Poison it?"

Frank nodded.

"With what? What do we have that could do something like that? And even if we had something like that— No." Lucinda grabbed the machete, stalking away from him. "No. There must be another way. There must be . . ."

She hacked at the jungle with renewed energy. He pulled himself up and loped toward her.

"I'll cut for a while—"

"You are too slow," she declared. "We must keep going, even after sunset. We can reach the waters by midnight if we keep this pace."

Frank nodded. For a moment, he watched her—a slender girl-woman wielding her knife against the wilderness—then limped after her, his mind turning on questions of destruction and contamination. He wished his father's work hadn't been taken by the Amazon when his laptop and camera sank. There might have been some help there—some clue. As it was, Frank wasn't sure that even something as toxic to humans as nuclear waste would be enough to do the job—assuming he could have gotten his hands on something like that in the first place.

Lucinda had stopped ahead of him.

"What's the matter?" he asked. "Are you ready for me to—"

She shook her head. "I want . . ." she began hesitantly, "I want you to tell me about her. About Jackie."

Jackie. Her image lurked behind every blink, her name hovered in each breath. He would have been overjoyed to talk about her—to anyone but Lucinda.

Frank sighed. Without looking into Lucinda's querying eyes, he grabbed the machete from her hands and held it between his teeth while he found the antibiotic cream and slathered it generously over her blistered palms. When he'd sealed each blister with an adhesive bandage, he put himself to work ahead of her on clearing the path.

"Frank." Her voice was insistent. "You must tell me."

"Why, Lucinda? What possible good could it do now? This is already really difficult for both of us—"

"Why didn't you come back?" she interrupted. "You promised . . . to return for me."

Pain laced her words. Frank stopped, compelled by her emotion.

"I'm sorry. I never meant to abandon you. The only explanation I have is that after my father died . . . everything changed. I was . . . lost. Shut down. For a long time. Longer than I really even knew—"

"And she . . . brought you back?"

Had she? Frank hadn't thought of it that way, but it wasn't wrong. Something changed on that flight from San Diego to Boston, and Jackie was a big part of it. Or perhaps it had been even more elemental. Perhaps, faced with the possibility of death, he'd simply decided to take a chance on truly living for the first time since he'd left the Amazon all those years before.

"I don't know," he said at last. "Maybe. I just know that when I'm with her, I'm different. I can face things I couldn't face before."

"Face?" Her expression registered bewilderment.

He tried to explain it, beginning with the plane crash and the crying toddler, then looping back into the past to connect the dots to his losses.

"I do not understand," Lucinda said with a sigh. "People we love die—just as we will die. It is the way it must be."

"You sound just like her right now."

"But not her, I know," she whispered. "You cannot know what the hope of your return has meant to me. It perhaps was foolish—a girl's romantic dream. Beautiful . . . but not real. I should have given up a long time ago, but I could not. And now, you return at last, but not for me—"

"Lucinda, please understand." Frank dropped the machete to grab her hands and pull her close to him. "Please. You were my first. My first love. That love is still there. It always will be. I won't leave this jungle without you—"

"I will not leave my children, Frank."

"Then they'll come, too. I promise."

"You have broken your promises before," Lucinda said dully and hung her head. "Besides, this Jackie. How will she feel when you return with me and my children? How will she feel to know you have invested so much in another woman? How will she feel when she learns of what we have done in the waters?"

Jackie's face appeared in Frank's mind in triptych, first accepting Lucinda with genuine care and concern, then with furrowed brow as she intellectualized Frank's position, and then finally, tear-stained with the pain of betrayal. Which face would he see if he returned home with Lucinda and her children in tow?

"I don't know," Frank answered honestly. "But I'm going to have faith in her. I'm going to believe she'll understand. Lucinda . . ." Frank forced himself to continue, even though he feared her answer. "You said you wanted to reverse this curse as much as I do. You mean that, right? You're still going to do this, even though . . . even though we won't be together afterward. You'll still do it. With me. When we get there. Won't you?"

"I do not know, Frank," she answered softly. "I think of José—and how quickly after he returned to the pool all its benefits left his body." She sighed. "My husband is a brutal man, Frank. I fear that it is only the recovery power of the pool that has protected me from death at his hands. For love, I would have risked much—even my own death—and trusted in you. But much as I long to 'reverse the curse' as you say, I cannot leave my children motherless. I cannot abandon them to his violence and caprice."

"We're just going to restart the clock, Lucinda. I don't think it's going to kill us—"

"Then you still do not understand, Frank. You have love—and you have hope . . . and I . . ." She offered him a sad smile. "I have neither."

Another several hours trickled past, steamed in heat. The forest—already dark under the canopy of soaring trees—deepened around them. Though Lucinda had said little to him, he could tell she felt they were close to their destination. Her eyes were shadowed with fatigue, but they glowed with determination. She allowed him to settle his headlamp on her head, but other than that she kept counsel with her own thoughts, leaving Frank to wonder if, after traveling all this way, she would refuse him at the pool's edge.

He wished for the ability to charm her: to tell her what she wanted to hear to get what he wanted. He wished for the heart of a true seducer: to be able to bring his passion alive for the moment, and then forget any responsibility for its aftermath the moment after she succumbed. But he couldn't do it. It was bad enough that he'd forgotten his promise and worse that every beat of his heart pounded out Jackie's name. He'd have to wait. He'd have to hope. He'd have to have faith. After all, she hadn't turned back. She was still leading him on, deeper into the jungle toward the pool and whatever fate awaited them there. Frank left her to her own heart's counsel, and communed with his own.

Do you trust me, my love? Do you have any idea how much I love you—or how far I would go to see you healthy and happy and safe? There is no limit to what I would do for you, Helen—none at all. To see you well, I would do anything. To see you well, I would happily bear your anger with me for any transgression.

That, and other mysteries of his father's letters, now made sense. His father had known he was breaking his vows, but he'd done what he had in the hope of achieving a greater good. In his mind, Frank added a codicil to his own letter to Jackie:

To get you back, I will happily bear your anger with me for any transgression. I know it's wrong, but it's the only way I have to make our future right. I hope you will forgive me. I hope you will understand.

The darkness made the heat closer and more stifling. Loud with birdcalls in the daylight, the jungle seemed even louder at night as hundreds of nocturnal animals awoke and went in search of food. Now was when the jaguars and other predators searched for prey. Frank heard more movement behind him now and thought of the giant boar—the Devil—Lucinda had spoken of. Once again, he wished for the pistol confiscated by Officer Garza in Panama. There was something about the constant rustling that made him feel like he was being stalked by something large, mean and hungry.

"Frank!" Lucinda cried from the darkness ahead of him.

"What?" Frank asked, stepping up beside her.

Lucinda pointed into the space ahead of them in dismay. "This could be bad. Very, very bad."

He expected to find Ari's thugs ahead of them on the trail, or some insuperable jungle obstacle blocking their path. But instead, a few feet ahead of them the trail ended completely—

And so did the rainforest.

Except for a few stripped logs that littered the path in front of them, the trees were gone. Ahead of them, the moon shone high and bright over wide-open space, cleared to flat, packed dirt as far as they could see—so completely leveled it was difficult to believe that there had ever been jungle there. The greens and browns had been bleached from the ground: it threw a dusty yellow gloom back at the moon. It reminded Frank of a massive construction site—a major shopping center or a recent East County San Diego housing complex in progress. The space was suspiciously silent; the jungle's night music had evaporated as though in respect for its dead.

"Who has done this?" Lucinda's voice dropped to a whisper, and the eyes she showed him were wet with dismay. "And why?"

"I don't know. I can't believe anyone would be building anything this far out. Unless it's a mining operation. Oil, maybe. I've read something about that. Peru has been issuing oil licenses in the deep western jungle. But . . ." He peered into the darkness. "I don't see any machinery. When was the last time you were here?"

"Many years ago. José was still alive."

"How far are we from the pool?"

She squinted across the clearing. "Five kilometers. Perhaps less. There was a tree with its trunk split in two at the bottom. That was the marker. If it has been cut down . . ." She gestured, helplessly. "I do not know if I will able to find it again."

"We'll find it. Five kilometers is about three miles," Frank calculated. "On the bright side, no more chopping," he added, trying to lighten the heavy sadness that had clouded Lucinda's face.

"If they have done this . . ." She gestured around her. "What about the pool?"

"I don't know," Frank repeated, staring out at the open space ahead of them. "But I don't like this. It's too . . . exposed." He thought of how quickly a jungle cat could cross this open plain and pounce on a couple of exhausted people, but then pushed the thought aside. "A helicopter could land here," he murmured instead. "If we've been followed—"

"We have not been followed," Lucinda asserted with finality. "And at least it is dark." She slipped the machete into Frank's hand as though she had read at least a few of the thoughts in his mind. "You hold this now. You fought off a caiman with your bare hands. Do you think you can slit a jaguar's throat with a machete?"

"I don't want to find out." He reached for her hand. "I think we should stick close to each other now. Can you imagine this with the trees? Which direction should we go to find whatever's left of the trunk of that tree? If there's anything left at all?"

Lucinda closed her eyes for a moment, then looked up at the heavens in part for prayer and part for celestial navigation. "Northeast." She gestured. "This way."

They stepped cautiously into the clearing and began moving quickly over the flat, scorched ground. The open space stirred the first breeze Frank had felt since he left San Diego. It would have been pleasant, had it not felt so wrong.

They trooped along in wary silence for half an hour.

"I don't see any roads," Frank said, hesitant to violate the silence with the sound of his voice. "If this was a mine site, they must have helicoptered in supplies and personnel—"

"And then just left?"

"Apparently."

Several minutes later, Lucinda aimed the headlamp at a spot in the distance. "What is that?" she asked, pointing at a white cylinder of concrete squatting a few hundred feet ahead of them.

"It's some kind of pipe . . . or the top of one," Frank murmured as they drew closer. "But it's been capped." He looked around him for something that might offer him more information, but in the darkness he could see no further clues. "I think this was an oil drilling site, Lucinda."

"But they found no oil?"

"I guess not. Either that or extracting it was too difficult. Look, I really don't know a lot about drilling for oil, but I do know this much. Drilling requires a nearby water source."

Lucinda's face crumpled with dismay.

"No, Frank. You do not think—"

"Do you think we might be close now?"

Lucinda sighed. "It is impossible to say. All of the markers are gone."

"I wish I hadn't destroyed my phone. I don't know if there's a cell tower within range, but I could at least try entering Dad's coordinates into the GPS—" He stopped, shining the light more closely at the ground. "Wait. There's a trench dug here." He pointed at the dusty ground, kicking at the dirt with his boot. A bit of pipe revealed itself. "Lucinda, this might be it."

"What?"

"This pipe might have been used to bring water to the drilling site. If they used the pool as their water source—"

"We can follow the pipe to find it—"

A sudden rush of sound split the darkness and silence around them. A spotlight hit Frank's eyes, momentarily blinding him just as he heard the sounds of footsteps, pounding over the seared earth toward him. On instinct, he sent a roundhouse kick into the darkness beside him and felt it make contact with some soft part of a human torso. As the air moved in front of him, he swung the butt of the machete forward and heard a crunch as it met flesh. He whirled around, sensing the next attack. Instead, he heard the clicks of several semiautomatic weapons cocked and loaded, and he knew without seeing them that he was their target.

"I'm sure you don't care much for you own life, but unless you want me to fill your lady friend full of holes, you'll drop that knife, Mr. Young, and stand very, very still," a steely voice said. "I will kill her. And that would be a great shame, considering she's the only one of us who knows where your father's great secret lake is."

Frank still couldn't see—someone was shining a large flashlight directly into his face—but he knew the voice.

"Leave her alone, Pandora," he said. "Lucinda!"

He heard the sound of scuffling, and then a thickly built man with a mass of shaggy black hair shoved her toward him. She stumbled, landing hard in heap on the ground. As she tried to stand, the man slapped her so hard, her head rocked on her neck, cursing in a language Frank didn't understand.

Frank lunged for the man, but he stretched his gun at him with the uncertain hand of one who had little knowledge of weapons. Frank stepped back, knowing well the danger of a gun in the hand of an angry and untrained hand. Instead, he pulled Lucinda up. There was blood on her lips and shame in her eyes.

"Are you okay?" he muttered.

Her eyes filled with tears, but she nodded, wiping her face with her hand.

"My husband . . ."

"He's been very useful," Pandora said, pacing toward

them. For the first time, Frank could see her. A safari hat covered her face and hair and sent a yard of netting over her shoulder and down her back as though she were posing for the cover of a magazine, not trekking the jungle. She wore a pair of lightweight linen pants and knee boots and somehow looked like she had managed to hike for a full day through the heat of the jungle without ever breaking a sweat.

"How long have you been trailing us?" Frank asked.

"Almost since the beginning."

"You found the map?"

"It took a while, but the smell of paint eventually gave me a clue. It was very clever, but . . ." She smiled. "I saw *The Da Vinci Code*, too, Frank. We were very excited by that, as well you can imagine. For a moment, you were . . . superfluous. Unfortunately, it appears that some of the coordinates may have been tampered with. That made it necessary to find you once again." She stalked up to him and paused. "We reached out to your friends, but . . ." She shrugged. "So distrustful. I'm sure you'll be happy to know that, as of yesterday at least, his doctors seem to believe Mr. Hughes will make a complete recovery."

"No thanks to you."

"I find him very rude, but I certainly wish him no ill will."

"Right," Frank muttered.

"And then, of course, Ari spoke to Jackie. To see if she had heard from you and to warn her of the sort of man she has become involved with."

His letter flashed in Frank's mind, but he tried to keep the thought from showing on his face.

"Really? And what sort of man is that?"

"The sort who is serially unfaithful. The sort who has sex with strangers for outrageous sums of money. The sort who would abandon her and fly off to the Amazon without so much as a goodbye."

Lucinda's eyes locked on Frank's face as Pandora spoke, searching for the truth. He couldn't explain it to her now, so he focused on Pandora instead.

"So where is your boss?" he demanded. "Where's Ari?"

"Oh, he really doesn't care much for hiking. Neither do I, particularly." She sighed dramatically. "But someone had to do it. At any rate, he should be here shortly. He'll join us for the last few steps of the walk. You see, he really wants to see this—what shall we call it? This 'mystical pool' of your father's. He wants to see it very, very much."

"I bet."

Pandora's chilly laugh floated toward him. "We can always count on you for the unexpected, Mr. Young, and certainly you outdid yourself this time. You should be quite proud of the amount of trouble you've caused me. This all could have been so very simple . . . but instead here we are, perspiring at the equator, looking for a source that, ultimately, makes you quite expendable after all." She flashed him another wicked smile. "Funny how things work out."

"Hilarious."

Her attention zeroed onto Lucinda. "Well, Ms. del Flores—or I suppose Mrs. Quispe is more appropriate, yes?" she asked, nodding toward the dark-haired man who still leveled his pistol at Frank's chest. "If you wouldn't mind, please do lead on while we have the help of the moon. I'd like to be back in Iquitos and in some air conditioning by daylight if at all possible."

"I do not know—the markers—they have been destroyed—"

Pandora shook her head. "I think not. I believe this"—she gestured toward the well cap—"will point the way. Oil drilling requires a water source, right, Frank?" She indicated the wide, flat expanse ahead of them. "And it can't be too far away. Start walking, Mrs. Quispe. I'm sure something will come to you—especially now that we're able to provide you with considerably more light."

Lucinda's shoulders sagged as she turned back to the water pipe, kicking at the dirt to track its path.

"I'm sorry, Frank," she murmured.

"Me, too," he replied. Her husband edged closer, eyeing Frank suspiciously.

"I understand now what you said earlier about these people," Lucinda whispered. "And you are right. If we can find a way, we must—"

"Oh dear," Pandora interrupted. "Still plotting? I'm afraid you two need to be separated. Mr. Young, you'll understand why I find this necessary. You are just too much trouble and you've proved you cannot be trusted, so—"

A hand grabbed his shoulders, roughly extricating him from his rucksack. An instant later, thick cords of rope tightened over his wrists, tethering him like an animal being led on a reluctant journey.

"That's better," Pandora cooed, inspecting the handiwork of her minions. "And oh, I believe I owe you a little something." Without warning, she leveled a surprisingly powerful right jab to his gut so forcefully, Frank doubled over, breathless with pain. "Consider that payback for that little tango on your front lawn. My ribs are still quite sore.

Seems only fair you should share the discomfort, yes?" She stalked away from him, satisfaction spreading across her feline features. "All right, Mrs. Quispe. You may proceed."

By flashlight and torch, their odd procession marched through the clearing: Lucinda led them, followed closely by her husband and another man who looked like he, too, might belong to their tribe. Pandora walked in the middle of the assembly in the company of a man whom Frank recognized as one of the goons he'd stopped at his home the day of his escape. Two more of Ari's men came after them and Frank stumbled behind them all, dragged by the cord looped so tightly around his wrists that he could barely feel his hands.

They twisted and turned, following the rut in the ground. The well must have been abandoned for quite a while, because in places, the pipe was invisible and the trench joined the rest of the site in a level plain. From time to time, Frank heard Lucinda's voice—a low murmur of words he was too far away to hear—and sometimes the answering sound of a slap, followed by hurried words in her indigenous tongue.

There's got to be a way out of this. There's got to be a way to stop this.

Those were the only thoughts in Frank's mind, but as hard as he bent his brain to their predicament, there didn't seem to be any help or escape.

The terrain changed. The clearing gave way to massive remnants of felled trees, some split and splintered, others nearly whole but lying rootless on their trunks. Frank lost both the pipe and the trench for the detritus of the rainforest's former greenery, now stripped and scattered in front of them. Lucinda ran her fingers along the bark of a thick kapok as wide as she was tall, now felled and broken. In another moment, ignoring the shouts of the men from her village, she had scrambled up it and was walking quickly and steadily along its surface. She stopped and turned back to them. The harsh white glow of the flashlights made her bruised face look ancient and sad.

"It is down there." Lucinda said the words in English first and then in her native language. "This is the ravine." She squatted. "The pipe ends there."

Pandora hurried toward her, peering into the darkness. "I can't see anything. Lights!"

The men rushed toward her, lifting flashlights and torches, peering down the steep slope of the ravine. Frank was yanked to the edge of a dark crater that was nothing like the steep hill of greenery he recalled bumping and sliding down with Lucinda fifteen years before. He closed his eyes, trying to remember. There had been so many trees then, but to his best guess, the drop was about forty feet—far enough and steep enough to cause a body serious damage if it made contact with a hard enough surface, like a rock or a tree. He inched closer to the edge of the crater. His pupils were still dilated by the sudden light that had been thrust in his face, and he closed his eyes as the others craned their necks and projected their lights into the darkness. When he opened them again, he peered in the other direction, away from the lights and into the impenetrable darkness below.

He couldn't see the bottom any more than Pandora could, but that wasn't exactly what he was looking for.

It appeared that the ravine, like the area surrounding it, had been deprived of all its green. No trees still stood on the slope, nor had any logs found refuge on the embankment. He could see dirt and a few gnarled roots, but other than that, the slope seemed to have been stripped smooth. There might be trees farther down in that deep, impenetrable darkness, but that was a risk Frank knew he'd have to take.

"I still can't see," Pandora said, pulling what looked like an old-fashioned two-way radio out of her pocket. She spoke a few words into it in a low voice, but Frank made out "fly," "Ari" and "spotlight" before she pocketed the device and turned her attention to Lucinda.

"How far is it down there? Is there a path or—"

Frank closed his eyes.

Three, two, one . . .

He didn't know where the sound came from, but to his own ears it sounded like the roar of an angry animal—only *he* was that animal and there was much desperation in the sound's origins as pure fury. He leapt forward, aiming two sure kicks at Pandora's muscle men before knocking the gun from Lucinda's husband's startled hands. It went off with a report that shattered the stillness of the night and sent Toro Quispe scuttling in crablike fear into the others.

Frank grabbed Lucinda with one bound hand.

"What—?" she whispered.

"Protect your head if you can," he murmured, gripping her tightly. Then, counting on surprise and gravity, he dove over the edge of the ravine and let the steep slope of darkness swallow them.

They hit the dirt embankment hard, rolling together, over and over, faster and faster as they plummeted toward the base of the ravine below. Frank's caiman-damaged arm was snagged by the hard remnant of a tree root, and the shock of fresh pain made him lose his grip on Lucinda. He heard the scrape and clatter of her limbs as she tumbled away from him, then the crack of gunshots in the air above them. Then, after ten body-jarring seconds, he landed with a shuddering thud in a heap of bruises and scratches at the base of the dark ditch.

For a moment, every muscle in his body hurt too badly for him to do more than lie there in a breathless, battered daze. But faint voices, shouting from the top of the ravine, roused him. There wasn't much time.

He pulled himself up to his knees, slowly and painfully, checking himself for new injuries and finding nothing more serious than a few deep scratches. Still, his very brains felt rattled as though something critical in his skull had been shaken loose.

"Lucinda!" he croaked, unwilling to raise his voice much above a whisper. He knew they were invisible from the top and it was crucial that sound not betray their location—or even that they had survived the fall at all. "Lucinda!"

He thought he saw something a few feet away and moved toward it, blinded by darkness. He bit at the end of the rope around his hands, loosening the tie with his teeth until, at last, his hands were free and he could crawl. He felt around in the darkness until he almost fell on her. She lay motionless on her stomach, her face pressed into the barren ground. "Lucinda," he murmured, but she didn't respond. Concerned, Frank found her pulse, then exhaled with relief as her chest slowly rose and fell.

Water.

He remembered it with a sudden sense of relief, turning away from her to crawl toward the pool.

But as his eyes acclimated to the darkness, he realized something was wrong.

Where the edges of the pool had once lapped cool water against the banks, there was nothing but the hard angles of a great quantity of logs. Frank pulled himself to his feet and peered toward the center of the basin, looking for the mystical waters of his memory.

There was water—a little—here and there, trapped between the rails of wood, but nothing like what he remembered and far too little for even the hope of swimming in it. Frank pulled himself to his feet and staggered toward a little eddy, cupping a bit of it into his dirty hands. It was thick and slick and silt-filled. He sniffed it, and the putrid smell of oil mixed with some chemical and the putrefaction of decay assaulted his nose. His worries about destroying the pool to keep it safe from Ari Kousakas had been for nothing. Someone else had already done it for them.

Frank sank to his knees, exhaustion and despair sweeping over him simultaneously, his heart filling with utter darkness. Without the pool, there was no hope, no reason to return home. He'd never see Jackie again—or Eva or Steve or Max and her family, either. The love—the hope—that had fueled him through the jungle seeped out of him. Frank covered his face with his hands.

I wish none of this had never happened. I wish I'd never come here. It would have been better for me, and better for Lucinda—

Lucinda.

Frank wet his hands and hurried back to Lucinda's side. The water smelled horrible, but when he ran his wet fingers along her temples, she moaned and opened her eyes.

She stared at him for a long moment.

"You are . . . crazy . . ." she said softly at last.

"Yes," Frank agreed. "Are you hurt? Can you sit up?"

She tried, then clutched her chest and winced.

"You're hurt."

"It's okay. Help me," she whispered, stretching her hands toward him.

Frank grasped them and eased her upward, bracing her body with his own.

She sat in his arms placidly, collecting herself. "We don't have much time. If we can get to the pool . . ."

"There *is* no pool. It's gone," Frank murmured.

"Gone? No . . ." She pulled away from him. Frank watched as she struggled to her feet with difficulty and limped into the blackness toward the basin's edge.

She was quiet for so long he grew worried. He stood up and staggered toward the pile of logs resting in what remained of the water.

Lucinda was crouched near a tiny square of trapped water, her hands over her face. Her sobs were soft as whispers and her shoulders shook in the dim light.

What could he say? What words were there for this moment that doomed them both to lives they didn't want—without any hope for improvement or change?

"I will just let him kill me." Her voice was a shattered, broken-sounding thing that hurt Frank more than the caiman's jaws or any punch he'd ever taken. "I do not wish to be young any longer." She stood suddenly, staring up at the top of the ravine. "If I call out now, he will come. This time, he will kill me. If I just let him kill me—"

Even though his own hope was crushed, Frank couldn't bear her despair.

"No, Lucinda. Please," he said, rousing the last of his optimism. "We'll . . . we'll have to find another way—"

"There is no other way, Frank!" she hissed. "The pool *was* the way, and now we have nothing!"

"You can't just . . . give up!" Frank grabbed her shoulders. "What about Helen and Frank? If you just quit, what will happen to them? Maybe there's another spot—or maybe underneath the logs there's still some uncontaminated water—or somewhere else—I don't know! My dad taught me there is always a solution. We can't give up—"

"What choice do we have?"

"You have to try for your children, Lucinda. And I have to try for Jackie and the hope of any kind of normal life. And the last thing either one of us can do is let any of those people up there get us, because if we do they'll—"

A familiar thumping noise filled the air, interrupting him. Frank craned his neck toward the night sky.

"*Shit*. It's their helicopter. It'll be here any minute. We've got to get out of here."

By the light of the setting moon, Frank made out that they were standing on the level banks of a deep crater of earth that had been the basin of the pool, its dirt sides compacted like a rock face from years of containing the waters. Even in the low light, he saw that what had been the pool's floor was now filled with everything that had been stripped from the land above them: logs, vines, mud and ooze tangled with each other like so many bodies buried in a mass grave. The remnants of once-proud trees leaned haphazardly against each other in broken tangles of wood. Some lay flush against the basin's floor, others at the angles in which they fell, looking too defeated and precarious for him to hope to climb—even if any of them had reached the top of the ravine. Clearly the pool had been much deeper than he had realized when it was filled with water. As far as Frank could tell from the moon's light, the pool had looked circular on the surface, but it was actually shaped more like a funnel: wide at the top but growing steeper and narrower as it tunneled down toward earth's core. With a perverse bit of imagination, he thought of a Hershey's kiss, inverted so they were standing on the wide chocolate bottom—and the pointy tip was down beneath them, plugged with tree trunks and branches.

Frank scanned the steep embankment they had just tumbled down with dismay. Without the bushes and trees that he and Lucinda had used to pull themselves back up fifteen years before, the slopes were nothing but slippery dirt. Even if he thought he could climb them, he wasn't sure Lucinda would be able to—and it would take more time than they probably had. Suddenly sliding into the ravine didn't seem like the best idea. They were sitting ducks here—and delving deeper, down into what once had been covered with water, offered no exit.

Lucinda dragged a dirty hand across her tear-streaked face. "We cannot stay here," she said.

"Yeah," Frank agreed, with a sigh. "And I guess we'll have to go down there and hope to find a way back up on the other side. I don't see any other way." He stretched out his hand to her. "Can you make it?"

She hesitated. The moonlight shadowed her face, softening the bruises and easing the lines of the scars. Frank saw her as she had been on that fateful night that had changed them both forever, and he was seized with a powerful feeling of remembered connection and deep regret.

"Lucinda, I've made nothing but mistakes. I never meant to abandon you—and I'm ashamed of how I've behaved. I—I can't blame you if you don't trust me. I can't blame you if hate me, but—" he began.

"Enough, Frank," Lucinda whispered, taking his hand. "Our destinies unfold as they are meant to. And you are right. We must keep going. We must try. We must find a solution. If not for ourselves, for the ones we love—"

The rotors grew louder. The dark shape of a military-looking aircraft crested the distant trees.

"Get down!" Frank cried, pulling Lucinda into the nest of dead branches just as the helicopter's lights swept over the ravine, then turned to sweep it again in the steady increments of an intentional search. "They're coming," he said. "And now they've got the helicopter's spotlight. We're going to have to try walking down there—along the silt at the bottom. At least there's brush down there. We can hide and hope to find a way to the other side."

Lucinda shook her head. "But it is so steep. And it is still very dark. How will we keep from falling?"

Frank looked around. His hiking poles were somewhere in the clearing above his head and impossible to retrieve. But something like them would do. He grabbed a few small tree branches and quickly stripped them, inspecting the wood for smoothness and strength. Satisfied that they were straight enough to be used as supports, Frank handed two of them to Lucinda and took two for himself.

"You're right. It's too steep to do standing," he told Lucinda. "And the banks might be soft from the water that used to be here. If it's wet, the dirt will just pull away and we'll fall." He peered at the logs and brush littering the bowl of the basin. "Something tells me it won't be as soft a landing as our last one." He lowered himself to the ground and positioned his branches, posting one on either side. "It will be like skiing. Or tobogganing."

Lucinda frowned. "Skiing?"

"Never mind." Frank shook his head at himself and his crummy analogy. After all, she'd spent her life in the Amazon jungle; she'd never seen snow or witnessed a winter sport. *If we get out of this, I'll take them skiing*, Frank thought. *Lucinda and her children.* The image of them sliding down the bunny slopes surrounded by white snow was a soothing promise of a better day. "Down on your bottom, and use the poles to ground yourself." He demonstrated. "Since there was water here, it's going to be a slow decline in places and then drop off sharply. It's dark, so don't go fast. You won't be able to see the drop-offs, so you have to slow enough to feel them and anchor yourself accordingly. You understand?"

She nodded, sinking onto the ground beside him with a small grunt of pain. "I am ready."

"All right," Frank said, managing to smile. "Together on three. One, two, three!"

He pushed himself forward, wishing for a toboggan or a boogie board or something to cushion his ass as he bounced slowly down the basin that had once held miraculous waters. Twisted knots of roots and rocks and debris from the efforts of the oil miners bruised him at every painful slide. In some places, the ground seemed so level he could have stood and walked, and it seemed silly to be bumping along the ground on his rear end. Then, suddenly, the terrain would change and he'd be clinging to his makeshift poles for dear life, his feet brushing the air while he slid desperately toward the ugly pile of killer logs at the pool's floor.

They traveled like that for what felt like a lifetime of agonizing inches as the gradient got steeper and steeper. Above them, the night sky began to lighten, the stars in the black sky fading into the gray dawn as, by slow degrees, the night eased toward day. Frank craned his neck toward the sky with a mix of gratitude and fear. It would be easier for them to make their way to the pool's floor with the aid of the sun—and easier for their pursuers to see them do it.

Help us, Frank prayed. He wasn't sure whom he was praying to, but he hoped that any God or benign spirit within earshot of his appeal would take pity on him. *Please, don't let them catch us. Help us find a way out. Help us figure out a way home . . .*

Something black loomed in front of them, blocking the path of their descent. Frank felt it with his feet before he saw it: it was hard and solid and too high to climb over. He touched it; his fingers scraped against bark.

"It's the kapok," Lucinda said. "The marker tree. Or what's left of it."

"There's no way we're getting over this," Frank muttered, inspecting the tree carefully. "It's got to be thirty feet high and there's nothing to grab or—"

He lifted his head, expecting to find Lucinda at his side, but she was gone.

"Frank . . ." Lucinda sounded far away.

"Where are you?"

"Inside. Down here. Inside."

He followed the sound of her voice, his shoulder pressed against the massive tree as he dug in with his legs to navigate his descent without falling. She was crouched in a hollow slit between the giant kapok and the silty ground, almost invisible beneath its splintered trunk.

"Remember, I told you it was split into two pieces at the base?" she said, gesturing. "It is nearly hollow here. The tree is wedged into the dirt. Almost like a bridge we can walk beneath."

"Can we get through? Going underneath?"

"I don't know. I do not see light from the other side—"

Rotors thudded to life in the gray sky.

"Come, quickly." Lucinda reached for Frank's hand and pulled him into the crevasse, just as a bright light pierced the basin's walls and the spotlight traveled slowly back and forth near where they had just stood. Frank and Lucinda shrank deeper into the awning of the felled giant, dropping to their knees as the space between the tree trunk and the ground grew smaller and tighter. Overhead, the helicopter's engine roared loudly, out of place in the silence of the abandoned drill site.

"Why don't they go? Did they see us?" Lucinda asked, crawling away from him deeper and deeper in the shelter of the tree trunk.

"I don't know, but my guess is they're trying to find a spot to land. Down here at the pool's floor."

"I do not think that will be possible."

"Neither do I. But they might be able to send a party down by ladder to look for us." He sighed. "We might be safe here for a while, but eventually—"

"We are hidden here, but we will not be able to get out on the other side. The tree is wedged too tightly. We cannot reach the bottom of the pool from here." Lucinda reappeared from the darkness, now smeared with mud and bark from her hair to her boots. "But we can reach the other bank. And unseen. And maybe there we will find another way."

Frank nodded. He didn't have the heart to point out that wherever they emerged, it was likely now they would be caught. Ari would tell Jackie how he'd cornered Frank like a rat in a hole. Frank could imagine him gloating over it . . . but when he pictured Jackie's reaction, he only saw her face at the hospital.

"This is my fault," she had said as solemnly as an oath. "But maybe I can keep it from happening again."

Ari was here, in the Amazon. Whatever Jackie planned for him either hadn't worked or had yet to take effect . . . and either way it didn't matter. If he saw the sunrise today, it would probably be for the last time.

"Frank? Are you coming?" Lucinda was ahead of him in their woody shelter and her voice was faint with distance.

"Yeah," he called, and made his limbs move.

The space grew more and more narrow and sloped dramatically downward. The tree must have been one of the tallest in the jungle—and nearly hollow for most of its extraordinary length. They went on and on, leaving all light behind them, but still there was room to continue forward. The soft mud of the pool's floor oozed between their fingers, and from time to time the unmistakable odor of oil burned Frank's eyes and stung in his throat, making his head ache. The fabric of his thin cargo pants tore and his bare knees scraped the ground.

Ahead of him, Lucinda stopped. "It ends," she announced in the impenetrable darkness. "I feel . . . just dirt. Mud."

Frank sank onto his belly, easing the kinks in his back and hands from the long crawl. He lay his head in the cool mud, and the last of his hope sputtered and died. *Which is better?* he wondered. *Death by dehydration or by discovery?*

Lucinda continued to move frantically ahead of him, digging desperately at the wall of soft dirt. "Stop. You're just exhausting yourself. You're not going to be able to dig us a way out of here, Lucinda," he muttered. "The tree's too big to lift and if that's the bank, there's just too much dirt."

"Yes." There was panic just under the surface of her voice, and her breath whistled through her mouth as she spoke. "I—I don't like . . . I can't—"

"Calm down—"

"No! There—there has to be a way—there has to be—" She kept going, flailing at dirt with her hands, tossing it aside desperately. "I cannot—we cannot—not like this—"

Her fingertips scraped something. The hard *scritch* sound of her nails against it told Frank it was too firm and solid to be dirt. "What was that?"

"There—there is something here!" He couldn't see her face, but he could hear the eagerness of relief in her voice. "It sounds like . . . like . . . wood. Almost like some kind of door . . ."

Frank reached for his pockets. Ages ago, there had been a lighter in one of them, but that time seemed to belong to another man in another lifetime—yet as he stuck his fingers into the matted fabric, the slim tube seemed to jump into his hand.

"I have a light," he told Lucinda. "But I'm not sure I should use it."

"I do not believe they will see it, Frank."

"No, but there's a lot of oil under here. I don't want to set us ablaze."

Lucinda guffawed, hysteria dancing on the edge of the sound. "I do not think that a fire would matter much now. We face death at all points here. Try it. We have little to lose."

Frank sighed. Death by fire wasn't on his top-ten list, but neither was slow starvation under a dying tree, let alone an untimely demise by firing squad. Besides, the smell of oil was less pungent here than it had been. He eased himself into the space beside Lucinda, closed his eyes and rolled the lighter's wheel.

The flame burst to life higher and brighter than he expected and burned robustly for several seconds—long enough for them both to see an oval impression was cut into the wall of the reservoir in front of them—a door that had once been covered by water.

The lighter flared higher, stretching to the length of a ruler, then sputtered out.

"Something tells me we shouldn't do that again anytime soon," Frank muttered, feeling the wall of mud for the outlines of the door and beginning to dig. "How does it open? Is there a handle or a pulley or—"

"From the bottom, I think. In our tribe, there are many doors with this design. The ancient temples and—" She stopped suddenly and though she was invisible in the pitch dark, when she spoke again her voice was bright with joy. "Frank!" she exclaimed. "I know where this heads! It leads to the ancient temple—the one you were supposed to see when you were here before but did not. The priests there were the caretakers and guardians of the pool." She pointed to the door. "This door must have been like . . . like a well or—"

"A cistern. An aqueduct, even. To bring up water for rituals or—"

"Yes!"

"Is there water there? In the temple?"

"I do not know. The structure is very, very old. Very unstable. Nearly part of the jungle itself. Papi—my father—said no one had been inside it for many, many years. He said it was unsafe to try."

Frank attacked the mud like a dog, pulling up handfuls of dirt and tossing them over his shoulder as fast as he could make his muscles move. "You think it's big enough for us to get through?"

Shouts echoed from above them. The voices were muffled by the breadth of the thick old tree.

"They're getting closer," Frank muttered.

"Dig," Lucinda whispered. "I do not think we have any other choice."

CHAPTER
Twenty-Two

Together they cleared the silt from the small opening and heaved it open just enough for first Frank and then Lucinda to wriggle on their bellies into the darkness behind it before it slid closed again, as though shutting its mouth to the outside world.

"They'll find us," Lucinda said softly as an even deeper darkness closed in around them.

"Yes," Frank said. "It's a matter of time." He felt around him, reaching for the walls and ceiling of their enclosure. "It's not a cistern. Feels more like . . . a tunnel. Not high enough to stand up in, but tall enough to crawl through—at least for now."

"But we cannot see anything." Frank felt her tremble beside him. "There could be anything in here . . ."

Frank hit the lighter, sending its feeble light down the

narrow dirt tunnel. "For as long as it lasts, it's better than nothing." He tried to smile. "Ever been spelunking?"

Lucinda frowned, bewildered by the word. "Spe..."

"Spelunking. Crawling around in caves."

She shook her head.

"Well, I guess you're in for a new adventure," Frank said grimly. "Scorpions, spiders, bats—they love places like this." He shut off the lighter to conserve the fluid and took his place in the lead, starting off down the mouth of the tunnel. "Stay close."

They made their way slowly along the dirt floor. Every fifteen seconds or so, Frank thumbed the lighter's wheel to assess the terrain in front of them and scare off whatever critters might be just ahead, but as far as he could see it remained uniform in width and height, smooth and uninhabited.

"Definitely some kind of aqueduct," Frank muttered over his shoulder. "The water must have flowed through here—"

"Into some kind of pool or container or something," Lucinda finished.

"How far is the temple?"

"Not more than one or two kilometers—but the terrain has always been difficult over land."

"Not going to be any fun to crawl it, either," Frank muttered. He touched the lighter again to survey the path ahead. Still the tunnel continued, straight and level and completely uniform, as though it had been created by a modern machine. Frank shut off the light and moved forward into the darkness again, ignoring the cramp in his knees and his wrists, grateful at least for the coolness of being underground and for the silence behind them. For now, at least, they were not being pursued.

At last, after a long and tortuous hour in the tunnel's darkness, the lighter revealed a dark opening in the tunnel a few feet ahead of them.

"Wait here," Frank commanded, inching closer to it. He lay flat on his stomach and stretched the lighter into the dark space. It flickered and went out before he could see anything. He tried again—and caught a quick glimpse of a wide ring of uneven stones.

"The lighter's dying," he called over his shoulder. "But it looks like a well of some kind."

He tried again, aiming the light toward the floor of the structure. This time, just before it died, he pulled his body through the hole.

He stood at the bottom of a stone well just wide enough for two people. The opening to the tunnel he and Lucinda had crawled through formed a hole in the well's stone lining about the height of Frank's chest and must have once been the conduit through which water traveled, but now even the floor was bone dry. A small circle of light shone like a beacon about twenty feet above Frank's head.

"It's okay, Lucinda!" he called, reaching back into the tunnel for her. When she joined him in the narrow stone enclosure, she stood as close as an embrace beside him on the dirt floor. Frank studied her face as she lifted her head to the dim light above, and his heart was filled with an emotion he could hardly explain. When she turned and her eyes locked on his, weary but determined, Frank had to look away to keep from pulling her into his arms.

Instead, he pointed to the faint orb above them. "Maybe if we're lucky there's some water up there. Enough to drink at least."

"But how will we get up there?"

Frank tested the stone in the walls with first his fingertips and then the toe of his boot. "Climb. The stones are uneven. I know you're hurt and tired. I am, too. But we're almost there. If we're lucky, there will be something that can help us there. And if not . . ." He shrugged. "Well, we can say we tried. We did everything we could."

Even in the dim light, Frank could plainly see the terror in Lucinda's face. "I don't know, Frank." Her voice quivered. "I-I don't think I can . . ."

"You can." Frank turned her toward the stones and stood behind her, guiding her hands. "Put your fingers in the cracks like this . . ." He placed her fingers and then lifted her slightly, his chest grazing her back. "And your toes here . . . and here . . . and pull yourself up," he murmured gently, his mouth at her ear. "Good. Keep going. Feel around for a place with a grip to pull yourself up. I'll be right behind you. I'll do my best to place your feet—"

"F-Frank . . . I'm scared."

"I know, but you can do this. Look at everything you've already done. It's just a few feet. I promise, I won't let you fall."

She swallowed hard and nodded, turning her face back to the uneven rocks, reaching out her right hand for the next hold. "Good!" Frank cried as she hoisted herself another few inches closer to the top. "Keep going! I'm right behind you!" He chose a spot to the right of where she had begun and dug his toes and fingers into the stones.

"Frank!" Lucinda's voice was a near shriek of panic. "I can't—"

"Hand, toe, hoist, hand, toe, hoist!" Frank called up at her. "Say it and do it. Hand, toe, hoist, hand, toe—"

"Hoist!" Lucinda breathed, pulling herself up another few feet. "Hand, toe . . ."

They said it together over and over until the well's opening was only a few feet away. Frank scaled ahead of her, pushing himself over the lip of stone with shaking muscles, but didn't pause to look around. He leaned back into the well, grabbed Lucinda by both wrists, and dragged her the last few feet up the stone ring.

"See," he panted. "You did it."

Lucinda squatted in front of him, breathing heavily, her hair a curtain concealing her face. But at last, he heard her chuckling with disbelief. She lifted her head to speak—but the words never came out. Instead, her eyes widened and her lips parted with amazement.

"Is that . . . gold?" she asked, pointing over Frank's shoulder.

It was just another circular wooden hut, thatched with a bamboo roof, through which they could see the beginnings of daylight as well as ropes of vines that had grown into the spaces where the thatch had worn away. The floor was dirt around the well and there appeared to be no other adornments . . . except for the platform that raised a small rectangular enclosure about the size of a Jacuzzi tub over the rest of the room. The tub reminded Frank of the canoes Native Americans made—a hunk of some sturdy tree, its center hollowed out and rubbed smooth—but covered by an ornate plate of shining gold. Posted on either side were two braziers whose fires had long gone dead and two huge bamboo buckets.

Frank mounted the platform reverently. The golden cover was decorated with images of people who all seemed to be bathing or drinking from the mystical pool. Some of the engravings seemed to depict a healing—while others envisioned darker endings. There was even a representation of a couple with exaggerated genitalia immersed in the water in a carnal embrace.

Lucinda caressed the carvings, her face rapt with wonder.

"I did not know this was here," she whispered. "Do you think my father knew?"

"Yes. I think he and my father found it. During his dig here thirty-two years ago. He wrote that it existed, but he didn't describe anything like this." Frank glanced at the vines enrobing the ceiling and snaking through the planks and thatch of the walls. "You said it was hard to reach—"

"It has grown back into the jungle. From the outside you cannot tell there is a structure at all, unless you know it is here."

Frank nodded. "That's kept people away. At least until now. Now that this area is being mined, the miners may end up discovering it eventually. If Ari doesn't find it first."

Lucinda didn't seem to have heard. She knelt by the tub, her face close to the golden images. She ran a finger over the figures, breathless with wonder.

Frank turned to the braziers and buckets. Beneath each brazier was a small piece of flint, but no steel and nothing to burn. When he picked up a bucket, the ancient rushes crumbled into a pile of wisps at his feet. Frank gathered a handful and lined the braziers before pulling the lighter from his pocket, praying for one last burst of flame. With a feeble flicker, a small thumbnail of blue flame caught a husk of thatch and chewed it eagerly, bringing one of the braziers roaring to life in a matter of seconds. With a bit of bamboo, he lit the other one. The twin flames sent shadows dancing over the golden plate.

"Do you think . . ." Lucinda began in a small voice. "Do you think there's water under there? After all these years . . ."

Frank shook his head. "I wouldn't get my hopes up. It probably evaporated long ago. But . . ." He fingered a corner of the golden sheet. "I suppose we can find out."

Lucinda stood, stiffly, her hand pressed against her abdomen. "We must try," she said, joining him at a corner of the wooden tub.

Frank surveyed her uneasily. Even beneath the mud and dirt that covered her clothing, her skin was pale. Evil scratches and bruises sliced her face and arms. Her eyes glimmered too brightly above the purple welts below them.

"Gold is heavy, Lucinda. And this is a lot of gold—"

"I think we can do it—"

Frank shook his head. "You're hurt," he said softly.

She smiled. "Yes. But if there is water . . ."

Frank hesitated, but only a moment. She was right: if there was water, she might be healed. If there was water, he might be free. If there was water, they might be able to go home.

"All right," he said. "But promise me, you'll be careful."

They put their hands on a corner of the plate.

"On three," Frank said. "One, two . . ."

Together, they strained against the weight of solid gold.

Frank dug in with his legs and pushed every muscle until he was screaming with the pain of the effort. It moved with a rusty, scraping sound, giving up only a few inches before they fell away, spent. Lucinda dropped to the ground, holding her side, grimacing. Frank stumbled backwards, sweating and breathless.

"Can . . . can you see . . ." he gasped.

Lucinda leaned closer, squeezing her hand into the black gap between the stone tub and the heavy gold. Frank watched as her face changed from excitement to fear, then shifted again with understanding and realization. Slowly, she pulled her hand out of the space and showed him her fingers.

They were wet.

"Water, Frank! And it is cold!" Her eyes misted over with tears of joy and relief. "Help me," she said, rising unsteadily. She pushed the cover's edge, straining her fully body weight against it, but it didn't move at all.

"Wait, Lucinda. Wait a minute. We're never going to be able to get it off that way. We're—we're not strong enough. We need something. Leverage or—"

Frank looked around for something—anything—to help them move the plate aside. But if there had ever been some kind of implement the ancient priests had used, it was long gone. The space was bare and decaying, lonely in its emptiness.

"Look." Lucinda pointed upward toward a couple of crude wheels buried amid the thatch and limbs that formed the roof of the structure. "Pulleys. They must have used rope or vines or something to lift it off. Maybe we could do that."

"If they still work. The roof has pretty much rotted away.

And even if they do, they won't do us much good. We don't have any line," Frank muttered. "Never thought I'd say it, but I wish I had the rope they tied me up with. When I got loose I just tossed it aside. We could sure use it now . . . what are you doing?"

Lucinda had stripped off her shirt. Beneath it, she wore nothing. Her breasts were as round and supple as he remembered. He could also see the scratches and bruises that covered her skin. Most of them, he knew, were the gifts of their harrowing journey together, but others were darker and older mementos of years of abuse. Anger and guilt surged to the forefront of Frank's consciousness again until he saw the angry purple patch of inflamed skin just below her rib cage. That was the spot she had been nursing—and instantly Frank understood how bad it was.

"Lucinda . . ." he breathed.

Lucinda ignored him. She was too busy ripping her shirt into long shreds.

"Take your shirt off and give it to me—"

"What are you doing?"

"Making a rope," she answered as if that should be obvious.

"Lucinda, I don't think that's going to be long enough to—"

"Then I will use my pants and yours as well," she snapped, her dark eyes flashing. "There is *water* here, Frank! We can do what we came to do at last! We must make enough rope to pull off that golden plate!"

"Then you . . . you're going to do it. With me. In the water."

She raised solemn eyes to his face. "I will always love

you. You are still kind and your heart . . . it is good. But every time I look at you, I see this other woman in your eyes. It hurts, yes. But I do not believe you would love a woman who was not also kind and of good heart. I believe you will keep your promise to me this time. That you will look out for my children—"

"And you, Lucinda," Frank added quietly. "All of you."

"Yes." Lucinda lowered her eyes. "Take off your shirt."

Frank didn't argue. He pulled his rank T-shirt over his head and ripped it along one seam, then tore it into long strips according to Lucinda's example. Within a few minutes, she had tied the fabric together, fashioning a makeshift length of rope several yards long.

"Do you think it is enough?" she asked.

Frank nodded. "It might be . . . but the only way I can reach the pulley is to stand on the cover."

"Then take off your shoes at least," Lucinda directed, sounding so much like a fastidious housewife that Frank had to laugh. He did as he was told and tossed the makeshift rope over the wheel easily.

"Can you tie it somewhere?" he asked.

"Yes . . ." She quickly snaked their rope beneath the plate and looped it through the other side, tying the two ends together in a knot. "Okay. Pull."

"I hope the pulley doesn't come down on us—"

"It won't." Determination added a gritty edge to her voice. "Pull."

He did. The heavy gold rose an inch and then another. Lucinda jumped into the space beside him and grabbed at the T-shirt rope, lending her strength to his, but even together, they were barely equal to the job. The cover's heavy weight lifted by slow degrees as they both strained their exhausted bodies against it. Finally, when they had raised it about six inches off its base, Frank asked, "Can you swing it away from the reservoir?" His face was red with strain and his hands were wet with sweat, but he gritted his teeth and set his feet, squatting deeply into the floor for leverage. "I think I can hold it alone . . . for a few . . . seconds . . ."

"I will try." Lucinda hopped back up on the platform and gave the plate a shove, setting it in motion like an oversized playground swing.

"Again," Frank grunted.

She pushed again, this time using all her weight, and as the heavy plate swung away from the water beneath, Frank let go. It crashed to the dirt floor, making the braziers shimmy with the force of its landing.

Lucinda scrambled to the edge of the basin and stared into the tub.

"Well?" Frank asked, when she neither moved nor spoke.

"It is enough, I think," she said softly, turning to Frank. "I think . . . it is enough."

Frank stood up slowly, his overtaxed muscles shaking so badly he could barely force his legs to obey him as he staggered the few feet to join her at the platform's edge.

Set into the wooden tub was a stone basin half full of clear water. It shimmered, reflecting the firelight and their own disheveled and wounded faces. Frank stared into it, awed and intimidated. Exhausted and overwhelmed as she was, Lucinda's fragile self-control finally dissolved. She covered her face with her hands and sank to the dirt floor, her slender body shaking with sobs.

"We found it," she murmured. "I cannot believe, after all of this . . . we found it . . ."

She lifted her face, her eyes communicating all of the feelings of his own heart: relief and fear, urgency and hesitation, hope and uncertainty, the thrill of rediscovery and the ache of farewell.

He reached for her, intending only comfort, but at the touch of her skin all of his feelings for her crested inside him. The infatuation of his eighteen-year-old self was there, but it was joined by something deeper, something stronger. Respect, gratitude, concern and admiration stirred inside him as he leaned forward, gathering a drop of salt as his lips brushed her cheek.

She wrapped trembling arms around his neck as more tears fell, but Frank no longer felt any hesitation. He lifted her easily, carrying her toward the basin and lowering her gently into the cool water. She was right: there was just barely enough left. Like he was bathing a child, he swirled the water with his hands, scooping it over her dirty hair, rinsing the grime and blood from her body while she sighed and shuddered at his touch. Then at last when her supple brown skin glistened from his ministrations, he stepped out of his shorts and joined her.

She pulled him against the cool wetness of her skin, her mouth covering his with a hunger that erased everything but the sensations of the moment. Frank surrendered as she climbed on top of him, pressing him into the shallow water that somehow seemed to touch every part of him like a gentle, soothing caress, easing his depleted muscles as it cleansed him. All the while, Lucinda's lips claimed his, enflaming his desire so quickly and so completely that he knew without a doubt that good angels had led them to this moment—and that there was no turning back. A part of him longed to take control, but a wiser, more knowing part understood her dominion over him was complete and that the climax was hers to shape as she would. When he thought he could wait no longer, Lucinda's slender fingers slid down his body and grabbed his hardness, guiding it deep into her softness.

She rode him with a fevered passion, slamming herself onto him with a recklessness that obliterated everything else from Frank's mind. Gifts and costs, powers and prices, youth and age, even life and death evaporated from his consciousness. Her wet hair swung wildly, raining droplets of moisture over his face, and her breath whistled through her teeth as she worked them both to the very brink of release and then over it at last.

"Frank!" Lucinda screamed his name and he felt her body convulse around his with desperate energy just as Frank released his own center. She collapsed against him, her face buried in the side of his neck.

"Jackie," Frank groaned as his desire drained out of him and he closed his eyes, embracing the beckoning darkness of exhaustion like a welcome friend.

He wasn't sure how long they slept, but when he awoke, the braziers had burned low. Lucinda lay still against his chest, breathing deeply, her mouth slack with sleep. Frank looked down at their intertwined bodies and realized with surprise that they were no longer soaking in cool water. In fact, they were almost completely dry.

"What?" Lucinda's voice was weak and soft. Her eyelids flickered but she did not open her eyes.

"The water . . . it's gone," Frank told her.

He craned his neck, peering over the rim of the sunken basin, expecting to find a puddle or some other clue. But there was nothing there to explain it. Frank shifted, glancing between his legs down at the smooth stone that formed the basin's floor. A crack ran down the center, nearly dividing the tub in two. Whether it been there all along or they had created it with their energetic lovemaking, Frank didn't know, but he could only guess that what remained of the mystical waters had seeped through it and merged with the earth beneath.

"Yes," Lucinda whispered, as though it were exactly what she had expected.

"And the fire's almost out," he added, suppressing a yawn. He tried to move, to rouse himself enough to tend to the dying flames, but nothing happened. His muscles wouldn't obey him any longer, no matter how hard he willed himself to action.

"I think . . . we did it," he said, and to his surprise he felt neither happy nor sad. In the place of either emotion was only an overpowering weariness that was beyond caring for anything but rest.

"Perhaps," Lucinda murmured into his chest without lifting her head. "Do not get up yet, Frank. Do not leave me . . . yet."

He needed no further encouragement. His lids fell over his eyes and once again he dozed, drifting between wakefulness and sleep as he waited for strength to return to his body.

When he woke again, the fires were out and the temple

was dark. From somewhere outside he heard the shouts of many voices and the movement of many feet.

"They're coming," he said, becoming fully alert and sitting up. His muscles ached, but he no longer felt too weak for action. "Lucinda." He shook her gently. "Wake up. They're coming. If we go back down the well, maybe we can—"

Her head lolled forward.

"Lucinda?" Frank shook her again.

Her arm dropped lifelessly from his shoulder. When he looked into her face, he knew. She was dead.

You return to the pool twice, you must pay the price—and it might even be life itself.

She'd said it at least a dozen times, and yet somehow Frank hadn't taken it seriously. How could he? She was hurt—he'd known that—but the pool should have healed her—not cost her her life.

"No . . . Lucinda . . . no . . ." Frank murmured, hugging her tightly as tears of guilt and loss welled in his eyes and rolled unchecked down his cheeks. "No . . ."

He wept, rocking her close to him, staring into her face. Her features were as lovely as they were the first day he'd ever seen her, but older and more mature. Somehow the waters had taken away the bruises, erased the scars and aged her into classic beauty. She looked as exquisite and peaceful as if she had simply fallen asleep.

He might have stayed there, holding her while his heart broke with gratitude and sadness, had it not been for the growing clamor from the jungle.

"There's something here!" he heard a distant voice say.

God damn you all, he thought furiously. *She's dead! Can't you leave her alone now?*

They were near. The pursuit was still on . . . and if he stayed too much longer, though the temple was ancient and unstable, Ari and Pandora would storm it anyway, even if the walls crumbled around them. And he'd certainly be caught.

A part of him didn't care. There were no more waters. Lucinda was dead in his arms, and more than likely his own powers of eternal youth were departed as well. What could Ari or Pandora do to him now? He couldn't bear to leave Lucinda. Not after everything.

But another part of him knew better. If Pandora and Ari found him, he could be sure they wouldn't just take his word that the gift of youth was reversed. He wanted to get home. He *needed* to get home.

He got up slowly and slipped on his pants and his boots before turning back to Lucinda. Gently, he arranged her body in the basin, combing her hair around her face with his fingertips. He wished for flowers, but their lack couldn't be helped. Instead, he took one long last look at Lucinda's perfect, thirty-something face and kissed her one last time.

"It's okay," he muttered, his voice cracking with grief. "No one can hurt you now. Don't worry about little Frank and Helen. I'll take care of them. I won't break this promise, Lucinda. As long as I'm alive, they'll always be safe."

He looped the golden cover with their makeshift rope and took his place alone, hoisting its heaviness back up into the air, maneuvering it carefully until it was in the proper position. He released it slowly, groaning with the effort, until it settled on the basin. Then he shook down the knotted T-shirt rope from the pulley and laid his hand on the golden coffin one last time.

"Goodbye," he whispered, and then hurried to the well, dropping over the edge to climb back down into its depths and retrace his way back through the jungle alone.

An hour later, Frank reemerged in the log-filled basin under the high heat of the afternoon sun, hot and cramped from crawling on his hands and knees, but other than that, none the worse for wear. As he stood up and stretched himself to his full height, he thought again of what Lucinda and Charmaine had told him about the price for having reversed the effect of their first swim in the pool . . . but except for his weariness at heart from the loss of Lucinda, he felt as strong as ever.

He peered out from the shelter of the fallen kapok, half-expecting to find the basin and ravine occupied by at least a few of Ari's machine-gun-toting goons, but it seemed quiet and abandoned. Frank studied the violated landscape, thinking of how Lucinda had wept at the great trees brought low and the water run dry. His heart twisted at the memory, bringing up a fresh well of sorrow that there was no cure for but to keep moving—to keep moving and find his way home.

He emerged carefully. The branches he and Lucinda had used to brace their way down the pool's shore lay where they had abandoned them, and Frank grabbed them. Now, he'd use them to carefully hoist himself back up to the clearing. With any luck, he'd be able to make his way back into the jungle unseen.

He climbed. The steep sides, loose dirt and lack of vegetation on the ravine's terrain made it impossible to ascend either quickly or invisibly—but he saw no other option.

I just want to get home.

Frank made the words his mantra. He dug himself a toehold and started to climb. The dirt was unforgiving and Frank had to claw his way into every hold. A few times, he hung by his fingers alone, nearly vertical to the ground, kicking at the slope until he loosened enough dirt to gain a foothold and advance. The hot jungle sun rose higher in the sky, beating down on his chest and head, blinding him with sweat as the mosquitos made a feast of his bare neck and chest, but he did his best to ignore that and kept going. *Hand, toe, hoist* . . . he thought of Lucinda and tears mingled with the sweat rolling down his cheeks.

I just want to get home.

At last, he reached out, curling his fingers for dirt, and found air. With a final fluttering kick of his feet, he flopped over the lip of the ravine and lay, gasping, in the clearing.

He raised his head to take in his surroundings.

Two helicopters rested a few hundred yards ahead of him, their rotors still. One was small—a lightweight-looking two-seater with a white body and a wide, clear window. The other resembled something Frank might have seen in a movie featuring some kind of military plot: darker and bigger—clearly meant for several passengers—with a sleek black exterior. That one, he was sure, was the one with the spotlight that he and Lucinda had been evading.

Frank lay still against the ground, wishing he could assume the color of dirt like some kind of chameleon. He peered toward the cabin of the small white craft, but from his vantage point, there didn't appear to be anyone inside. He couldn't see anything at all through the heavily tinted windows of the other vessel.

There was nowhere to hide, nowhere at all, and the jungle sun was like fire on his bare skin, but Frank pulled himself to his feet and started moving, focusing on the smaller helicopter. It looked like one of the newer turbine-engine models that would be relatively easy to pilot. If the door was open—and chances were good that, in such a remote spot as this, it would be—all he needed was to turn on the fuel, set the throttle and press the "start" button and let the onboard computer system do most of the work. Landing it would be difficult—he'd only had a few flight lessons while working on a travel article a few years before, and helicopters were far different from airplanes—but he'd deal with that after he got out of the jungle.

I just want to get home.

He darted forward, staying on the periphery of the impromptu airfield, running quickly until he reached the smaller white copter and concealed himself as best he could behind it. There didn't seem to be anyone here—most of his pursuers were in the jungle, searching for him—but someone had to have been left behind. He needed to act and soon, before they knew he was here. Before they could muster the forces to stop him.

He was about to make a move when the rear doors of the black helicopter swung open. Frank ducked, crouching against the smaller aircraft. All he could see was a pair of legs in a powder-blue flight suit. The legs started walking and Frank moved, too, circling the small craft to stay out of sight. The owner of the legs walked past him, toward the ravine, without noticing him—but Frank recognized her instantly.

Lilly, the owner of Elite Air Services, strolled the clearing, stretching her arms and legs like she'd just completed a long flight.

Fuck, Frank thought, berating himself. *I trusted her! Ari's probably one of her clients. When I gave her my letter she probably went straight to him.*

The betrayal infuriated him—even though he knew he had been foolish to trust her just because she seemed so kind. But her presence erased any hesitation Frank had about stealing the helicopter. He eased out of her line of sight, watching as she paced away from the helicopters toward the edge of the ravine. Then, he carefully lifted the handle and eased himself inside the small vehicle.

The interior was sticky and hot, the air baking from the light of the jungle sun through the wide windows. The instrument panel was more complicated than he remembered, but the throttle was at the driver's left hand and he quickly found the "fuel on" switch. He was scanning the instrument panel for the "start" button when he heard them.

Voices.

Angry voices.

The doors of the black helicopter flew open again and Ari Kousakas emerged from its interior, his gray ponytail glinting in the sun. He wore a white T-shirt cut close to his body and a pair of khaki shorts, and he was screaming at the top of his lungs at someone inside.

"Never! I don't care what you say! Never—"

He stomped away from the helicopter like an angry child, crossing his arms over his barrel chest, cursing vehemently in an odd mix of English and Greek.

Frank ducked, lowering his head so as not to be seen

through the windows. The stifling air burned his lungs. Sweat poured from his body, and his head felt light.

"Come back here, Ari!"

Jackie?

It sounded like her voice, but Frank didn't trust his ears. He was exhausted and dehydrated . . . and probably hallucinating.

"You're beaten this time, Ari. You hear me? This time, you're not bullshitting your way out of it. The only play you have left is to sign the papers and leave Frank alone—or I swear to you, I *will* do this. Murder is hard jail time. Not a nice corporate dormitory with private rooms and a swimming pool."

Frank couldn't stop himself. He sat up, wiping sweat out of his eyes, and stared out into the clearing.

It really *was* Jackie. She stood less than ten yards away, her long dark hair swept off her neck in a loose bun. She wore jeans, a light long-sleeved top over a tank top and a face full of righteous indignation. When she lifted her left hand to shade her face, the sun caught the tiny stone on the fourth finger and showered the space between them with a rainbow of refracted light.

His mother's ring. She was wearing it.

She's forgiven me. She's forgiven me. The words circled in his brain and heart. Frank covered his face with his hands. Gratitude and relief joined grief and exhaustion, and more tears might have fallen if there had been anything left inside him to give.

Frank sat up and popped open the helicopter's door, his imagination already fixed on the joyous reunion.

"All this for some... boyfriend?" Ari was shouting. "What about family, Athena? You are my daughter, my heir—"

"Don't talk to me about family, Ari. You don't know the meaning of the word—"

Ari rounded on her. "What are you trying to say, Athena? Is there something you want to say to me?"

Jackie backed away from him, her battle with her courage showing on her face. Frank read it clearly—and so did Ari. He advanced steadily on her, swaggering with confidence. "You have nothing to say. And you will not do these things you threaten." He jerked the papers out of her hand. "That is enough, Athena. Don't you ever, *ever* bring these terrible accusations to me again or—"

Do it, Jackie, Frank thought. He closed his eyes and tried to transmit his convictions to her. *Do it.*

"This is the end, Ari," Jackie said firmly. "What you've done to Frank is the last straw. I saw you, Ari. I saw you at his house. You destroyed the place—you did everything but set it on fire!" She pulled her phone from her pocket and thrust it at him. "See the pictures I took?"

Surprise flitted across his face before he mastered it and resumed his usual faint amusement.

"What were you doing there?"

"I went to apologize to Frank. At first I was ... freaked out ... by his 'power.' I just couldn't imagine a life for us. And then I realized ... I realized that he's part of me. Since we met on the plane it's been as though we belong together. I don't even feel like myself unless he's near—"

"Completely ridiculous," Ari chuckled. "Do you hear yourself? 'We belong together.' You've barely known the man a month—"

Jackie glared at him, her lips folded with suppressed anger. "Never mind. You wouldn't understand. You don't know what it means to love someone enough to sacrifice everything for that person. You just know how to corrupt and destroy. After Lilly brought me Frank's letter and told me that she thought he was in big trouble, I knew all I had to do was watch you—and I'd know where he went. And then Gregory said—"

"Gregory!" Ari said contemptuously. "He works for *me*, foolish girl! I hired him six months ago to help me keep up with you. I have always had someone near you. *Always*. He will not go against me."

Jackie studied him coldly. "No, Ari. You *think* Gregory works for you. And that's what we wanted you to think."

Ari's eyebrow lifted. *"You* wanted?"

"Yes. Gregory is a former police detective and now a private investigator. I hired him about a year ago to help me catch you, Ari. The whole plan was to get you to hire him—or think you had hired him—so that he could get close enough to you to find out what I've always known was the truth. And a few weeks ago, he found it."

"Found what?" Doubt frayed the arrogance of Ari's tone.

"He found Dr. Garajan's file. On Zander."

Ari's mouth opened and closed before he found the power of speech. "I-I don't know you're talking about. What file? Zander's death was a family tragedy, nothing more—"

"I don't think you meant to kill him . . . I know you loved him. We all loved him. He was such a sweet, sweet kid. You miss him. I know you do . . . and that's why this has been so hard for me. I *know*, Ari. How you felt—how you still feel. But you just couldn't leave him alone. Let him be what he was. You just couldn't stand that the great Ari Kousakas had a son who would never be able to take over the empire. You and your Old World bullshit. So you had to play God . . . and Zander's life was the price. Enough is enough, Ari. It's time to end this."

Ari stared at the ground. "You could never do it, Athena. You have a daughter's heart for me. Even now."

"Maybe. But with this stuff with Frank you've proved to me that you've learned nothing. Nothing." Jackie shrugged. "Gamble on my soft heart if you want. Or maybe you'll just bump me off, too? Terrible accident in the Amazon—billionaire's daughter killed. Poor Ari Kousakas. Do it, Ari. The feds will be waiting for you at the gate when you get back to the United States. Because this time, I've set it up like you would. If he doesn't hear from me in twenty-four hours, Gregory takes the files to the appropriate law enforcement agencies. He's spoken with Dr. Garajan—and the good doctor's conscience bothers him. He doesn't like what you did to Zander. He's ready to talk."

Frank could not see Ari's face, but his expression must have been priceless because Jackie laughed.

"Don't look so surprised, Daddy dear. Be proud. You've taught me well. For the things you've done, you deserve to rot in Hades. You're still my father and it's not for me to send you there. But jail? I can send you to jail. I only wish I'd done it sooner. Before you nearly killed Frank's friend. Before you and that awful Pandora chased Frank out to this godforsaken place and I had to get on plane after plane just to stop you. Thank God for Lilly. Frank sent her to me: he knew she would help me get here."

Ari was silent. Frank could see him clearly now: his eyes were on the ground and for just a moment, Frank thought the older man had surrendered. But when he lifted his head, he saw the shift in both his face and his voice. Frank grabbed the door handle of the helicopter and slid out, intending to leap into the fight. But his knees buckled beneath him and for a moment the Amazon sun stole his sight.

"Tell me, Jackie." Ari's voice was filled with venom. "Did your Mr. Young tell you exactly what it was he came here to do? Did he tell you what he would have to do to reverse the power in his loins? You know he came here to fuck that native girl again. Right now, she might be riding his pole—"

"Close your filthy mouth!" Jackie shouted, covering her ears.

"Ah . . . I see he did not give you those particular details," Ari said, his voice unctuous with concern. "How hard it must be to know that he can find the will to screw almost any woman but you—"

"I'm not playing any more head games with you, Ari," Jackie said, her expression hardening with distrust. "Sign the papers. Go back to Greece and leave us alone. Or go to jail. It's up to you."

The father and daughter stood, staring at each other in silence for a long, heated moment. The classic images and music of that old film *High Noon* surfaced in Frank's mind. If his mouth hadn't been so dry and his head so light, he might have whistled the tune, accompanying the tension of the moment with an appropriate soundtrack.

"I see," Ari said slowly. "You think are smart . . . but you are a foolish girl. A very foolish—"

Ari lunged, slamming his daughter's slender frame against the hull of the helicopter so hard her head rocked on her neck. The papers sprayed the ground like litter. "You stupid little bitch!" Ari shouted. "You really think you can beat me? You really think I'm going to just let you take over what I spent my whole life building? Do you? Do you—" His hands closed around her throat, squeezing furiously.

Frank's head cleared. The helplessness he'd felt as Lucinda's husband slapped her reemerged in his mind and in the space of a breath he sprinted toward the man, his fingers already curled into a fist, his heart pumping wildly in his chest.

"Get off her!" he screamed, laying both his hands on the older man's shoulders and tossing him aside like a rag doll. He stood over him, his fists raised, aching for contact. "Don't you ever touch her again or I'll—"

Ari's tanned face kaleidoscoped from anger to amazement to contempt. "See, Jackie—he's not dead. Or hurt. Your hero. Tell me, Athena," he chuckled from the dirt. "Are ready for a life without sex? Or will you fuck him after all? Claim youth for yourself and deny it for everyone else—"

"Shut—your—filthy—mouth!" Frank grunted, slugging the man with every word. Blood spurted from Ari's nose and mouth, but Frank couldn't stop. He thought of Steve and Eva. He thought of Lucinda and he punched the man again and again, long past the moment when Ari sagged to the ground, silent at last.

"Frank!" Jackie's voice finally pierced his consciousness and he stopped, his arms heavy and his knuckles raw. "Oh thank God! You're alive—"

"Jackie . . ." he breathed, his heart still racing with adrenaline and joy, relief and fury. "Jackie. What are you doing here?" He staggered to his feet, gasping for breath as he opened his arms to hold her. "What—"

A hot poker of pain stabbed the center of his chest, stealing his breath and blurring his vision. Frank stumbled, hunching forward against it, praying for the agony to subside. Instead, a second violent squeezing arrow knocked him to his knees.

"Frank! What is it? What's wrong?" Jackie screamed, rushing to his side. "Frank!"

There's a price, Frank. We take the pool and the gifts it gives at a cost . . . Lucinda seemed to be standing at his shoulder, whispering the words in his ear.

At a cost . . . The pain in his chest intensified and radiated throughout his body, killing the power of thought. Frank fell face forward into the dirt, straining his lungs with the effort of breath. Jackie's face was beside his but her features were doubled and distorted. Her lips were moving—she was screaming something—but the words were muffled and garbled as though he were hearing them from someplace deep below water.

Help me—I don't want to die. The thought was a prayer offered to any god or angel who might be near. *Help me. I don't want to die—*

The pain twisted inside him again, relentless and inexorable. He couldn't see anything anymore, couldn't hear anything but the pounding of his heart, racing faster and faster like a train headed for derailment, trackless and out of control. Then, just as it seemed his chest was about explode from the pain, the frantic beating stopped. Jackie and Ari, the jungle and the clearing, the pain and his breath—all of it disappeared. Silence consumed him and Frank surrendered to it, body, mind and soul.

CHAPTER

Twenty-Three

A movie theater.

Within a few seconds of opening his eyes, Frank recognized the place—the old General Cinema in San Diego. But that couldn't be. That theater had closed in the late 1980s, replaced by the multiplex in the Fashion Valley Mall. Still, when he looked around, Frank recognized the old-fashioned single-level sloped auditorium and the black curtained stage. How many movies had he and his father seen here when he was a little kid? He remembered the excitement and adventure of being seven years old and captivated by *The Princess Bride*, and how he'd begged his father to see Arnold Schwarzenegger in *The Running Man*—only to have bad dreams about it for weeks afterward. He was even sitting in his favorite spot—dead center of the fourth row from the top—in an old crimson-upholstered seat that smelled of age and stale popcorn. The rest of the theater was dark and empty. The massive screen in front of him was blank.

"Is this seat taken?" The voice was unfamiliar. Girlish and light, teasing and sweet, with an edge of wry, intelligent humor. Frank looked up.

He had expected something different. Someone with angel wings, maybe—like a Victoria's Secret model. Or in some kind of white-robed costume from the old days of Hollywood before everything was created on computers. But instead, she wore the same long denim skirt, the black vest over some kind of slouchy top and the fedora he'd seen a million times before in one of the photos his father had kept in his study. Her brown hair curled exuberantly around her twenty-five-year-old face and she wore bright lipstick and smoky eye shadow. Something about the look reminded Frank of Madonna in the movie *Desperately Seeking Susan*, even though she'd skipped the fishnets and tutu skirt.

She was a young, attractive woman . . . and she was his mother.

"This was always one of my favorite outfits," Helen Young said, as if reading his mind. She adjusted the hat rakishly and grinned. "Like it?"

Frank nodded, too bewildered to speak. Questions circled his brain—so many he hardly knew where to begin. He stared at her for a moment, taking in every detail—the big curly bangs on her forehead peeking out from under the black hat, the chipped nail polish on her left hand, the smell of some fruity perfume that floated toward him as she settled into the seat beside him and crossed her legs—feeling both intrigued and uncomfortable at the same time.

"Oh good," she said, nodding toward the screen. "The show's starting."

He glanced at the screen, foolishly anticipating one of the movies his father had told him were among her favorites: *It's a Wonderful Life*, maybe. Or *Annie Hall*. Or—

"Frank!"

On the screen in front of him, Jackie screamed his name in surround sound. He saw himself lying in the dirt, his eyes closed and his face ashen. Jackie straddled him, pumping on his chest with her palms, sweat dripping off her face. "We have to get him to a hospital!"

"I'll radio for help!" Lilly replied, running toward her aircraft.

"Hurry!" Jackie yelled after her; then, with the grim determination of a wartime medic, she leaned forward and covered his mouth with her own, blowing her breath into him before continuing her work on his sternum.

Frank stared at the screen in horror.

"What—" he began.

"You're having a heart attack," his mother answered calmly.

"Am I going to die?"

She smiled, showing him a pair of clear brown eyes and white teeth beneath the bright lipstick. "Of course, silly. Everyone dies eventually. But if you're asking me if it's *today* . . ." She shook her head. "I'd gamble on 'no.' But I'm not in charge, so . . ." She shrugged, communicating wordlessly that anything was possible.

Frank turned back to the screen.

"Come on, Frank . . . please, baby . . . please hold on . . ." Jackie repeated the words over and over, like a prayer. Tears and sweat in mingled drops rolled down her face, but she ignored them. She blew into his mouth again, then resumed her vigorous CPR. "Come on, Frank. Please . . ."

"I can't watch this anymore. I have to get back there—" Frank stood up, looking around him for an exit sign or a door. There was only darkness.

"It's okay. We don't have to watch it. We all know you want to go back. You don't want to leave her. And I'm pretty sure that, unless you change your mind about it, you'll get back before . . . well, you know." His mother nodded toward the screen and it went black again. "It's tough to watch, but since you like movies as much as I do, I thought it might help you understand."

She patted the seat beside her and Frank reluctantly lowered himself back into it.

"Understand what? Where am I? What's happening to me?"

Helen laced her fingers through his. "Understand why things happened the way they did. Why your father did what he did. And what might happen next. Things are about to change, Francis—and you're going to find those changes to be very difficult." She smiled sadly. "I want you to be ready for it. If anyone can help you with this . . . well, I guess it's me."

Frank waited, but for a long moment, she simply stared at him, pride and love radiating from her eyes.

"You look so much like your father! And you're like him in so many other ways, too . . ." she began. After a long pause, she continued. "I'm sorry, Frank," she said. "This is harder than I thought it would be. Your father wanted to come—maybe he should have—but I told him that this was my fault, so it's my job. But now that we're sitting here . . . it's hard. I mean, we don't really know each other—or I guess I should say *you* don't know very much about *me*. Francis—your dad—didn't tell you very much, unfortunately. I was mad at him about it at first, but . . ." She smiled. "I could never stay mad at him for long. He couldn't talk about me. It hurt too much."

"Is he here?" Frank cast another glance around the theater.

"He's near. But for now, it's just us." She released his hand and sat up straight in her chair with fresh determination. "Okay, Frank. I'll cut to the chase. Do you know how I died?"

Of all the things he had expected her to say, that wasn't even in the top one hundred. Frank blinked at her for a shocked second before he stammered, "I know you died . . . having me, I guess. I know you were sick, but beyond that . . ." He shook his head, embarrassed that he'd never pressed for more details. "No."

Helen rolled her eyes. "Honestly, Francis Young," she muttered, and Frank understood that it was his father—not him—who was in big trouble. "You could have told the kid *something!*"

"I guess he just—"

"It's okay, Frank," Helen continued, brushing off her annoyance with a gentle toss of her head. "I had a heart condition. A genetic thing that runs in my family. I was born with it. It's a rare condition with a long name that I'm sure the doctors will tell you all about when you get back. Some people with this particular kind of heart defect are basically healthy until one day"— snapped her fingers—"the heart just stops. And others are never particularly strong. That was me. In the hospital . . . out of the hospital . . . in the hospital . . . out of the hospital. Your father has his faults, but he has the patience of a saint." She adjusted her hat a bit lower on her head so that it shaded her face a little. "I had been warned against getting pregnant. The docs didn't think my ticker could handle childbirth." She giggled a bit, a cheerful sound that matched her twenty-something-year-old exterior and distracted Frank's attention completely from what she was saying. "And it turns out they were right! But it doesn't matter. I wouldn't change a thing. I couldn't imagine the point of living without a child. I couldn't imagine dying without leaving behind someone your father and I made together. It wasn't fair—I know. But I think you two did quite well." She raised an eyebrow. "Do you understand what I'm trying to tell you?"

Frank shook his head. "I'm sorry. I'm listening, but—" He lifted his hand, gesturing toward the screen and the theater around them, and then Helen herself. "This whole scenario is just so bizarre. I mean, how is this happening? How am I here and . . ." His eyes slid to the blank screen again. "There. Am I having some kind of near-death experience or something? And if you're some kind of ghost or dream or hallucination, why are your hands so warm? Why do you seem so real?"

She laughed again. "You and your father! Both of you have such trouble with existence beyond existence. So wedded to your science and your observations that you can't really *see* anything!" She squeezed his hand again, intensifying the pressure on his fingers so that it almost hurt. "Of course *this* is real, Frank." She waved a hand toward the movie screen again. "And so is *that*."

"Help is the on the way!" Lilly slid into the dirt beside Jackie, lifting a defibrillator out of a white case marked with a red first-aid cross. "Here," she said, handing Jackie two adhesive electrode pads. "Put them on and then get clear—"

Helen waved her hand and the screen darkened again.

"You have the same heart defect that I have, Frank. Unfortunately, in the genetic crap shoot, you and I lost. Welcome to your new reality."

"But I've always been healthy!" Frank protested. "As a kid I . . . well, I didn't play sports or anything but I went on a million digs with Dad. And as an adult, I've done even more extreme stuff! Since I was eighteen—"

Eighteen. The number resonated in his mind. When he was eighteen . . . he made a journey to the Amazon. When he was eighteen, he swam in a crystal pool of mystical water.

"I remember you, in this forest, years ago before we swam together. You struggled to keep up," Lucinda said in his memory. But after the pool . . .

"You were a healthy kid—mostly," Helen said. "But concern for you was the reason your dad kept you so close. It's why you were always with him on the digs—why you spent more time on the road with him than in regular schools with regular children. And that's why your father sent you to Peru. To José. He hoped José would take you to the waters and that they would protect you. He couldn't bear to lose you. He didn't want you to die young like—"

"Like you did," Frank finished, understanding at last. His father had sent him to Peru hoping José would lead him to the pool... but instead it was Lucinda who had taken him there. And in their youthful attraction they'd unintentionally accepted one of the sacred water's more unusual powers. He replayed his life in his mind: he'd run his first marathon at nineteen, started mountain climbing around the same time. Took up martial arts in his mid-twenties, embraced extreme travel after doing a triathlon at twenty-six—

All of it was after that swim with Lucinda under the light of the moon.

"Did he know he was dying?" Frank asked suddenly. "And he aged. I thought the waters stopped or slowed the aging process?"

"The mind is the most powerful pool of all, Frank," Helen said softly. "If you understand that, you understand everything I have to tell you. My poor Francis. He was dying from grief from the day I passed and no water—no matter how mystical—was going to change that."

"So you're saying he was able to undo the effects of the pool with his own mind?"

She nodded. "Yes, something like that. But you, my son, have a very different problem now. The pool that you swam in had great power—it's true. But that power is likely gone now—forever. What is happening to your body—the heart defect you were born with and the episode your body is experiencing right now—they are real. Without the effects of the pool . . ." She shook her head. "I'm sorry, but I don't think you'll be able to do the things you are used to doing. Not without putting your very life at risk. Without the gifts of the mystical waters, the man you were is gone."

"Lucinda—" Frank's voice quavered with the freshness

of her loss as he said her name. "Lucinda said something like that."

"Ah, Lucinda. I just met her not too long ago. A lovely woman. Very strong—though not quite as tough as your Jackie. You've made an excellent choice for the next stage of your life journey."

"The next stage of my life journey?" Frank asked, suspicious of the New Age phrasing. "Which is . . . ?"

"Learning to rely on others." She quirked a parental eyebrow when he rolled his eyes. "Don't look at me like that. You've been incredibly self-reliant. Too much so—though lately, you've been improving. It's good to see you open up to Eva and Steve and the others. It's good to see you let yourself love and be loved. This heart attack will change the dynamics between you. It's very likely that you will have to change your role in X-Treme Travel. And your friends will be there for you, if you do."

X-Treme. For all the months of worrying and working on funding the company, the idea of letting it go washed over him without distress. He opened his mouth to ask another question but the words seized in his throat.

Bright, eye-searing light filled the dark theater as though an invisible hand had torn the roof off the dingy place and let in the full strength of the sun.

Frank lurched in his seat as his chest twisted with violent pain. "Shit," he cursed, breathlessly, his body beading with sweat.

"Come on, Frank. Come back, babe . . . come back . . ." Jackie said into his ear, and he thought he felt her hands on him—then, just as suddenly, darkness settled around them again.

"What was that? What's happening?"

"Your time is up. Jackie is bringing you back. If you want to go."

Sunlight dazzled them again and once more, Frank's body torqued with pain. When darkness settled again his body felt heavy, as though massive weights had been fastened to his arms and legs.

"I told you she was tough," Helen said softly. "You see, as we're sitting here getting to know each other, your heart is not beating. Your brain isn't getting any oxygen. Every second that passes, the greater the potential for even more debilitating damage—"

"What are you telling me? That when I wake up from this heart attack, I'll be a vegetable or some weak, sick old man?" He shook his head. "I wouldn't do that to her, Mom—"

Mom. The word tumbled easily out of his mouth, bringing with it a strange sense of peace. From the wide smile that Helen beamed at him, Frank saw how much the word meant to her. "I love her, Mom. I couldn't do that to her."

"She loves you, too, Frank. You say you don't want to burden her . . . but somehow, I think dying *now* would be a heavier one."

"But—am I going to be some kind of useless invalid?" Frank demanded. "Am I—*arrgghh* . . ."

Light crashed down on him and he found himself struggling against it, even though he knew Jackie waited for him on the other side. There were too many other questions—too much he still didn't understand. Too much he wanted—needed—to know.

But this time, the light didn't die. The theater began to

disintegrate around him as light shot through the screen and the walls. The center of Frank's body throbbed and screamed and as hard as he tried, he could neither move nor stop it.

"Mom—please—tell me—" he panted, reaching out for her with the last of his strength. "What—?"

"I don't know the future any more than you do. That belongs to God or Buddha or Karma or whatever you believe in. You may have a day, or a year or a lifetime, left to live. You may live it in a coma, or perhaps you will climb a mountain again—I don't know. No one knows." She stood up, and now the light edged around her like a halo. "You take your chances in life, Frank. We all do. The beauty of God's love is that whatever we choose, He works it for the best." She leaned over and dropped a gentle kiss on his forehead. "You go on now."

"But—"

"I'll always be near you, Frank," she said, but her voice was little more than a whisper as light surrounded him and a bone-crushing fatigue dropped over him. He felt the hard ground on his bare back and smelled Jackie's hair on his face.

"Oh Frank . . ." He could hear Jackie sobbing and feel her kisses on his cheeks and neck. "Thank God . . . You're gonna be okay. Help is on the way . . ."

He wanted to answer but found he couldn't, not yet. His limbs felt like granite, and even moving a finger was a two-man job. Lifting his eyelids was more effort than he could manage. They felt stuck—as if someone had taped them to his cheeks.

"You're going to be okay, babe," Jackie said again and again. "You're going to be okay."

"Don't forget your promise." Lucinda sounded like she was at his elbow. He couldn't see her, but he made his lips move.

"I won't," he tried to say, but no sound came out.

Faintly, like the softest echo in his ear, he heard another voice, gentle and sweet: "She's right. You're going to be okay, honey," and then even softer, "Your dad says to kiss our grandchildren for us..."

Their grandchildren. His children. His and Jackie's. Frank sighed, a feeling of peace sweeping over him like a welcome breeze. It would be different... but they would be together, he and Jackie. Suddenly, he wanted nothing more than to see her and read the future in her face. Ignoring the sputtering pain in the center of his chest, he marshaled all of his strength and opened his eyes.

Acknowledgments

As I was writing my first book, *The Power Curve: Smart Investing Using Dividends, Options, and the Magic of Compounding*, I thought to myself, "... I can't wait until I can work on a novel; it will be so much easier..." In writing *Forever Young* I learned quickly the grass is not greener on the other side, especially when it comes to literary genres. Even something as solitary in nature as writing a book requires a village, or at least a tribe, and I was fortunate to have many people assist in making my dream of creating a novel a reality. My first thanks goes to Karyn who understood immediately that the concept for the work held potential well beyond a light romantic comedy. Our brain storming sessions over a glass of wine were some of my most creative hours to date. To my parents, Bob and Barbara, prolific authors themselves: thank you for inspiring my love of the written word from

ACKNOWLEDGMENTS

an early age. Thanks as well to Lisa Wolff for her editorial expertise. Praise to Greg Smith, whom I have now had the pleasure to work with on two books, for his artistic prowess. Kristie Langone deserves credit for the initial cover design concepts. My colleague here at Coastwise, Seneca Hampton, proved invaluable in assisting with myriad logistical matters including building the web site www.FYnovel.com. Finally I must give a heartfelt thanks to Charmaine for listening to me describe *ad nauseam* every twist and turn and plot change late into the night.

Made in the USA
Lexington, KY
13 March 2014